EMBRACED BY
BLINDING PASSION

The flounced dress came off much more quickly than it had gone on. With her arms around Hugh's neck, her lips urgent against his throat, Arabia threw it aside and he lifted her and carried her to the bed, laying her down on it while he quickly got rid of the burden of his clothes. Her body was lithe and creamy. She was a wanton, writhing crescendo of desire, and he threw himself at her with utter abandon. Downstairs raucous laughter and infrequent singing could be dimly heard, but in the silence of Hugh's room there was only the creaking of the bed, the soft rustling of bodies swaying on the coverlet, the sighs and gasps and, finally, Arabia's deep, throaty laughter.

Never once did Hugh think of Louisa...

SANDENNY

MARYHELEN CLAGUE

CHARTER BOOKS, NEW YORK

SANDENNY

A Charter Book / published by arrangement with
the author

PRINTING HISTORY
Charter edition / May 1986

ISBN: 0-441-75348-5

Charter Books are published by The Berkley Publishing Group,
200 Madison Avenue, New York, New York 10016.
PRINTED IN THE UNITED STATES OF AMERICA

PROLOGUE

England, 1778

THE DAY PROMISED to be cloudy and overcast. In the fields below the clearing gray tufts of fog still clutched at the tops of the damp trees and the limp hayricks. Slapping his arms back and forth underneath his cloak, Hugo St. Dennis tramped across the wet grass, thinking how appropriately the weather suited the occasion. A few feet away he could see Rob Earing standing beside Dr. Mallory, both men murmuring quiet words to each other. He could not make out what they were saying but then he did not need to. He could repeat every word himself, he had heard them so often:

"For God's sake, Hugh, it's still not too late. For once put aside your damnable pride and apologize to the man. He is not worth the risk you're taking. Apologize!"

And he knew what his answer would be as well as they did. He would not apologize. He had gone too far to back down now. Besides, for too many years he had suffered Pelham Stoakes' snide remarks and veiled insults. The man was a boor and a clod and—though he had not been able

1

to prove it—Hugh was more than a little certain that he cheated at cards as well. It was time someone took him down a notch or two.

His steps brought him abreast of his two friends, close enough to see that they were examining the brass-handled dueling pistols that were his pride. Their shiny metal gleamed in the wan light. This was not the first time they had been taken out for such an occasion.

Dr. Mallory handed him one of the pistols to check over. The doctor's round glasses had slipped halfway down his nose and were flecked with the heavy dew but the sober eyes that peered over the rims at Hugh's face were filled with a mixture of anger and frustration. Inwardly he had already sworn that this was absolutely the last time he would stand by and see this mettlesome cub through such a disgraceful incident. Sympathy for Hugh's difficulties at home had always before overruled his reluctance but this time was one too many. He remembered bringing Hugo into the world, the last of several children of Earl Lindsay and his party-loving wife, Caroline. From the first he had felt that Hugo had a promise that none of the other St. Dennis children evidenced but that had now been all but obliterated by a stern, disapproving father and Hugo's wastrel ways. Over the years the harshness with which the Earl handled his son's every misdeed, far from bringing him into line, had only made the boy more recalcitrant. Hugo was not one to be cowed into submission by punishment and the more overbearing his father grew, the more daring and insufferable became his actions. He had already killed one man in these foolish duels and had only managed to escape the consequences through the efforts of his friends and the high station of his father. If he killed another there would be no escape. And his opponent today was one of the Stoakes, whose family was prominent in the area and whose uncle, it was rumored, had the ear of the Prime Minister. Sir Lionel might well cast his son off altogether if this duel went on as planned.

He had barely opened his mouth to say as much when Hugo stopped him with a wave of his hand.

"I'm not backing off, Dr. Mallory, so save your breath.

And don't bother to remind me how furious my father is going to be. If I am killed he will only be relieved, while if I kill Pelham, it will give him the excuse he has sought for years to drum me out of his life. Either way, it is nothing to me."

Mallory shook his head, jerking open the top of his medicine box with an impatient yank. "I expected you to say as much. A piece of foolishness! Sometimes I think you want to be killed!"

"I concur in that," Rob said quietly, his brown eyes searching his friend's face. "And for what? A careless remark that any other man would have passed off with a shrug."

"He called me a coward and a blackguard in front of my friends."

"You forget I was there, Hugh. He never used your name directly and if you hadn't downed so much brandy you would have realized that."

"His remarks were most certainly directed at me. He's done that before, the sniveling little bastard. He hasn't the courage to insult me to my face. It's time he learned that hiding behind vague threats won't wash. It's time someone made him stand up and act like a man."

"And this is acting like a man? God's blood, Hugh, though you are my best friend you'd try the patience of a saint, I must say. You are too hot-headed and impulsive by far and someday it is going to land you in a situation far more serious than you bargained for. Let's hope this is not it."

Hugh turned the pistol over in his hand. "I've no wish to kill the little insect—he's not worth it. I just want to teach him a lesson he'll not soon forget. We'll both have a quick shot at one another then you and I can go along to breakfast."

Hugh's cavalier words might have been reassuring on other occasions, but today Rob could not help but feel that his friend's hand was too visibly unsteady to put much trust in them. The truth was that Hugh had consumed far too much brandy last night and when he was tipsy one could never tell just how aware he was of his own actions. Did he really mean for things to go this far or had it all simply evolved from a few careless remarks? He had risen early enough this morning to put his affairs in some kind of order, which suggested he was more alert than he seemed. But Rob could not remember when he had seen Hugh's hand this unsteady.

At the soft crunch of horses' hooves on the leaves below the fringe of trees surrounding the clearing Hugh looked quickly up. So Pelham was coming. He had wondered if the fool might refuse to show.

As the sound of the approaching riders grew louder Hugh swept off his wool cloak and began unbuttoning his coat. By the time the two men rode into the clearing he was standing in shirt-sleeves and waistcoat looking down the barrel of his pistol. Over its tip he noticed that Pelham's face was even whiter than usual as he sat in the saddle looking down at Hugh. Yet pistols had been Pelham's choice of weapons, no doubt because he knew that though he was not a particularly good shot, he was even worse with a sword.

Pelham Stoakes lumbered down from his horse and worked at the frog on his cloak with nervous fingers. His puffy, stodgy figure was as ungainly on foot as it had been in the saddle and his pasty complexion looked gray in the dim light. But Rob noticed that his eyes were burning as dark and angry as Hugh's had been last evening. He had a score to settle here this morning too.

"Gentlemen," Dr. Mallory began. "One last time I ask you—beg you—to reconsider."

The two adversaries glared at each other. Pelham shook his head vigorously. "No," Hugh barked.

Mallory turned away in despair. "Very well, then. Let's get on with it. Fourteen paces, one shot each. On the count of fourteen, attend, present, and fire. Fools!"

The two seconds stepped up to offer a last minute adjustment to each duelist. Hugo could hear the low voice of the other second as Rob helped him load and prime his pistol. No doubt Pelham's friend was doing his best to talk his man out of this also, to no avail.

"I've a button caught on my cuff, Rob. Can you help me with it?"

As his friend bent to push back the deep lace ruffle on his sleeve and unclasp the button, Hugh glanced over his head to where Pelham Stoakes stood only a few feet away. The light was a little brighter now, enough to allow visibility in the clearing. He could see that Pelham was trying to appear brave but the tightness about his white mouth and the way his little eyes darted around from one side to the other told Hugh clearly enough what the man was truly feeling. Had Pelham, too, made certain that his papers and letters were where they could be easily found? Had he too pulled together his clothes and some ready money in case he had to make a sudden exit from the country?

Hugh had a sudden disconcerting image of his own body lying torn and bleeding on the damp grass and he gave an involuntary shudder. In all his twenty-three years he had never really thought about dying, expecting always that it would be the other man who was hurt. It was suddenly very clear to him that he did not really want to kill Pelham Stoakes even though he had detested the man for many years—since they were boys together.

How had he managed to put himself once again in this dreadful position? What dark destiny had led him once again to a place where he was risking his life on the vagaries of a single shot, incurring the wrath of a father who already thoroughly hated him, alienating friends like Rob and Dr. Mallory who had seen him through so many bad times? What devil drove him to set up these situations where he could not win? What depth of pride or fallacy of judgment landed him in a place where he was sure to be hurt once again?

Though his life often seemed meaningless yet he had always felt that he had a destiny lying somewhere over the next horizon. He truly believed it was there, undiscovered and unknown, waiting for him. But not if he should die now, here in this damp, gray, barren place.

Dr. Mallory barked an order and Hugh found his feet carrying him to the center of the clearing to stand back against back with Pelham Stoakes, his pistol held before him. Against his tall back he could feel the squat flabby softness of his adversary, nearly a foot shorter than himself. Well, with any luck they would both miss and then he and Rob could go to breakfast at the Bell and Crown with the risk safely run and honor satisfied.

"One . . ." Mallory's voice rang through the quiet air. A flapping of wings and a sweet chirrup in the trees above them signaled the morning chorale of a nest of robins. From the other side of the clearing came a musical explosion as an exuberant wren added her welcome to the day.

"Thirteen, fourteen. Attend."

Hugh's heel dug into the soft earth as he turned to face the man on the other side of the clearing. The abrupt motion almost threw him off balance and he wavered a single instant before regaining his footing.

"Present."

Holding the gun at arm's length he looked down the gleaming barrel. A single ray of sunlight caught the brass and careened off it, brighter than the coming day.

"Fire!"

The wren's lovely song broke the silence, only to be deafened in mid-chorus by the roar of the pistols' loud retort.

Chapter 1

AFTER CRUISING SMOOTHLY along the coast of England for
two days, the *Windward* hit a spell of fierce weather just
after losing sight of Land's End. It was a sorry beginning
to the voyage and passengers below decks were calling it a
bad omen, further proof, as if any more were needed, that
the long, bitter war between the King and his American
colonies had been a dreadful mistake from the beginning.

Louisa Culpepper kept mostly to her cabin, a tiny cup-
board of a room which she shared with her maid and her
cousin Cecily Davenport. Poor Cousin Cecily, who had been
seasick since the moment she stepped on board, survived
the storm by moaning and retching in the close confines of
the cabin until the stench drove Louisa above decks. She
found little solace there with the cold spray blowing in her
face stinging like fine ice and the wind twisting her skirts
around her ankles. Twice she slipped on the wet planks,
clinging wildly to the ropes that had been stretched between
every mast and groping her way back to the gangway and

7

the comparative safety below.

Then, just when she thought she could bear it no longer,
the angry clouds blew away, the sea settled into a peaceful
roll and the sun reappeared to dapple the waves with silver.
The decks filled with haggard but grateful people breathing
deeply of the clean air and smiling and nodding to each
other with the camaraderie of those who have shared a
common danger.

"Isn't this a glorious morning, my dear," her father said
as he reached out a plump hand to help her up the last of
the stairs. "I'm relieved to see you up and about, Louisa,
and none the worse for wear of the storm. How is your
cousin?"

"A little better but not well enough to leave her bed yet.
She suffered terribly in the bad weather. But you look as
though you did not."

"Ah, well, one must expect a bad spell now and then on
a long voyage." Thomas Culpepper smiled at his daughter.
"Perhaps we have had ours early and will now have a settled
and smooth trip the rest of the way. A good sign for our
return to Georgia."

Louisa fastened her hood beneath her chin and gave her
father a cursory once-over. He was neatly dressed in his
favorite coat of rose brocade and his white bagwig was as
smoothly combed as if he had just left their London house.
A plump, round man with a face that fell into a natural
smile, Thomas Culpepper seemed the picture of good health.
Yet Louisa knew he suffered from shortness of breath and
occasional severe pains in his chest and she watched over
him like a mother hen, looking for any sign of stress. She
was relieved to see that the severe storm had not dampened
his customary good nature.

Resting her hand on his arm the two of them set out
slowly around the deck, carefully avoiding the sailors who
were busy at their tasks and the small clusters of women
and children sitting in scattered groups. Most of the men
promenaded near the taffrail, as eager for the sociability as
the exercise.

"The Captain has invited us to dine with him tonight,"
Thomas said. "Now that the storm is over he can begin to

entertain guests and wishes us to be among the first. I believe it is something of an honor."

"That is kind of him."

"Sir Ralph has been invited as well," Thomas said guardedly, watching for any change of expression on his daughter's lovely face.

"Oh dear. Must we be there the same time as Ralph Stoakes? Is there no way you can rearrange it?"

"Now, Louisa, you do the man an injustice. He is the premier aristocrat on this ship and we should be flattered to be included in his company. I am sure he probably asked for us."

"But Papa. You know how I have disliked the man since the first time I set eyes on him."

"Well, I think you are letting your girlish imagination run away with you. Sir Ralph is a very eligible and attractive gentleman."

"Eligible perhaps. Attractive, no."

"He is a widower with a fortune and a title, something every young girl longs for."

"Not this young girl, as you know well."

"You have taken a foolish dislike to him, based on I know not what..."

"Papa," Louisa cried in growing distress. "Must we talk about this man when the weather is at last perfect and the sea is so beautiful. You know how I feel about him. You won't think of..."

"There, there, my dear," Thomas said hurriedly. His soft heart could never bear the sight of his beloved daughter in tears. "Very well, we will say no more of Ralph Stoakes for the moment. Just promise me that you will be pleasant to him when you are in his company. That is all I ask."

"I will try, Papa. I promise." Tucking her arm in his, she leaned against him, thinking how very convenient it was that they both tried so hard not to upset the other. Perhaps that explained why she got along so well living with her father all these years since her mother died. He was as unromantic a figure as any man could be and yet she had never met a gentleman to equal him in pleasantness and congeniality. Certainly not Sir Ralph Stoakes—a severe man with thin lips, hard eyes and an elegant manner masking a heart which Louisa suspected was made of flint.

"How long do you think it will be before we reach Georgia?" she asked her father, knowing the thought of going home would drive away all other subjects.

"Oh several weeks, I believe. But isn't it comforting to think that every thrust of the waves brings us that much closer. I confess, Louisa, sometimes when I think of setting foot on Savannah streets again my heart quickens within me. It has been too long. Too long. Don't you feel that way too?"

Louisa thought a moment before answering. "I'm not sure. I have missed the town and the colonies. But London was a great pleasure and the situation at home was so difficult when we left. I wonder if it will be any better now?"

"It may. If it is really true that the British are sending an army to retake Savannah then we might find an atmosphere as congenial as the one in London. It would solve a lot of problems.

"Yes, but suppose they lose? There was so much bitterness when we left, it could only be worse by now. I hope we are doing the right thing by going back."

"I'm sure we are," he said, patting her arm affectionately. "I just feel it in my bones. Oh, look. There is Mr. Warren. My, he still looks a little green from the seasickness, doesn't he. Come, let's go wish him a good morning."

Louisa stood to one side looking out over the taffrail while her father chatted with a tall man in a worn brown velvet coat. A wide expanse of beautiful green ocean stretched out in all directions, crowned by foamy lace where the plunging bow of the ship creased the waves. The sky was a pale, soft blue, free of clouds. The strong wind had just a touch of chill in it that was not unpleasant. Under full sail to take advantage of the wind's strength and direction, the ship cut through the water, its huge sails billowing above like great piles of snow. Louisa stepped toward the rail under the shadow of the poop deck.

"Well, Mr. Sandenny," a voice boomed down from above her. "Feeling better are you? I'm glad to see it for I don't care to have my passengers keep to their beds the whole crossing."

Glancing up Louisa saw Captain Leeds leaning down over the rail, speaking to a gentleman standing just behind her. Her eyes flitted briefly over him, taking in that he was tall, broad shouldered, wearing a black broadcloth coat with a tricorn hat over brown hair that was swept back and tied in a ribboned queue. For a moment she thought he might be a Quaker. Then his eyes met hers briefly and she saw that the latent mischief in them in no way fit that sober personality.

"Why, thank you, Captain," the gentleman said, doffing his hat. "As a matter-of-fact, I am feeling much more fit now. The quinsy wore off just as the storm brought on the seasickness, but both are well disposed of by this excellent weather."

Louisa found herself studying the young man even more closely at the sound of his voice which was deep and mellifluous and held genteel accents that did not fit his sober attire. He was very pleasant to look at, with long lean cheeks and a merry mouth, wide and shapely. Though his coat was rather worn, she noticed the lace at his throat was fine Valencia and beautifully done up. He must be able to afford an excellent manservant, she thought, before the young man turned his intense gaze away from the Captain and back to her. Blushing she turned away and fastened her gaze on the water.

"Well, sir," the Captain went on, "When you have a moment free from sauntering the decks, would you be so kind as to step up here and have a word with me?"

"I should be happy to," the young man answered more solemnly. Louisa turned a little, catching him as he stood watching her, obviously wondering whether or not to speak. She smiled shyly and made a step forward as though she had settled the matter for him.

"Louisa, my dear," her father called as he stepped suddenly between them. "Where did you get to? I looked around and you were gone. See here, my child, Sir Ralph has come up from below and wishes to walk with you."

Dismayed, Louisa watched the young man turn away and disappear to the other side of the deck while Ralph Stoakes, glittering in a yellow brocade coat and striped waistcoat, stepped up beside her at the rail. In the bright sunlight the scars of an old siege with smallpox stood out glaringly on Stoakes' sallow skin. He wore an elaborate yellow-dyed wig underneath a plumed hat, and the buttons on his coat and shoes were of beaten silver. To her discomfort she saw he was carrying the staff he was never without—a sinister thing of ebony with a gilt snake winding its length and the head at the top. Two tiny sapphire eyes looked out of a gold dome while its open mouth displayed silver fangs and a narrow ruby tongue.

"Good morning, Miss Culpepper," Stoakes said, smiling thinly and making her an elaborate bow. "I was hoping to have the pleasure of your company for a turn around the deck. Such a lovely day for it."

This was not a prospect Louisa would have welcomed under the best of circumstances. Now, annoyed at the way Stoakes had interfered just at the moment the interesting young man was about to speak to her, she found it difficult to remember her manners at all.

"Thank you, Sir Ralph, but the truth is I was just thinking I might go below. I feel the headache coming on . . ."

Her father threw her a warning glance which Louisa ignored.

"And my poor cousin has been so disturbed by the bad weather. I really should look in on her."

"Nonsense," Thomas spoke up quickly. "I'll have a stop below and check on Cecily. You enjoy the fresh air. There is no better remedy for the headache."

Stoakes smugly offered her his hand as Louisa, glaring at her father, recognized defeat. "Well, perhaps just a few steps," she muttered as he led her off. Stoakes made no effort to hide his pleasure at squiring the prettiest girl on the ship, convinced as he was that they made the most attractive couple. He was not unmindful of Thomas Culpepper's connivance and it pleased him to know the father was almost as anxious for his suit as he himself. Time would bring the girl around.

"I must admit, Miss Louisa," he said smoothly, "that with such a charming companion as yourself on this tedious voyage I almost grow reluctant to reach Savannah at all. I have made this trip before but never under such advantageous circumstances."

"You are too kind," Louisa muttered, fastening her eyes on the blue vista of water off the right bow.

"What about yourself? Are you looking forward to returning home? I understood your father to say that you left in some hurry."

Louisa thought for a moment, wondering how much she should share with this man who, for all his high station, she did not really trust.

"Well, of course, Savannah is my home and I will be happy to be there again. I love our old house and there are several servants who have cared for me since I was a child whom I shall be glad to see once more. But it was such a troubled city when we left that I sometimes wonder if we are doing the right thing to go back before the war is settled, one way or the other. The divisions were so terribly strong. And when the patriotic party finally gained the upper hand it seemed there was nothing to do but to leave for England. I wonder how much that has changed in the year and a half we've been away."

"Your father shared with me some of the concern he felt, being a true subject of the King. I understand that dreadful rabble once threatened to burn down your fine house."

"That is true," Louisa said, wishing her father had not been quite so open.

"Horrible! There is only one answer for such a mob. Hard, swift, severe justice. Fear is the only way to keep order and if my dear friend, Sir James Wright allows me a post on his council as he has promised, I shall certainly see that that rule is enforced."

Louisa smiled to herself thinking how this arrogant man knew nothing of the stubbornness of native Savannahians. "But Sir James has not been the Royal Governor for two years. I'm afraid his promises are rather thin considering the circumstances."

Ralph looked down on her, a thin veil of irritation in his

eyes. Lovely as she was, Louisa Culpepper could learn something about the proper submission of women. She was far too outspoken for a young girl—a result, no doubt, of the way her father coddled and spoiled her.

"Yes, but that will surely change once the regulars retake the city, as they are sure to do."

Louisa bit back a reply. She had not missed that quick flare of annoyance. "Of course," she murmured, not interested enough to argue. Ahead she spied a group of men, all of them dressed like sober merchants, smiling and nodding where they stood by the boxes and crates piled near the forecastle: As they moved away she saw that behind them, leaning on his elbows on the rail, was the young man she had noticed earlier. He was looking broodingly out to sea, taking no part in the conversations around him. Yet, judging by his dress and manner he was probably another merchant seeking trade in the colonies. Her heart sank slightly. A man of trade, no matter how attractive, was no competition for the glittering aristocrat at her side. Her father would never indulge her to that extent.

Ah well, it was only a wistful idea anyway. No doubt she would not even like the gentleman had she the chance to know him. In spite of his pleasant face he would probably be as lacking as all the other young men she had ever known.

"My dear you are woolgathering," Stoakes broke into her thoughts. "I was asking you about Georgia."

"Oh, excuse me, Sir Ralph. It's the headache again. I would be so grateful if you would excuse me. Perhaps we can continue our walk some other time."

The irritation flitted back across Stoakes' eyes but there was nothing he could do but give in. "Of course, Miss Culpepper. Why don't you rest until supper. We can continue our conversation then."

He led her to the hatch where he bowed politely. Louisa bolted down the stairs as quickly as their steepness and narrowness would allow, vowing to stay below until the dinner hour.

In spite of the fact that Sir Ralph promised to be the only interesting man at the table, Louisa took great pains with her dress. She was feeling better than any time since their departure and her natural good spirits welcomed the chance to look her best. She slipped on a brocade dress of deep forest green that accentuated her coloring and the golden sheen of her hair. It was cut deeply in front, allowing a tantalizing hint of the cleft between her breasts and was ruched with blonde valencia lace. She piled her hair high with several long curls at the back instead of wearing it loose and free as she had that morning, emphasizing the long slenderness of her neck. There was a tinge of ceruse on her cheeks and lips and a tiny black patch signifying her loyalty to the King to one side of her face. Then tying a thin strand of green velvet ribbon around her neck and picking up a hand-painted fan of translucent chicken skin, she smoothed her skirt and went down the narrow hallway to the Captain's cabin, followed by her cousin who continually moaned to herself that she would never be able to look directly into a plate of food.

The door to the Captain's cabin was open and through it Louisa caught a glimpse of the soft glow of a lantern swinging gently with the roll of the ship. It threw long shadows on the dark paneled walls. The table was laid with silver and translucent china on a fine damask cloth. An ornate silver teapot securely anchored to a side table had been polished to a gleaming patina of reflected light.

Louisa moved into the room to meet Captain Leeds who quickly came around the table where he had been standing talking to two other men, her father and Sir Ralph, who had exchanged his yellow coat for one of an elegant indigo blue satin.

"Ah, Miss Culpepper, I am honored," Leeds said, bowing over her hand. "And this must be your cousin. Madam, I hope you are feeling better since we have been blessed with this spell of fine weather."

Cecily Davenport, ordinarily a vivacious agreeable woman, had suffered such misery on his ship that she merely murmured a response and bobbed the Captain a curtsy. He, taking Louisa's arm, led her toward the table.

"Your good father preceded you. Sir Ralph you know . . ." Louisa nodded while Stoakes made her an elaborate bow . . .

"and this young gentleman is also bound for Savannah. May I present Mr. Hugh Sandenny."

Louisa looked up to see a figure emerge from the shadows behind Stoakes and step out into the light. Instantly she recognized the young man she had seen on deck earlier that day.

"Miss Culpepper," he said, bowing slightly and smiling at her. Once again she noticed how his eyes held a mischievous glint not in keeping with his sober dress and manner. He seemed taller in the low ceilinged room and the shadows set his face in craggy lines. His hair was pulled back and tied with a simple black grosgrain ribbon and his dark clothes and the indifferent quality of this lace at his throat made her wonder for an instant why the Captain had included him. Yet he obviously had bearing and gentility and was very handsome. She gave him a shy smile all at once very glad she had taken pains to dress so well.

"Mr. Sandenny. An unusual name."

"Yes," he murmured. "I suppose it is."

"Surely not English?"

"I believe it was once French."

His hand was strong holding hers and his eyes never left her face. She was suddenly very sure that he was as taken with her as she with him.

"My dear Miss Louisa . . ." Stoakes said as he came between them. "Allow me, I believe this is your place."

Reluctantly Louisa turned to Sir Ralph and let him lead her around the table while Captain Leeds motioned the others to their places. She was relieved to be sitting next to her father while Stoakes was across the table next to Sandenny. He paid scant attention to the young stranger and concentrated so much of his attention on her to the exclusion of all the others that she found herself more and more embarrassed as the meal wore on. Hugh Sandenny sat saying little and picking at his food while Cousin Cecily spoke rarely. Her father, in his usual gregarious style, expressed an opinion on every subject from the King's health to the price of indigo on the English market. When Stoakes volunteered a comment it was with the arrogance that suggested his was the final word and no one had better disagree with it. Finally at a break in the conversation Louisa leaned across the table and spoke to Hugh directly.

"Are you staying in Savannah, Mr. Sandenny, or do you plan to move on from there to some other part of the Colonies?"

Hugh set down his wineglass. "As a matter-of-fact, I plan to stay in the city as long as my business keeps me there. Do you plan to settle there?"

"Oh, Papa and I are already settled there. In fact, we are going home after two years in England. Savannah is my home."

"Oh, I see. I wonder that you left it."

"Why, we had to, my boy," Thomas broke in, waving his knife. "It was no longer a safe place to live. The Whigs had complete power and their vindictiveness toward anyone who disagreed with them was so terrible that I feared for my daughter's safety. My own loyalties were too well known to pretend to be one of them. Had we not left when we did my house would have been burnt down around us. Even now, I tremble to think what I will find when we finally arrive."

"Than why return?" Hugh asked, tearing his eyes away from Louisa's face.

Ralph Stoakes turned in his chair to peer down at Hugh. "You sound as though you know nothing of the war going on in the Colonies. Are you not aware that a British army has been dispatched against the coastal cities of the South? We are confident that by the time we arrive it will have secured Savannah and Charleston for the crown."

"I have not paid too much attention to it, I confess," Hugh said with great patience. "Matters in England took precedence."

"Sir Ralph has been promised a position by Governor Wright once he is reinstated," Culpepper said to Hugh. "Better get on the good side of him, young man. It may stand you in good stead once you are living in Savannah."

Stoakes gave Hugh a smug smile. "You must have had grave matters indeed to prevent you from being aware of the important nature of the war George the Third is waging to hold on to these valuable colonies. It has dragged on far too long and cost too much in money and lives. People even dare to criticize the crown for his so-called stubbornness. Do you really mean to say you have never given the matter any thought?"

"Well, I had problems of my own. Naturally I would support my King in any endeavor. Beyond that I really do not much care."

"Oh, you'll have to do better than that, my boy," said Culpepper, "once you set foot in Savannah. Why men have been tarred and feathered for expressing such a lukewarm lack of conviction and by both sides!"

"Feelings run high then?"

"High! Why sir, I am a Savannahian, born and bred, so I can speak about my own where I would take another man to task for doing so. And I tell you, there is no more cantankerous, stubborn, narrow-minded bunch of mules to walk the earth than the Georgians! You'd best polish up your Tory creed or you won't last a day on Bay Street."

"Papa, I fear you will give Mr. Sandenny a poor impression of our town," Louisa said soothingly.

Hugh smiled at her. "I shall try to work up an argument that will do justice to the sentiments of a native Englishman." Louisa caught his teasing tone though her father and Stoakes seemed not to.

Captain Leeds came to his rescue. "I suspect Mr. Sandenny has not thought these matters out because he has been ill. He came aboard with the most dreadful case of the quinsy. But all's well now, eh sir? Have some more of this Portuguese Madeira. Nothing like a good wine to cure a man of all ills, I say."

The cabin boy leaned over Hugh's shoulder to fill his glass while Sir Ralph reared back, raising his pince-nez, searching Hugh's features through the glass.

"Just what is the nature of your work, Mr. Sandenny?"

Hugh ran a finger around the edge of the wineglass. "Ah . . . well . . . I am employed by the firm of Worth and Collins, dealers in fine silver and gems. They are thinking of setting up a branch in the Colonies and want me to look over the territory."

"Seems a strange time to be expanding, I should think," Stoakes muttered, trying to remember if he had ever heard of the company.

"By the way, sir, speaking of gems, I noticed you were carrying a very interesting piece on deck this morning. The walking stick with the serpent's head."

"Yes, very novel, that piece," Stoakes replied, obviously pleased. "A connoisseur would notice it, I should think. It's from India. Very valuable."

"It looks so."

"And cleverly made. The entire head and a shaft below it can be removed allowing a thin blade to project from the stick in case one meets with footpads or purse snatchers. Most convenient in the streets of London."

Louisa, who had been half listening to the conversation, was suddenly aware of Sandenny's eyes on her. Glancing up she caught a most blatantly sensual look fastened upon her, one that caught at the breath in her throat. She dropped her eyes, feeling her cheeks burning hot, not with indignation but with delightful anticipation. The mutually-felt interest that flowed between them was like a current in the room. Let Stoakes try to monopolize her all he wanted. Let Hugh Sandenny continue to make indifferent conversation with the others at the table. They both knew where their real interest lay.

After the other guests had left and the cabin boy had cleared away the table, Hugh lingered behind to have a last glass of Madeira with Captain Leeds, indulging in that most delightful of post-party pastimes—gossiping about the others who had been there.

"That was a close one," Leeds said, puffing at his pipe and loosening his jabot a little. "If Stoakes had asked me what kind of work you were in, devil take it if I'd of known what to say. What made you pick gems and silver?"

"That stick of his. I remembered it as a valuable piece. Also, he is so vain I knew he'd be flattered to have it noticed. Have to admit though, I held my breath that he'd not know Worth and Collins. They're a small firm dealing mostly with the family royals. My father has used them once or twice. They'd be most surprised to learn I was a member of their staff."

"No doubt. Look here, my boy. I took you on board as a favor to young Rob, but I'm not comfortable with this bit of false names and deeds you won't talk about. Whatever it is you've done that forced you to leave England, it seems to me that you'd do better to make a clean breast of it. Your father's got influence. Surely he could hush up any scandal. You young blades are always in some kind of trouble or other."

Hugh slowly turned his wineglass admiring the ruby liquid.

"You don't know my father very well, Captain Leeds. He dislikes me intensely. I seem to have a penchant for getting into scrapes and this would have been one too many." He raised his glass. "But I'm conscious of your help and grateful."

Leeds waved an indifferent hand. "I'll keep up pretenses. Though I wonder why you didn't pick a ship for New York rather than Savannah. T'would make a lot more sense."

"I said as much to Rob but he was afraid I'd be recognized there. After all, it's bursting with soldiers and half of them are younger sons of good houses. He's probably right."

"Well, you'll find Savannah a mite tame for a man-about-town like yourself. New York would have been a thousand times more lively."

"Oh, I don't know. I wonder if New York would produce as lovely a young woman as that Louisa Culpepper who graced your table tonight."

"And that's another thing. I saw your eye on her. You'd do best to forget about the Culpeppers."

"Why?"

"Because they're an old Georgia family—as old as any family can be in a province that was only settled fifty years ago—and she's the spoiled apple of that old gentleman's eye. He's an amiable sort but I wouldn't want anything happening on my ship to upset him."

"I got the impression she could wrap him around her little finger."

"That's true enough—to a point. That nobleman, for example. Sir Ralph. Had a wife that died only six months back. It's obvious he's staked the fair Louisa out as the replacement."

"She did not seem too delighted at the prospect."

"Don't believe she is. But that's neither here nor there. It's only the fact that her doting father won't give her to any man against her wishes that prevents the marriage banns from being called. Not the way to bring up children a'tall, I believe."

Hugh gave a chuckle under his breath, remembering the haughty iciness of Louisa's manner toward the arrogant Stoakes. He had been pleased and relieved to see it, for unless he missed his guess, Louisa had been as taken with him as he was with her. He remembered suddenly the picture she had presented that morning standing at the taffrail looking out to sea. Her head was turned away but the way she stood with the wind whipping her skirt against her tall, lithe body drove all other womanly images from his mind. Her hair was loose, streaming out in soft waves above the fall of her hood. The dress sculptured her body in the wind, outlining a tiny waist and small, dainty breasts. The lift of her skirt revealed delicate ankles clothed in rose colored stockings. She had raised one arm to hold back her streaming hair and her lacy sleeve fell away revealing a porcelain forearm, pale as warm cream. Then she had turned to catch his stare, her eyes large in her heart-shaped oval face. She was the loveliest thing he had ever seen.

And he still thought so after seeing her tonight in her shimmering green finery. The serene good manners she had shown throughout the difficult dinner only made him more certain that she was the most perfect woman he had ever met. She had none of the silly repartee of the London salons nor the simpering flirtatiousness of the rouged women he met in them. The openly pleased look she turned on him was as honest as the cold one with which she met Ralph Stoakes' advances. He was enchanted.

The thought of Stoakes quickly turned his joy to misery. It had only taken him a few moments after hearing the name to remember that this nobleman was the "uncle in high places" Pelham Stoakes was so fond of bragging about. Hugh even remembered meeting him once as a boy, though thankfully that was too long ago for the uncle to recognize him.

Pelham Stoakes! What a terrible blunder that had been. He only meant to teach the blockhead a lesson, graze him a little, just enough to frighten him. He never meant for the ball to go so close. Never meant to kill him. He wasn't even worth killing.

Now, because of Pelham Stoakes' idiocy, his whole life was in shards, he was exiled from his family and his country and forced to go as a pauper and an impostor to a backwater town in the backwater province of a wild and uncivilized country! And on the same ship as Pelham's detestable uncle. What an unlucky throw of the dice that was!

Yes, but beautiful Louisa was also on this ship, his optimistic voice reminded him. And, since he had left England so hurriedly, Ralph Stoakes could not possibly know yet of his nephew's demise. With any luck, and if Hugh could remember to continue to answer to the name of "Sandenny", Stoakes might never connect him with it at all.

The pompous peacock! His attitude toward Louisa was one of absolute ownership even though it was obvious that she had no use for the man. Even the thought of so sweet a creature in those cold arms was enough to raise Hugh's hackles. Yet because Stoakes was Pelham's uncle, it would be the better part of wisdom to have as little to do with him as possible.

Captain Leeds studied the profile of the young man's face against the flickering light of the lantern. He had known many such young men. Younger sons of the idle rich, they were all of them reckless, daring life, courting danger, too easily bored and too light-minded for their own good. He had no aversion to helping one who'd gotten himself into a scrape but he did not want any quarrels with titled noblemen on his ship. Nor did he wish for the seduction of a young lady of quality who was traveling under his care. Better by far if young Mr. Sandenny kept to his cabin.

His reverie was broken by the sounding of bells from above.

"Well," Leeds said, straightening his stock. "Time to check on the watch."

When Hugh continued studying the table without answering, Leeds reached forward to touch him on the knee.

"You're woolgathering, my boy."

"What? Oh, your pardon, sir. I was thinking about Miss Culpepper."

"Well, just make sure thinking is all you do. I want no trouble on board the *Windward*."

"You needn't fear, sir. I would not so abuse your kindness to me. But just so I won't be tempted, I think I shall stay below most of the way. And, much as I appreciate your hospitality, perhaps I had better not be invited to any more of these pleasant suppers."

Leeds nodded gravely, pleased that their thoughts took similar lines. "I understand. I can always say you've suffered another attack of the quinsy."

Chapter 2

THE GOOD WEATHER held until they were nearly halfway across the Atlantic—an unprecedented occurrence this time of year according to Captain Leeds. Louisa took it as a favorable omen for her future. She was going home to a country and a town that she loved above all others and, as if that were not enough, fortune had smiled upon her and sent a most interesting and attractive young man as a passenger on the same ship. Everything she had noticed about Hugh Sandenny at the Captain's supper party had reinforced her first impression that he was a gentleman of breeding and refinement, though probably a bit rakish as most young men were. She had sensed that he was just as impressed with her as she was with him. She was pleased that it did not seem to bother him that, though she was only a daughter, she was intelligent and educated rather than silly and simpering like most girls her age. It was a stroke of good fortune that they had been thrown together, for had she endured this voyage with only the fawning attention of Sir Ralph Stoakes, she was sure she would have thrown herself into the sea.

And yet as beautiful day melted into beautiful day and
Louisa walked the decks alongside the other promenading
passengers looking in vain for a glimpse of Hugh, she began
to wonder if her fancies had carried her away. Never did
she set foot on deck without Sir Ralph appearing at her
elbow, ready to hover over her with an infuriating solici-
tousness that frightened off everyone else. Hugh would not
have been intimidated by Stoakes, she felt sure, but Hugh
was nowhere in sight. Finally she broached the subject with
the Captain and learned that he was back in his bed with
the quinsy. Her irritation was vented on Stoakes who seemed
impervious to it. She barely spoke to him and when she
did, it was to bring up some unpleasant subject such as his
late wife or the persecution of the loyalists in Georgia. To
the first he was completely without feeling while, as to the
second, he was so arrogant as to think he could handle any
threat of violence to his person. Louisa clenched her teeth
and hoped that he would soon learn how wrong he was.
Thankfully, her father almost always accompanied them and
she was able to leave most of the conversation to that amiable gentleman.

Everything changed once the weather turned again. Louisa
kept mostly to her cabin, as did the other passengers, venturing up on deck only when the sea was calm enough to
lessen the threat of being swept overboard. She soon learned,
however, that returning below wet to the skin and shaken
to the core was not worth a brief respite in the cold, salt
air.

There was a momentary return to clear weather on the
day they sighted the second ship. She was the *Oriana*, ten
days out of Charleston and on her way to England. Her
captain, Martin Forbes, was a good friend of Leeds' so the
Captain had the jolly boat lowered and was rowed across
for a brief visit. Louisa was standing with a group of people
on the deck watching the little boat bobbing about on the
pewter-colored water when she looked up to see Hugh lum-
bering up the hatch and stepping unsteadily out on deck.
He looked very pale but otherwise unaffected by his long
spell of illness. She pushed the fur-lined hood of her blue

velvet cloak away from her head and moved to where she stood next to him.

"Mr. Sandenny. How nice to see you up and feeling better," she said, smiling up at Hugh. His eyes narrowed as he looked her over with obvious approval. The red fox fur of her hood set off the vivid pink of her cheeks and the shining flecks of gold in her eyes—eyes that seemed to have grown larger in the small oval of her face during his enforced separation. He stepped quickly up beside her.

"It is very pleasant to be feeling better, Miss Culpepper. The recent weather has been so damp and disagreeable that I don't suppose I missed much by staying below. I hope it did not trouble you."

"Oh, no, I am never seasick. It was so nasty however, that I stayed dry and warm in my cabin and solaced myself with a copy of Mr. Pope's poems."

"I had one of Fielding's stories to help me while away the long hours," Hugh answered, his eyes bright.

Louisa gave him a teasing smile. "I daresay both reflect our respective tastes."

Hugh laughed. "No doubt, since I am not over-fond of Pope's florid prose and you are far too much the lady for one of Fielding's racy stories."

All at once Louisa stepped back, pulling her hood close around her face. "Oh, dear. Here comes Sir Ralph. I had hoped to avoid him for a little while at least."

Stoakes, ebony stick in hand, was bearing down on them through the crowd that had thinned out along the rail. The despicable man, Louisa thought. After so many days of not seeing Hugh at all she had been looking forward to a leisurely stroll and a chance to renew their acquaintance. Now Stoakes would surely drive him away as he did all the others.

"Good morning, Miss Culpepper," Ralph said coolly, making Louisa an elaborate bow. "How very nice to see you about again. I feared you were indisposed."

Louisa gave Hugh an embarrassed glance. "Thank you, Sir Ralph. I find that my strength is not what I thought it was. Perhaps I should return to my cabin—"

"Oh, don't leave yet, Miss Culpepper," Hugh said quickly, stepping forward to take her arm. "A little turn around the deck would do more to restore your health than hours spent in a stuffy cabin."

Deftly he maneuvered her away from the scowling nobleman.

"Don't you agree, Sir Ralph?"

He threw the remark over his shoulder as he almost pushed Louisa down the deck. She hid her happy relief by pulling her hood around her face and tucked her arm in his.

Glaring at their backs, Ralph turned on his heel and started in the opposite direction. He had lost one round and had learned that this Mr. Sandenny would bear watching. Glancing back, he saw Louisa smiling happily up at Hugh in a way that he never saw her smile at him. Yes, Hugh Sandenny would certainly bear watching

Captain Leeds returned within half an hour, big with news.

"The King's forces have taken Savannah," he announced to the passengers who crowded around him. "They attacked the town in late December, a few days before we sailed, and easily overcame its weak defenses. A British army occupies it and the royal standard flies over the Council House once again."

Thomas Culpepper, standing beside his daughter, bounced up and down. "Capital! Excellent news. Did you hear, Louisa? Savannah is the King's city once more."

"Yes, Papa. I'm so happy."

"My, now it will be like old times again. Great news, isn't it, my boy," he said, slapping Hugh on the back.

"Yes, I suppose it is. Great news," Hugh muttered. He really did not care who occupied the town as long as he could find a haven there while his father's anger cooled.

"And what of Governor Wright?" Stoakes asked, pushing forward through the crowd. Of course, Louisa thought, that would be his main concern.

"I believe he has been reinstated as royal governor. Yes, I'm sure Captain Forbes mentioned that."

Standing across from Stoakes, Louisa got the full benefit of the satisfied smirk that settled on Ralph's thin lips. He looked directly into her eyes. There now, he seemed to be saying. My appointment is as good as made.

"No doubt the Whigs have fled to the wilderness," Thomas said. "Well, good riddance. They were nothing but a parcel of trouble from the beginning. Egad, I cannot wait to get home again!"

Hugh, standing on Louisa's other side, leaned one elbow on the taffrail and studied Ralph Stoakes' face.

"Well, Sir Ralph," he said lazily. "I suppose this means you will be appointed to the Council."

Fussing with the sleeve of his coat which had caught on a rough splinter of the rail, Stoakes beckoned to his valet, a thin, wizened fellow in a gray frizzled wig, who was standing on the other side of the deck.

"Very likely."

"You are to be congratulated. These appointments are great plums, I hear."

There was something in Hugh's tone which was anything but congratulatory. Ralph Stoakes sensed it at once.

"Just what do you mean?"

"I have heard it said that the King's ministers in the provinces have *carte blanche* to rob the government blind and build up a tidy fortune for themselves with which to ease their return to England."

Stoakes visibly bristled. "I beg your pardon, sir!"

"Come now. It is well known that a man in the right position can easily arrange to make a profit for himself in every transaction in which supplies are purchased for the army. It is almost a scandal in New York, I've been told. One fellow returned with two hundred thousand pounds."

Stoakes went very white about the lips. "Are you suggesting I am a thief, sir," he said in a cool, clipped voice.

Louisa caught her breath and looked imploringly at Hugh. Too often she had witnessed the beginnings of quarrels which always seemed to end up on a dueling ground. It was obvious that Hugh was flirting on the edge of one such now. To her relief Hugh seemed to recognize it as well. Straightening up, he bowed and said politely, "Why, no, sir. I meant no offense at all. I was merely mouthing a lot of rumors I picked up in London. Second-hand rumors, I might add. Please accept my apology for any unintended offense."

Ralph glared at him with a look full of daggers, then decided not to press the matter any further. He had no wish to get involved in a challenge either, just when events were taking so favorable a turn. A man with a title, a position, and a fortune could hardly be turned down by any woman, no matter how indulged.

Keeping a close watch on Louisa to make certain she appreciated how magnanimous he could be, he accepted Hugh's apology.

"Very well. But you'd do better to watch that tongue of yours, Mr. Sandenny, or you may well find yourself in a very uncomfortable position. Not all men are so quick to forgive."

Though the words stuck in his throat, High forced them out. "Thank you for your excellent advice. I shall remember it."

"See that you do."

Taking Louisa's arm, Hugh ushered her quickly away towards the poop deck. Behind them, Arthur, Stoakes' valet, who had come running at Ralph's signal and had heard the whole exchange, struggled to remove his master's sleeve without tearing the expensive brocade.

"Insolent dog," Stoakes snapped, as furious at Hugh's carrying Louisa off once more as he was with the verbal exchange. "I should have beaten him within an inch of his life."

"You should have indeed, my Lord," Arthur agreed, although he had never seen Hugh before that moment. "He's got a fresh tongue on him, that one."

"He is not at all what he pretends to be, I'll wager," Ralph said, frowning after Hugh, "although I cannot quite place what it is about him that bothers me so. He has a little too much arrogance for a man of his low station. And he is increasingly in my way. It is beginning to make me very annoyed."

Working the sleeve free at last, Arthur leaned close to Sir Ralph's shoulder.

"He could have an accident if your Lordship wants," he whispered. "They happen all the time on ships like this, if your Lordship takes my meaning. Just say the word and it can be arranged."

Ralph looked down his long nose at the man, turning this delicious thought over in his mind. No, it was too crude, like the person who suggested it.

"I think not. It might serve to draw too much attention to the scoundrel. There will be other opportunities for accidents in the colonies if he should continue to be a problem. Life there can be very uncertain, I'm told. In fact—"

He rubbed a long finger along his narrow chin. It could not hurt to plan ahead, to set events in motion on the ship which would not see fruition until they were back on land.

"I think I may have a better answer. Yes, that would do nicely. Now listen, Arthur, I want you to do something for me."

Chapter 3

AFTER STRUGGLING FOR two days through a second winter storm off Cape Hatteras, the *Windward* limped in along the coast of the Carolinas and made for the Savannah River. Hugh and Louisa, grateful to be out of their cabins and anxious to set foot on solid ground again, hovered at the rail, devouring the distant horizon. Hugh was fascinated by the strangeness of the land that slipped by them. It was not at all what he had expected. Flat, low sand dunes, long stretches of scrawny pines standing like a forest of ship's masts on end, an infrequent glimpse of a cottage roof interrupting the green monotony of the wilderness—it was so different from England that he began to wonder why he had chosen to come. But then he had not chosen. It had been chosen for him.

Louisa, by contrast, was filled with an overwhelming happiness as she watched the familiar landscape slip by. Until this moment she had not realized just how much she had missed this harsh, tough wilderness, so enthralled had she been with the verdant beauty of the English countryside. But this was home, with its rugged, unspoiled primeval magic. There was a newness, an excitement, a "becoming" about it that one never caught in settled old England. And it was where she had grown up. Her only memories of her mother were here in the little town whose church spire was just visible on the bluff in the distance. Her breath caught in her throat as the ship moved sluggishly toward Savannah and she wiped at the misty tears that welled behind her eyes.

Moving slowly through the outer islands, the *Windward* edged up the river and toward the town wharf, threading its way among a whole fleet of British warships. Leaning on the rail by Louisa's side, Hugh was not encouraged to see the rooftops and steeple of the town emerge through the hazy air. It was much smaller and flatter than he had anticipated and he began to wonder how he was going to bear an exile in so provincial a place for the year or two it would take before it would be safe for him to return home again. From the ship's deck they could make out the bright smear of the British soldiers' scarlet coats, the green jackets of the Dragoons and the black leather helmets of the Hessians. Hugh consoled himself with the thought that a town that housed this many foreign soldiers was bound to be a little lively.

Louisa's father soon appeared to call her below to supervise the unloading of her boxes. With his portmanteau under his arm, Hugh was one of the first people to crowd down the gangway to the wharf where he dallied around the area hoping to speak to Louisa once more before she was swallowed up by the town. Perching on one of several bound bales of cotton stacked on the cobbles of the street near the wharf, he sat watching the slow procession of passengers off the ship.

He soon spotted Sir Ralph, looking around with haughty disdain at the cluttered wharf as he swept down the gangway followed by several men who were obviously officials of the town. Soon Louisa and her father appeared and headed straight for a hansom carriage waiting near the dock where a Negro driver decked out in satin livery sat on the driver's seat. The man recognized them at once and jumped down from his perch smiling broadly.

"Welcome home, Mista Thomas, Miz Louisa. Ain't it good to see you ag'in."

"Hello, Nathan," Hugh heard Culpepper respond as he motioned toward several boxes. "It is good to be back home. Everything is still as we left it, I trust."

The driver began piling their boxes in the boot, talking all the time.

"No suh, not quite, but you gets to see soon enough. Them shells when the English soldiers come, done lots of damage. Not so everythin's gone but like so it's been hurt some."

"Oh dear, dear. Well, come along Louisa, my child, we may as well know the worst."

Handing a large hatbox to Nathan, Louisa was about to step up on the carriage when Ralph Stoakes moved up to her side. Hugh who had been pushing through the crowd to speak to her himself hung back while they exchanged a few words. When Stoakes turned away toward a second carriage waiting behind the first, Hugh nearly knocked over a Scottish corporal trying to reach her before she disappeared into the dark interior of the coach.

At the sound of his voice Louisa paused and stepped down.

"How fortunate I was able to catch you before you left," Hugh said smiling down at her. "I was just on my way into town to find a tavern but I wanted first to tell you how very much I enjoyed your company on the *Windward* and how much I hope we shall meet again here in Savannah."

Louisa's eyes were very bright. "Why, thank you, Mr. Sandenny. May I say that you have helped to make the voyage very pleasant for me as well."

"Miss Culpepper . . . would it be, that is, may I call upon you at your home some afternoon, once we have all got settled?"

"Of course. I should be very pleased if you would. We live on Abercorn Street near Reynolds Square so you should have no trouble finding us. In fact, I was hoping to invite you before you left only I thought I had missed you."

Hugh felt a warm sensation of pleasure spreading through

his chest. So, she had been searching for him all the while he was waiting for her.

"One afternoon next week, perhaps. Say, Monday?"

"Monday. That would be excellent. I shall look forward to it."

"And I," Hugh said, lifting her hand to his lips and looking deep into her lovely honey-colored eyes. She smiled shyly, then turned to the waiting Nathan to step up into the carriage. In a swirl of her camlet cloak she was gone and Hugh went back to where he had left his box, his heart singing.

Finding the Tondee Tavern, which had been recommended by Captain Leeds, turned out to be a simple procedure since Savannah was not large and was neatly and precisely laid out in evenly spaced streets surrounding several squares.

The day was warm, much warmer than the damp penetrating chill of a customary February afternoon in England, and Hugh strolled the streets near the wharf fascinated by the new things he saw. The roads were very clean for a bustling town, the houses neat and pleasant, and the people, for the most part, busily engaged in some kind of activity. Away from the shore the squares were filled with thick shrubs and trees. He was especially fascinated by the live oaks which spread their huge limbs like splayed fingers out thirty feet and were draped with a gray fungus he learned was called Spanish moss. Flowering shrubs and vines were everywhere, like an English spring, only larger and more exotic. He was amazed at the number of negroes on the streets and slightly appalled when he remembered they were probably slaves. Before he found Broughton Street and Tondee's, he passed three Indians in brightly colored turbans and beads. Hugh stared at them with an intensity he knew branded him as a yokel.

A sign hanging over the door marked Tondee's Tavern and judging from the number of men going in and out, it was a popular place. Hugh passed through the entry hall and entered a room in which a blazing fire at one end warmed the air and threw shadows on paneled shelves glistening with polished pewter. It was cozy and comfortable and all at once Hugh began to feel very hopeful about his stay in the Colonies.

Since it was already into the afternoon he was very hungry. He asked for a private room in which to sleep and have a solitary supper, but Mistress Tondee, the widow of the tavern's famous proprietor, informed him that there were none and he would have to share a bed in a room with seven other men. It was that or nothing, so Hugh put down his money and followed a potboy who carried his box upstairs to a room strewn with the belongings of other travelers. Stowing his box under one of the beds, he splashed a little water on his face and hands, brushed his coat and headed down the hall to the stairs, anticipating a hearty meal.

Halfway down the hall he was brought to a stop by the muffled sound of a woman screaming. Hugh stopped, trying to place where the cries came from. Most of the rooms off the hall had their doors open but there were two near the end which were closed. As the screams grew in intensity and distress he hurried toward them. The first was locked but across the hall the cries were muffled by the door on the right. Without thinking Hugh tried the handle and found it gave under his hand. He threw it open.

There was a long table across the room near the window. A man stood with his back to Hugh bending over the struggling figure of a woman stretched out flat on the surface of the table. A second man stood on the other side, one knee on the top, half bending over the struggling woman whose stockinged legs and frothy petticoats thrashed around him.

Racing across the room Hugh tripped on a tray of dishes and a green bottle laying on the floor below the table. He recognized well enough what was going on. This girl had brought these two men their dinner and they had decided she would make a capital dessert. There was nothing wrong in that—he had tasted many such a delicious morsel in taverns back in England—but this girl obviously objected. And that, to Hugh, was not sporting.

With obvious relish he grabbed the man nearest him by the coat collar pulling him away from the table and knocking him to the floor. The second man had straddled the girl whose hands, freed when Hugh pulled off his friend, pelted him furiously. Grabbing him around the throat, Hugh dragged him off the table and slammed him down beside his companion, banging his head against the planks several times for good measure. Then he stood back looking at them both thoroughly disgusted.

They were older men, decently dressed with the trappings of gentlemen. One of them wore a gray frizzled wig which now sat askew over one eye. The other had a face so scarred with the pox that even Hugh was appalled. No doubt he had to force a woman because he could never get one willingly.

"Get out of here, both of you, or I'll haul you downstairs and throw you into the street myself."

"Who the devil are you," one of the men groaned, rubbing the back of his neck where Hugh had jerked him off the table.

"What right have you got to come meddlin' in other folks' business."

"No right," Hugh snapped, "except that the lady was loudly inviting someone to come in and help her. Next time pick on someone who wants your attentions, if there is any woman that desperate in this world."

"I'll have the magistrate on you for this," the second man muttered, sitting up to pull up his stockings which had come loose in the fracas.

"Go ahead. I'll be very sure to tell him how it was the lady's screams that brought me here. Or is rape not an offense in the Colonies?"

"Lady!"

"And she'll back me up, I've no doubt."

Staggering to their feet and glaring daggers at Hugh, the two men straightened their coats and reached for their hats, shuffling to the door.

"We'll get back at you for this," one of them threatened, quickly retreating as Hugh made to follow them into the hall.

"I'm trembling with fear!"

"I'll speak to Mistress Tondee . . . It ain't right . . ."

"Neither is forcing a woman."

"Woman! Slut, more like!"

Still muttering they slunk down the hall toward the stairs, and Hugh, laughing, looked after them until he was sure they were gone. Only then did he turn back to the room to see how the victim was holding up.

The room was gray with the shadows of the afternoon, but there was enough light to clearly see the girl who stood, clothes and hair disheveled, leaning against the table. She was tall and full breasted with a mane of auburn hair flecked with flame. Her figure was voluptuous. Wide at the hip underneath the thickness of her skirt and petticoats, tight waist laced into a bodice that tapered out at the top to support the heavy mounds of her breasts, barely concealed by the low cut of a white linen blouse. With a gesture that was unconsciously provocative she raised a creamy arm and pushed back the flowing waves of her hair, completely free and undone in the confrontation with her attackers. Her face was rather square, her lips full and shapely, her green eyes slanted like a cat's under the dark crescents of her brows. A deep widow's peak in the center of her forehead accentuated the feline quality that was almost an unconscious part of her nature. Hugh felt she could spring silently and quickly as a cat would or on the other hand, she might curl up into a chair purring with creature contentment. She did neither. She simply stood, looking up at him from under her long lashes, her lips parted, bold, assessing, earthy.

All at once Hugh had the craziest desire to throw her back down on the table and mount her himself. Then he caught himself and gave a brittle laugh.

"Sir," she said. "I can't thank you enough."

Tearing his eyes away from her figure, Hugh fussed at straightening the cuff of his sleeve which had been slightly torn in the scuffle.

"Think nothing of it. Glad to be of help."

"Oh, but it was something. It was a lot. There aren't many men who would come to the aid of Arabia Tillman, no matter what the reason. I'm that grateful to you, sir, I am indeed."

That is probably true, thought Hugh. Most of them would simply get in line and he was not so sure but that he might have too, had he seen her before he rushed in.

"Arabia? Is that your name?"

"Aye, sir. Arabia Tillman."

"Well, Arabia. I think you had better collect that tray and get yourself back downstairs where there are people around to spare you this kind of indignity. I'll explain to Mistress Tondee what happened, if you'd like."

"Would you sir? It would help for I fancy Mistress Tondee will say it was all my fault for leading those gentlemen on. But I swear to you it ain't so. I come up here only to bring them their supper like they asked and I never dreamed . . ."

To Hugh's surprise she turned away, wiping at her eyes with the hem of her skirt. Looking more closely he could see that the poor girl was shaken, though this sort of thing surely must have happened to her before. One could not be a serving wench in a busy tavern without having to fight off the advances of many men. A girl like this one had to be experienced. But then again, she was young. Very young.

"Now don't cry, Arabia," he said gently but without trying to comfort her. That he didn't trust himself to do since it had been some time since he had lain with a woman. "It's all over now and you're none the worse for it. Put it aside and go about your business. And the next time men like that ask for a private supper send up the ugliest wench in the place. Either they won't want to attack her or, if they do, she'll be grateful."

"Thank you, sir. I appreciate what you say. Is there . . . is there anything I can do to show you how grateful I am. Anything at all?"

Was this an invitation? Hugh looked her up and down and decided it probably was, although a safe one since he was sharing a room with seven other men. Besides, there was Louisa. When he thought of all her beauty and goodness, a fling between the sheets with the likes of Arabia Tillman seemed a little degrading.

"No, there's nothing. And you mustn't give it another thought. You owe me nothing."

"But sir, I really wouldn't mind," she said quickly, sensing his displeasure. "I mean . . . I wasn't talking about . . . well, you know. I meant can't I hang up your clothes, or

carry your wig to be combed, or polish your shoebuckles—
anything at all."

The girl was quite serious and would probably devil the
life out of him till he thought of something. "Well, you
could press my shirts. They have been folded in my box
for the better part of two months and are frightfully wrin-
kled. Will that make you feel that all debts are honored."

She smiled and began stuffing her thick mane of auburn
hair under her cap, obviously pleased. "Thank you, sir. Yes,
indeed, that will be fine. And I'll see that they're washed
too. I'm very grateful Mister . . ."

"Hugh . . . Hugh Sandenny."

"Mr. Hugh. I'll see to it right away."

Hugh took a moment to point out his portmanteau to the
girl then left her to go downstairs and take his supper. He
was ravenous and the meal turned out to be simple but so
delicious that he forgot all about the brief incident. It was
only when he left the fire later that evening to go upstairs
to bed and found his shirts hanging neatly over the bedpost,
that he remembered and smiled to himself.

Hugh had expected to sleep like the dead but, in fact,
he lay awake for what seemed like hours, tossing on a rough
mattress uncomfortably stuffed with corn husks and listening to the snoring and coughing of the other occupants of
the room. At one o'clock he heard the watchmen crying the
hour in the street outside his window, then at last drifted
off into an uneasy, restless, half doze. It seemed he had
barely slipped into the first stages of a dream when he was
awakened by a loud thumping on the door below. Turning
on his side and pulling the blanket over his head to block
out the noise, he tried to muffle the muted voices of several
men in the street followed by Mistress Tondee's answering
at the front door. None of it was his concern and he wanted
only to be allowed to go back to sleep. It persisted as an
annoying undercurrent to his fitful dozing until suddenly he
was roughly shaken by the shoulder and looked up to see
his landlady bending over him, the lantern held high to throw
its light on the round moon of her face inside the ruffle of
an enormous nightcap.

Hugh squinted his eyes against the glaring light.

"What the devil..."

"Mr. Sandenny," Mrs. Tondee said in a loud whisper. "Very sorry to bother you, sir, but the magistrate is downstairs and wishes to have a word with you."

"With me? In the middle of the night? Odd's blood, what's this all about?"

"Don't really know, sir. Just that he said it was extremely serious and that ye'd better get dressed and come downstairs."

Hugh pushed the lantern away to ease the glare in his eyes. "Can't it wait until morning? This is damned inconvenient."

Mrs. Tondee, uncertain as to whether or not she was dealing with a gentleman or a criminal, reluctantly pulled on Hugh's arm.

"It is inconvenient, I know, Mr. Sandenny, but it is the magistrate after all. I think you had better come."

"Oh, very well, But I intend to give the man a piece of my mind for this!"

Groggily Hugh pulled on his shirt and breeches, and slipped on his shoes. He was not quite so brave as his indignant attitude made him appear for he was almost certain that the two gentlemen whose heads he had knocked about earlier that day had returned to bring the law down on him. Following behind Mrs. Tondee, he moved down the hall, noticing in the shadows near the head of the stairs, a shawl wrapped around her nightdress, the girl who had been the cause of all this trouble. Hugh glared at her, wishing he had minded his own business. She probably brought that whole thing on herself anyway and now it was his hide to be nailed to the barn door. So much for good deeds!

Behind him Arabia shuffled down the first two stairs, then sat down in the darkness where she could not be seen but could hear the loud voices of the men in the barroom below.

To Hugh's surprise the two miscreants he had dragged off Arabia were nowhere in the room. There was a burly, tall, thick gentleman with a heavy moustache and an air of authority that he immediately identified as the magistrate. With him were two soldiers in scarlet tunics with white cross straps carrying muskets. The fourth man—a narrow-faced, skinny fellow with pipe stem legs and a face like a ferret—took him a moment to place. Sir Ralph Stoakes' valet—what was his name? Arnold? Arthur? Yes, that was it. Arthur. What on earth was he doing here?

"There he is," the valet cried as Hugh stepped into the taproom. "That's him, ready enough. A thief! Bold as brass. Arrest him."

Hugh, completely mystified and still only half-awake, stared at the man. "Thief? What are you talking about? What's this all about anyway? What are you doing here?"

"Are you one Hugh Sandenny?" the magistrate asked, stepping between Hugh and his accuser.

"That is correct."

Keeping his scrawny body safely behind the magistrate, Arthur poked his head around, shaking a bony finger at Hugh.

"I knew he was a thief the moment I set eyes on him. Says he works for a jewelsmith. Works indeed! Steals for 'im, more like."

"Now see here," Hugh snapped, beginning to be annoyed with this scurvy little man. He took a step toward him intending to poke him in the chin but the magistrate stopped him with one thick arm.

"Arthur Helms here is gentleman's gentleman to Sir Ralph Stoakes. The same Sir Ralph who, I believe, arrived in Savannah this morning on the *Windward*. The same boat that brought you to our town, I believe, Mr. Sandenny."

"That's correct. We shared the voyage. So did about fifty others."

"Well, Mr. Helms here says that Sir Ralph is missing a very valuable piece of property—a piece that you were known to have admired and asked about. Further, one that you would immediately recognize as valuable."

"I don't know what you're talking about. What piece of property?"

"Describe the piece, please, Mr. Helms."

"He knows well enough. He looked it over enough times with those covetous eyes. It is the top to a walking stick in the shape of a serpent. Carved out of pure gold, it is, with sapphire eyes and a ruby tongue. Worth two hundred pounds at least. This so-called Hugh Sandenny—if that's his real name—knew right away what it was worth and that it could be screwed off the top of the stick. Nobody else would 'ave known that!"

"Do you recognize the piece he is describing, Mr. Sandenny?"

"Yes. I saw it once or twice. And Sir Ralph himself volunteered the information that the head came off the stick. I never asked about it and I certainly would not think of stealing it."

"Don't you believe 'im," Arthur cried, hopping around Hugh but careful to keep the magistrate between them. "Where's 'is box? Search it. He'll 'ave it there right enough. Go to 'is room and look through 'is luggage and I'll warrant you'll see who's telling the truth."

"Now see here," Hugh cried, growing more outraged by the minute, "I am not a thief. This is preposterous."

"Do you have any objection to having your box gone through?"

"Of course not. Why should I?"

"Would you please be so kind as to bring it down?"

"No! No! He'll take it away before we see it. Go right on up now and look for yourself before he has a chance to hide it again. You'll discover where it is. There's not a doubt in the world."

"You're very sure, aren't you," Hugh snapped. "I resent this—this whole thing. Obviously this man is persuaded that I have something of his when I don't even know what he is talking about."

"Nevertheless, we'd better have a look at your box. Will you be so kind as to show us the way?"

Swallowing his pride, Hugh led them back up the stairs. A sense of dread was beginning to spread through his chest. If the scurvy fellow was so damned sure of finding the jewel hidden in his portmanteau then it could only mean he had planted it there. Now if the magistrate found it, no matter how much Hugh protested he was innocent he would never be believed. The palms of his hands were beginning to grow damp as he remembered the black, resentful looks Ralph

Stoakes had favored him with that day on the deck. But would he go to such lengths to be rid of him? If that serpent's head was found in his box it would be Ralph Stoakes' doing. This Arthur was only his instrument.

He dragged his box out from under the bed and watched soberly as the magistrate went through it, carefully setting aside his clothes and the smaller parcels that held his buttons and coins. A curious crowd of the other sleepers in the room who had also been awakened by the noise collected to peer over the man's shoulder.

"I'm afraid I don't see anything here that fits the description you gave, Mr. Helms," the magistrate said, with something like disappointment.

"Then look again. It's there. I know it's there. You're not examing the thing closely enough. Nobody else could have taken it. It had to be him!"

"Then look for yourself," the magistrate said, standing back. Helms rushed to the bed and grabbing up the box, dumped its contents on the quilt, Hugh, struggling to keep his composure, barely restrained himself from yanking the man back by his collar and dumping him out the nearest window. After shaking out every item in the box, Arthur began tearing at the paper lining.

"Now see here!" Hugh cried, jumping forward. Once again the magistrate held him back but had the decency to take the box away from Helms' destructive hands and began to feel around the lining himself. After what seemed like hours he stepped back, closing the lid.

"There is nothing hidden in this portmanteau. I am afraid you have made a mistake, Mr. Helms. And you may tell your employer so."

Arthur's eyes glistened white in the lamplight. "But it has to be there. You have to look again."

"There's no place else to look. Come now. This is enough. I'm afraid we disturbed your sleep for nothing Mr. Sandenny. My apologies to you, sir. And to you, also, Madame Tondee."

The landlady shrugged. "I'm glad at least that we won't have a thief dragged from the premises in the middle of the night. Not good for the reputation, you know."

Hugh was too enraged and at the same time too relieved to speak. He followed the others out into the hallway, hoping to get an opportunity to kick Arthur Helms down the stairs. Instead he watched with pursed lips as they went muttering down to the floor below and out into the night. Absorbed as he was, for a moment he did not notice the shadowy figure that stepped up beside him.

"I believe this is yours, sir," Arabia said, making sure that there was no one in hearing distance. Reaching out her fist she dropped the gold head of a snake into Hugh's hand. He stared down at it, gaping, his eyes full of questions.

"Where . . . ?"

"I saw it this afternoon when I went to get your shirts from your box. It was underneath a loose corner of the lining. When I heard them talking downstairs I knew they'd be searching your box for it so I slipped in and took it out."

"Arabia." Hugh exclaimed, looking at the gold glimmering in his hand then back to the triumph in the girl's green eyes. "I hardly know what to say. I didn't steal this. I've never stolen anything."

"I know that, sir."

"I have no idea how that got into my luggage but I know well enough what would have happened had it been found there just now."

She stepped up to whisper close to his face. "Yes, sir. You'd have been hauled off to jail and maybe hanged. They don't hold with thievery in Georgia."

"I owe you a great debt."

"Why, sir, it seems to me that just about makes us even."

She was standing so close to him that he could feel the pressure of her breasts through the thin stuff of her night-dress. Her smile even in the darkness was provocative, her eyes inviting. Hugh bent toward her ever so slightly and impulsively she reached up and kissed him full on the lips.

The bar clanged into its slot downstairs and Madame Tondee came muttering to herself, her slippers shuffling along the plank floors toward the stairs. Pulling himself away from the girl's willing embrace, Hugh stepped back to put space between them.

"I hope to show you my appreciation sometime, Arabia, in a more appropriate way."

She smiled up at him from under her long lashes.

"I look forward to that, sir."

Mrs. Tondee, nearing the top of the stairs, saw them standing together in the shadows. "Arabia," she snapped. "Go to bed!"

"Yes, madam," she answered demurely, slipping away up to the next floor where she shared a room with the cook. Hugh looked after her, hoping that Mrs. Tondee would not think she was somehow mixed up in a robbery, but his landlady's concern about Arabia was entirely of a different nature.

"That girl! Just too attractive for her own good, she is. One of these days I'll have to let her go. Only keep her now because she'd be in the street but for me. Hope she wasn't botherin' you, Mr. Sandenny."

"No, no. Not at all."

"That's good. With all the trouble she causes me, I'm fond of her. Good night, then."

"Good night."

Hugh looked longingly at the ladderlike stairs that led up to Arabia's tiny room then down at the glittering gold in his hand. Shaking his head he went back to his bed. There would certainly be no more sleep this night.

Chapter 4

LOUISA ROLLED OVER on her feather mattress wondering
where she was. Opening her eyes she saw the bright sunshine spilling through the wide windows of her bedroom
onto the faded Turkey red carpet. Then she remembered.

She was home. In Savannah, in the colonies. Home.

Waking, she jumped up, and rang the small bell on the
table next to her bed to summon Olana her black maid.
Seeing Olana again after almost two years of exile in England had been one of the best things about coming back to
this comfortable house. Her feet were already over the side
of the bed and she was pulling on her housedress when her
maid wobbled through the door wearing a checkered scarf
around her head and an expansive white apron over her
winsey-woolsy dress.

"La, Miz Louisa, you don' sleep no time," Olana greeted
her, slipping on her shoes and tucking the robe around her
shoulders. "I expects you to be in this bed till past noon at
least and ever'day you been up with the sun."

Louisa stretched her arms high over her head, exalting in the tightness of her lithe young frame. "I'm too happy to be home to waste time sleeping, Olana. There's too much to do. Too many people to see again." With a light step she moved to her dressing table.

"Tha's true," Olana said picking up a brush to work at Louisa's long hair. "But a young gal needs her sleep if'n she goin' to stay pretty. And you too pretty to go t' seed so young. 'Sides, all them peoples, you don't need to see them so much as they bothers you. Takes up too much of your time."

"Come now, Olana. How would you have me spend my time? Sewing? I hate it. Drawing? I'm too impatient. Gossiping with the other young ladies of the town? They're silly creatures."

"Learn'n how to run a decent house like any self-respectin' gal do if'n she 'spects to be a good wife." Olana grabbed a handful of long, spun-gold hair and pulled the brush through it, bringing it alive in her dark hand. "'Specially when your Daddy don't have no wife to run it for him."

"Oh, Olana," she said watching her maid's reflection in the mirror "how I missed your fussing over me while I was in England. Just think, for nearly two whole years I didn't even think about marriage."

"Humph," Olana grunted. "Ain't natural for a young gal not to think about marriage."

"It will come in time," Louisa replied thoughtfully. "But there are other things I want to do first. A married woman has nothing but her husband and her house and her children to look after. I intend to enjoy myself before I get buried under all that."

"Where you learn such things? Not from Olana, that's for sure."

Louisa laughed, teasing a slow smile from her maid. "Come now, make me look extra beautiful for today I'm going to have a very special visitor. I want you to curl my hair and maybe add one of the artificial flowers I brought from London. And I think I'll wear my yellow dress—the one with the striped underskirt."

"Peers to me some young gentleman comin' by. Peers maybe you not so set 'gainst marriage as you tries to sound."

"Oh, this young man is not interested in marriage either. But I like him and he likes me. I'll be glad to see him again."

"He tell you he not interested in marriage?"

"Oh no. We never talked about it. I just know he isn't but I don't know how I know. It doesn't matter anyhow," she said, jumping up from the dressing table to run to her clothes press.

"Hurry now, Olana, and take this to be ironed. I want it to look especially nice."

Clucking her tongue Olana drew the yards of fabric together in her arms and started toward the door.

"Never worked so till you come back, Miz Louisa! Didn't know what peace was while you was gone."

Louisa, smiling after her, turned back to the mirror to hold several earrings against her cheek trying to decide which would look the prettiest with the yellow dress.

It was a beautiful sunny day, she was home in Savannah and Hugh Sandenny was to stop by this afternoon to call on her for the first time since they left the ship together. She was very happy.

Straightening his tricorn hat, Hugh took a deep breath and vaulted up the short steps to Louisa's front door. The house was small by London standards and not quite so fine as the Dunning house just down the street. But it had a welcoming look to it, from the white lace curtains shading the long front windows to the pots of geraniums at the top of the landing. There was a handsome fan light over the front door and the brass knocker was polished to a gleaming gold. He pulled on the handle and waited, wondering why he of all men should feel this sense of giddiness over calling on a young lady. Rob would have said he had outgrown such youthful fancies long ago, and he rather thought he had too.

The door was opened by a young black girl in a gingham turban. Hugh asked for Louisa, mentally making a note to have some cards made up with his new name. Either the girl expected him or was unusually friendly for she ushered him immediately inside and into a handsome parlor. Sitting across the room on a sofa in a cheerful yellow dress was Louisa, looking up at him with a smile in her amber eyes. With something of his old aplomb, Hugh sailed in and kissed her hand.

"It's such a pleasure to see you again," Louisa said, allowing her hand to linger in his a little longer than was necessary.

"My dear Miss Culpepper, may I say the same for seeing you again. You are just as lovely as I remembered."

Louisa flushed a little, retrieving her hand. "You Londoners, you are always so gallant. Won't you sit down, Mr. Sandenny, and have some tea. Anna, bring in the tray please."

Hugh was so intent on examining her face once more that he backed toward the opposite sofa, catching the warning glance Louisa threw his way just in time: Glancing around he saw he was not alone. Ralph Stoakes, resplendent in white wig and a deep burgundy velvet coat heavily laced with gold braid, sat in the corner Hugh had intended to take, one leg crossed over the other, twirling a glass on a red ribbon. The long look on his face told Hugh readily enough that his appearance had been an unwelcome interruption.

"Sir Ralph," Hugh said, making his most elaborate bow.

"Mr. Sandenny. How nice to see you again," he drawled in a tone that clearly said it was not nice at all.

Hugh settled on the other end of the sofa trying to mask his own irritation. He had certainly hoped to have Louisa to himself.

"Are you quite settled in Savannah by now, Mr. Sandenny?" Louisa asked as Anna laid an elaborate silver tea service on a tray in front of her.

"Yes, quite comfortably. At the Tondee Tavern," Hugh said to Ralph, "but then you are aware of that, aren't you."

Stoakes gave a discreet cough and raised a lace-trimmed handkerchief to his lips. The eyes looking over it were cold as ice.

"I'm sure I do not know what you mean."

"You must be careful at the Tondee," Louisa went on. "It was a notorious meeting place for the Liberty Boys before the British took the town. I suppose it is safe enough now but do keep your ears to the ground and don't let them draw you into their schemes."

"Oh, I rather doubt that they would bother with such an obvious King's man as I. Especially one just off the ship." He turned back to Stoakes. "Did you get that matter of the missing top to your cane cleared up?"

"Humph. Yes. As a matter-of-fact, it was delivered to me by post just yesterday. I was not able to trace who sent it."

"I'm so pleased. No doubt the scoundrel who took it found that Savannah is too small a town to try to sell something so distinctive. It would have come to your attention at once."

"No doubt," Stoakes answered, glaring at Hugh.

"Why, Sir Ralph, did you lose part of your stick?" Louisa asked.

"It's no matter," Ralph answered, waving his handkerchief. "A trifle. My valet is a careless fellow and he probably misplaced it where some enterprising fellow picked it up. The whole thing is forgotten."

Hugh glared at the man over the rim of his cup. Had it not been for Arabia's quick thinking, he would have been in jail right now and likely to stay there. "Your valet seemed very convinced that I had taken it," he said, sticking grimly to the subject.

Louisa, looking from one to the other, realized that something more was going on than a lost trifle. Ralph Stoakes leaned forward to take the cup she offered him, glaring back at Hugh.

"Well, fellows of that class tend to distrust one another."

There was a clatter of china as Hugh's cup rattled against the saucer. His fingers tightened on the cup to keep himself from flinging it in Stoakes' face until he recognized the look on the man's face. He was testing him, teasing him along in order to goad him into betraying his origins. He would like nothing better than for Hugh to lose his temper and throw the contents of the cup at him.

Relaxing, Hugh leaned back on the sofa and smiled with satisfaction. "Unfortunately, that *is* a characteristic of a certain class. But we must learn to adjust to it now that we are in a country that intends to abolish such distinctions."

"That idle hope is bound to have as little success as the rebel defenses of this city had against Sir General Clinton's army. Don't you agree, Louisa, dear?"

Louisa concentrated on her cup. "I suppose I must agree, though I'm bound to say, liberty and equality are most attractive ideals. Impractical but attractive."

"Once we rally the true loyalists in the Georgia countryside," Sir Ralph went on, "and clean out those nests of treasonous vipers, who continue to disrupt our peace, there will be no question but that the order of the mother country is the proper and productive one."

"I had no idea you were so involved in Georgia politics," Hugh said with just the slightest touch of sarcasm. "Or so knowledgeable about recalcitrant Whigs."

Louisa, noting that his comment sounded more like a challenge than a question, broke in quickly.

"General Prevost has offered Sir Ralph a temporary appointment with the Council until Governor Wright returns to Georgia. One of his first concerns is the security of Savannah."

"My congratulations," Hugh murmured. "But I was under the impression that the colony was already in the hands of the loyalists. Do you mean there is still some question about its leanings?"

"Unfortunately this war is more a civil strife than a rebellion," Louisa replied sadly. "Brother against brother, family against family. Feelings run so terribly high. Neither side wants to give an inch and I'm very much afraid they won't even now, when the British have taken Savannah. We were not even able to hold on to Augusta more than a month."

"Augusta?" Hugh asked.

"Yes. A small town far up on the Savannah River near the Indian country. You see, Mr. Sandenny, our poor colony of Georgia is surrounded on all sides by enemies. The Indians to the west, the Spaniards to the south, South Carolina to the north—who would love to extend her boundaries beyond the Savannah River—and, meanwhile, we fight and kill each other over loyalty to the King on the one hand or to Congress on the other. It doesn't make much sense, does it?"

Stoakes, anxious that Louisa not direct too much of her attention to this interfering young man, broke in hurriedly.

"I do believe this internal squabble might be cleared up very quickly were it not for these detestable men who deliberately keep it fermenting: Robert Sallette, the Fews, father and son, John Dooly. If we could catch them and hang them, the colony would settle back into the old order at once."

"And who is Robert Sallette," Hugh asked, wondering how Ralph Stoakes had learned so much about Georgia in so short a time.

Louisa reached for his cup to refill it. "He is a former Savannian who was burned out and his family killed by a Tory mob. Now he has a group of men with him and they live in the swamps near the Florida border from which they make raids on Tories and British regulars. It is said they are without mercy when a Tory falls into their hands."

"Trash. Nothing but trash," Ralph muttered. "But we'll soon have them under lock and key. I have some ideas . . ."

His voice trailed off expectantly as if waiting for them to ask him what they were. When Hugh, who cared nothing at all about the strong feelings between Tories and Whigs, sat without answering and Louisa concentrated on pouring the tea, Ralph went on as if determined to impress them.

"Even now I am planning to mount a new attempt to catch that fox, Sallette. He's eluded every other because his friends always get to him before we do. But this time that will not happen. This time the whole plan will be carried out in strictest secrecy."

"I'm sure you will be successful, Sir Ralph," Louisa said soothingly. "Of course, you do realize, I hope, how very inhospitable that terrain is—all swampland and bogs. I believe that is the reason Mr. Sallette has managed to avoid hanging up till now. He knows the area so well and we town folk know it so little."

"Nonsense. It cannot be any worse than some parts of England. But I shall see that for myself. I plan to coordinate this entire operation with the military and will be at the head of it myself, along with Colonel Brown, of course."

"I should truly love to see that," Hugh muttered, smiling innocently at Stoakes who glared back at him over the rim of his cup.

"Well, I avoid that area like the plague," Louisa spoke up. "I only went through it once, to visit St. Augustine— which, by the way, Mr. Sandenny, is a very interesting old town and one you should see some day—and I shall never go through that discomfort again. Some of Olana's people live there and are very good about bringing me the hearts of palm which I do enjoy eating."

"I suppose even the most inhospitable country has some redeeming virtue," Hugh said good naturedly. "I have found that to be generally true of Savannah. Even the Tondee Tavern has its share of pleasantries."

"I'm sure you don't find hearts of palm on the bill there," Ralph drawled.

"No, but we've other delicacies—oysters, crabs and ten different rice dishes. Arabia tells me they also serve green turtle when they can get it."

"Arabia?" Louisa's hand stilled over the handle of her silver teapot.

"Yes. Arabia Tillman, one of the serving wenches at the Tondee.

Something in Stoakes' manner perked up ever so slightly. "I was not aware that gentlemen are customarily on a first name basis with serving wenches in taverns."

"It is not so unusual in London, I assure you," Hugh answered, rattling his cup against his saucer. He leaned forward and laid it on the table. "Arabia Tillman has been a friend to me when I needed one badly."

Ralph's laugh had a touch of slyness. "No doubt."

"Not that kind of friend," Hugh glared back at him. Too late he saw that he was only getting himself deeper. Louisa came to his rescue.

"A most unusual name," she said, in her gentle way. "Won't you have another sweet meat, Mr. Sandenny?"

"No thank you, Miss Culpepper. I've had quite enough

and I really must be going. I do hope you will allow me the honor of calling on you again."

"Why, I hope you will and very soon too." She rose, looking, Hugh thought, a little unhappy to be left alone with Ralph Stoakes. "Perhaps I shall see you in the town. It's not large, you know, and I often go abroad to . . . to look over the books at Mr. Waxman's store."

Hugh looked up at her telling her with his eyes that he had noted the name.

"I too enjoy browsing in bookstores," Hugh said softly. "Perhaps we shall meet there some morning. Good day, Miss Culpepper."

In the kitchen of the Tondee Tavern, Arabia Tillman laid her small pressing iron on its trivet near the hearth and folded the sleeve of one of Hugh's ruffled shirts. Ten feet away, stirring a long wooden spoon in one of the kettles over the fire, Margery, the Tondee's cook, glanced up and caught the look on Arabia's face. She chuckled, showing the gaps between her yellow teeth.

"Why don't you cover it with kisses," she said, the greasy blouse shaking like a blob of jelly with her silent laughter.

"Be quiet, old woman," Arabia snapped.

"I can see," Margery cackled. "I got eyes. It's lovelorn you be. No doubt about it, you'll be in the gentleman's bed 'fore old Mrs. Peter knows what's 'appened. Mind ye be careful tho. Them gentlemen what come from London, ten to one they bring the pox along with 'em."

"Mind your own business, you old crone," Arabia said, more angry at herself than the cook for allowing her feelings to show on her face. Laying the shirt on top of a stack of several others, she carried them across the room to the deeply set window where she could turn her back on Margery and smooth down the folds without being seen.

"Ha, ha," Margery said, bobbing up and down. "Our girl's gone and lost her heart to the fine London gentleman what's not goin' to give her the time of day. And all because he treats her like a lady."

"He's not such a fine gentleman. He's got very modest

means, or he wouldn't be staying here. And he doesn't treat me like a lady. He's just nice to everyone. And you're no better than a gulla black!"

"Yes, sir, better warn old Mrs. Peter," Margery went on, amusing herself. With an exasperated shrug, Arabia flounced down on the window seat and stared at the street which was just above her.

The stupid old crone was right, of course. She had lost her heart to Hugh Sandenny, and all because he had been kind to her and saved her from a mortifying situation. He was far above her and she could expect nothing from him, yet telling herself this bold truth had not eased her longing in the least. He was a handsome and fine gentleman and she felt more drawn to him than to any man she had ever known. Though he seemed to admire her, so far he had made not the slightest effort to get her into his bed, a fact which caused her some chagrin.

Jody, the little Negro kitchen boy, sat down by the hearth pulling at a long willow stick with a blunt knife. Sensing the cook's joke, he joined in.

"Why don't you take those shirts upstairs now, Miss Arabia? Maybe you find that nice gentleman all alone. You changes his mind for him mighty quick, I think."

"She won't find him upstairs now, no way," Margery said, reeling back and standing like a man-o'-war with both hands on her hips. "He's out. I heered it myself from Robert, the oustler."

"That's right," Arabia said nonchalantly. "He went out calling on some friends he met on the ship. He told me he was going."

"Yes, on that Miss Louisa Culpepper, Robert says. Now there's a pretty girl, as fine as he is himself. And rich too. Couldn't do much better, he couldn't." Collapsing into a chair near the plank table, Margery cackled, low and self-congratulatory. "Now that's got her, hasn't it, Jody. Sittin' there with her mouth hangin' open like a fish just off the hook. Didn't know you had such high-toney competition, did you Arabia?"

"Louisa Culpepper is in London," Arabia said in a tight voice. "She's been there these last two years."

"Well, she's not there now. She come back on that same boat ye'r fine gentleman come on. The two of them's thick as thieves, no doubt."

Flouncing to her feet, Arabia carelessly grabbed up the stack of Hugh's shirts, crushing them in her arms.

"I don't believe it. You're just telling lies to tease me."

"Land sakes, if it ain't true, may I die on the spot this moment. Ain't it so, Jody. You said yourself, Jerral told you the mistress was home again when you saw him in the market yesterday."

Jody nodded solemnly. "Tha's right. He did so, indeed. And Jerral knows. His ma, Olana, done worked for them Culpeppers mos' her life."

Arabia threw back her head and stared at the two of them, two red spots on her cheeks. "Well, so what if she is. Mr. Sandenny's only paying his respects after the trip, like any gentleman would. And you two are nothing but a couple of gossips. There must be better company in this place and I intend to find it."

She stalked to the door and started up the low stone steps to the main floor above. Behind her she could still hear Margery's cackling until the noises of the taproom drowned it out. As little anxious to face the crowd there as she had been to linger in the kitchen, Arabia waited until she felt no one was looking, then slipped up the stairs to the rooms above. In a moment Madame Tondee would be calling for her since this time of day business usually began to pick up, but with any luck she might yet have a few more precious moments to herself. She quietly slipped into the empty bedroom where Hugh's portmanteau stood beside one of the beds, opened it and laid the shirts inside, smoothing them down with her hand. About to close the lid, she glanced up to be certain the room was empty, then picked up the topmost shirt and held the smooth linen against her cheek, imagining it had something of Hugh's scent about it still. Gently she slid the cloth down her cheek and against her lips, savoring it, imagining it was Hugh's skin, Hugh's lips.

Louisa Culpepper!

Arabia jerked the shirt away, threw it in the box and slammed down the lid.

Of all the women in world, why Louisa Culpepper! God must have singled her out for some special kind of mean trick. From below she caught Madame Tondee's high pitched yell. It was time she got back to work. Enough foolish dreaming. What was the use of it anyway. While she had lovingly washed and pressed Hugh's linen, he himself had been calling on Louisa Culpepper. What was the use of anything.

By the middle of the next morning Arabia had thrown off her depression. Hugh had returned that evening feeling so happy that he made those around him happy as well, including Arabia. Her attempt to be cool to the gentleman was soon overcome by his kindness and charm. By the time they went to their respective beds she was as besotted with him as ever.

Hugh had mentioned that he would be leaving the tavern by midmorning and Arabia made certain she was there when he stepped out of the door, her straw hat tied securely under her chin and her market basket over her arm. Hugh could not help but notice how attractive she looked with her long dark hair streaming down her back and the white fabric of her blouse straining over her full, luscious breasts. For a moment she drove all thought of Louisa from his mind, until he remembered his errand of the morning.

"Might I accompany you, sir," Arabia said, casting her eyes at Hugh coquettishly. "I was just on my way to the market to pick up a few bits and pieces for Margery, the cook. She often asks me to since it's hard for her to walk with her great bulk while I like nothing better than a good stroll."

"Why, I should be honored, Arabia," Hugh answered, tipping his hat. "As a matter-of-fact, I have not yet learned to find my way around this town and you could direct me."

"Why that would be my pleasure, sir," she said, setting off beside him on the narrow street. "Savannah is not very large, I suppose you've noticed. Nothing like London I should imagine."

"Certainly not as large and a great deal cleaner. Although one does not see some of the unusual sights in London one does here. I'm almost beginning to get used to them. For example," Hugh said, gesturing with his cane to two Yamacraw Indians on the path ahead of them. "Gave me quite a start the first time I passed them," he said, lowering his voice as they neared. "All those feathers and that smeared ocher. Do they ever start hacking away at the inhabitants?"

Arabia followed him as they crossed the street and started in the direction of the river. "Sometimes out in the wooded areas they can turn savage and kill a farmer or two, but generally the ones who come into the town are peaceable. And it's said they like the British better than the Georgians. Besides, Yamacraws are not so bad. It's the Creeks you must watch out for."

"I'll try to remember that, though I confess I cannot tell one from the other."

"It's all in the way they dress."

"You seem very knowledgeable about Georgia province, Arabia. Have you lived here all your life?"

"Oh, yes, sir."

"Where did you ever get a name like 'Arabia'? It is a country, you know, full of sand and bedouins and camels. Were you named for it?"

"No. Nothing like that. My Ma came from a small village called Stonearabia in New York province. Just after she was wed she and my Pa set out for Georgia to make their fortune. When I was born I guess she already knew coming here was a mistake and she was so homesick she named me for the town. My Pa died when I was only three and after that she had a hard time finding work so's she could care for me. She always wanted to go back to New York but could never put enough shillings together to get there. She died when I was eleven, just worn out and too sad to go on living. Do you have a mother, sir?"

Hugh laughed. "To be sure I had one, but I can remember so little of her she might as well have died when I was an infant. She did not get along with my father and they seldom met. I lived with him."

"La, sir, I never heard of such a thing."

"People have some strange customs in the old country, Arabia."

Two British dragoons approached them from around a corner, their eyes widening approvingly as they blatantly looked Arabia over. Hugh took note of how the girl absently threw back her shoulders and walked with a slow, undulating movement yet at the same time refused to look them directly in the eye, glancing away as though their attentions embarrassed her. She was something of an enigma, he thought. There was a sensuality about her every movement that had something of innocence and naiveté underneath. He could not quite believe it was real. She drew men on even as she pushed them away. Was it part of a carefully orchestrated maneuver to bank the fires even more, or was it possible that she didn't realize she was doing it. He simply could not make up his mind.

Tucking his cane under his arm, he glared at the soldiers until, discouraged, they passed by on the other side.

"There are an uncommon lot of troops in this town, Arabia," Hugh commented, seeing another group approaching, their interest caught by the girl at his side.

"That's just since the bloody-backs took it back," Arabia answered nonchalantly. "I don't mind the British so bad but those Hessian Mynheers—Ugh! All greasy pigtails and thick moustaches. And not a word of English among them."

They were drawing near Market Square where Hugh expected to lose his companion.

"I see the market is just ahead so I expect you'll be leaving me here. But can you direct me to the bookstore before you go? I thought I would have a look at it to compare it with the ones in London."

"It's down Queen Street, I believe," Arabia said, straining to remember. Since she read poorly she had little interest in the store but had heard it mentioned enough when the Whigs were so vociferous in Savannah. "I think it is two streets over. You shouldn't have any trouble finding it."

"Thank you, my girl. Have a good morning and watch out for those soldiers. They'll take advantage of you, given half the chance."

"Oh, I shall, sir."

She watched him saunter off smiling happily and nodding to anyone on the street who looked kindly at him. Almost too happy. And why a bookstore when most any self-respecting gentleman before noon would head straight for the first coffee house.

It took her only a moment to make up her mind. Ignoring the cries of the vendors in the stalls on Market Square, she set off hurriedly behind Hugh, keeping to the shaded side of the street in case he should look round.

Twice Hugh stopped to ask directions before disappearing into the dark depths of Waxman's Book and Confectionary Store. Arabia lingered awhile across the street looking longingly at the entrance filled with an uneasiness she could not identify. She had almost decided to retrace her steps back to the Market Square when she heard her name called and turned swiftly to look behind her.

There stood Louisa Culpepper, elegant in a calico ruffled dress with a colorful sunshade over her beribboned straw bonnet. Her light hazel eyes were wide with surprised delight.

"Arabia Tillman. Surely it is you."

Arabia's eyes narrowed and she took a quick step back.

"Miss Louisa," she said grimly.

"Arabia," Louisa said, stepping up to her and laying her gloved hand on her arm. "You cannot know how many times I've wondered about you and longed to see you again. How have you been? You are looking so well and beautiful as ever."

"I'm fine, thank you, Miss," Arabia muttered.

"I've been away, you know. In London. My father and I just returned to Savannah about a week ago. Oh, I missed it so, Arabia. London is nice enough but it is not home."

"Yes, miss," Arabia said, wondering how anyone in their right mind could wish for Savannah when they were in a great city like London. How typical of Louisa.

"Are you well, Arabia?" Louisa asked, the girl's coldness finally dampening her effusive greetings. "That is, are you well placed? Is there anything you need?"

"I'm very well, thank you, Miss. I have a position in a tavern."

"Do you like it?"

"Well enough."

Louisa peered closer into the girl's face. "You know you have only to speak and you can have a place with us. Any time at all. I should adore having you in our house. Everything would be as it used to be. I remember those times so dearly."

Arabia's stare focused on the pavement. "That's very kind of you, Miss Louisa, but I'm very well where I am."

"All right. But you will remember, if ever you need another position, come to me first."

"Yes, ma'am. I'll remember."

"Oh, Arabia, it is so good to see you again. It quite brings back my girlhood days. Do take care of yourself."

Arabia nodded, still staring at the cobblestones. Louisa, finally put off by her reticence, gave her arm a gentle squeeze and started across the street. Arabia stared after her, her eyes narrowed, watching as the door to the bookstore opened and the bell jingled merrily.

For Arabia all the light had gone out of the day. With her shoulders drooping and her lips grimly pursed, she set off back to the market.

To Hugh's surprise, when he returned to Tondee's later that day he found a handsomely scrawled note from Sir Ralph asking him to stop round at the Council House where he kept his office. Full of curiosity, he changed his shirt, powdered his hair, and walked down Broughton to Reynold's Square and the new Council House. He found Ralph Stoakes waiting for him in a small office stuffed with elegant furniture. He was all affability as he led Hugh to a mahogany chair and offered him a glass of the finest Portuguese Madeira.

"You are no doubt wondering why I asked you here," Ralph said as he resumed his place behind a table of brightly polished cherry wood.

"I confess I am most curious," Hugh answered, crossing his legs and studying the man opposite him. "Somehow I feel certain that it is not out of affection or friendship."

Stoakes smiled at him, no humor in his narrow eyes. "I won't pretend that it is. But when there is something which needs to be done I believe in using the best man for the job, regardless of my feelings toward him. It seemed to me this matter might be of interest to you as well as of service to me."

"Oh? And what is that?"

"At Miss Louisa Culpepper's home yesterday we spoke of the small Spanish garrison at St. Augustine and, I believe, you expressed some interest in seeing it firsthand. Well, as it happens, I have some dispatches which must be carried to that garrison. If you are truly serious about visiting it, I would be most happy to offer you an escort, providing, of course, that you guarantee me that you will deliver my dispatches into the hand of Governor Tonyn's secretary and no other. What say you?"

Hugh thought a moment. His first reaction was admiration for how cleverly Ralph had concocted a way to get him out of the city.

"How long would this trip take?"

"Oh, I shouldn't think more than a few days. Unless you decide to linger there, savoring the delights of what I am told is a very interesting and ancient little town."

"I shouldn't like to be away from Savannah too long," Hugh said cryptically.

Stoakes gave a wave of his hand. "As you wish. I assure you I have no motive except to be certain that my letters get to Governor Tonyn. After that you are free to come or go as you please."

"But why me? There must be soldiers whom you would trust more."

Stoakes studied him a moment before answering, tapping his fingers lightly on the polished surface of his desk.

"The nature of these letters are such that a military courier would draw too much attention. A civilian traveling to the fort as a visitor, on the other hand, could not interest anyone. I remind you, Mr. Sandenny, we are at war and sometimes we must take precautions which in peaceable times would not be necessary."

Hugh looked warily at the man sitting so easily across from him. He could detect no trickery, no ulterior motive,

but that did not mean there was none there. He did not trust
Ralph Stoakes and something told him it would be wise not
to.

On the other hand he was curious about the old Spanish
city. And a few days could not hurt.

"Very well, Sir Ralph. I shall deliver your dispatches. I
warn you, however, that my interest in the city will not be
sufficient to linger there much longer than it will take to
hand them over to someone in the Governor's office. When
shall we depart?"

"Good, good. I hoped you would agree. I can have an
escort ready by tomorrow morning."

"So soon?"

"Well, there is some urgency in getting these letters down
there."

Setting his glass down Hugh rose. "Very well. Tomorrow
morning it is then."

"They will wait for you at the Trustee's Garden Gate just
beyond the old powder magazine. Do you know where that
is?"

"No. But I'll find it."

"Take along a pistol if you have one. You do have one?"

Hugh had started for the door but something in the man's
voice made him turn back. "Yes, I do."

"Good." Stoakes stood up behind his desk. "Terrible
things pistols. They can cause so much harm. Why only
this morning I had news from a ship just arriving from
England that my young nephew Pelham Stoakes was recently killed in a duel."

Hugh's hand was on the knob. He paused, looking back
over his shoulder. "Oh?"

"Yes. Terrible thing. Such a fine young gentleman. His
life snuffed out like a snap of the fingers. So difficult for
my poor brother."

"I'm sorry to hear of it," Hugh said, facing Ralph squarely.
"Now if you will excuse me, I suppose I'd better be getting
a few things together for the journey."

"Of course. Good luck to you. And my thanks."

Hugh gave him a quick, shallow bow and slipped through
the door, closing it behind him and leaning against it.

So word had come and so soon. But did Stoakes' obvious comments mean he knew of his involvement in Pelham's death? He might be suspicious but, thinking it over, Hugh felt certain he had no direct proof or he would not have been so formally polite in the interview just ended. Stoakes had almost certainly sent an inquiry back to England—he might even have written the firm of Collins and Worth for all Hugh knew. Perhaps it might not be such a bad idea after all to leave town for a while.

On the other hand, once he left Savannah Sir Ralph had no competition for Louisa's company. Hugh frowned as he walked down the steps of the Council House. It might be better if he went to St. Augustine but, by heaven, he would not stay there long.

Chapter 5

HUGH WAS UP before dawn readying his haversack for the
trip. He took along a change of linen, a small bottle of wine,
some bread and cheese, and, for good measure, his dueling
pistols, powder and balls. At the last moment he threw in
the stub of a candle and a flint, then drew his cloak about
his shoulders, set his hat on his head, and slipped down the
hall to the front door. There he was met by Jody whom the
night before he promised an English ha'penny to light his
way with a lantern through the still sleeping streets.

It had rained during the night sending a thick fog rolling
in from the river to turn the air damp and cold. Ghostly
shadows thrown by the lantern danced along the empty
streets as Hugh followed the small boy across town to the
city's old garden gate. Once far off he caught the mournful
wail of the night watchman crying the hour, but the only
other sounds to break the calm were sleepy roosters and the
early chattering of the awakening birds.

He found the soldiers waiting for him, stamping their

boots in the cold. There were three of them, a British grenadier sergeant from Yorkshire with a thick, northern country accent and two German mercenaries from Westphalia, one of whom spoke a little English and the other none at all. They were fierce looking sights with their tall furred helmets, their huge waxed moustaches and long pigtails bound in stiff leather. Hugh was rather grateful they were on his side.

The north country sergeant wasted no time getting started and before the sun was risen they had already left the rice fields and outlying plantations of Savannah far behind. The first day's journey proved to be easy going for the road that led south to Fort Barrington on the Altamaha River was a fairly busy one. The following day they were up at dawn again but once across the river they were tramping through terrain that was like none Hugh had ever seen before. The path was a rude affair, hacked out of thickets and dense underbrush thick with a forest of long palm-like plants the sergeant called 'palmettos'. These gave way to endless flats of pine growing close and tall. Dry as a desert in some places, it could as quickly change to marshy bogs, mired in mud. Sergeant Linton, who had made this trip several times, explained to Hugh how grateful he should be that the day had remained cloudy, for the heat could be truly fierce when the direct sun beat down on the scrub like this.

Other than these comments on the weather the Sergeant had little to say and the Germans nothing at all. Shortly before noon they came to the first of several large bodies of water, sleepy brown streams that meandered with a serpentine grace through the surrounding marsh grass and palmettos. Hugh looked across to the pine flats far on the other side and wondered how they were going to get there. Behind him he heard the first slap of the hatchet and turned to see the two German soldiers hacking at several saplings, preparing a raft.

"Is this going to happen at every body of water?" he asked Sergeant Linton dryly.

"No. We've a couple o' canoes hidden away in several places if the Indians haven't got 'em. But there's a deal o' rivers 'tween here and Fort Augustine and when we've no canoe, we make a raft."

Hugh tried to assist but soon found that his inexperienced attempts got in the way more than they helped. It was amazing how quickly the three men stripped the tree limbs and lashed them together in a kind of serviceable platform, complete with a long steering pole. They clambered aboard and Linton gave a push with the pole that sent them out into the brown water. They were well out into the river when they heard a sharp cry behind them. Turning Hugh stared at the unexpected vision of a girl standing on the shore they had just left, waving frantically. He had to stop himself from rubbing his eyes. It couldn't be!

But it was: Arabia Tillman, the ends of her shawl crossed over her dress, a floppy straw hat over her black hair, frantically waving and calling to them.

"God!" Linton exclaimed. "A white woman. Out here?"

The two German soldiers began to chatter in their own language, gesturing excitedly and smiling a little too broadly Hugh thought.

"I know that woman," Hugh said. "She's from Savannah. She must have been following us."

"What does she want—that we should turn back?"

"I expect so." He was beginning to feel the first tinges of real annoyance. The nerve of the girl thrusting herself on him this way.

"What's to do?" Sergeant Linton looked to Hugh for an answer, a little confused by such an unaccustomed problem.

"Well, we can't leave her there," Hugh said, thinking to himself that it would serve her right if they did. "Can you get this thing back to shore?"

Linton, without answering, poled the raft around and into the shallow water. Without hesitating, Arabia slipped out of her shoes, lifted her skirts and waded into the lake to the raft, grasping Hugh's hand to clamber aboard.

"I thought you were going to leave me here," she said, steadying herself against Hugh's arm. "In this wilderness."

"What the devil are you doing here," Hugh snapped, not even trying to hide his irritation. One glance took in her obvious traveling costume, the homemade knapsack she carried tied to her back and the heavy leather shoes she held in her hand. "Why did you do this? Were you following me, Arabia, because if you were..."

"Maybe I was and maybe I wasn't," Arabia snapped back, pouting her ripe lips and tipping her chin to look down at him from her slanted eyes. "Maybe I just wanted to visit St. Augustine myself, and this was as good a time as any."

"I don't believe you. Really, this is too much."

"Better keep your shoes off, ma'am," Linton said, pushing back out into the water. "We didn't make this raft to carry five and it's going to be a wet trip across."

Hugh caught the lascivious leer with which the Germans and even Sergeant Linton were taking in the girl's appearance and his irritation flared.

"This your woman?" Linton said curtly.

"She certainly is not."

The soldiers nodded and giggled and Hugh added quickly, "But she is a friend and as such I suppose she is under my protection."

"Well then, what do we do, Mr. Sandenny? Better make up tha' mind. Do we go on or leave her here, or maybe all of us go back to the city."

"No. We've come too far to turn back. Besides, I have to get to Fort Augustine. I have important business there. The devil take you, Arabia, you've made this trip too complicated by far."

"I won't be any trouble, Mr. Hugh, I promise. I'll stay out of the way and I'll keep up. I'm light and fast, you'll see."

"Well, I suppose there's nothing for it but to drag you along. Go on Sergeant Linton. Take us across. I'll do my best to see that she doesn't get in the way."

"Oh, thank you, Mr. Hugh," Arabia said, her smile lighting her face. "You won't be sorry. I promise you won't."

Hugh muttered something to himself, noticing that the Germans, while still devouring Arabia with their eyes, had obviously caught on to the relationship between them. Stepping back to balance the rickety raft, they made only one or two incomprehensible comments on the trip across the river, but seldom took their eyes off the girl.

Arabia was as good as her word once they pulled the raft ashore and set off down the narrow path again. Hugh put her in the rear where her distracting presence might be ignored, but every time he looked around she was right with them, as agile and quick as a young deer. If she tired before they did she was careful not to show it and she was the first up after their brief rest stops in an occasional shady clearing.

Hugh spent the last hour of the day's trek wondering how they were going to manage when they made camp but as it turned out he was pleasantly surprised. Once a fire had been started Arabia stepped in to make a passable communal supper out of the provisions each of them had brought along. She was the only one to remember to carry cornmeal and using some river water and salt she fried a flat cake that tasted delicious. With great decorum Hugh improvised a frame covered with palm fronds and pine branches behind which Arabia could spend the night. He then rolled up in his cloak next to the fire keeping on her side of the camp while the other three men took the far side. He anticipated a possible problem but found there was none. Though the soldiers admired Arabia, they had the decency to honor another man's protection and had concluded she was off limits to them.

To Hugh's chagrin, Arabia seemed to manage the trek through thicket and bog better than he, her strength gaining as his ebbed. As they neared Florida territory each day grew warmer and Hugh, who was more accustomed to long rides than long walks, threw himself down at night with muscles stiff and feet sore and blistered. His clothes grew stagnant with the sweat that poured down his body during the hot afternoons. Occasionally a sudden squall would bring relief until it passed on and he had to walk in sodden clothes steaming from the renewed vigor of the tropical sun.

But he forced himself on, too embarrassed to show his weaknesses and discomfort in front of this slight girl who never seemed to be fazed by the miles or the weather.

Privately he consoled himself with the thought that she was used to it, having lived here all her life while he was a raw newcomer.

And then one morning they broke out of a thick brush of scrub palmetto and pine to confront a vast panorama of open sea stretching to the horizon before them. It was such a sight as Hugh imagined must be the nearest thing to paradise. A sea, green and translucent as jade, rolled noisily against the shore in reams of glistening froth. Above it the sky lay vast, vividly blue and empty for endless miles. On the undulating acres of dunes sea oats waved lazily in the warm breeze.

With a joyous cry Arabia tore off her hat, slipped off her heavy shoes and ran, her arms outstretched as to embrace the beauty of the scene, to stand in the milky froth of the waves. Hugh glanced around to see the almost contemptuous smiles on the soldiers' faces but then thought, "Oh, what the hell," pulled off his boots and ran to join her. The sand squishing between his toes felt delicious and the water, cold as only the ocean can be, was balm to his aching feet. With only a little encouragement Arabia would have torn off her clothes and dived into the rolling waves, Hugh close behind her. But both of them knew better while the three soldiers, obviously accustomed to the sight of pristine beach and surf, sat lolling under a palm tree waiting for them to finish.

By the next day when they reached the old city of St. Augustine, the sight of the emerald water and vast blue sky had become more familiar. Thankful to be at last among the civilized amenities of house and bed, Hugh barely noticed the old ponderous fort and narrow streets of the town itself. All he wanted was a hot bath, a clean shirt and a comfortable bed in which to sleep for two days straight.

But first he had to see that his dispatches were delivered and Arabia was settled. Sergeant Linton led him straight to Government House where he left off the pouch given him by Ralph Stoakes and made an appointment with Governor Tonyn's aide. After that it was to the nearest decent inn to book a room for Arabia and himself. The burly owner, a bearded ox of a man in shirt-sleeves and a dirty apron, insisted on putting them in the same room and it was only with difficulty that Hugh was able to finally pay for a tiny cubicle where the girl could stay privately. Afterward Linton explained that it was not seemly for a lady to stay in a tavern alone and Arabia would be better served to put up with a family in the town.

"But I don't know any families in the town," Hugh said, wishing the whole problem would go away and he could take that longed for bath.

"Speak to the Governor tomorrow when you see him. He'll know of someone. It's not uncommon, you see."

Hugh explained to a disappointed Arabia that she would have to make-do with one night in the inn but that by tomorrow he would see she had a respectable place to stay for the rest of her visit. The look she gave him was so enigmatic that had he been less tired he might have gone looking for the Governor at that moment. But, God's blood, he hadn't asked her to come along. If she found herself in a difficult position for one night, it was her own fault. He had done all any gentleman should be expected to do.

Hugh awoke the following morning to long bands of sunlight streaming through the wooden blinds of his window, laying neat stripes on the straw carpet. When he sat up he realized at once that his body was not going to lose its stiffness for some time to come, yet in spite of that he felt renewed and invigorated by the good sleep and the hot bath of the night before. He shaved, combed his hair and tied it in a queue, put on his best linen and went downstairs to enjoy a breakfast of porter and steak on a patio surrounded by a trellis thick with trumpet vines.

He looked for Arabia but she did not appear before he was due at Government House. By now he had a fair idea where that building lay in relation to the rest of the town and he enjoyed walking there through the narrow streets lined with quaint coquina houses built in the Spanish style with walled gardens and overhanging wooden balconies.

The British Governor made short work of him, obviously having more important things on his mind. After a few questions concerning the state of affairs in Savannah which

Hugh, a too recent arrival, was unable to answer, the Governor gave him a letter for General Prevost in Savannah and ushered him to the door. Hugh only barely remembered to ask about a place for Arabia to stay and was given the name of a widow who had a respectable house on St. Francis street where young ladies visiting the town were often accommodated. Hugh walked the streets until he found the place and made arrangements for Arabia to arrive early that afternoon. Then, with difficulty, he found his way back to the tavern.

He found Arabia sitting at one of the patio tables nursing a cup of chocolate. Her long hair was tucked up under a cap and the fischu at her breast was clean though badly in need of pressing.

Hugh ordered up a cup of coffee for himself and sat down opposite her.

"Did you enjoy sleeping in a real bed?" he asked cheerfully. "I must say I did. I had almost forgotten how good a feather mattress could be."

Arabia looked up at him from under her dark lashes, scowling.

"Where I was it was too noisy to sleep. All night long those soldiers, singing and swillin' their drink. I would've had to be dead to be able to sleep through all that din."

"You poor child. I didn't hear a thing."

"Maybe you were in a better part of the tavern," she said sullenly.

"Perhaps. But you will not have to put up with such inconveniences again. I made arrangements this morning for you to stay at a house in town. You'll be better off there and safer."

"I can take care of myself."

"I don't doubt that. But I've spent a good part of the morning walking around this place and it is full of military men. It's no place for a girl alone."

Arabia shrugged. "Can't be any worse than Savannah."

Hugh found himself growing impatient. "But you know Savannah while here you are a stranger. Now look Arabia, I won't feel easy about your being here unless I know you are in a safe place. Mrs. Totten's house will do fine for you.

You'll have a clean bed, good meals and security. I must insist that you go there."

To his chagrin he saw her eyes fill with tears. Throwing him a black look she turned her head to hide them.

"I know why you want me to go there. You just want to put me some place so you can forget about me and go and do what you want. You'll be having a high old time and I'll be stuck in that dreary house with an old widow and two or three mamby-pamby girls who do nothing but talk about what dress to wear next."

"Now that's not true."

"Yes, it is. You won't give me a thought. Maybe you'll even go back to Savannah and leave me here!"

Her voice broke on a sob which she choked back. The tears began to inch their way down her cheeks but she held her chin high and struggled to hold them in. Hugh admired her for that even as he fought to keep from reminding her that she had invited herself along in the first place and if he did leave her high and dry it was no more than she deserved. But she was so obviously miserable that he could not bring himself to be so cruel.

"Look here, Arabia," he said more gently. "I promise I will not put you in Mrs. Totten's home and forget about you. I'll come every day and we'll see the town together."

She gave him a questioning sidelong glance. "Truly?"

"Yes, truly. After all, you are the only friend I have here in this town, with the exception of Sergeant Linton and I don't exactly call him a friend. How would you like to have supper together tonight," he added, in a rush of benevolence. "We can walk around the shops this afternoon, see the sights, then you can go back and change and I'll pick you up and take you to supper. How does that sound?"

Arabia's expressive face went from the depths of despair to a shining joy. "Would you? Oh, Mr. Hugh. I would love that."

"Good. That's settled then. Finish your chocolate now like a good girl and we'll collect your things and walk across to St. Francis Street. Oh, and you might as well stop calling me Mr. Hugh. Just plain Hugh will do since we're to be fellow sojourners. Hurry up now."

Arabia, her face shining, gulped down the rest of her chocolate not even noticing how cold it had grown.

Anxious not to keep Hugh waiting, Arabia bundled up her few belongings without giving a last glance at the tiny room where she had spent such a miserable night. Had she told the truth, it was not only the boisterousness of the inn's clientele that kept her awake during the previous night. The truth was she was bitterly disappointed at the way things had gone since that fateful moment when she had thrown caution to the wind and followed Hugh from the Tondee's Tavern in Savannah. To begin with it was obvious that he had not been very happy to see her. For a terrible moment she had feared he was going to send her back. Then he had been so awfully polite about fixing her a bed alone and apart from the others. That was to be expected, probably, with three soldiers along, but her only consolation had been the thought that when they reached St. Augustine, surely he would book a room for the two of them together. And then last night he had shunted her off to this lonely attic by herself without even seeing that she had her supper first. Now he was determined to put her in a respectable house under the nose of a widow who would make sure she never got out at night alone. She would have been better off here at the Inn where she might have been able to sneak into his bed some evening. It was very discouraging that she had spent most of her life fighting off men who wanted nothing so much as to take advantage of her while the one gentleman she longed to give herself to was determined to treat her like a lady!

Yet her happiness at the thought of sharing the rest of the day and the supper hour with Hugh in new and fascinating surroundings almost did away with her disappointments. Even Mrs. Totten's house did not seem so bad once they stood in the street looking up at it. Like all the houses in the town it was built in Spanish style of coquina stone, the patio door flush with the street and with walls on either side behind which lush greenery suggested cool gardens. The lady herself was British and very prim, with a tiny pair of spectacles balanced on her thin nose. She had a pleasant manner and a warm smile and she ushered Arabia into a room which, though tiny, was as clean and pretty as any she had ever seen. And after Hugh had left them with a promise to return in two hours, the good widow called her servant, a strapping black woman with a gingham kerchief, and ordered her to draw up a hot bath for Arabia and even wash her hair for her.

Perhaps, she thought, it was not going to be so bad to be a lady for a while

When St. Augustine was ceded to the British along with the rest of Spanish Florida in 1763, the Spanish inhabitants of the town, three thousand strong, picked up and moved to Havana. As a result though the city was still Spanish in flavor, the inhabitants were almost exclusively English. A few Spaniards remained and Latin visitors were frequent. Many of their young ladies had boarded with Madame Totten and she had come to greatly admire their dark beauty and flamboyant style. When she stood back and looked at Arabia she was struck immediately with how closely the girl favored these Latin ladies, even though there was no Spanish blood in her background. Madame Totten suspected she was not quite a lady either, but in these frontier outposts one soon learned not to adhere too closely to distinctions which in England would have been absolutely paramount. The old widow had something of a subdued romantic nature and when she learned that the nice gentleman was returning to take the girl to supper she threw herself into preparing Arabia to look as smashing as possible.

So it was that two hours later Arabia stood staring at herself in Madam's long mirror, not believing what she saw. Her dark hair, clean and sweet smelling, was swept up on her head and fastened with a long ivory comb from which fell the graceful folds of a black lace mantilla. There was a large flower, some sort of hybrid rose perched over one ear. She wore big gold hoops on her ears, borrowed from Madam herself, and her dress, left by one of the former visitors and hastily tucked in in the appropriate places by Mrs. Totten's hand, was a lovely cascade of bright flounces and ruffles, deeply cut in front to allow for an almost indecent exposure of white bosom.

She was splashed with the fragrance of distilled gardenia water, her stockings, also borrowed, were the thinnest lace and her shoes, slippers of Moroccan leather.

"If that don't set him back on his heels," Mrs. Totten breathed with satisfaction, "then I don't know what will. You'll draw the eyes of every man in the place."

"I don't know how to thank you, Madam," Arabia said, still not quite believing that the ravishing beauty she saw before her eyes was actually herself.

"You can thank me by taking care of all them things— so the next girl can use them, don't you see—and by not letting it go to your head. Don't let them take advantage of you, my girl. Let 'em look, but that's all. Of course, Mr. Sandenny, he seems a right enough gentleman so I don't think you'll have any problem with him. But the town's full of soldiers. You must watch out for them."

With an almost motherly hand she carefully pulled one long strand of Arabia's dark hair over her shoulder and down the front of her dress. Then making sure the rest was neatly caught on top of the girl's head, she straightened the mantilla and stood back with her hands crossed over her waist.

"As neat a job as I've ever done," she said. "Oh, my goodness and there's the bell. Only just in time we were. You stay here my girl and I'll go let the gentleman in."

Arabia waited in the room trying in vain to quell her pounding heart. What would Hugh think of her? Would he feel she was putting on airs, aping her betters? Would he command her to strip all this finery off and put back her old tattered dress which was all he had ever seen her in? She had convinced herself to expect the worst by the time she heard Mrs. Totten call her. Timidly she walked to the door down the hall and to the stairway which gave out onto a walled patio. Supporting her trembling knees with her hand on the rail, she went down the stairs to face Hugh.

The look on his face stopped her halfway down. Thunderstruck, he was staring up at her as though he was convinced she was the wrong girl.

"Good evening, Mr. Hugh," she muttered, hoping her

familiar voice would dispel the delusion of a strangeness. "I mean, good evening, Hugh."

"My god," Hugh muttered when he finally found his voice. "Can that really be you, Arabia. What have you done to yourself?"

"It was Mrs. Totten's doing," she cried, ready to run back upstairs and strip it all off. "I . . . I can change if you want."

"No, no. Don't touch a thing. I'm just amazed, that's all. So unexpected."

Politely he moved up the stairs and took her hand, bowing over it. He kept it in his own while Arabia's heart continued to thud. "You look really lovely. An amazing transformation. I shall be the envy of every man in St. Augustine."

All of Arabia's confidence began to flow back. With shining eyes she allowed him to lead her into the formal parlor and twirl her around to get the full effect. She even began to believe that she might really look beautiful and her heart flowed out in gratitude to Mrs. Totten.

Hugh muttered a few words to that well pleased woman then ushered Arabia downstairs. He walked beside her through the narrow streets without speaking, trying to take stock. Something had happened back there when he first saw Arabia descending those stairs which he would prefer to ignore. Up to that point he had not realize that the girl was so beautiful. Dressed up like that, clean and neat and smelling of that heady scent, she was enough to drive a man wild. He glanced over at the deep cleavage of her breasts barely hidden by the tight bodice of the dress gently swelling with the rhythm of her breathing and his whole body began to tingle. He had known, of course, that she was a tasty morsel since that day he first saw her disheveled and holding her ripped bodice together in the upper room of Tondee's Tavern. But he had subdued that impulse filled as he was with admiration for Louisa's ladylike, golden beauty. It had lain somewhere in his mind, unable to disturb more important concerns. To hell with supper. He wanted to go straight to his rooms, throw her on the bed and take his fill of her. And yet . . . .

Arabia turned to catch him staring at her bodice. Smiling coquettishly, she slipped her arm through his, pressing against him.

Why not? She was willing, she was experienced, and Louisa was far, far away. Everything would be different when they got back to Savannah. Hugh reached over and took her hand, squeezing it gently.

But they did not go straight to his room. First they walked the Plaza green and then down St. George Street, arm in arm, looking at the interesting wares in the shops. When Hugh learned that the comb and mantilla were borrowed he bought her one of her own—a tortoise shell comb of translucent amber and a red silk shawl. To top it off he added a small pewter hand mirror that Arabia thought was the lovliest present anyone had ever given her. Then they walked to the Blue Bell where they shared a long, leisurely supper, with several wines and the most delicious green turtle soup either had ever tasted. It was dark when they left the tavern and Hugh suggested they walk the short distance to the grounds of the old Spanish castillo where the last vermilion tinges of the dying day were glistening on the water.

"This has been the happiest day of my life," Arabia sighed, breathing deeply of the heavy salt air. To have Hugh's undivided attention for a whole afternoon and evening would have been enough alone to make her happy, she thought. But the way he had treated her since he saw her descending Mrs. Totten's stairs—offering her the condescension due a lady while at the same time so obviously transfixed by her charms—it was almost more than she could bear.

"All that because of a few trinkets?"

"No, of course not. Though I love the comb and shawl, they are the finest gifts I've ever had. But . . . being with you like this, in such a pretty place . . ."

He slipped an arm around her shoulder and she turned, leaning easily against him. Laying a hand gently on her throat Hugh tipped her face up and kissed her lips which opened slightly under his. There was no hesitation in her. She was as ripe for it as he was himself. They were not even aware of the other couples strolling nearby.

Hugh lifted his head from Arabia's full, luscious lips

only to face a demon within himself. He wanted her and she wanted him—there was no denying that fact. But what about Louisa? He felt certain he was in love with that golden, enchanting girl. Could those strong feelings be set aside and ignored for one evening's pleasure?

Arabia's arms slipped sensuously around his neck. "Take me back with you," she whispered against his cheek, her breath warm and tingling on his skin. With a will of their own his hands searched out her shoulders and wandered down her back. The blood was pounding in his head and loins and he could barely heed the small voice that cried within that he was being led along a garden path.

"Where? Not Mrs. Totten's, certainly."

Her lips moved softly, sensoulsy against his face. "Your room. No one need know. We can be . . . discreet . . ."

"Oh, Arabia," he groaned. Would it be so terrible? Louisa was far away and he didn't know that she would even care that he took another woman to bed . . . especially a servant girl.

She found his lips and flicked her tongue against them, licking them gently and softly urging them open.

"Take me, Hugh . . ." she breathed as though there was nothing on earth but this flaming desire.

He grabbed her hand and hurried her across the street and through the gates of the city to the inn where he kept his rooms. Arabia ran with him, her heart singing, light as air. All her dreams and hopes were coming true. He wanted her and once he had her he would never think of the golden Louisa again. When they reached the inn Hugh glanced around the doorway long enough to make certain that the innkeeper was looking the other way then he ran across the open patio to the stairs, pulling her after him. The hall was empty and they hurried down its darkened recesses to his door, slipped inside and bolted it after them. Hugh leaned against it, realizing for one stark moment that he had come so far that he would never be able to turn back. Arabia gave him no time to think, pressing her body against his against the wood of the door, tearing at his coat and jabot with eager hands. Her eyes were heavy-lidded, her lips parted, as she looked up at him with an undisguised longing. Without allowing thought to intrude on the overwhelming feelings that possessed him, Hugh reached up and pulled the tall comb with its frothy lace from her hair, throwing it aside and allowing her dark hair to spill around her shoulders. With light fingertips he traced a line down her neck and between her breasts while she shuddered with delight. He filled his hands with the heavy fullness of her breasts and buried his face in their sweetness. With a deft movement Arabia slipped the flounced dress down around her ankles and never once lessened her grip around his neck as he bent and picked her up and carried her to his bed. She lay there, lithe and creamy and wanton while he pulled away his clothes and fell upon her with an utter abandon.

Downstairs raucous laughter and infrequent singing could be dimly heard but in the dark quiet of Hugh's room there was only the creaking of the bed, the soft rustling of two entwined bodies on the coverlet, the sighs and gasps and finally, Arabia's deep, throaty laughter. He did not think of Louisa again until he woke the next morning.

Chapter 6

DAWN WAS JUST breaking when Hugh delivered Arabia, all properly reinstated in her finery, to Mrs. Totten's door. After enduring several black looks which this lady fastened upon him—though she did not dare to speak her thoughts—he closed the door to the street and walked back to the town for his breakfast. It was going to be a warm day but at this hour the air had a softness about it that was almost cool. The emerging light shimmered on the gray-blue waters of the harbor and gave a glistening quality to the green of the palms and the whiteness of the sand. Later on the heat would be heavy and oppressive but at this wonderful hour all of nature seemed reborn with the new day.

Hugh did some hard thinking during his long solitary walk. He knew it had not been fair to give in to Arabia's demands last night. It was not a question of enjoying their mutual pleasure, for he certainly had. But this morning he felt ashamed. Nothing told him so much as this that his pleasure had been a selfish one and neither kind nor loving.

He was rather amazed at his own feelings for certainly the passions of a serving wench had never bothered him before. Most of them were accustomed to being used and discarded. Yet somehow he could not feel so light this time. Arabia herself was partly to blame. She was a passionate girl, true, but she was also very much in love with him. He could sense how much even when she tried desperately to keep from saying it in so many words. And he was not in love with her. He liked her, admired her beauty, was grateful to her for the help she had given him, but he did not love her and never would. His heart was true and surely taken by Louisa Culpepper. What he would have given to have spent such a night as last night with Louisa!

Yet that thought, too, made him ashamed. Louisa was a gentle and refined lady who would never hop into bed with him on an impulse of the moment. And somehow that integrity of character made last night's wallowing in sexual abandon seem shabby and small.

Somehow he would have to make all this clear to Arabia. He was not going to take her on as his mistress. He might have before knowing Louisa, but that was impossible now. Poor girl. He really did not wish to hurt her.

Arabia woke later that morning as if from a dream. She looked forward to meeting Hugh later that day, to browsing through the shops of the old town, to walking its twisted narrow streets, and then to lying hot and spent in Hugh's arms in the evening. She stretched and smiled to herself as she thought back on the evening before. Though Hugh Sandenny was not the first man she had known, he was certainly like no other. She felt a new sense of worth she had never known before. Peering into her hand-mirror she thought that she had never looked prettier. She was happy, and she was his, and while they stayed in the city she would remain this new creature, never allowing by so much as a glimmer a memory of her old life and her old self to intrude.

So it was that she was bitterly disappointed when that afternoon Hugh announced his intention of returning to Savannah the next morning. He longed to see Louisa again and he was anxious to see if Ralph Stoakes had come any closer to recognizing his true identity. It would not do to be too long away from the city for who knew what gains that insidious nobleman might make in his suit for Louisa's hand while the competition was out of sight.

He tried to be diplomatic in breaking the news to Arabia and even suggested that perhaps she might wish to remain in St. Augustine and seek her fortune there. Those hopes were quickly dispelled.

"But I want to be with you," she cried. "I thought . . . I thought I could stay here with you,"

Hugh tried to make his voice sound kind. "That cannot be, Arabia."

"But last night . . ."

"Last night was lovely and I am grateful to you for sharing it with me."

"Grateful!"

"But it cannot be, Arabia. I can't take you as my mistress. Even if we managed it here in St. Augustine, it would be impossible in Savannah and it would complicate my life in a way that I simply cannot afford at the moment."

"I love you, Hugh," she said, her eyes stinging with tears.

"I . . . appreciate that, Arabia. You do me a great honor. I wish I could return your love, truly I do, but it is impossible. And besides, it would not be to your advantage. Think of your reputation."

"What do I care for my reputation," she answered bitterly. "I only want to be with you. No one ever thought of me as a lady anyway. I'm not like your . . . like your Louisa Culpepper."

She spoke the name guardedly and was aware of a moment's irritation in his eyes. "She's not my Louisa," he muttered "not yet, anyway. The truth is, I do have a very special regard for her. It is even my hope that someday . . ."

"But last night—how can you turn me away after what we had? How can you?"

"I'm not turning you away. Look, if you want to go back with me I'll take you. And as long as you are with me you'll be under my protection. I won't abandon you and I won't let you be hurt. You can trust me."

Arabia caught her full underlip between her teeth. She

wanted to cry out in anguish that she was hurt, terribly hurt by what he was doing. But her pride had gotten the better of her and she turned away, tossing her dark curls. "I'll accept your protection because I need it, but you won't have me in your bed again without begging for it, Mr. Hugh Sandenny. I can be just as choosy as you!"

She tried to believe her own brave words, telling herself that there was still plenty of time before reaching Savannah to entice him back into her arms. That afternoon, as they browsed through the shops, admiring the Spanish beaten gold and silver jewelry and fancy imported British goods, she pretended not to notice as Hugh quietly selected a pair of pink opal earrings that were designed to set off golden hair and a creamy light complexion. He slipped them into his pocket and Arabia, biting back her tears, fingered the lovely comb he had bought her the day before when there seemed so much promise between them. Then Hugh took her with him when he walked down to the dock to see if he could purchase passage for them on a ship going north. When it turned out that the first ship to sail would be in two weeks time, he led her over to the castle to speak to Sergeant Linton about hiring an escort, perferably the same one that had brought them down.

They found the sergeant sitting in the dark, dank guard-room of the old fort, a cavelike hole bored out of coquina stone and sweating the damp coolness of a tomb.

"Tis not possible," Linton said, mopping up his tin plate with a piece of hard bread. "I'm set here for the time being, until the Gov'nor tells me different."

"What about those Westphalians of yours? Can't they accompany us?"

"They've gone back already. You might wait until the Governor has a dispatch to send and pick up an escort to go along with ye, but, for my part, I wouldn't bother."

"Oh? And what would you do?"

"You know the trail more or less. Ye came down it right enough. And you've those fine pistols. Take along some gear and some powder and walk it yourself. Even better, get a horse and get there sooner."

Hugh rubbed his chin absently. "I think a horse in that

jungle might be more trouble that it's worth. And Arabia doesn't ride."

At the casual mention of the dark, smoldering beauty by his side, Sergeant Linton leered upward as if to say he would gladly trade places with Hugh given half the chance. "Seems to me she handled the trail better than you did on the way down. And with such company, I don't think I'd care if I ever made Savannah again or no."

Hugh hurried Arabia out of the sergeant's slavering presence, his mind made up. They would start back alone the next morning and make their way back the same way they had come down. He still had a crude map the sergeant had given him with marks on it where showing where the canoes were stashed near the St. Mary's and Great Satilla rivers, the two largest they must cross before reaching the comparative civilization of the Altamaha. As to the smaller streams he had helped to put together those rafts enough times that he felt sure he could manage it alone. Even with his limited experience of the woods he was vastly more knowledgeable than when he had first left Savannah. They would set out in the morning and with any luck, be back in Savannah by the end of the week.

The need to be up early was his excuse to return Arabia back to Mrs. Totten's protective hands immediately after supper. Though she wanted to be barely civil to him she disguised her irritation under a calm, matter-of-fact complacency. She may have lost out on this one night, but there were still several others before they reached the Georgia city where she would be alone with Hugh in the wilderness. She had not lost hope yet.

They set off early the next morning. The first part of the trail as far as Fort Prince William was well traveled and they were accompanied by several mounted guardsmen escorting a wagonload of provisions. Wobbling along among the barrels and boxes Hugh enjoyed the leisure of this first part of their trip and was almost sorry to reach the fort lying next to the green ocean and white beach which had been so enchanting on the way down.

To Arabia's disappointment, Hugh arranged separate rooms for them in the fort that evening. Early the next

morning he roused her out of bed and without pausing to
eat breakfast started with her down the white sandy path
that wound through the palm and thickets. They did not
stop for breakfast until the sun was well up. Already they
were well into the wilderness they must cross before reaching Savannah. With civilization left behind and the Georgian
city far ahead there was nothing between them but miles
and miles of jungle teeming with wild animals, alligators
and snakes, not to mention an occasional Indian. Yet he felt
confident and excited. It was good to be hacking one's way
through the wilds again, good to have a sturdy girl like
Arabia at his side and good to be going back to Savannah
where Louisa waited for him. He was not the tenderfoot
who had first stepped of the *Windward* to face a strange
new colonial world. He was experienced and now wise in
the ways of the forest. He felt sure there was nothing ahead
of them that he could not handle.

Although the night had been chilly, the day promised to
be one of those perfect harbingers of spring that made winter
bearable. Hugh pushed Arabia hard, knowing all too well
that by midafternoon the sun would be strong enough to
make walking through the swampy forest a misery. But they
made good progress and found the first canoe still hidden
underneath the thick brush Linton had put there on the way
down. Several alligators lay stretched on the mud banks
sunning themselves but they scurried into the dark, coffee-
colored water at the first thrashing sounds of human feet.
Arabia breathed a sigh of relief when Hugh at length shoved
the light, bark-covered vessel out into the water and began
paddling it toward the overhanging thickets far on the other
side. Glad to rest, she lay back with her face turned to the
sun, savoring its warmth. Midway across Hugh rested the
oar on his knees and allowed the boat to drift awhile, content
to rest and enjoy the peaceful river. The strident cries of a
flock of gulls and an occasional bark of an inland fox broke
the soft stillness, and now and then the surface of the water
was creased by the plopping of fish. Insects hovered in lacy
networks over the river's tranquil surface while from the
thickets on either side of the river a chorus of tree frogs and

crickets sang an accompaniment to the easy motions of the boat. Though Hugh did not allow himself this respite for long yet he found that being on the placid river like this gave him a sense of satisfaction, a feeling of peace with the world and with himself. For the first time since he had set foot on Georgian soil he began to feel a sense of compatibility with the strange wilderness of this peculiar English colony. For the first time he was genuinely glad he had come.

Once on the far bank they pulled the canoe ashore and camouflaged it for the next travelers, then set off down the almost indistinct trail once again, slapping at mosquitoes and accompanied by the ever present sand flies.

"We've done well so far," Hugh said, stepping out briskly ahead of Arabia. "At this rate we should reach Savannah by the day after tomorrow at the latest."

A startled cry behind him brought him suddenly to a halt. Arabia was standing, staring beyond him into the woods, her face a white mask, transfixed with terror. There on the trail ahead stood three figures, blocking their way. Their heads were encased in greasy turbans vivid with bright reds and greens. Their chests were bare and bronzed. Leather leggings covered their legs above moccasins elaborately worked and beaded. There were long swatches of paint across their faces and one of them had a silver loop through one ear.

"God in heaven," Hugh breathed. Arabia gave a choked cry behind him and he whispered hurriedly: "Don't move, don't cry out." He stood resolutely looking the Indians over and trying to remember how Linton had advised him to act if he should ever come face to face with savages like these.

"Oh . . . oh," Arabia's muffled cry behind him warned of her growing hysteria.

"For God's sake, keep calm," Hugh hissed at her. "Very easy now, move up close to me."

She was behind him almost before he finished speaking, clinging to his coat. The three sets of black, intense eyes fastened on them, looking, he felt sure, for the slightest sign of fear. His hand itched to slide to the handle of his pistol, but he knew that the slightest movement in that direction would bring one of the axes barely concealed in the sash around a waist flying at him. He was almost certain they were Creeks and not the poor looking Guales or Ya-macraws he had seen in Savannah. They were healthier, immensely more dignified and fifty times more threatening. But were they friendly?

He stood frozen to the spot, afraid to break the momentary stalemate. Then the warrior standing in the center spoke a few guttural words that meant nothing to him. He searched his mind for an answer but the only word he could remember was "English" and that would be no help at all if they were pro-American. What was the Creek word for "friend?"

The Indian on the left gave a throaty chuckle and said something in reply to his companion's remarks. Moving quick as a snake he glided forward and clamped a hand around Arabia's arm, pulling her out from behind Hugh. She screamed in terror and Hugh, acting unconsciously, grabbed at her to pull her back. Before he knew how it happened, the other two braves had him pinned to the ground while the third, holding Arabia by her long hair, had forced her to her knees. She was panicky now, screaming wildly over and over. Hugh twisted under the iron grip of the hands that held him until with a cry and a swift motion one of the Indians jumped astride him flashing a knife at his throat, his fingers digging into his scalp, yanking at his hair.

Hugh struggled wildly, filled with fury that death could come like this, so swiftly, rendering him helpless, just at the moment when he felt so good about the world. The implacable face of the other brave standing over him, the wild joy on the eyes of the straining man flashing the knife, the terrible screams of the girl to the side—these were to be his last images.

There was a crashing roar that reverberated through the trees. Suddenly the Indian astride Hugh arched his back, his head twisted grotesquely and his grip slackened. He slumped to the side as a second volley roared through the woods and the figure bending over Hugh disappeared into the pines. He raised up to see the third Indian trying to drag Arabia with him while she clutched wildly at the narrow trunk of a young pine. Though his throat was in an agony of constriction, Hugh rolled over and grabbed at her ankles, holding on for dear life. Then the gun roared again and the Indian's body doubled up, crashing at her feet.

Arabia, in the throes of panic, started to run. Forcing himself to his feet, Hugh took off after her, catching her only a few feet away down the trail where the underbrush was so thick she could make no headway against it. He threw his arms around her, holding her close and speaking to her gently until she calmed down enough to realize the Indian threat was over. Then she dissolved in tears against his chest.

The two painted figures lay sprawled in the dirt a few feet away. Hugh looked around, wondering if the third Indian would come screaming out of the thicket any moment, bringing his whole tribe with him. Then, without the rustling of even a twig a figure stepped out from the pines, a man of medium height in a fringed linen shirt and a battered round hat, cradling a slim rifle in one arm.

Hugh's body sagged with relief. Here was help indeed. A white man, a woodsman, and very much in command of the situation.

"Sir, I am very much in your debt," Hugh muttered.

"I should think you are," the man answered, a thin smile on his lips. Hugh looked him over, impressed. His hair was long and neatly groomed. His face was chiseled like an old statue, with a sharp aquiline nose, wide mouth and firm chin. His eyes were slightly squinted, creased at the corners, and very blue. There was something of humor in them, Hugh thought, yet there was also a hint of a coldness that could turn deadly. He seemed to find the sight of two terrified English compatriots almost comical.

"I am Hugh Sandenny," Hugh went on with as much dignity as he could summon, "recently from England, and this is Arabia Tillman."

If he expected his rescuer to politely introduce himself in return he was quickly disappointed.

"Gentlemen newly arrived from England ought not to go messing about with Creek braves," the man answered, his eyes narrowing.

"Believe me, sir, I had no intention of 'messing' with

them. I didn't know they were within miles. We are on our way back to Savannah after a visit to the garrison at St. Augustine and . . ."

"I know who you are and where you've been," the man interrupted. "And you're some kind of a fool if you think to go traipsing through these woods without meeting trouble. Indians or other."

There was a gentle rustling noise and Hugh looked over Arabia's head to see shadows emerging from the trees surrounding them. His relief began to take on elements of a new concern.

"Nevertheless," he said, "you saved our lives and I'm grateful to you."

"I saved your scalp, and the girl here from an unspeakable slavery. I accept your thanks."

Hugh found his sense of unease growing as the figures surrounding him became clearer. They were a scraggly looking lot, all of them bearing rifles, grim faced with eyes that moved restlessly about.

"I . . . I don't believe I've had the honor," Hugh said lamely to the man who had killed the Indians.

"Robert Sallette," he answered, his thin lips still in that half-mocking smile. "Of the Georgia Continental Militia. And you, sir, are my prisoner."

They walked for hours. Hugh lost all sense of time and place, with no idea of where they were except that he thought they were moving away from the ocean, further into a wilderness of pine barren and palmetto that grew more impenetrable with every mile. Though he had been quickly relieved of his pistols and the letter to General Prevost from Governor Tonyn, he was not mistreated. He was amazed at how the men surrounding them seemed as much at home in this jungle as if it had been a drawing room and they never hesitated about direction. It was nearly evening when they at last halted, breaking from the thick brush into a small clearing that was obviously some kind of primitive camp. Makeshift tents were scattered around a central fire with one tattered marquee off to the side, marking the headquarters of the chief—Sallette's, no doubt.

Immediately he was thrown into the depths of one of these tents. It was tiny and stifling with the heat permeated by the pungent aroma of a bear skin that covered half the ground and which he assumed served as a bed. He was so weary that even that felt good. Yet he had barely stretched out on it before one of the men who had accompanied him stalked in, tied his wrists and without saying a word left him there.

Though he was beginning to feel desperately hungry having not eaten a bite since that morning, he was weary enough to doze fitfully. When he woke it was dark inside the tent and beginning to grow cool. Outside he could hear the crackling of a fire and catch low voices of several men who must have been sitting near the tent flap.

Edging his body near the door Hugh strained to catch what they were saying. His anxiety was laced with questions. Who were these men and what did they plan to do with him? Where was Arabia? Was she safe? And, having gone to all the trouble of saving his life and bringing him here, why didn't they bring him something to eat.

"Prevost don't know how to do that," he heard a voice say. Scrouging his face down near the ground he found he could almost follow the conversation. A delicious odor of stewed meat tantalized his empty stomach but he tried to ignore it and concentrate on the voices.

"I wouldn't say that. He fought well enough down in St. Augustine. Must have been there nearly a year before Savannah fell."

"Yeah, but he's Regular. They don't know nothin' really about fightin' in these woods. Sallette's got the right idea. Prick 'em and run till they get so sore they give up."

"Humph! I wouldn't count on that."

"Well, leastways, it keeps the damned Tories runnin' scared, blast their black hearts. And the more of 'em we can keep from taking the oath the sooner the damned redcoats'll learn they can't have Georgia."

"Some of them Tories was friends, you know, when the circumstances was different."

"Tories is like Indians. The only good one is a dead one!"

The soft clang of a spoon on a tin plate reminded Hugh

of how hungry he was. The two men scuffled in the earth as they moved away out of earshot, leaving him to wonder at what he'd heard. Obviously he was the captive of one of those American bands Louisa had spoken of. But if they hated Tories so much why had they spared him? With his British citizenship and coming from St. Augustine he would be considered an enemy. Unless he could convince them he was friendly to the American cause. Perhaps that was what Arabia had done.

He rolled over on his back just as the tent flap opened and a tall gaunt figure stepped inside holding a plate. Roughly Hugh was pulled to his knees and his hands released long enough to wolf down the stew which under other circumstances he would have thought frightfully gamey, but now tasted absolutely delicious.

After the first few gulps Hugh took the time to look over his guard, wondering if he might get some information out of him. The man sat by the door glaring at him with such narrow-eyed hatred and suspicion that he soon gave that idea up. Almost before he had finished the last bite the plate was yanked away, his hands retied and he was left alone again without a word. He spent the next hour straining for more conversation but only caught a few sentences:

"Ought to string him to the first tree. Waste of time . . ."

"What's he waiting for anyway?"

"Oliver . . . some kind of . . ." the speaker moved away and the rattling noises of the woods took over. A little later he caught the name "Oliver" again: *"Yes, but Oliver says . . ."*

More confused than ever Hugh squirmed his way back onto the bear skin and tried to sleep. The bonds around his wrists and the cramps in his arms added up to a restless night, not helped by the frequent shrieks of wild animals in the woods, sometimes too near for comfort. Early the next morning he had a visitor, one he had been hoping to see. Robert Sallette pushed open the flap and stood over him, his hands resting on his rangy hips.

"Good morning, sir," he said politely. "I trust you rested well."

"I'd rest better if my hands were free," Hugh answered gruffly.

With a motion so quick it startled Hugh, Sallette bent and cut through his bonds, freeing his hands. Rubbing his wrists Hugh sat up.

"I'm obliged to you," he muttered. "But aren't you afraid I'll try to escape?"

Sallette smiled and sat down on the ground facing his prisoner, resting his hands on his knees.

"You wouldn't get far. If you were able to get past me, then past my men, where would you go? These woods are very dense and I don't think I need to remind you that there are savages out there."

"No, you do not. I was grateful to you yesterday for saving my scalp from two of them. I'm not so grateful this morning after the way I've been treated here."

"Why, sir, don't you know you are lucky to still be alive. My friends out there would have been happy to let the Creeks have you or, failing that, to hang you themselves. It is not an uncommon fate for Tories who fall into their hands."

Hugh studied the enigmatic face. "Then why am I still alive? I confess, none of this makes sense to me. It seems I went from the 'frying pan into the fire' as you provincials say."

Sallette chuckled as though from some private joke.

"I had no wish to hang you. I had a suspicion you might be worth preserving."

"I don't understand why. I never set eyes on you before in my life."

"Nevertheless, it was my hunch and it proved correct."

"What happened? Did 'Oliver' confirm it?"

For the first time he caught a hint of angry surprise in Sallette's eyes. He had got him there.

"What do you know about Oliver?"

Hugh toyed with the idea of pretending he knew a lot in the hope of finding out more. But, on closer reflection, he decided not to. His position was precarious enough without adding bluster to it.

"Nothing," he shrugged. "I heard your men mention the

name. It seemed to have something to do with the fact that they were not stringing me up to the nearest pine tree."

"That would be O'Reily," Sallette said, "His family was burned out and his eldest boy murdered by Thomas Brown's Florida Rangers a year ago. He's fierce where Tories are concerned."

"Where is Arabia? You didn't hurt her, did you?"

"You mean the girl who was with you. No, she is quite safe. Quite a tiger, that one. She was determined to get to you so I sent her away. By this time she should be back in Savannah."

"Thank God," Hugh breathed. "That's good judgment on your part. She's only a woman and not involved at all in this partisan struggle."

"I wanted to be certain of that before I let her go. She convinced me."

"I'm relieved to know it. Look here, Mister . . . whatever your name is, Mr. Sallette. Since the girl is gone and you have only me to contend with and since you do not seem to be in a hurry to dispatch me to my heavenly reward, would you consider accepting my parole? It would be a great relief to just be able to walk about."

"Why should I? This is not the Continental Army you're dealing with, in case you haven't noticed. 'Gentlemen's honor' often goes by the board in the kind of warfare we're waging."

Hugh bristled at Sallette's tone. "Well, for that matter, I am a civilian, in case you haven't noticed. I have nothing at all to do with the British military."

"You went to St. Augustine, a Crown province, in the company of three military personnel. And you were returning from there when you ran into those Creeks. Why should I not believe you are a spy?"

"A spy! Now see here, that is just a bit too much. I have nothing to do with this rebellion. As far as I'm concerned these colonies can belong to the Crown or can run themselves. I only came to Georgia because . . ."

Hugh stopped just in time. He'd almost blurted out his whole story to this renegade and that could be dangerous.

"Yes," Sallette offered.

"Because I was in trouble with my father. I'm here to kill time until he cools down and I can go home again. Believe me, I am not interested in politics."

Sallette leaned back and crossed his arms over his chest. In spite of the amiable smile on his thin lips Hugh had an impression that those cool, dark eyes saw a lot further into a man's mind that the pleasant manner would suggest.

"Since you are here, Mr. Sandenny, perhaps you'd better begin to accept a few facts. There is a war going on, a bitter, divisive, civil war. People who once all called themselves Americans are now trying to kill each other with a vengeance. So many cruelties and injustices have been perpetrated on both sides that murder compounds murder. Thomas Brown, for example, was tarred and feathered as a loyalist in Augusta back in '75. His latest revenge was to hang thirteen Whigs from the staircase of his house so he could watch them die from his bed.

"A sizable British army sits in our capital city, threatening to overrun the entire province. A second British force harries our southern border. An American army waits just across the line in South Carolina, ready to fight when the time is right. And just to help matters along, the Creek nation, long courted by the British, are playing both sides to their own advantage, which is to scalp settlers and discourage immigration into Indian territories."

"Well, I never assumed it was a tea-party," Hugh said lamely.

"No. It is not a tea-party. Like it or not you are caught up in this war and you'd better determine where you stand. I'm going to send you back to Savannah, not because I wish to but because someone else wishes it."

"Oliver?"

"Once there I suggest you stay safely within the town. Because if you venture back across the Altamaha, I promise you you won't go back a second time."

Sallette stood up, towering over Hugh in the tiny tent. "Good day, Mr. Sandenny," he said stiffly and turned on his heel. Hugh watched the flap close and sat back.

The nerve of the man! A common brigand, reading him a lesson like that. The humiliation of it was irritating. And

yet, as his anger subsided he began to see the sense behind
Sallette's words. He had been naive, thinking he could traipse
through this wilderness without compunction, oblivious to
the very real dangers of renegade Whigs, Indians, and even
of wild animals. His obsession with his own problems, his
attraction for Louisa and his dislike of Ralph Stoakes all
had preoccupied him, blinding him to other more significant
events taking place all around him. He had come to Georgia
seeking a diverting place to while away a few months.
Instead he had landed in a part of the world where something
far beyond his personal concerns was taking place. He knew
he would have to think more about this, face it squarely
when he got back to Savannah.

At least he *would* be going back to Savannah, thanks to
Sallette. And Oliver, whoever he was. And at least his hands
had not been retied. In spite of all his seething emotions,
he began to feel better.

Some time before noon, one of Sallette's men poked his
head in the tent and beckoned Hugh out. He was given a
brief meal of bread and cheese and a bitter porter to wash
it down then placed between two armed woodsmen and
marched out. They walked for most of the afternoon, through
thickets worse than any he had seen before. Toward evening
they came to a clearing on the banks of one of the dark
creeks so prevalent in the area. There was a small cabin
there built of tree limbs lashed together, the bark still on
them.

The cabin served as a primitive way station and was run
by a grizzled old man named Joe Tyman. Sallette's men
left Hugh there and faded away into the brush before darkness set in. Hugh spent a miserable night on a straw mattress,
scratching fleas but at dawn Tyman had him up and on his
way. He ferried him across the creek and directed him along
a path that turned out to be an actual road, assuring him
there were settlers along the way and that by afternoon he
would reach Fort Barrington on the Altamaha where he
could probably rent a horse to ride back to Savannah the
following day.

Tyman's directions proved accurate and Hugh, on the

evening of the second day, rode into Savannah on the back
of a half-winded nag borrowed from the small garrison at
Fort Barrington. He had never been more happy to see the
towers and chimneys of London than he was to see the
scattered low rooftops of Savannah that cool, lovely evening. He felt as though he had never before so appreciated
all the blessings of civilization. He went straight to Tondee's
where he fell into the welcoming arms of an ecstatic Arabia
and ordered her to make him up a bath before he would
even so much as give her a hug.

Chapter 7

THE FOLLOWING SUNDAY, as Louisa and her father came out of Christ Church after the morning service, they ran straight into Hugh. He had waited for her, sweeping off his hat and bowing politely as he blocked her way down the low stairs.

"Why Mr. Sandenny," Louisa said, hoping her pleasure was not too apparent. "I was not aware that you had returned from St. Augustine."

"Good morning, Miss Culpepper," Hugh answered, thinking how lovely she looked in her dark blue cloak and feathered bonnet. "I returned early last week."

"And you haven't been around to call on me. For shame, Mr. Sandenny. You shall have to do better than that to stay in my good graces."

"Forgive me, madam, but the rigors of the journey left me a little indisposed. May I escort you home."

Louisa gave her father a meaningful smile and took Hugh's arm, falling in behind Thomas Culpepper's rotund figure as he strolled alongside Colonel and Mrs. Mulryne.

"In that case, I forgive you. Actually, I am pleased that you are back in time for the assembly which is to be held next Friday in the long room of Mrs. Tondee's tavern. You will be there, won't you?"

Hugh tore his eyes away from the tantalizing dimple in her creamy cheek. "Wild horses could not keep me away. Will you save me a dance?"

"Oh, you may have several. I am very partial to dancing, especially the country frolics. Papa says I wear out all my partners."

"That is a challenge I shall happily accept."

He was looking very smart, Louisa thought, studying him from under her bonnet. The trip had been good for him. He was tanned and handsome and looked more fit than before. And there was a new assurance in his manner—or was she perhaps just getting to know him better. Her heart seemed to turn loops when he smiled at her and she mentally gave herself a good shake. It was lovely to be walking with such a fine looking gentleman, especially one who was so amiable and interesting but she mustn't let it get the best of her judgment. That road only led to broken hearts.

"My goodness," she said lifting her skirt to expose trim ankles in silk hose decorated with scarlet clocks. "This path is very sandy today. My slippers are full of sand. We need a rain badly."

"I've noticed that in Savannah the rain only turns the deep sand to a quagmire. Still, I agree, rain would be welcome. The woods I came through were very dry."

"And what did you think of our Georgia wilderness? Did you have any trouble? Indians, wild animals?"

Hugh hesitated, a little relieved to spot the Culpepper's door not far down the street. "No, nothing to speak of. A little brush with Indians, that was all."

"Oh. How fortunate that you met nothing worse. Now promise me you'll stop by one afternoon this week. I want to hear all about St. Augustine."

Hugh kissed her hand lightly and smiled up into her soft enticing eyes.

"Tomorrow afternoon?"

"That would be splendid."

It seemed to Louisa that she had never seen Savannah so gay as that spring and summer. Outside the city there were the shortages and the ravages of war but in Savannah itself, those difficulties were below the surface, eclipsed by a constant round of assemblies, soirees and tea parties. The sizable British army that had taken over the city meant hordes of attractive young officers looking to be entertained. Many of them were Germans and another large group were Scotch. The frequent forays outside the city toward the wilds of Augusta or the loneliness of Port Royal, or the occasional marches south in the creek-ridden wilderness along the Florida border still left enough soldiers within the limits of the town to inspire a new round of parties, plays and dances each week.

The large military force that descended on a town the size of Savannah also made for more unpleasant problems. Housing was at a premium. Even with the large barracks built on Bull Street, nearly every private home was pressed into boarding one or two British officers or was taken over completely for their use. The crowding was made even worse by the flood of Tory refugees that turned to the city for safety when their homes had been destroyed by the fighting in the up-country.

Staples like rice, corn and potatoes were hard to come by since much of the plantation life that supported them had been uprooted. With the harbor open to English goods, luxuries were easier to obtain. It might be difficult to get flour but the finest Madeira could be easily purchased on the waterfront beneath the bluff.

Louisa saw much of Hugh Sandenny that lovely spring. They rode out to visit her friends who had homes in the outlying districts surrounding the town. They attended so many parties together that Louisa's friends became almost accustomed to think of them as a pair. Although she made every effort to remain uncommitted to any one beau, Hugh was such a frequent companion that the elderly ladies began to make sly remarks twittering at how soon they might expect to hear "the good news." As summer came on Louisa began to give Hugh more serious thought. It might look to others as though she knew him well but she knew that in fact they both knew very little of the other. She was at great pains to keep a part of her life to herself and he seemed to feel the same. She suspected from the first that his story about coming to Georgia to inspect sites for a firm dealing in gems was false but he never offered her any other explanation. On the ship he had pretended to be a merchant but it was obvious he was a gentleman from a long line of gentlemen. The strong animosity between Hugh and Ralph Stoakes was a mystery to her. It seemed far too deep to be merely the result of a rivalry for her hand.

And she had heard about Arabia. That Hugh might make a mistress of a serving wench was perhaps not unexpected, but that it had to be Arabia Tillman, of all people, was almost enough to make her want to break off their friendship altogether.

Yet that she could not do. In fact, the more she saw of him, the more she felt herself falling in love—something she ardently wished would not happen.

She sat back in the low boat, her sunshade over her head, watching Hugh as he poled their small vessel along a coffee-colored stream, overhung with massive live oaks, trailing their long wisps of Spanish moss in the water. They had come to Westerly, a plantation belonging to her father's friend, Joshua Long, on a brief visit, mostly to show Hugh how the rice crop was harvested. It had been a warm afternoon and there were many other visitors in the house, so after a sumptuous dinner, when most of the other guests had retired to their beds for an afternoon doze, they had fled to the river to paddle up its mysterious spiraling paths in quiet and peace.

For a long time they glided gently along the surface of the water without speaking. Then Louisa abruptly broke the silence.

"Will you be going back to England soon?"

Hugh stared around at her, taken aback by her question. England had been the last place on his mind just then. In fact, he had been thinking of how very beautiful the dark river was with its heavy shadowed growth and exotic plants. It had just dawned on him that he was beginning to be very fond of this strange, primitive Georgia as well as the lovely girl who had so captivated his heart.

"Why, I hadn't thought about it. Why do you ask?"

Louisa shrugged. "Only because I remember that on the ship you said you would not be staying in Savannah long."

"It's true that I did not plan to linger but as I've come to know the province, come to know you..."

Louisa smiled and trailed her fingers in the water. "Please don't mistake me. I have no wish for you to leave. In fact, I've enjoyed our friendship more than I can say."

Hugh looked away. It occurred to him that this was a perfect opening to suggest that their relationship might move on to something more than friendship and yet he was reluctant to speak. He was half-afraid of being refused and half-reluctant to offer anyone his heart when his life was so unsettled.

"You've never said much about your life in England," Louisa went on, "and I've no wish to intrude on your privacy. But I feel I must tell you something which it might be wise for you to know. Governor Wright is expected to arrive back in the city early next month and Father told me it is almost certain that Ralph Stoakes will be appointed one of the Commissioners of Claims. That means he will have official authority to judge who may remain free and who should be considered a threat to the King's peace. I know there is no love lost between the two of you..."

"That is certain."

"I do not know why and have no wish to. I only want you to be careful."

"Why, Miss Culpepper, you don't fancy I'm a secret rebel in disguise, do you?"

"Of course not. You seem as loyal as any other Englishman only recently arrived in the colonies. It's just that Ralph Stoakes, I believe, is not above using his office to carry out personal grudges, and he seems to have just such a grudge against you."

Pulling the pole from the water Hugh easily let himself

down on the seat opposite Louisa and allowed the boat to
drift.

"You are right, of course. I am a loyal subject of the
King and Stoakes does have a grudge against me. I cannot
tell you why right now but someday I hope I shall be free
to. I . . . I think he suspects that I injured a young kinsman
of his in an argument."

Louisa's light eyes darkened as she studied him. It was
not difficult to surmise that Hugh was talking about a duel,
for all his reluctance to call it that.

"At any rate," Hugh went on, "I agree with you that he
is the kind of man who would be happy to throw me in jail
on some trumped up charge and I appreciate your warning.
And your concern."

Louisa twirled the handle of her sunshade lazily. "It is
no more than I would do for any friend."

"I would like to think it was more than that." He reached
for her hand but his sudden movement set the boat rocking
crazily. Louisa seemed preoccupied with her sunshade and
he quickly backed off, discouraged.

"Just do be careful what you say and to whom you say
it," she went on, pretending not to notice. "The town is so
full of rumors—some believe the British garrison in New
York will arrive here for a southern offensive, others that
the French will send an army to help the American rebels
retake the city. It is difficult to know who to believe."

"What do you think?"

"Oh, I don't give too much thought to military matters.
Savannah is very lively right now with all the soldiery there
so I simply enjoy it and try not to remember there is a war
going on."

Hugh rested his elbows on his knees, giving her a quizzical look. "I'm not sure I believe that. It was you, after
all, who told me about all the Whig activity in the countryside. Even tried to make me see their point of view."

"Well, being a mere woman does not mean one must
never use one's mind. And you forget, I grew up in this
town. Some of the people who have suffered on both sides
are—were friends of mine. That is why I try not to take
sides."

"Louisa . . ."

"Come now, let's not talk any more of serious matters. It is such a beautiful afternoon and the river is so peaceful. Mary Long told me at dinner there is to be a frolic tonight with a fiddler come all the way from Charleston. Think of all the dancing!"

Without saying another word, Hugh carefully stood up in the boat and set the pole back in the water. He was disappointed that he had not been able to interject a word about his feelings for her, yet he was very much aware of her warning. He would have to watch out for Stoakes now more than ever. And in spite of the way she cut him off, he felt certain that behind that warning was a genuine concern. It was a small consolation but it made him happy nonetheless.

In July Governor Wright sailed triumphantly up the Savannah River to a tumultuous welcome. He had always been a popular man, even when the town was bitterly divided by conflicting loyalties. Now that it was once more a Crown province occupied by British regulars and Tories, no man could have been more favorably received. He immediately took up his old residence in the Council House and set about making appointments and convening the Council.

As Louisa had warned, Ralph Stoakes was among the first group of men appointed to serve as Commissioners of Claims. Because of the severe fighting in the outskirts of the city and the up-country settlements, there were many more claims than the Commissioners could handle. To Hugh's relief, it seemed as though Sir Ralph would be so swamped with the demands of his new office that he would have little time left for intrigues and personal vendettas against private enemies. At the same time the increased traffic between England and her southern province made him feel almost certain that Ralph had probably received some kind of confirmation as to his true identity. It would have been an easy matter in the months since he arrived for a letter to go back to England asking pertinent questions about the whereabouts of one Hugo St. Dennis, and for an answer to have been received notifying anyone who was interested that the young man had not been seen for some months and was rumored to have fled the country. Hugh took particular pains to avoid Ralph whenever possible.

But that was not always easy. Governor Wright's return had set off a new round of social affairs complete with splendid feasts and illuminations over the river to which Louisa fully expected him to escort her. Since he could not bring himself to forgo that pleasure and watch some other attractive gentleman have the honor, he took the chance, dancing, eating sumptuous suppers, walking the terraces and gardens, and standing on the bluff watching the fireworks, always as near to her as she would allow.

Yet he was not unmindful of the way Stoakes watched him on these occasions, or the suspicious, scurrilous, snide little comments he made when the two of them could not avoid meeting. As July moved into August, Hugh grew certain that his identity was known and why Stoakes had done nothing about arresting him he could not fathom.

It had been a brutally hot summer with three weeks in which the temperature had gone from stifling to unbearable. Hugh fully expected that with the coming of fall cool weather would descend and no one told him that September was often as enervating and uncomfortable as summer. Early in August he arose one morning to find the air of his tiny room already suffocating. A merchant brigantine from London had been sighted off Tybee Island the evening before and as much to seek relief from the heat as anything else, Hugh hurriedly dressed and made his way down the bluff to the harbor. The dock was already crowded with workers, soldiers, and new arrivals crammed in among the barrels and boxes of supplies being unloaded from the ship. In the confusion and crowd the heat was just as bad as it had been above in the streets of the town and Hugh decided to make his way back up to Tondee's and have a leisurely breakfast. It would be no cooler but it would give him a chance to see Arabia.

He had turned toward the cobbled walkway and steps that framed the bluff when he heard his name called.

"Hugo! Hugh, is that you?"

A tall figure in a black cloak was knocking aside pedestrians on the dock trying to get to him. Hugh took a closer look, gasped and hurried toward him.

"Rob Earing!" he cried, slapping his friend on the back. They all but embraced in their mutual delight.

"How in heaven's name did you get here? What are you doing here?"

"I thought I recognized you but I wasn't sure until you turned and then it looked as though you were leaving. Hugo, old friend, it's so good to see you."

"Hugh! It's Hugh now, remember. God's eyes, I'd forgotten how good it could be to see a face from home."

"I'd hoped to find you but I'd envisioned searching through all the taverns and brothels first. What a piece of luck to come across you here on the wharf."

Hugh laid an arm around his friend's shoulders and turned with him toward the steps. "I heard a ship was due in last night and thought I'd come down and look over the cargo. Never expected to find you among the barrels and crates. Come, have some breakfast with me."

"Capital idea. Just give me a moment to speak to the First Mate. Want to leave Elizabeth word where I've gone and that I'll be back for her."

"Elizabeth? She's with you?"

"Yes. It's a long story I'll tell you about it over breakfast. Be right back."

He disappeared among the crowd for several minutes leaving Hugh to wait and wonder at this news. Rob's sister, Elizabeth Earing, he recalled, was a timid little creature, the least likely person to sail away from England for a country in the midst of a war. How had Rob ever talked her into accompanying him, and why?

He did not get an answer until later when they were seated at a secluded table at the King's Arms coffee house. Rob Earing ordered up an enormous meal of fish, steaks, eggs and cider then loosened his stock and sat back fingering the handle of his pewter tankard.

"I hope you're prepared to help pay for all this," Hugh said grimly. "Not that I wouldn't be happy to stake you under other circumstances, but the truth is . . ."

"Running a little short, are you?"

"Frankly, yes. What I brought with me is about gone and I've no idea where I'm going to get more. I've even considered the dreadful thought of going to work!"

"Well, I can postpone the horrible calamity for you for a while. I've some money with me from your father. I went to see him when I knew we were coming here and he unbent enough to help you out."

"I can't believe that."

"It's true. I think he thought sending you money was preferable to seeing you return. He's not anxious for that, I'm sorry to say."

Hugh shrugged. "I *can* believe that. I must admit, though, I'd hoped enough time had passed by now that I could quietly slip back into England."

"I wouldn't advise it yet. Besides, I am here out of choice. Why should you want to return?"

"I've been going over in my mind all the possible reasons why you could have come to Georgia and I confess I cannot come up with one plausible explanation. Why did you, Rob?"

"Elizabeth and I are *émigrés,* of course. Bet you never considered that. My father died last spring, you see, and unknown to either of us. His estate was heavily encumbered with debts. It took most of what was left to pay them off. With so little to support us, we both decided we would seek our fortune in the colonies, as so many others have done. So, here we are."

"But you knew there was a war going on?"

"It has to end sometime, doesn't it? And when I heard that the King's men had retaken Savannah, and hopefully the rest of Georgia to follow, I thought what better place to stake out a new life. Elizabeth took some convincing but in the end she chose to stay by my side. So, here we are."

"You foolish fellow. I'm afraid your optimism is a little premature. Georgia is still bitterly divided. Whole sections are under the control of the rebels, particularly the uplands in the west. We were counting on the Indians and the loyalists to rise up and reclaim the colony for the King but it hasn't happened and now the Rebels have their own government parallel to the Crown's. Two governors, two councils, two Chief Justices. It's true we control Savannah and St. Augustine but not much else."

Rob rubbed a finger along his square chin.

"We could have gone to New York but I'd heard such terrible stories about the overcrowding there and lack of basic necessities. And then, too, I knew you were here."

"I'm overjoyed to see you, make no mistake about that. It's just that I wonder you chose such a time to emigrate."

"Well," Rob said, holding up a fried oyster, "if I can do nothing else I'll offer my services to the Army. In the meantime I can at least get to know something about the place." He popped it into his mouth.

"You'll probably like it, knowing you. The town is a lively place right now because of all the officers and regulars."

"Any pretty girls?"

Hugh hesitated. He was not particularly anxious to have another rival for Louisa's fair hand. "Very many and very pretty. I'll introduce you around." He pushed the food around on his plate. "There's one special girl . . ."

Rob looked up at him with a knowing smile. "She's got your brand, maybe?"

"I see we understand each other."

"As always. What's her name?"

"Louisa Culpepper and she's a beauty. Fair, lovely eyes . . . I met her on the ship coming over."

"I believe I met her once in London. Her father was with her, a portly man who talks a lot."

"That's correct."

"And another fellow, always hanging over her—gaunt, uppity, always looks like he smelled something bad."

"Ralph Stoakes. He likes to think Louisa is his but the truth is she can't abide him. Seems to be fairly pleased with me, though."

Rob's brows creased in a sudden frown.

"Ralph Stoakes wouldn't be Pelham's rich uncle, would he?"

"The same."

Rob threw down his knife. "God's eyes, Hugh! You've walked right out of the den and into the lion's mouth. Does he know who you really are?"

"I think he suspects."

Rob made a clucking noise with his tongue. "We shall have to watch that. Well, at least you've a friend nearby now to help you if he causes trouble. But please, dear fellow, no duels!"

"I've been very good about that since I arrived here, Rob. Not a challenge or even a sharp word to anyone. You wouldn't know me."

"Love must have its compensations. See you keep it up. Now, can you advise me of a decent place in this town where a gentleman and his sister can hire rooms? I know Elizabeth will be anxious to get ashore and get settled."

"That may be a problem since we're almost as over-crowded as New York. Of course, there are always the inns. But I think the thing to do would be to go and see Louisa. She might even be kind enough to let your sister stay with her and that would be infinitely more pleasant than a tavern. Meanwhile, you could put up with me temporarily. Finish up your coffee and we'll walk around to the Culpeppers."

"Good. Good."

Rob shoveled down the rest of the food on his plate and took a long swig from his mug.

"I understand what you mean about overcrowding," he said when he could speak again. "I don't think I've ever seen this many soldiers in one place in my life. Any possibility of their bringing an end to this war soon?"

Hugh shook his head. "The more I learn about the colonies the more I despair of peace. Too many men want independence and are willing to fight and die for it. There is even a rumor now that Admiral d'Estaing might intervene on the side of the Americans. If he should attack Savannah, it would all be over in a short time."

"But surely he's in the West Indies."

"The last we heard. But make no mistake, there has been a lot of pressure put on the French to take an active part in the fighting."

"Well," Rob scoffed, "when did a true-born Englishman ever regret a chance to fight the French! And from what I hear, the American army is a ragtag sort of affair without enough bullets or even shoes. You don't really think they could whip Prevost's regulars, do you?"

"I don't know," Hugh said, laying some coins on the table and walking with Rob to the door. "I only know that the defenses in this town have been pretty much neglected. And a good portion of the 71st regiment, 'the flower of the Army,' is up at Port Royal, leaving us undermanned to face any kind of concentrated attack. However, perhaps the frogs won't have the initiative to make one. The talk is they won't, and talk is the only involvement I have in all this. I'm not terribly interested in becoming a soldier. Never was."

Rob paused on the doorstep to fasten his cloak around his shoulders but noticing how the heat had increased since they entered the coffee house changed his mind and threw it over his arm instead. Together they walked out onto the sandy street.

"Too bad. Anyone as anxious to fight duels as you ought to be invaluable to the army."

Chapter 8

AFTER HER INITIAL surprise Louisa decided that the idea of entertaining a visitor from England was worth considering. The officer who had been billeted with them had only a week ago been sent to Fort Cornwallis in Augusta and she had been waiting every day for word that some new arrival would take his place. Elizabeth Earing's presence might at least postpone the inevitable.

When at last she met Rob's younger sister she was more than ever convinced of the wisdom of her decision. Hugh had warned her that Elizabeth was a shy, quiet child. What he had neglected to mention was that she was also gentle, pretty and eager to oblige. Furthermore, she was no child but a young woman, very small in stature but with a doll-like fragility and youthful beauty. Louisa found her enchanting and was convinced from the first that they would get along famously. Elizabeth, for her part, was so grateful to have a friend and a pleasant home that she would have gladly taken on any task Louisa asked of her. She had been seasick most of the voyage from England and simply to be back on solid earth again was like a gift from heaven.

The end of the summer went out with a flurry of entertainments that left Elizabeth wondering at the quiet life she had led at her family's rural home in Somerset. In the space of just a few days Louisa talked Hugh and Rob into squiring them to a performance of *The Captain's Dilemma* at the Broughton Street Theater, to a Jockey Club race to watch Stephen deLancey capture the purse, as usual, and to a brilliant assembly at the home of Chief Justice Stoakes.

Across town, in the dark rooms of Tondee's Tavern. Arabia Tillman went about her duties with a grim determination. Her life had also changed dramatically since the morning Hugh ran across Rob Earing of the Savannah quay but not in the pleasant, gratifying manner of Louisa's and Elizabeth's. Not once since that now long ago trip to St. Augustine had she been able to entice Hugh back into her bed though she had tried every trick she knew to do so. Between all the time he spent elsewhere and Mrs. Tondee's watchful vigilance when he was around she had known only discouragement, hurt, anger and disappointment. Yet she could not give up. The memory of that one lovely night in Florida was still too strong. She knew she ought not to care—that she had only to crook her finger to have any man she wanted in Savannah. But she wanted Hugh and the more he treated her with a friendly civility the more desperately she loved him.

And now, since he and Rob had hired rooms together at Mrs. Strickland's boarding house, she barely saw him anymore. He seldom took his meals at the tavern, leaving her in a jealous agony to wonder where he was and who he was with. Gradually her disappointment seemed due more to Rob's appearance than to Hugh's reluctance and, given the opportunity, she would have gladly tried to scratch out the newly arrived Englishman's eyes.

This had gone on for nearly a month and Arabia thought her misery could grow no worse when one morning she left Tondee's to set off down Whitaker Street to the market on an errand for Mrs. Tondee. Though it was only the third day of September it was as hot as all of August had been. Already the streets were choked with dust stirred up by the horses and carriages of civilians and military alike.

As Arabia turned onto Bay Street, intent on her thoughts, she was nearly run over by a small carriage being driven at a fast clip by a Negro slave in full livery. The horse was pulled up abruptly, shied and jerked sideways, and in trying to get out of its way Arabia tripped and fell to the ground. Cursing under her breath, she picked herself up and began brushing the sand off her skirts.

Louisa Culpepper peered around the sides of the carriage and threw back a long gauze veil over her hat which had kept off the dust.

"I'm most frightfully sorry," she called. "Are you hurt?"

"No, ma'am," Arabia muttered, too furious to look at her.

"That should not have happened. Nathan, you really must be more careful. You could have injured this poor girl."

"Sorry, Miz Louisa," Nathan said, pulling back on the reins, "but this animal, he skittish when he not be out for several days."

At Louisa's name Arabia's eyes shunted to the carriage. The two women stared at each other, Louisa's eyes widening as she recognized her former serving girl.

"Arabia! Is that you?"

Jerking her shawl around her shoulders Arabia stepped back against the protective cover of the Merchant's Exchange buildings. But Louisa was already out of the carriage in a flurry of blue chintz skirts and ruffles, brushing at Arabia's sandy skirt with her gloved hands.

"I'm so very sorry, I had no idea. Are you certain you're not hurt?"

"No, I'm not. It's all right. Please let me go," Arabia cried, trying to get out of her way.

"Nonsense," Louisa said, pausing to look directly into her face. "I've longed to talk to you since that brief conversation we had some months ago. I even thought of going round to call at Tondee's but . . ."

"I must be going along. I've marketing to do."

"Let me walk with you, just to the market. Nathan, take

the carriage on to the Market Square. I'll meet you there."

"You sure, Miz Louisa?"

"Yes, yes. Go along now. I'll be all right. I'm just going to walk along with Arabia. It's only two blocks."

Reluctantly Nathan slapped the reins against his anxious horse's back and disappeared in a fog of dust. As she fell in step beside her, Louisa glanced over at Arabia's grim face, knowing her presence was unwanted but determined nonetheless. She had been hoping some day she might come across Arabia like this.

"You really shouldn't do this, Miss Louisa," Arabia said through pursed lips. "It isn't fittin', walking alongside a serving girl."

"Nonsense," Louisa answered briskly, taking Arabia's arm and propelling her toward the square. "We were friends, remember. Why, you were the best, the only friend I had when I was a little girl."

"That was a long time ago."

"Oh, Arabia, you can't know how many times I've wished . . ." There was no softening of the hard lines around the servant girl's mouth. Louisa felt her unyielding hardness but she was not ready to give up yet.

"Do you know that when my mother died I don't think I could have gone on living if it hadn't been for your mother and you. You were all the comfort I had. You'll never know how much you meant to me."

She felt Arabia's arm stiffen under her hand. Far from having a softening effect, her words seemed to make the girl more angry.

"I remember."

"I think about you so often and wonder if you are all right. You still could work for me any-time, you know. Your mother was such a good, faithful servant to my family, you would always be welcome."

"I told you I have a position in a tavern," Arabia said very formally.

"Do you still like it? Does Mrs. Tondee treat you well?"

"Well enough. I've no complaints."

They walked in silence for a moment then Arabia turned,

speaking directly to her for the first time.

"How did you know I was at Tondee's?"

"Hugh Sandenny told me."

"You know Mr. Hugh?" Arabia said innocently, knowing full well that she did.

"Why, yes. He's a good friend. He told me a little about how you were but still I longed to know for myself."

"Do you know Mr. Robert, too?"

"Rob Earing? Yes, I do. His sister is staying with me until such time as they get settled."

Arabia's head shot around. "Mr. Rob has a sister?"

"Yes, he does. A lovely, quiet young thing. She's been such excellent company."

They were nearing the bustle of the market place. Arabia, yanking her arm away, pretended to fuss with her bonnet strings.

"I have to go now. There's some shopping I have to do for Mrs. Tondee. Good-bye, Miss Louisa."

Once again Louisa reached out and laid a hand on the girl's arm.

"Oh, Arabia, what did I do to make you hate me so. You were such a dear friend. I was so fond of you and I thought you were fond of me. Then—I don't even know why— you began to hate me. Why? Why?"

Arabia looked into the earnest face so close to hers. How pretty she was with her fair skin, soft lips, large liquid eyes. How she exuded caring and kindness. For a moment her animosity wavered under the genuine concern in Louisa's face.

But why shouldn't Louisa be kind. She was rich, pampered, spoiled and beautiful. She had everything while Arabia Tillman had only one thing—Hugh Sandenny. And now this petted aristocrat threatened to take even that from her, just as she had taken everyone and everything else Arabia had ever loved.

She pulled her arm away.

"I have to go," she muttered and darted off into the crowd. Louisa stood looking after her, dejected, embarrassed that she had allowed her feelings to show so openly to someone who treated them with such contempt. Then she turned away and started back down the street, looking for Nathan.

Later that day the sleepy peace of the town was shattered by a report that French ships had been sighted off Tybee Island. It was only a small flotilla of six ships but when an attempt was made to get a closer view of them from a pilot boat they immediately drew out to sea.

"That says it all," Hugh remarked dryly when he and Rob met in Louisa's drawing room. As in so many other houses of the town, the ships were the only topic of conversation.

"Obviously they hoped to slip by without being seen."

"But how can they be sure they were French?" Louisa asked.

"Lieutenant Lock plainly saw the men on one of the frigates wearing French uniforms. There's no doubt at all."

"Oh dear," Elizabeth Earing sighed. "I hope it doesn't mean there will be any fighting. I'm terrified of guns and the awful noises they make."

Her brother reached out and gently patted her small hand. "Take heart, Elizabeth. A few ships are not a whole fleet. They may have been on their way to carry dispatches to Charleston or Philadelphia. I think everyone is making too much of this sighting."

Hugh shook his head. "They were certainly French and therefore part of d'Estaing's fleet, but what they are doing this close to Georgia is anyone's guess. General Prevost was vastly relieved when they sailed away but I for one think his relief may be premature."

"Please, Hugh," Rob said softly. "No need to frighten the ladies."

Hugh glanced from the white-faced Elizabeth to Louisa sitting calm and curious beside her on the settee. One of the ladies was certainly not frightened. But out of deference to his friend and his sister he said no more.

At daybreak a few days later Governor Wright was awakened by a note from General Prevost informing him that there were forty-two French war ships in sight, most of which appeared to be very large.

Word raced through the streets of the town. Dragging Rob out of bed Hugh hurried him to the Council House where they joined the crowd gathered there waiting for news. It was obvious to Hugh, at least, that the French now intended to attack the city though General Prevost was trying to quiet the civilians with the suggestion that they were only on their way to Rhode Island or New York.

Yet it was still difficult to believe that a mighty French fleet would bother with "this miserable sand pile," as Hugh had so often heard the Hessian officers describe Savannah. Why not Charleston or even New York? D'Estaing obviously thought the town was an easy fruit for the plucking, a victory to add to his recent one at Grenada, or perhaps the Americans had convinced him that by taking Savannah the whole of Georgia would follow. Whatever the reason, there was no doubt now that they were in for it and Hugh found his blood tingling with excitement.

As he and Rob worked their way back out of the crowd standing on the edge of the Common, they came across Louisa and her father sitting in an open carriage.

"What news?" she asked Hugh as he took her hand and raised it to his lips.

"There is no doubt it's d'Estaing," he answered and she noticed how unusually bright his eyes looked. "And there are rumors that a sizable American army is marching down from Augusta and over Zubly's Ferry from South Carolina to join his forces. We're going to face a joint attack, there's no doubt about it."

"Oh dear, dear," Thomas Culpepper said anxiously. "And the city so woefully unprepared. No defenses to speak of, half the army off at Port Royal . . ."

"They've been ordered to return but who knows if they'll be able to get through. Surely the French will blockade the water passage and I'm told it's impossible by land."

The look Louisa gave him held as much excitement as concern. "What do you think will happen?"

He still gripped her hand. "I'm no soldier but it seems to me that if the French attack immediately, the town is theirs. If they wait and entrench, then we may have a chance to use the delay to our advantage. What do you say, Rob?"

"I don't know this town well enough to guess. How is my little sister, Miss Culpepper?"

"She's at home with the sal volatile. Perhaps I should have stayed with her but I was so anxious for news. I'll go directly to her when I get back."

"I'm grateful to you. Tell her I'll come as soon as I'm able."

Louisa caught something in his tone of voice. She looked suspiciously from him to Hugh. "Where are you going?"

"We've agreed to offer our services to the army until the crisis is past," Hugh answered. "I suppose they'll find some use for us. They've already begun commandeering the slaves to build fortifications. We can help with that if nothing else."

"Good show, my boy," Thomas said, leaning forward to clap Hugh on the shoulder. "Wish I was younger. I'd join you."

"You just take care of your daughter. And Rob's sister."

He half expected Louisa to say she wished she could join them too. It would be like her. But she was far too preoccupied at the moment with more practical matters.

"I suppose we'd better send Nathan and Sam along too. You will let us know if there is anything more we should do?"

"I won't have to. You'll hear soon enough. If the French do come ashore it is going to take all the men *and* women in this town to hold it for the King."

Louisa shifted her hand in Hugh's so that she was gripping his fingers. "Do be careful, Hugh."

"I promise."

While Louisa plied a prostrate Elizabeth Earing with comforting cups of tea on one side of town and sullen Arabia aired the linen bedding at Mrs. Tondee's insistence on the other, Hugh and Rob made their way to the Council House where they presented themselves at Headquarters. After several false starts they finally stood before a Colonel Lamb, smartly attired in a scarlet coat and white brigadier wig. The searching look he favored them with showed he was not nearly so impressed with them.

"Want to help, do you? Well, you look able enough though a trifle soft." He peered closer at them. "You're not gentlemen, I don't think?"

"Yes," said Rob.

"No," answered Hugh.

"No matter. You'll be doing hard enough work. Too many idle young men think they should be handed a cornetcy for stepping forward at times like these. I'll send you to Captain Moncrief at the Governor's Mansion. He has a few ideas about how to defend this town. Right now he's about to dismantle Governor Wright's barns to make platforms. He could use two able-bodied fellows like yourselves."

"Well, sir," Rob said, "I had hoped . . ."

"What? That you'd be in the fighting itself? There'll be time enough for that. Once the 'Monsieurs' attack we'll all be swinging a sword."

Captain Moncrief turned out to be a moving bundle of energy. He had more than just a few ideas for defending Savannah, he had a whole brilliant plan. "And if the French-ies only begin using a spade, it'll work too," he said to the crowd of men who were tearing down the rice machine and adjacent barns on Governor Wright's property next to the Common. This was only the beginning. Four days later when the French troops began to disembark at Beaulieu thirteen miles below Savannah, the hard pressed workers had come to alternate between despair and renewed effort. The British had 1,200 troops to man a line surrounding the town that was more than 12,500 feet in length. Everyday hope rose with the sun that Lt. Colonel Maitland and the troops from Port Royal would come marching in and by evening those hopes had receded once again. Talk on the lines was mostly how the British might surrender with as little disgrace as possible yet the work went on, impelled by Captain Moncrief's vigor and the thought of a large French army three times their size sitting just outside the fortifications.

Setting out from Tondee's late on a gray morning, Arabia thought she had never seen such chaos on Savannah's streets. It was a town in turmoil. The clatter of hammers and axes never ceased. The streets were thronged with people, all of them in a hurry. Voices of men crying impatient orders mingled with the crash of falling timbers and the thud of wood piled up for hauling to the line of defense. A cannon taken from one of the ships under the bluff was dragged laboriously through the sand. Yet the confusion in the town was as nothing compared to that on the lines. It took nearly an hour for her to find the redoubt where Hugh and Rob were working and even then she only discovered it by asking several times. There was an air of excitement, almost of good fellowship along the lengthy sweep of the defenses being raised in front of the town. Every able-bodied man had turned out to help, most of them rather cheerful considering the threat the French army posed. Arabia was not too concerned for hadn't she come through the British sack of Savannah last December? She knew how to take care of herself and the French, after all, were just the gentlemen to appreciate a woman like her. Her real fear was for Hugh who was more enchanted every day with the thought of an actual battle. If he should be hurt she would care for him but if, God forbid, he should be killed, she would no longer care what happened to herself. The French could do anything they wanted with her and with Savannah.

She finally located both Hugh and Rob at the bottom of a trench struggling with several long poles whose ends had been sharpened into deadly points. Spying her looking down at them from the end of the pit Hugh waved and wiped his sleeve across his brow. Leaving the logs to a group of sweating negro slaves both he and Rob climbed through the deep sand.

"I've brought your lunch," Arabia said, indicating her basket. "Can you stop to eat it now?"

Hugh reached for the basket hungrily. "We will. After all, they can't flog a volunteer for taking time to eat a meal. It wouldn't be good form. Come over here in the shade."

"There's a bottle of wine, a cheese and some of Margery's corn cakes. You're lucky to get those. She's very particular about them."

"We pay Mrs. Tondee well enough to send out our dinner,"

Hugh said, resting against a stack of logs. "It had better be worth it."

"The bearer alone would be worth it," Rob smiled at Arabia. "How did you get away?"

She settled on a barrel beside them. "There was nobody else to come. They've taken all the men, even young Toby. Of course, he wanted to go. There was no holding him. The Madam wasn't a bit happy about sending me but fat Margery would never be able to walk this far."

"We would rather have you anyway." Hugh replied, lifting the bottle of wine in her direction before taking a long swig from it.

"How is the work going?"

"Very well." Rob said with enthusiasm. "I'm amazed at what we see rising around us everyday. If General Prevost can only stall d'Estaing long enough Savannah will never fall."

"I think you're being slightly optimistic," Hugh muttered as he sliced a hunk off the cheese. "If the Frenchies should attack now we'd be in trouble. The longer they wait the better prepared we'll be," he said to Arabia.

"What are those things?" she said, pointing to the stack of pointed logs.

"Fraises, to be used in the earthworks. Makes them very difficult for troops to storm."

"You're digging trenches but back closer to the town they're building platforms. I just hope you know what it's all supposed to add up to."

Hugh reached out and squeezed her hand. "Trust us. Even if we didn't, Captain Moncrief does and that is all that matters."

Arabia, pleased that he had taken her hand, studied Hugh for a moment. He was working in his waistcoat and breeches, his shirt open at the throat revealing the light brown hairs below the neckline. His face was deeply tanned from working in the warm Georgia sun and his hair untidy even though he had tried to confine it in a band at the back of his neck. He looked healthy and strong, full of vitality even with the damp perspiration along his brow and standing on his wide upper lip. Her heart turned over and she looked quickly away to hide her feelings, hoping the flush on her skin was not noticeable.

But Rob, chewing his bread and cheese, had seen it though Hugh had not. "Any news of Maitland?" he asked Arabia, more to help her recover than from curiosity.

"None that I know of. The talk is that the French continue to come ashore. So many of them!"

"We hear nearly four thousand. Four to one against ours," Hugh said. "If only Colonel Maitland could get through from Port Royal, it would make all the difference."

"What's happening back in the town?" Rob asked.

"Several buildings have been taken over for hospitals, I was told. Women are running around trying to store up rice and flour against a siege. A lot of confusion."

"You should be careful coming out like this," Rob said gently. "People are unpredictable. Anything might happen."

Arabia tossed her head. "I can take care of myself," she answered. "Ask Mr. Sandenny about St. Augustine."

Hugh gave a short chuckle. "Yes, you should have seen her tracking through that wilderness, Rob. She was much better at it than I."

"All the same . . ."

The prevailing sense of urgency in the air allowed them little time for their meal. After a few more minutes, Hugh bundled the remains back in Arabia's basket and rose to his feet, stretching his arms above his head.

"Time to get back to work, Rob, my friend."

Reluctantly Rob pushed himself up. "Every muscle in my body aches and he never even feels tired. It's not fair."

"It's that dissolute life you've led at home," Hugh said good-naturedly bending to peck Arabia's cheek. "Thanks, love."

"Will you stop in at Tondee's for supper?" she cried, clutching at his sleeve.

"I don't know. It depends on how much we're needed here."

She frowned then, her dark eyes narrowing, tucked the basket on her arm and turned away with a swirl of her skirts. As she disappeared among the crowd of soldiers working nearby one or two called out to her, a half-ribald pleasantry which she ignored.

Walking beside Hugh, Rob shook his head.

"Hugo, my friend, two of the loveliest beauties in Savannah and you must claim them both. Don't you ever have pity on other men?"

Hugh laughed. "Trouble is the one I really want isn't too interested."

"And the other?"

"Arabia? She's something of a puzzle to me, Rob. She's in love with me, I know, but try as I may, I cannot love her back. I'm fond of her and perhaps if it were not for Louisa . . ."

"You could always make her your mistress on the side. It's done all the time."

"That's just it. For some reason I don't want to. I would only be using her and that would not be fair to her or to myself. Of course, there was a time when I would have made her my mistress without a second's thought. But no more. Louisa would despise me for it if she found out."

Rob glanced over at Hugh's lean face, thinking how much he had changed for the better since leaving England. Not only was he more responsible toward these two women who cared for him, but there seemed little left of the foolish young rake who wasted his life with dissipation, challenges and duels.

"I know I should not encourage Arabia," Hugh went on. "I know it would be wiser to remain distant and cool. But I like her. She's a lively girl with a lot of feeling and a need for friends, even if she isn't a lady like Louisa."

Rob shook his head. "Just because a girl is a serving wench doesn't mean she can't feel things deeply, my dear Hugo. I don't think it would be wise to take her devotion too lightly."

Hugh increased his step. "I'm trying very hard not to hurt her. However, right now we both have more important things to be concerned about. If the French and Americans have their way in the next few days, we may all of us be too busy saving our skins to worry about matters of the heart!"

* * *

Though she struggled to remain calm, Louisa soon found that the panic among the women around her was beginning to tear at the edges of her composure. It made her that much more grateful when Captain Langley approached her about helping to organize a hospital in one of the meeting houses of the city. Not only would it give her something productive to do but, more to the point, it might be a way of involving her houseguest in something that would help her to forget her fears.

For Elizabeth was having a difficult time. When she agreed to come to America she had known there was a war on but she felt certain it would never involve her. In fact, she had been told that it was only important to those few areas where the two armies met. Now she found herself not only in the throes of a siege but in the path of an impending battle. Her worst nightmare had become reality and her fragile nerves were close to collapse. Louisa tried to understand and pity her even as she struggled to hold in her exasperation. If all the women of the town took to swooning there would be no way to save Savannah.

She longed to do something to help and this was the best answer she could find. So, much against Elizabeth's will, she dragged her each morning to the meeting house to roll bandages, count supplies, or any other useful activity that came to hand. And, gradually her efforts seemed to work. Captain Langley was pleased, Surgeon Walsh was pleased and even the two young subalterns who had been assigned to help her had ceased grumbling that they would prefer to be working on the defenses and willingly ran to do her bidding.

Every day reports raced through the town detailing how much closer the French had moved and how much farther General Lincoln had advanced with his American army. Neither side had any secrets. The loyalists in Savannah knew when Count Pulaski, the dashing Polish cavalryman who had offered his services to the Americans, met with Admiral d'Estaing on the 14th. It was recounted with horror in the drawing rooms of Savannah how the French had ransacked the Habersham plantation on the Ogeechee Road, pillaged the Morel home, and carried away from Bethesda steers, cows, sheep, hogs and Jamaican rum. Like a cloud of locusts they advanced, devouring the countryside. On the other hand, Admiral d'Estaing knew full well that the British were building up their defenses but it did not bother him very much. He had so much faith in his own invincibility, was so contemptuous of the American allies he was supposed to be helping, and so aware of the feeble position of the town and its defenses that he was already picturing his triumphant return to Paris. It was common knowledge that he expected little more than symbolic support from General Lincoln who was hurrying with his army down from South Carolina.

Thus it was not surprising when, even before General Lincoln arrived, the Count advanced his French troops to within three miles of the town and on the morning of the 16th, sent in a capitulation that it surrender. The word swept through the lines. No one seriously expected General Prevost to concede to this high-handed demand, though there were those to whom the four-to-one advantage held by the French spelled only defeat who urged that in the name of common sense there was no alternative. The General himself was known to be uncertain, feeling that if the Americans were allowed to join with the French, the garrison in Savannah would be so outnumbered there would be no possibility of defending the town.

And then, shortly after noon word raced through the streets and houses of Savannah that boats had appeared on the river below the bluff—longboats filled with rows of men in scarlet coats, their muskets like masts rising above their heads. Up the bluff they marched, weary veterans filing off to join their regiments. The reinforcements from Port Royal had come at last. For some unknown reason, neither the French nor the Americans had thought to block the channel out of Port Royal and Lt. Colonel Maitland had brought his 900 crack troops through by avoiding the sea and weaving their boats through channel and marsh. At one point they had carried them on their shoulders across a cut of land that separated the creeks.

There was no holding back the joy of the civilians, soldiers and sailors who crowded into the streets to welcome these hardy veterans, cheering and shouting them on.

Now there was no more talk of surrender. When the twenty-four hour truce which Prevost had requested was up, he sent word to the French Commander that he was determined to defend the town. And now, with the defenses rising all around and the arrival of Maitland's reinforcements, feeling was high that he might well succeed.

Chapter 9

ONE OF THE first buildings to be dismantled for use in the town's defenses was the large barracks the British had rebuilt for their troops. Had it been still standing Hugh and Rob would have taken to sleeping there. Instead they gradually got in the habit of collapsing with fatigue on a pallet in the shadow of one of the redoubts, too weary to walk back into the town.

It was there, shortly after General Prevost's decision to defend Savannah, that Hugh was surprised early one evening to look up and find Olana wending her way through the crowd of working and lounging men, asking for him.

"Olana," he called waving to her. "Over here."

"Mistress wants to see you, sur," Olana said, waddling over to his side.

Hugh looked down at his dust-stained clothes. "I'm in no fit state to see any young lady."

"She say, don't matter how you look. Very important that you come. She tell me not to come back home without you."

"Is anything wrong?"

"Don't know, sur. Just know she say you gotta come."

"All right, I'll be there. But you must allow me time to wash and change first. We'll go back by my rooms. God's blood, I don't feel like it."

Still grumbling, he set out for the town with Olana following along behind. Too weary to hurry, it was nearly an hour later that he presented himself at Louisa's door, cleaner and neater than before though by no means the dandy he used to be when calling on Louisa. She did not seem to notice.

"Hugh, I'm so grateful you're here," she said, taking his hands and leading him inside the drawing room where she closed the door. "I've an errand to go on and I want you to come with me."

"You know I'm happy to serve you, Louisa, but I hope whatever this is, it doesn't involve walking very far. I'm about at the end of my strength."

"We won't walk then, we'll take the carriage."

"Where are we going?"

Louisa hesitated. "To the American camp," she said her eyes glinting mischievously. At his openmouthed reaction she hurried on. "I have a letter from my father to General Lincoln and I have General Prevost's permission to deliver it in person, under a flag. He doesn't wish to send troops with me so he allowed me to pick my own escort. I chose you."

"But you're mad Louisa! Even if the Americans let us in, they may never let us out. They might consider us spies."

"But we're not. My father has known General Lincoln for years and I met him myself when I was a child. He'll see me and I'm certain he'll give me a safe conduct. Sometimes diplomacy can be better served by friends than by general's adjutants."

Hugh, weary as he was, found himself fascinated by the thought of walking boldly into the center of the Continental Army. "But what do you hope to accomplish? Aren't they afraid we might bring out information that could be used against them?"

"Hugh, you must know that there is a great deal of traffic

back and forth between the camps of the allies and ours. Why, I saw two French officers walking along Broughton Street just yesterday. Besides, I'm not going there to try to learn anything. I'm going to ask a favor. And at night, too. How much could I see at night?"

"What favor?"

"General Prevost has made a formal request to d'Estaing that the women and children be allowed to leave the city before any hostilities begin. He thinks if a friend of Lincoln's can put in a word on their behalf it might help sway d'Estaing's decision."

"Prevost is thinking of his own family," Hugh answered, taking a seat opposite Louisa on the brocade settee. "The French are building batteries and so are we. There's bound to be some kind of bombardment soon. But do you think our plea would help?"

"I don't know but it's worth a try. Many of the rebels have family here in town, too, and they'd be happy to know they're safe. Will you go with me?"

Hugh smiled at her with a gleam of mischief in his eye. "My dear girl, I am so weary I could drop here on your Turkey carpet and go to sleep, yet wild horses could not hold me back from a chance to walk right into the American camp. Of course, I'll go."

He reached for her hand. "Besides, if you should be successful in your mission, it would mean you would be safe. I would be vastly relieved to know you were out of this. For that alone I'd go along."

It was dusk by the time Louisa's small carriage rolled smartly along between the orderly rows of tents in the wood before Savannah where the American army had established their camp, well to the left of the larger French cantonment. Hugh tried not to be too obvious about observing everything yet his fascinated gaze took in every detail. His experience with Robert Sallette had accustomed him to the fringed deerksin shirts and leggings that many of the Continental soldiers wore but the mixed assortment of military coats, homespun shirts and breeches, round hats and tricorns with one side pinned raffishly up was a wonder to him after the smart precision of the British and Hessian forces. There was also an air of informality on every side which he had never seen in any cantonment before and which suggested a lack of seriousness about the whole thing.

Many of the accoutrements were those to be seen in any army camp anywhere. The orderly rows of tents, the iron pots over rough campfires, the muskets propped against tree trunks, the myriad smells and noises. Groups of men lounged on the grass playing at checkers or sharing a bottle or a pipe. But over all lay such unmilitary, casual informality that he found himself wondering if the defense of Savannah was not going to be an easy thing after all.

They were stopped several times, questioned then directed on their way until at length an orderly in a smart blue coat heavy with silver lace escorted them to General Lincoln's marquee. He disappeared inside for a few moments then returned to lead Louisa and Hugh through the flap opening.

A camp bed stood in the corner, two empty chairs sat before a small plank table in the center. In front of it facing a wooden writing desk open before him sat a heavy-set gentleman in a a blue coat and powdered wig. He rose as Louisa extended her hands.

"My dear Miss Culpepper. It's been so many years. What a lovely young lady you've grown up to be."

"General," Louisa said, curtsying deeply. "Thank you for seeing me. I too was glad of this opportunity to renew old acquaintances. I remember you so well from when I was a child."

He engulfed both her hands in his huge paws and patted them gently. "That was a long time ago. So much has happened since . . . And how is your father, that good man?"

"He does very well, thank you," Louisa said. She brought Hugh forward and introduced him.

"Sandenny?" Lincoln mulled over Hugh's name. "Don't remember ever meeting any Sandennys before. You're a friend of Louisa's?"

"Yes sir. We met coming over on the ship. I've only been in America a short while."

"Another Tory, eh. Well, well, we don't hold that against

you, not yet, anyway. Please my girl, sit down. I'll have my orderly bring us some wine."

"No thank you, sir," Louisa spoke hurriedly. "I must be very brief." Reaching into her cloak she drew out her father's letter and gave it to the General. "My father requests you read this, General, and, if you will, send us back some hope that our concerns will be met."

Like many hard pressed, busy men, Lincoln did not offer the courtesies a second time but seemed glad of the chance to get on with the business at hand. Breaking the seal, he spread the letter on the table and glanced quickly over its contents. Then, stepping quickly to the door, he spoke a few words with the sentry outside.

"You know what your father writes?" he asked Louisa, as he came back to the table.

"I know something of it, sir. We are all concerned especially for the children. Several of your own men have families in Savannah, I believe."

"I know. I know. Ah, come in, Count."

A tall man stepped inside the marquee. His eyes lit up at once on seeing Louisa standing in the middle of the tent and the smile that flitted across his lips had a light in it Hugh did not relish. He was dressed in a brilliantly flamboyant uniform and wore a thin moustache which branded him a foreigner.

"May I present Count Pulaski," Lincoln said. "He has come all the way from Poland to serve us a legion of cavalry. Miss Louisa Culpepper, Count, and Mister . . . ah . . ."

"Sandenny," Hugh said stepping forward. The Count bowed to them both—a precise military bow—but his attention was obviously all for Louisa.

"So pleased, Mademoiselle," he said with a heavy accent.

"Miss Culpepper's father has written me to ask for my help in convincing Admiral d'Estaing that the women and children of the town be allowed to leave before hostilities erupt. You've seen more of d'Estaing than I, Pulaski, and you speak his language. Do you have any idea whether or not he will agree to this?"

The Count shook his handsome head. "My General, I

do not believe he will. He was more than a little miffed by criticism of the twenty-four hour truce he allowed General Prevost before your excellency arrived and I fear it is anger rather than mercy that is uppermost in his breast at the moment."

"Humph!" Lincoln snapped. "The criticism was just, but this is not the time to discuss that. Louisa, my child, go back to your father and tell him I will approach the French commander on this subject but that I fear there is little hope he will allow it. Matters have gotten too far beyond us."

"I only wish the decision were up to me," the Count said gallantly, raising Louisa's hand to his lips.

She smiled at him and retrieved her hand. "I understand. Thank you for seeing me, General Lincoln. I hope that we will meet again under better circumstances."

"My child, my advice to you is to keep to the cellars. And try to keep your father there also, if you can."

"You know he will not do that. Nor I, for that matter."

"Then, be careful. I should hate to think that these dreadful divisions among our countrymen caused harm to you or your father. But that is what we have come to in America. So very sad . . ."

His heavy eyes drooped. For a moment Hugh thought he was going to fall asleep on his feet. Weariness is not exclusive to the British, he thought.

It wasn't until they were safely back inside the British lines that Louisa explained to him that Benjamin Lincoln had a habit of falling asleep suddenly, sometimes between sentences as he dictated a letter. It often caused men to think he was not very understanding or quick when actually the opposite was true.

"I remember him as so very kind. How terrible that we should be enemies."

Once they returned to the town there was little time for visiting and Louisa lost all contact with Hugh. All Savannah was aware of how the French and Americans were both feverishly digging trenches and building batteries in the outlying areas while the British were just as busily throwing up fortifications close to its perimeters. Louisa kept busy with preparations at the hospital and meanwhile thought over

General Lincoln's advice. When her father had built the Culpepper house he had not bothered with a cellar, thinking it was not needed in such a sandy, warm place. Louisa had never regretted not having one until now when she was forced to go across the street to her neighbor, Melissa Stratham and ask if she might store some personal things in the commodious, solid cellar underneath her house. Though it was already half filled with the assorted belongings of the two officers and a Councilman who were billeted there, Melissa generously gave in to Louisa's pleading. Two afternoons later Sam and Nathan carried two trunks, several casks of wine, four wheels of cheese and a keg of pickled beef across the street to be added to the Stratham collection.

"Do you really think that was necessary, my dear," Thomas asked her that evening as they sat playing chess in the back parlor. "This is a very solid house. Surely it can withstand a few French shells, assuming they even get this far. Besides, you know Ralph Stoakes has begged us to share his quarters which are even farther out of the range of any French guns. He would be happy to accept any belongings we might wish to store there."

Louisa leaned on her hand and stared at the figures on the board. She was finding it difficult to keep her mind on the game.

"I know he would, Father, but I didn't want to ask him. Mrs. Stratham doesn't mind, and her house is so much more convenient."

"You really should not be so shy of Sir Ralph. He thinks only of your welfare. My goodness, Louisa, do you really want to make that move? I shall take your bishop right away, if you do."

"Oh. I didn't see that."

"My dear, you are not playing your usual game tonight. Are you tired? You haven't looked yourself for several days."

Louisa sat back and tried to smile at her father knowing it was a poor attempt. "A little tired, perhaps, but I'm really all right. Captain Moncrief has kept us going steadily the past few days."

"Tsk, tsk. Not at all the way a lady should be spending her time. Sometimes I regret returning to Georgia. I should have kept you in London where you'd probably be married by this time."

"Nonsense Papa. I love being busy, especially with something worthwhile. I'm just a little weary tonight."

"Well then, you must get to bed early," Thomas said, picking up the chess pieces. "We can have another game when you're rested."

"I think I will go to bed," his daughter answered, moving to the window and pulling back the drapes. Though October had come and the swamp maples were turning blood red, the heat was still oppressive. The thought of her soft bed with its protective netting against the mosquitoes suddenly seemed very welcome.

Almost at once she fell into a deep, dreamless sleep lulled by the friendly chatter of the night insects. Two hours later she was jarred awake by a thunderous roar that set the house shaking and rattled the windows. Louisa sat straight up in bed for a moment not sure where she was. Then she was on her feet, pulling her robe around her as the door burst open and Olana came flying into the room.

"Miz Louisa! Mercy, Lord God, what's happenin'?"

Louisa met her halfway across the room. "It's all right, Olana. The French must have begun their bombardment. Where's my father?"

The roar grew louder with every new blast, Olana threw her hands over her ears screaming, "It's a judgment! Lord have mercy . . ."

Gripping her arms Louisa gave her a good shake. "Stop that, Olana. Nothing is going to be helped by you standing there yelling. Come along, now, and get the other servants together."

Louisa pushed her terrified maid toward the door and into the hall just as a shell crashed against a side wall of the Culpepper house. As the house shuddered Olana began to scream louder. In the hallway Louisa met her father running from his room, still dressed. Behind him Sam and Nathan were pounding up the stairs.

"Louisa, are you all right?"

"Yes, yes, Papa. But I don't think we should stay here," she said, trying to dodge the plaster dust that drifted off the ceiling like rain. "Nathan, help Olana get the rest of the servants together. We'll go across the street to the Stratham's cellar, at least until things quiet down."

"But leave my house! I don't think—"

"Papa, we've been through all this before. It's the safest place to be. Don't change your mind now."

Thomas looked miserably around as the house shuddered from a blast in the street, which rattled the crystals in the candelabra on the downstairs landing.

"Very well, but I don't like it."

His grudging consent was followed by the horrified vision of his daughter traipsing down the stairs with her robe billowing behind her and he flatly refused to budge until she went back to her room and threw on some decent clothes. Not even the French shells could overshadow the spectacle of his daughter out in public in her nightdress. By the time the two of them followed the rest of their household across the street toward the Stratham cellar the bombardment had stilled momentarily. A few houses away Louisa caught a brief glimpse of flames roaring above a roof but Thomas pulled her into the security of the Stratham cellar before she could see how bad the fire was. She was not unhappy to get out of the street even without the constant roar of cannons. The shrieks of women and children were terrible to hear. People were dashing wildly from doorway to doorway and down near the corner there was a small shadowed lump in the street that looked too much like a body.

Inside Mrs. Stratham's cellar they found chaos. Much of the space had already been filled with trunks, boxes and casks and now what was left was crammed with neighbors, for the Culpeppers had not been the only ones to seek the safety of a substantial cellar. There were several neighborhood families—fathers, mothers and children, and a number of their Negro servants, all crammed together in various stages of distress. The roar of the firing began again, a little muffled by the thick tabby walls of the house yet just as terrible and frightening. Louisa tried to help by quieting some of the children, hoping to take her own mind off the shuddering of the walls of the house and the shrieks which could be heard outside in the street.

They huddled in the damp cellar until daylight came and the bombardment stopped long enough to convince everyone that there was going to be a respite. Louisa ventured outside to such a spectacle as she had never imagined. Two gaping craters in the sandy street were all that was left after two shells had landed there. The walls of her father's house had been hit in three places, but, thankfully, no fire had resulted. Even more important, the stable was still safe though the horses were frightened out of their wits. Even as the Culpeppers walked around their yard the street began to fill with others venturing out while they had the chance and Louisa began to hear some of the extent of the damage done by the guns.

"They say a shell passed right through the Laurie house on Broughton Street," John Sparks who lived at the corner house told her. "They say it killed two women and children but I haven't yet been able to learn if that's true."

"Four Negroes in a cellar were burned to death when a shell burst right at their feet."

"I tried to get to Yamacraw, out of range, but only made it to the trench on the Common the Governor's slaves dug. Fell right on my face right alongside them, I did, and was glad to get there!"

After a lull the roar of guns began again, forcing everyone off the street and back into their dark holes. Louisa and her father sat out most of the day there, helping to put together enough food and drink that everyone might have a little. Late in the afternoon what they had feared all day finally happened and a shell burst near the door of the cellar, shattering it and flinging the three people who were sitting near it back into the room.

Running to the shattered opening, Louisa ignored the screams of the other women as she helped two of the victims to their feet. Though badly bruised their injuries were mostly superficial. However, the third victim, a black woman who had been sitting near the door cradling a baby in her arms, lay without moving, lumped grotesquely over her screaming child. Easing her over, Louisa carefully picked up the frightened baby and tucked it up against her. The mother's lifeless eyes stared up at her, surprised, startled. As two of the men bent over the woman's lifeless body, Louisa turned away, overcome by the terrible reality of death which had been all around her for hours but which now for the first time became starkly real.

The bombardment which took such a heavy toll on the town, for the most part went over the heads of the men in the fortifications the army had thrown up. When an occasional shell did hit, the battery was quickly replaced and the breastworks reinforced with the ever abundant sand. As loss of life among the civilians continued to climb, the soldiery suffered only a few wounded and one dead and it was soon wryly commented around town that it was safer to be with the army than on the streets of Savannah.

Hugh spent the first two days of the bombardment helping to load and fire British guns which were pointed toward the French trenches. He was finally able to slip away, grimy and sweaty, during a lull on the second afternoon when a hovering, black thunderstorm threatened to unleash its torrents on the area. He made straight for the Culpepper house where he found both it and the stable empty and so dented by cannon and small arms fire that his heart sank. The street lay as empty as the houses and was even more damaged. He called and pounded on the door to no avail and finally not knowing where else to go, headed across town to Tondee's Tavern.

The taproom was crowded with men drinking as though they expected no tomorrow. Arabia moved among them, her clothes disheveled and her glum unhappiness in sharp contrast to their forced merriment. When she looked up and saw Hugh standing in the doorway her misery dropped away like a cloak. Throwing down a tray on the nearest table she weaved through the crowd to his side, ignoring the ribald comments of the men around her.

"Hugh," she cried, throwing her arms around his neck. A loud guffawing went up around them and Hugh hurriedly pulled her into the hall to a corner behind the stairs.

"Oh, Hugh," she crooned, her lips searching his face until they found his, kissing him with fierce longing. "I was so afraid for you," she murmured. "You should have let me know you were all right."

"I couldn't." He pulled away from her and disentangled her fingers from behind his neck. "I cannot stay now, Arabia. I only came to find you and Miss Culpepper and make sure that you're both safe."

At Louisa's name Arabia stepped back, her dark eyes turning as black as the clouds outside the window.

Hugh pretended not to notice. "The talk on the lines is that the women and children are going to be evacuated to Hutchinson's Island where they'll be safe. I intend to make certain that you both get there."

"I won't go! Mrs. Tondee won't allow it."

"She'll allow it. She's a fool not to go herself. It's a miracle you haven't both been hurt already. Now go and get your things."

Arabia jerked her head away. "I won't go. Not with her! I won't."

Grabbing her arm Hugh's fingers dug into the soft flesh beneath her sleeve.

"Stop this, Arabia. There is a war going on and any minute those guns are going to start up again. I came away from the redoubt where I ought to be right now for only one reason—to make certain that you and Louisa are safely out of the line of fire. Now either you come with me right now or I'll wash my hands of you and you can manage on your own. I've no more time to give you."

Never before had she seen him so angry. For the first time she began to see that his preoccupation with the fighting left him little concern for either her or Louisa. Further, it was certain that if he left her here it would only be to search out Louisa Culpepper and take *her* to Hutchinson's Island.

"All right. I'll come. But you'll have to explain to Mrs. Tondee."

"To the devil with Mrs. Tondee. You've got two minutes to get whatever you want to bring."

While Arabia flew up the stairs, Hugh made several inquiries of those few men he recognized in the taproom and learned that the Culpeppers had been keeping to Mrs. Stratham's cellar across the street from their house. With a silent Arabia in tow, he made his way back across town to their house. By this time the lull in the bombardment and the easing of the threatened storm had lured the inhabitants outside and he found Louisa sitting on the grass cradling a young child surrounded by a number of women, both black and white.

Hugh thought she had never looked more bedraggled or move lovely. Her hair fell straggling under her cap and her plain, drab dress was sooty and stained from the cellar. Nearby several of the servants worked at filling empty casks with sand to roll up against the sides of the house. Spread across the grass among the reclining figures lay an assortment of featherbed mattresses collected from houses up and down the street.

Arabia hung back near the road while Hugh made his way through the figures spread on the lawn to where Louisa sat. Though her smile when she looked up and saw him was preoccupied yet he could tell she was happy to see him.

"I prayed you would escape injury," Louisa said, reaching out to him with her free hand.

"I've been in less danger of injury than you, it seems," Hugh answered, unwilling to relinquish her fingers. "Was it very bad?"

She stared out over the yard stroking the dark hair on the child sleeping on her lap.

"Terrible. The mother of this baby was killed yesterday when a blast shattered the cellar door. We've had no chance to find a relative so I've been caring for her."

Hurriedly Hugh explained his errand and discovered almost at once that his forcefulness had none of the effect on Louisa that it had on Arabia.

"I cannot leave these people," she cried. "Nor Papa. I couldn't desert him."

"Then bring the women with you. I'm sure your father is able to care for himself."

They argued for several tortured moments before he was able to convince Louisa of the wisdom of leaving. Then just when he thought he had succeeded Melissa Stratham refused to abandon her house to "a parcel of Negroes who would rob her of everything." At that point Thomas Culpepper returned, adding his voice to Hugh's and assuring Mrs. Stratham that he would keep a watch on the contents of her cellar.

So it was that within an hour Hugh was able to shepherd the entire crowd of women and children to the wharf where a flatboat waited to carry them across to the Island. Arabia, mollified somewhat by the fact that she shared her rescue with a crowd rather than just with Louisa, gave him one of her long languid looks and deliberately brushed against him as she stepped into the boat. Hugh hardly noticed, so intent was he on getting back to the lines. He watched the boat pull away, was left with a momentary image of Louisa looking back at him over the head of the child she still held, her eyes full of gratitude, then he turned and loped quickly back up the cobbled walk to ascend the bluff.

The relief the women felt at leaving Savannah was dissipated a little when they arrived at James Graham's plantation and saw that the garrison assembled there to protect them was made up of Cherokee braves with tomahawks stuffed through their belts, and, worse yet, Negro slaves carrying guns. The spectacle of armed slaves was unsettling to even the most liberal of Savannahians and there was much murmuring among the evacuees at this misjudgment on General Prevost's part.

Somehow order had been established out of the assortment of refugees who had flocked to the island for safety and a kind of communal meal of rice, pork and Indian corn was served that evening. At last Louisa could sit and listen to the crashing and shriek of the shells over the city without being afraid. She turned her small charge over to Olana then took her plate and sat down on a bench where Arabia was bending intently over her supper. Looking up the girl hesitated before shifting to make room for Louisa.

"This must be a far cry from what you're used to," Arabia said after several minutes of silence.

"Hunger makes the best sauce. And after two days in a cellar making do with pickled beef and two-day old bread, this is delicious. How did you escape the guns?"

"The first night I went with Margery the cook and Mrs.

Tondee down to the river under the bluff."

"Was it safe there?"

"Safe enough from the bombs but not from the river rats. The noise had them as frightened as the people. They were in some frenzy and I didn't like it much."

"I should think not."

"Then when that French ship started shelling the bluff we scrambled back up and made for Yamacraw. But Mrs. Tondee wouldn't hear of leaving her place for long and nothing must do but we go back. After that when it got too heavy we headed for the trenches on the Common."

"It does not surprise me that Mrs. Tondee would not leave her place of business. She's kept it going since Mr. Peter died through a rebel government and now a British one too. She's not going to let a little thing like French guns drive her out!"

Arabia smiled, the first genuine smile Louisa had got from her in years. Then, remembering, her face grew sour again.

"We gathered featherbeds from all the houses on the street," Louisa went on cheerfully, "and piled them around the walls of the cellar hoping to protect ourselves. All it did was make the mattresses damp and dirty."

"I expect they will still serve well enough," Arabia answered, thinking that she had never once in her life slept on a featherbed. Picking up her wooden trencher she got to her feet. "I'd best go and see if they need any help with cleaning up. That's the one thing I know how to do well."

Louisa watched her walk away, disappointed that their first friendly exchange in many years had ended so abruptly. Getting past Arabia Tillman's hostility was no easier than the French driving the British out of Savannah, she thought grimly.

"Why Miss Louisa," a voice said at her elbow. "How relieved I am to see you here."

Louisa looked up to see a group of men drawing abreast of her bench. She recognized most of them—Governor Wright and several members of his council, Mr. Habersham and Colonel Mulryne and, bending over her searching for her hand, Ralph Stoakes.

"It has vexed me sorely these last two days that my heavy duties with the Governor prevented me from seeking you out and making certain you got away. I confess I was worried. Several of our young ladies have thrown themselves on the mercy of the French and I hoped you were not among them."

Louisa retrieved her hand. "I have no love for the French, Sir Ralph."

"And the Americans? I know you have friends among them."

"Yes, I do. After all, I am an American, born here and bred here."

"Ah, but a *loyal* American. True to the Crown."

"Yes. I would never desert my father to ask for asylum among rebels."

"Miss Culpepper," the Governor said, walking up to where she sat. "How wonderful to see you safely here. How is your father?"

"I hope he is safe. I left him at Mrs. Stratham's caring for the people who are still seeking sanctuary in her cellar. I was there myself until this afternoon."

"Oh, you are so much better off here. I wish your father had come with you. And where is the divine Melissa," Sir James said, his eyes searching the crowd. "I must be sure to speak to her. A time like this is especially trying to a widow."

"You are very kind, sir."

The Governor gave her one of his warm smiles and moved off, spreading his comforting presence over more of the refugees. Squeezing her hand Ralph leaned into her face.

"I shall see you again. We are kept very busy trying to keep order in the town and prevent fires from spreading. But we are managing. This foolish bombardment so far has accomplished little besides wasting French and American ammunition. If there is anything you need please do not hesitate to send for me.

"Thank you. You are too kind."

As he moved away, she rose and worked her way back through the crowd toward the spot where she had left Olana with the child. If she thought about it there were probably

many things which she could ask for and which they might
well need while this shelling continued. But somehow she
did not wish to be beholden to Ralph Stoakes. She would
just put up with a few discomforts. It might even be good
for her!

Chapter 10

AFTER FIVE LONG days of constant shelling the guns at last fell silent. There was so much clandestine traffic back and forth between the two opposing camps that long before the end of the bombardment Hugh and Rob had learned almost as much about the state of affairs within the allied cantonment as they knew of their own. They knew, for example, of the high-handed way Admiral d'Estaing made decisions without listening to his French officers, much less to his American allies. They knew of the contempt he felt for nearly every American except George Washington. Of the way American soldiers were arrested if they so much as set foot in the French camp. Of the misery on board the boats which bobbed at anchor while the Admiral sought to win laurels for himself on land—the lack of food, the sailors lying sick in the holds, the thirty or more bodies thrown overboard every day. They learned that supplies were running short even among the land forces and they knew the strength of their own works, still strong in spite of the long bombardment. And they knew, as did the French and the Americans, how dangerous it was to keep a fleet lingering on these shores during the hurricane season, not to mention the threat posed by a British fleet that roamed nearby somewhere in the West Indies.

Then, finally, they learned that the French commander had made the decision against all the advice of his staff, to storm the British lines in one last desperate attempt to take the town.

"A sergeant in the militia heard it," Hugh said in astonishment as he pulled Rob up from a pallet where he had been resting. "He just stood outside the Admiral's marquee posing as a guard and listened bold as brass to the plans being laid inside. Then he hotfooted it back here to lay it all out before General Prevost."

"What a way to run a war!"

"Isn't it. Makes you wonder how these military men ever manage to get anything done. We know that he's planning to send his strongest lines against our right while the left will take nothing but a feint."

"And where will you and I be?"

"In the thick of it. I managed to get us assigned to Lieutenant Tawes and he's put us with the Carolina Tories. Get your cartridge belt and musket and let's be off."

Rob needed no urging. "I'll be there before you are," he cried, grabbing up his arms and racing to the door of the makeshift barracks.

"Here, take this," Hugh called, throwing a balled up shirt after him.

"God's blood, why?"

"You'll see."

It was dark by the time they got to the Spring Hill redoubt. They found it crowded with English redcoats, Scotch Highlanders, and Carolina Tories in fringed deerskin, each intent on readying his musket and ammunition. Hugh and Rob were assigned to a corner on one of the parapets where they scrounged down and tried to rest, too keyed up to sleep. Hugh recognized the same feelings he had often experienced on the night before a duel—that finely honed sense of excitement and danger that thrilled him like nothing else on earth. He gave no more thought to the possibility of dying than he had when he was to face a duelist at fourteen paces. If it happened, it happened. The real thrill was in out-maneuvering the other fellow to prevent it from happening.

Long before dawn broke the men in the redoubt were peering over its walls searching for signs of the French column. When the faint echo of drums was finally heard, the Highland pipers set up their customary yowling just to let the French know that their enemies were expecting them. The first faint glimmer of dawn gave a clear view of the long lines of troops sluggishly moving through the swamps and along the Ebeneezer road. Yet it was nearly an hour and a half later that the combined forces of Louis Roi's finest troops and the rebels of His Majesty's colonies in America finally drew up their lines to storm the defenses of Savannah.

Hugh propped his musket against the wall and buttoned an extra linen shirt over his coat.

"Now do you see why I told you to bring a shirt," he said to Rob who sat watching him.

"I figured it out long ago. The French wear white uniforms and we want to confuse them."

"Exactly."

Rob pulled himself up and reached for his linen shirt. "Let's just hope our lads don't confuse us for them!"

Off to the left came the crackling and popping of musketry, the signal for the feint upon the British left. There was the sound of muffled drums carrying across on the cool morning air. From the gloom of the mist beyond the abatis came the pounding of feet and the cries, growing ever louder, a cacophony of voices screaming, "Vive le roi!" Hugh's finger tightened on his primed musket as his eyes searched for the first clear figure. On either side the cannons began to boom, sending shudders through the parapet. The thunder of the batteries grew deafening. Out of the mist white shadows began to materialize as the first French grenadiers climbed the abatis and thundered toward the walls, swarming up the glacis in front of the redoubt.

Then there was no time for anything but firing, priming and firing again. The force of the attack carried the first troops up the steep sides of the parapet where they hurled themselves at the men defending the walls. Hugh caught them out of the corner of his eye swarming into the redoubt on his left. He could hear Lieutenant Tawes at the top of his voice ordering his men into the breach and he saw the flash of his sword as he hurled himself in the thick of them. Throwing down his musket, Hugh pulled out his own sword and with a whoop threw himself into the thick hand-to-hand fighting, parrying blows to his right and left and thrusting his sword into any undefended body he could reach.

A French soldier went down before him, adding to the churning mess under his feet. The ground was alive with men, some of them struggling to rise, others lying grotesquely still. He had no idea how long it went on but it seemed endless—an eternity of slashing and dodging, cutting down one enemy only to have another rise up above him. He caught a glimpse of a flag that went down under a swarm of men. Stumbling to dodge a musket aimed at his face, he knocked against another man fighting furiously with his sword. Briefly he recognized Lieutenant Tawes, his sword blood-red. Through it all the guns continued to roar and the air grew so thick with smoke that Hugh hardly knew if he was battling friend or foe.

Then the storm over the parapet began to slacken as the French fell back, unable to storm the works without support that had not appeared. The fighting along the walls grew more desperate as those who were abandoned attempted to follow their comrades. The main body in the retreat were cut down by murderous fire from the batteries on the British right. When finally Hugh had time to lower his sword and lean gasping against the walls he could see beyond the breastworks nothing but blood and carnage. The batteries were firing canisters now filled with chains, nails, bolts— anything that would cut savagely through the mass of retreating forms. The causeway near the road was thick with dead bodies while the retreating men were falling back on a new column which now, too late, was attempting to storm in behind them.

The mist lifted enough to reveal a new swarm of troops sweeping up the glacis and onto the breastworks. Hugh was still out of breath from the first foray and briefly wondered if he would have the strength to face this new onslaught. But Colonel Maitland had seen the threat and to Hugh's relief a whole new body of English troops came running in to help support the redoubt. There was savage fighting all around him. The clash of metal merged with the thunder of the batteries. Arms were severed, bodies run through, he grimaced as an officer's nose was cut off, cries and shrieks surrounded him in a tumult of fury and pain.

An American flag was planted in the glacis below where Hugh was standing. Forcing a sword from the hand of an officer lying dead at his feet, Hugh threw it with all his might at the Continental soldier trying to shove the staff into the soft earth, catching him through the chest. The flag went down but was caught immediately by another hand and raised again. Hugh got a glancing blow on the shoulder and turned to face a French dragoon, swinging a short sword at his head. Ducking quickly he deflected the blade which slashed down his arm, streaking blood. The Frenchman doubled over with a shot in the chest from somewhere behind as Hugh slumped down against the wall gripping his arm. Then the second charge finally drew away, as unsupported by their fellow troops as the first grenadiers had been.

In the ditch below the glacis Hugh saw that an American column had advanced, hoping to storm the walls. They were caught there and held down by the thunder of the British guns but bravely returned to the attack though every attempt was repulsed. A glimmer of admiration flickered across his mind before he was caught up again in the onslaught of a third charge by the combined French and American column.

Once again the allies fought furiously, storming the flimsy redoubt only to be repulsed by the men entrenched there and the murderous fire of the batteries on either side. The reserve army beyond them was in chaos, half of them mired in the swamps along the road, others caught in the advancing and retreating columns stumbling over each other on the causeway. After what seemed endless hours, but had in fact been only one, the retreat was sounded.

It was no sooner heard than Maitland ordered his troops in pursuit. Hugh, still slumped down against the parapet, gripping his arm where the sword had slashed it, watched the hordes of Highland Scotch, royal American Rangers and Hessian dragoons swarm over the breastworks and decided he did not have the strength to join them. Instead he watched as they were held off by a rear guard of French reserves while the main French and American armies retreated back through the pine barrens and swamp to their camps.

At last the guns grew silent, the air still. Pulling himself up, weary and dizzy from loss of blood, Hugh looked out on a sight like no other he had ever seen.

There were men spread around his feet, the dying and the dead. The ditches outside the walls were thick with bodies. Men lay caught, hanging grotesquely from the shattered abatis. The causeway beyond the breastworks was littered with men, some still moving and crying, many lying mutilated and cut nearly in half by the canister. Blood covered his shirt and congealed on the boards under his feet. The fields outside the redoubt ran with blood. He could taste blood in his mouth and felt it behind his eyes, veiling his sight. There was nothing but blood and death in all the world.

Ten feet away he recognized the body of Lieutenant Tawes, his hand still clutched around the hilt of his sword which was thrust in the body of a Frenchman lying across him. In places the bodies were piled three high, some without limbs, others mangled beyond belief by the grapeshot.

There was no excitement now, no thrill of danger, no glory in defying death. It broke on him like a revelation how overjoyed he was to still be alive. How could he have wanted this, how could he have sought it? It was sickening and obscene, a stupid waste of good lives.

He heard his name called and looked up to see Rob peering down at him, his face black with soot and a stained rag wound around his head. Did he look that frightful too, he wondered.

"Hugh, you've been hurt. Let me see that arm."

Gratefully Hugh slumped into the arms of his friend as his vision began to blur.

"That's a nasty wound," Rob said, supporting him with one arm and gently pulling away Hugh's sleeve with the

other. Propping him up Rob tore away the bandage around
his head and tied a tourniquet around Hugh's wounded arm.

"We'd better get you to the surgeon right away. Can you
walk?"

"I think so. What's happening, Rob. Is it over?"

"It's over for now. We beat them back, Hugh. It's a
glorious day for the Royal Army."

"Will they come back?"

"I very much doubt it. They were decimated by our guns.
Rumor is that d'Estaing and Pulaski are wounded and Pulaski is near death. DeBrowne was killed just below here
at the entrance, and an inestimable number of rebels as well.
God knows how many men the French lost."

"They were brave lads," Hugh muttered, fighting back
dizziness.

"But poorly led, I think. Come along now, Hugh. We've
got to walk a short ways back to where the surgeon has set
up a field hospital. Lean on me, now. We'll make it."

Hugh tried to smile. "I made it this far," he said wearily.
"I shan't go under now."

As Hugh opened his eyes a face materialized out of the
blur before him—a dark, broad face with full smiling lips
and eyes bright beneath a scarlet bandana.

"Olana?"

His voice was a cracked whisper. He dimly saw the full
lips part revealing strong white teeth.

"That's right, Mista Hugh. It's Olana all right."

He made an effort to raise up with no result. He was in
a bed that was wide, heavenly soft and starchy clean. From
beyond he caught an image of blue sprigged linen ruffles
at a window bright with daylight.

But Olana's face had gone. Closing his eyes he sank back
against the pillow. From across the room a door scuffed
open and there was a rustling of soft skirts. At the cool hand
that lightly touched his brow he looked up again and saw
Louisa bending over him.

"You, here?"

"Yes, my dear friend. You're in my house. We brought
you here after the siege was lifted."

"I don't remember..."

Louisa sat carefully down on the bed beside him, taking his hand in her own. "Of course you don't. I found you in the field hospital nearly out of your mind with fever. Your wound had putrefied and we were afraid for a while you might lose your arm. But, thank the merciful God, you did not. I insisted you be brought here because that foolish surgeon was determined to bleed you at every turn. It seemed ridiculous to me that someone who had already lost so much blood should have what little was left drawn off. So you can blame me if you do not recover."

Hugh tried to speak but was overcome with dizziness. Grasping her hand he thought with amazement at how weak and puny his own grip was.

"Serve you right if I died," he whispered, smiling faintly.

"Oh, you mustn't do that. Not after all you've already survived."

"And the French?"

"Gone. Vice-Admiral d'Estaing decided he had no more time to give to the American cause so he took his army and his fleet and sailed away. It was a wonderful victory, Hugh. Six thousand allies against two thousand British and you whipped them soundly and sent them off blaming each other for the defeat."

A horrible memory came rushing back—bodies impaled on the shattered abatis, the cries of those still living...

Hugh turned his face away. "It was horrible. No victory. Horrible."

The look on his face gave Louisa pause. She had suspected from his raving when the fever was upon him that there would be scars worse than those on his arm left from this battle. Now she was certain. Laying her cool hand along his cheek she spoke gently:

"Don't think about it now, Hugh. You've been very ill and you need time to recover your strength. Don't think about anything else but that. Dr. Wade left you a little laudanum and I'm going to fix you a small dose so that you can sleep. Everything will be all right now, I know it."

For an answer Hugh tried to grip her hand. She was so strong and so healthy. If he could only hold on to her perhaps his own strength would come back.

Within a week he began to believe Louisa's optimistic prognosis. Within two he was taking small hesitant steps up and down the steps and sitting outside in the garden swathed in an eiderdown quilt to protect him against the cool breeze off the river. It was almost November now and though the afternoons were still warm the early evenings and mornings could take on a brisk snap.

"Well, at least the cool weather has chased away some of the mosquitoes," Rob Earing said sitting opposite Hugh in the sheltered confines of the Culpepper garden. Nearby Louisa worked briskly with a set of pastels at the drawing she was making, while on her other side Rob's sister Elizabeth, bundled in a heavy fringed wool shawl plied a listless needle at her tatting.

"And the flies," Hugh added.

"What do you think of our patient, Miss Culpepper?" Rob went on. "Would you say he's improving?"

"Oh, I certainly should. All he has done these last three days is complain about the service and express his determination to be out of here at once. That is a sure sign of good health, is it not?"

"Now that's not fair," Hugh began.

"Oh, but it is. Who nearly threw poor Olana into a panic shoving her from the room and pitching the medicine bottle after her. It wasn't me, I assure you."

"Well, I don't need that vile concoction anymore. I'm really very fit."

"Hugh, you didn't," Rob cried in mock horror. "And Olana so anxious to please you, too. For shame."

"I don't wish to be pampered. After all, I cannot remain here taking charity from you and your father forever. It's only right that I get back on my own soon."

"Oh, Mr. Hugh," Elizabeth spoke up, "please don't speak of accepting charity from Louisa or I shall have to leave also. I've been a boarder here far longer than you."

"That's not the same thing at all."

"Now see here," Louisa said briskly, "I won't have any more of this talk of charity." She reached over and squeezed Elizabeth's tiny hand. "You have been delightful company for me and you are welcome here as long as you wish to stay. And as for you, Mr. Sandenny . . ."

"Oh dear," Hugh said, "now I'm in for it. When she calls me Mr. Sandenny I know I might as well quietly fold my tent and steal away."

"You may leave with my blessing when I am sure you are well enough. That is the least I can do for one of our brave soldiers."

"What about me," Rob cried. "I was a brave soldier too."

Louisa tossed her curls. "But you were not wounded. On the other hand you are welcome to stay in our house too."

"Louisa, you had better be more guarded or you'll have half of Savannah moving in on you. After all, yours is one of the houses that was the least damaged by the siege guns. You ought to be more jealous of it." Hugh shifted his weight in the uncomfortable chair and flexed the fingers of his hurt arm. There was still very little strength in that arm and it inclined toward a stiffness he had never had before. It was a great consolation that at least it was not his sword arm.

"I appreciate your offer, Miss Culpepper," Rob said, "but I am very well ensconced at Mrs. Strickland's and I rather think I'd better stay there to hold on to our rooms until Hugh is well." He turned to Hugh: "The walls of the house were quite shattered during the siege but your room is safe. Our landlady inquires about you nearly every day, as does Miss Tillman. In fact I have grown a little weary of these daily reports on your health."

"Arabia stops by? And how is . . . Miss Tillman?" Hugh asked guardedly.

"Yes, how is Arabia?" Louisa said. "I haven't seen her since we were on Hutchinson Island together. Why don't you tell her she is quite free to come by and visit Hugh here. I wouldn't mind at all."

"As a matter-of-fact, I told her that I was certain you wouldn't but she didn't seem to want to. So instead she plies me with questions every morning."

Elizabeth's large eyes went from one to the other, "Who is Miss Tillman?"

"You remember the serving girl who came with us in the

boat to the Island. Dark hair, very pretty?"

"Oh, with the handsome figure. Yes, I remember her. She was more than pretty, she was quite beautiful. But common, of course."

"I shall tell her you said she was beautiful, Elizabeth," her brother said. "It will please her."

"It's only the truth."

Hugh made to rise. "Well tell her for me I'm quite well and I shall soon be back to prove it to her. Now, I think this is enough fresh air for one afternoon. It begins to grow cool out here. Want to join me inside, Rob, for a game of backgammon?"

"That sounds capital. Will you ladies excuse us?"

Louisa nodded and watched as the two of them moved toward the parlor door that opened on the small terrace. For all his brave words Hugh still moved gingerly, rather like an old man and seemed glad to accept Rob's arm to lean on. Yet he was right about one thing. It would be only a matter of another week or two at the most before he would insist on leaving in spite of her caution. Already she was dreading the day. There had been something so very pleasant about having him around all the time, about caring for him, touching him. She thought back to the times when she laid her fingers on his brow, when he clung to her hand for strength or consolation, when she cradled his head in her arms to pour some frightful concoction down his throat. Of the moments when she read to him or shared an easy game of cards, or just sat quietly without talking.

Her pastels lay motionless in her lap, her eyes staring into the distance. His leaving would cause a void in her life, she knew that now. He would still come to visit her but it would not be the same at all. She had tried to keep their relationship light and friendly, affectionate but unencumbered by anything deeper and, perhaps because he had been so ill, he seemed to want it that way too. Now she recognized in herself the same longings and love for Hugh that she had sensed in Arabia. But it was wrong for her. This was not the time to fall in love. She had greater concerns right now. Besides, by giving in to these stronger feelings for Hugh she was putting herself once more in competition with the one person she least wanted to be. Even the thought of it made her feel a little sick.

"My goodness," Elizabeth Earing said brightly. "I believe it *is* getting a little cool out here. Why don't we go inside too, Louisa. Louisa . . . ?"

"What? Oh, yes, I suppose we should."

"You were miles away."

Louisa smiled and laid her pastels back in the box.

"Not so far, really."

A week later Louisa informed Hugh that she and her father were going to leave the next day for a visit to Bonaventure plantation.

"You're welcome to come with us," she offered. "I'm certain Colonel and Mrs. Mulryne would say the same if I asked them."

"Please don't. It's really time for me to be getting back to my rooms anyway. I've far outstayed my welcome."

"You know that's not true. Actually, this is not purely a social visit. Bonaventure was terribly ill-used by the French who made it into a hospital and plundered it of its cattle and stores. It's only now been partially restored. One of the reasons we're going is to help with its reorganization. So, it would not be very pleasant for you."

"All the more reason I must stay in Savannah." He was silent for a moment, studying her. Then, quickly, he pulled his chair closer. "Louisa, I cannot tell you how much it has meant to me to be here in your home. To be with you . . ."

Louisa looked quickly away, her cheeks growing warm. "Please, Hugh. You mustn't speak this way."

"But why not? I long to tell you all that is in my heart. I've felt it for so long . . ."

She laid her fingers against his lips. "No. This is not the time. Please humor me in this."

His eyes searched her face. "But when will there be a better time. I must know if you feel the way I do. I've suspected you do have some tender feelings for me. Just tell me that you feel as I do then I can wait for a better time more easily."

Louisa rose from her chair and moved away from him. "I cannot tell you that. Please believe me, this is not the time for such things. Our lives are too unsettled, too . . . too," she made a hopeless gesture with her hand. "I just cannot say that now!"

There was such anguish in her voice that Hugh half believed she was forcing herself to rebuke him.

"But surely the war is nearly over. With the victory we won last month the whole of Georgia is firmly in the hands of the Crown. They are saying now that General Clinton will soon send an expedition against Charleston and that should certainly clinch the matter. Why must our happiness wait upon generals and armies?"

Louisa walked to the window, clenching her hands together in front of her. "You are presumptive, Mr. Sandenny. I don't remember confessing that my happiness depended on your feelings for me."

Hugh went white about the lips. "Forgive me," he said in a clipped voice. "I was so certain that you felt as I do."

Impulsively Louisa turned back to his chair, smiling her familiar lovely smile. "I've offended you. Forgive me as well. Please trust me when I say that I cannot be concerned with matters of the heart right now. Can't we just go on being friends as we have been in the past? That's as much as we can hope for right now."

"Very well," Hugh said, reluctantly. "If that's as much of you as I can have now then I accept it. But you must know that once this thing is settled . . ."

"There will be time enough to talk of feelings then. Come now. We'd better start packing your box."

Early the next morning the Culpepper carriage pulled away from the house followed by a wagon loaded with several boxes and one or two pieces of furniture. Shortly afterward Hugh and Rob set out for the walk across town to Mrs. Strickland's house, Olana's ten-year-old son, Jerral wobbling along behind them carrying Hugh's portmanteau.

It was the first good look Hugh had had of the city since the bombardment and he spent most of the way gawking at the scarred houses and craters that still pitted the streets and yards. Though some repairs had already begun, evidence of the destruction was everywhere. Through the efforts of the fire watchers only two houses had been completely burned, but there was not one that did not show some evidence of destruction by cannon or small shot, and several that had been struck as many as fifty times.

"I've learned since then that the citizens of the town grew rather used to the bombs before d'Estaing gave it up," Rob said at Hugh's exclamations of horror. "Some of the Negro children even grew proficient at running into the street to cover the shells with sand before they went off. Then when they cooled they sold them to the British who promptly dispatched them right back to the Vice-Admiral. Isn't that right, Jerral?"

"Yes, suh. It's right, sure enough. I gots three myself."

"And what did you get for them?"

"Six pence each," Jerral said smiling broadly.

"You're lucky you didn't get a lost arm or leg," Hugh commented dryly. "That was a dangerous game."

"Yes, suh. I suppose so."

"But you'd do it again, given the chance."

"Yes suh, I would. Six pence is hard to come by in the ordinary ways of things."

Mrs. Strickland met Hugh at the door, giving him a motherly hug and looking him over until she was satisfied he had recovered sufficiently. Then, promising him to send up a bowl of tansy tea, she shooed him upstairs to rest.

Hugh looked around his small room feeling almost happy to be there since it meant his life was back in its normal routine. Rob stowed the portmanteau under the bed, then hurried out the door promising to return in an hour.

"But where are you going? Let me go with you."

"No! You have to rest after your walk here. Don't want you to overdo things the first day. I'll see you later."

Hugh watched the door close, briefly debated following his friend and then decided that after all he did feel a little tired. He pulled off his coat and stood turning back the covers on the bed when there was a knock at the door. At his answer it was thrown open and Arabia sailed into the room, her skirts billowing out behind her.

"Hugh!" she cried, as she threw herself into his arms.

The force of her body swung him around completely while she clung to him, her arms tightly wound around his neck and her lips covering his face with kisses.

"Hold a minute," he said laughing but attempting to pull her arms away. "You shouldn't have come here, Arabia. What will my landlady think?"

"I don't care," she answered, her eyes devouring his face. "Oh, Hugh, how thin you are. And those dark lines under your eyes. Didn't she feed you right? Didn't she take care of you? I knew you should have come back to Tondee's and let me watch over you."

"Certainly," he said, pulling her arms away. "I suppose this is how you'd have cared for me. I would have been dead in the space of a week."

She smiled provocatively. "Yes, but what a nice way to die!" Slipping her arms around his waist she leaned her head against his chest, savoring the good feel of his body. Out of weariness Hugh rested his chin on her hair which smelled clean and scented, reminding him poignantly of Louisa.

"Oh, I missed you so," Arabia sighed. She took his face between her hands. "I'll wager you never even thought of me with that golden-haired Louisa Culpepper around."

Abruptly Hugh pulled away to sit on the edge of the bed. "And I'm surprised you thought of me with all those British officers in and out of Tondee's. They kept you busy, I suppose."

Arabia mentally cursed herself for mentioning Louisa, the name that always caused an inviolable wall to descend between them.

"They're gentlemanly for the most part and they spend their money very freely," she said in an offhand way as she sat down beside him on the bed. Her hand slid up his back, warm against the linen of his shirt. "But they never took my mind off you. Not once."

He smiled down at her. "Somehow I cannot believe that."

"Well, it's true. You know it's true." She had the uncomfortable suspicion that he secretly hoped she had been with those officers—that they might have taken her thoughts away from him.

Hugh fell forward, resting his elbows on his knees. All

at once he was so weak and tired that he wished only to fall in bed, shut out the world and sleep for days.

"Forgive me, Arabia, but . . ."

She ran her fingers lightly over his hair. "Poor dear. You need to rest. I'll go along then but I'll be back tomorrow when you're stronger." Deftly she helped him stretch out on the bed and pulled the quilt over his legs. Kissing him lightly and lovingly on his lips she stole quietly from the room. Hugh was asleep before she reached the door.

Arabia made her way back across town to Tondee's feeling more at peace with the world than she had in weeks. It was a happiness that was mirrored in the people she passed on the streets and in the high spirits of the men in the tavern rooms and coffee shops. The feeling of euphoria that was still so strong among the soldiers and civilians in Savannah was partly a result of the amazing victory over vastly superior odds and partly the conviction that because of it, this unhappy war was bound to be over soon.

Later that day as Hugh and Rob made their way to the tavern they too were caught up in the general feelings of good will and hope that was so conspicuous in the people they met. As they walked up to the tavern door they could plainly hear outside the laughing and talking of the men in the supper rooms and taprooms. Hugh, who had enjoyed a long, restful sleep, was feeling contented and happy. It was good to be back among the congenial companionship of the clubs and taprooms and he looked forward to a good supper with stimulating conversation. He even anticipated with pleasure the sight of the lovely Arabia moving invitingly about on the edges of the crowd.

As he stepped into the doorway he careened into Ralph Stoakes who was just exiting the tavern. The force of his blow knocked Ralph's silver wig and lace-trimmed tricorn askew. The nobleman glared at him, suppressing a start of surprise when he recognized who it was.

"Mr. Sandenny," he said coolly, straightening his hat. "This is a surprise. I understood you were wounded in the siege."

"I recovered," Hugh snapped, stepping back to let him pass.

"How fortunate for you."

A heavy-set gentleman in a green coat stepped up behind Stoakes, tapping his shoulder with the end of an ebony cane.

"Move along, Sir Ralph. You're blocking the entrance," he said, good-naturedly forcing Stoakes out on the step. A second gentleman, thin and gaunt with a beaver hat over a grizzled bagwig, followed on his heels.

"Colonel Brown," Stoakes said, indicating the green coat, "Mr. Hugh Sandenny, from London. And this is Mr. Wyatt, senior."

"Good day, gentlemen," Hugh said tipping his hat politely. "May I introduce my friend, Robert Earing. Also from London."

"Earing? Earing?" Wyatt said. "The Somerset Earings?"

"The same, sir."

"Had a cousin who married into that family. Good blood there. Old blood."

Rob stole a quick glance at Hugh.

"Don't know any Sandennys though." Wyatt went on. "Never heard the name."

Ralph Stoakes' eyes never left Hugh's face. "Colonel Brown is the commander of the Florida Rangers. If you haven't had enough fighting, I recommend him to you. You'll see brisk action with him, I assure you."

Hugh's smile was enigmatic. He had heard of Brown. An avowed loyalist, he had been tarred and feathered in Augusta a few years before and his hatred of Whigs and rebels was legendary, as was his cruelties toward them. But he was a good commander and his regiment of loyalists had acquitted themselves in the recent siege very well.

"I've had quite enough brisk action for the time being, I assure you," Hugh said. "But I'll remember your suggestion."

"Come now," Ralph's thin lips fell into a tight-lipped smile. "I would have thought a young adventurer like yourself could never have enough action—especially of a violent kind."

"Oh. And where were you during the siege," Hugh snapped.

Rob grabbed his arm. "Excuse me, gentlemen, but we really must be getting on. Have some friends waiting inside, don't you know. So pleasant meeting you."

Propelling Hugh through the doorway, Rob left the glaring Sir Ralph and his friends behind. Brown clapped his hat on his head and gave a short laugh.

"That's an upstart young man," he said, "but with spirit. Wouldn't mind having him ride with me."

Stoakes was not smiling now. "We shall have to see what we can do about that."

Chapter II

THE SUCCESSFUL DEFENSE of Savannah by the British galvanized the hopes of the loyalist population that the rebellion might soon be over. With each passing week rumors grew stronger that General Sir Henry Clinton would soon be sailing from New York with a fleet of ships crammed with troops to seize Charleston. The oath of allegiance which the British offered to all misguided rebels induced many to change their stripes, for expediency's sake if for nothing else. Those who remained defiant found themselves entombed on prison ships below the bluff or forced to make their escape into the backcountry. Even there, it was said, the rout of the French and American armies had so discouraged the common people that England could now claim that nearly the entire province had been returned to royal jurisdiction.

With the coming of winter it began to be clear that this had been an optimistic judgment. True, Savannah and Augusta were firmly under the control of the Crown. But the stubborn, obstinate, independent frontiersmen in the western reaches of the province seemed determined to continue the rebellion, no matter how discouraging the odds.

They soon learned that their most formidable foe was not the British soldier but the Georgia loyalist, men like themselves fueled by a desire for revenge upon their own countrymen, men who for the sake of "liberty" had been hounded from their homes, abused and their lives wrecked. As so often happens in a civil war, injury fed on injury until it seemed as though some demonic force was loose in the land.

Hugh began to sense all this before he experienced it first hand. He listened to men like Brown, Governor Wright and James Grierson and he made his own deductions. There was not a little class snobbery in their hatred for the rebels. To them democracy was a "broth in which the scum rose to the top." Liberty was liberty only for those who agreed with their ideas. The crimes committed by a nameless mob in the name of freedom still lurked strong in their memory and indeed, when Hugh listened to Brown describing how he had been tarred and feathered and dragged through the streets of Augusta in an open cart, he could not blame the Colonel for his zealous hatred of rebels. When he thought back to the loutish looking men he had seen at Sallette's camp and those military-farmers running before the guns near the walls of Savannah, he was inclined to agree with the Georgia loyalists.

However, he had a more pressing concern with the political situation in Georgia. As his health returned and he walked more about the city he found that everywhere he went he ran into Stoakes or one of Stoakes' servants. Arthur, Sir Ralph's valet, was his most frequent companion. Nearly every time Hugh ventured into the streets the man was lurking somewhere nearby. Hugh grew so accustomed to discovering his gaunt figure leaning against a lamppost ahead or studying a window behind, that he almost missed him when he did not appear. At first he was amused, then irritated and finally, as the weeks wore on, concerned. He had the feeling that unseen eyes were watching his every move. Increasingly he felt an unnamed anxiety, as though

Stoakes, knowing his real identity and his part in Pelham's death, was only waiting for the right moment to strike him down.

He was almost relieved when he received a summons early one morning to appear at Colonel Brown's headquarters. Though it could possibly mean he might be destined for one of the prison ships, at this point even that would be better than waiting for the axe to fall.

Two hours later when he met Rob in the coffee house, it was apparent from the jaunty way he threw his hat and cloak at the nearest chair that whatever Brown had wanted, it wasn't anything threatening.

"I hope you are reconciled to becoming a soldier," Hugh said as he sat down opposite his friend. "Colonel Brown informed me this morning that General Prevost is preparing a proclamation that all unmarried men will henceforth have to give half their time to the service of the King. So, either you marry or take up a musket."

"Unfair!"

"Perhaps, but when did that ever bother generals? It seems certain that Clinton will soon begin a Southern campaign. His first step will be to besiege Charleston and when he does, he is going to need all the men he can get."

"And just why did Brown favor you with this information?"

"He wants me to join the Rangers. He's mentioned it before but I've never been too keen on taking up his offer. Now, faced with a choice, he thinks I might agree."

"And will you?"

Hugh drummed his fingers on the rough surface of the table. "I don't know. It strikes me that Colonel Brown is just a little too thick with Ralph Stoakes for my own good health. However, I did agree to go to Ebeneezer tomorrow with one of his men. Do you know a Morrel Curry?"

"No. I can't say that I do."

"He's some kind of loyalist lieutenant. A Georgian who's been with the Rangers since their early days. Perhaps the Colonel expects him to bring me around during this trip."

"Ebeneezer is not too far away. He'll have to talk fast."

Hugh waved to the potboy who was dodging a customer

just entering the door. Staring closer, he recognized the ever present Arthur, his narrow, pinched eyes darting suspiciously around the room. The good-natured smile on Hugh's face faded as he looked back to his friend. Rob was studying the table, frowning.

"Odd's death, there's my shadow," he muttered. "What's wrong?"

"I was just thinking that perhaps I wouldn't mind carrying a musket again. That experience at the Spring Hill redoubt still holds a horrible fascination, even in the face of all reason." He looked up and gave Hugh a quizzical grin. "Of course, I could ask Louisa Culpepper to marry me instead."

Hugh did not smile. "You do that and there'll be another meeting at the Dueling Grounds early tomorrow morning."

When Hugh met Morrel Curry face to face the next morning his worst fears were confirmed. He was at least six feet three inches tall, gaunt as a scarecrow with broad shoulders slanted in a permanent stoop, and as rangy and stringy as old beef. He wore the woodsman's fringed shirt and overalls so common among provincials and had a white hat with a strip of brown bearskin dangling over the wide brim crammed over his hair which was pulled back and tied with a buckskin thong. The backcountry drawl evidenced in the few words he mumbled as a greeting were no more than Hugh expected from his appearance. He watched as Curry effortlessly threw himself onto the back of a chestnut mare and thought that he was not going to enjoy this trip very much. Just about the only advantage to it was that here at least Arthur could not follow him.

The road they took led from Savannah to Ebeneezer then continued on to Zubly's Ferry where one branch forked off towards South Carolina and the other continued through miles of pine barrens and red clay toward Augusta. It was one of the most well traveled roads in the province. Ordinarily it would have been filled with travelers—farmers carting produce into town, small bands of troops and their mounted officers, carriages of the well-to-do traveling to and from their plantations, Indians headed into the western lands, frontiersmen and their families trudging inland to strike up a new life on some forested ten-acre spread.

Today Hugh and his companion passed only a few small bodies of troops on their way back to the main post in Savannah. For the most part they rode in silence, Hugh lost in his thoughts, and Curry, his eyes darting back and forth restlessly searching the woods and swamps that lined both sides of the road.

Hugh had become so accustomed to the lack of conversation that he was startled when Curry kicked his horse up alongside his and said in his country drawl:

"Woods is quiet today. I recall when you could tell you was nearin' this road by the noises of the traffic. You'd hear it long afore you saw it."

"I take it you've lived here all your life," Hugh asked, more to make conversation than because he was really interested.

"Most of it. My Pa moved us down from North Carolina to Georgy when we was just young'uns."

Hugh began to grow uncomfortable under Curry's direct stare as their horses walked easily along. The man had disturbing eyes. Deeply set in his cavernous face, they were like cold pools, very still in a body that was constantly poised to spring.

"I'm from England," he said self-consciously.

"Figured as much."

"How could you tell? My speech?"

"That and t'other things. Knew right off you wasn't no woodsman. Have the look of a young dandy about you. The Colonel says you fought well though when the Frogs tried to take Spring Hill."

There was something in the way he spoke that implied he would not be here today had Hugh not acquitted himself well in that battle. Hugh noted it with amusement. The arrogant fellow!

"Have you been with the Colonel long?"

"Since '77. My Pa died afore the rebels turned loose all this trouble on us. Now I only got a sister livin' near the Ogeechee. Her old man is a died-in-the-wool rebel who'd rather traipse around in Lachlan McIntosh's footsteps wavin' a musket than stay home and take care of his wife and young'uns. Never could stand him though my sister's right enough. You got family?"

"An elder brother back in England. And my father. But we don't get along."

"Many a man and his Pa don't. Now mine was all right. He'd as soon box your ears as look at you but he was always fair. I'm kind of glad he never lived long enough to see what this country's come to. What was the problem with your Pa?"

It amused Hugh that his companion was growing almost garrulous. And the idea of the arrogant, proud, beetle-browed Earl of Lindsay as his "Pa" was almost more than he could take in.

"Not fair. On the other hand, I must admit that when I look back at my own conduct, I gave him plenty of cause to dislike me. It was just that he was so damned determined to make me into what he wanted me to be and I was just as determined to be what I wanted. So, we never got along."

Curry turned another searching stare on Hugh but was careful not to ask if this disagreement with his father was the reason why he left England.

"Thought I might ride west after this business is done in Ebeneezer and look in on my sister. She sent me word a few weeks ago that there was trouble in the area. If you want to ride along, I'd be pleased to have the company. Give you a chance to see somethin' of the backcountry."

Hugh turned the invitation over in his mind, flattered that Curry would make it at all. It was tempting. He would like to see some of the more settled sections outside of Savannah. And it would keep him out of Stoakes' orbit that much longer.

"Thank you, Mr. Curry. I'd like that."

"Morrel," Curry said and abruptly kicked his horse forward, taking the lead in the narrow road.

After that effusive conversation Morrel Curry seemed to have exhausted his store of words and they rode most of the rest of the way in friendly silence. Hugh's respect for the man began to increase as he noticed the many small indications that told how aware he was of every little thing

that went on around them, from the smallest sound in the
forest to the rumblings of other travelers on the road. Nothing surprised the man, for long before any movement appeared to Hugh he had deduced what was coming and from
where. Hugh decided that if he was going to travel into the
backcountry, he could have no more trustworthy guide than
Morrel Curry.

The tiny German settlement of Ebeneezer had become
one large British outpost. It was crammed with soldiers and
officers all moving with brisk officiousness as they went
about the business of running a camp on the edge of a hostile
wilderness. Hugh and Curry were given a good supper and
a place to sleep and their horses were cared for. Early the
next morning Morrel shook Hugh awake while it was still
dark. In the woods the loud chirping of awakening birds
told that daylight was imminent.

It was bitterly cold. Hugh noticed that even Morrel had
pulled a kind of animal skin jerkin over his fringed shirt.
He wrapped his own heavy cloak close around his chin
before bounding into the saddle.

Curry seemed even more preoccupied today than the day
before and at least an hour went by before Hugh discovered
why.

"Was havin' a smoke last evenin'," he mumbled, "and
one of them fellows with the 69th told me McGirth's men
have been cuttin' a swath through the Ogeechee country
burnin' out rebels. Don't like the sound of it."

"But McGirth's a loyalist, isn't he? He wouldn't harm a
member of your family."

"Who knows what he is. He was movin' around and
pickin' up information for the Georgy militia until they
decided they wanted his horse and cooked up a court-martial
for him. Whipped him somethin' fierce, they did, till he
took off with his precious 'Gray Goose' and joined the
British. Now he just wants to get even. He strikes first and
asks questions later. And he's got some Cherokee braves
travelin' with him, they say."

"I've noticed there seems to be a lot of movement back
and forth between the rebel and loyalist lines. Makes it

difficult to tell just where a man's loyalties lie."

"That's true, and you won't find no more confusion any-where than right here in Georgy. Can't neither side make a move without some rascal or other runnin' to tell of it. Never know who you can trust."

Hugh's horse cantered nervously ahead at a sudden noise in the deep woods around them. He pulled up on the reins and dropped back to Curry's sedate walk.

"Does the name 'Oliver' mean anything to you?"

Curry gave him a narrowed glance. "Where did you hear about Oliver?"

"Some time ago I got myself caught by a band of rebels on the way back from St. Augustine. They were led by a woodsman they called Sallette."

"Robert Sallette. You was lucky to get away from him alive, and bein' an Englishman and all. Sallette would as soon skin a Tory as a skunk."

"I got the impression that it was only because of this Oliver person that he let me go and I've often wondered why. Whoever the gentleman is, I'd like to thank him some-day."

"You'll have a deal of trouble doin' that. 'Oliver' is a kind of pen name for a damned spy who leaks information to the rebels as fast as it's decided on in the Council. It's my belief that he's really two or three people because as fast as we catch and hang one feller who seems to be him another pops up. He's either got nine lives like the polecat he is or his signature is passed along. Don't know which."

"So he's a spy?"

"By Tory standards I'd reckon so."

Hugh brushed aside the bushy branch of a hickory limb that overhung the narrow path. "I cannot imagine how a rebel spy would know anything about me or care whether or not I lived or died. It's something of a mystery."

Curry looked carefully at both sides of the road, his wary eyes taking in every nuance of the dark woods.

"Just be glad he knowed of you," he said. Then added softly: "I just hope there's a similar kind of friend to my kin somewhere with McGirth's Cherokees."

* * *

All that day Curry's worried preoccupation followed them like a shadow along the winding trails that led through the swampy bogs near the river and along the cleared fields, still dotted with the stumps of burned trees. They passed several houses, some lonely and isolated among the pine trees and corn fields, others huddled together like a cluster of cattle in a field. There was almost always a woman or two in the cabins and usually a parcel of ragged children running about. They saw very few able-bodied men. It seemed to Hugh that all these people looked alike. The women were drab and rangy with lanky hair and deep-set eyes that looked fiercely out at the world as though expecting trouble to strike at any moment. The few men wore ragged shirts and round hats and seemed bowed with constant toil. Morrel assured him that had he made this trip five years ago he would have been met with warm hospitality at every worm-eaten cabin, but that was certainly not the case today. At every bark-covered log hovel they met open distrust if not hostility. Even when Morrel was recognized, as he was in several places, they were given a few reluctant words or an outright order to go away. By late afternoon when they neared Morrel's sister's farm they began to pass shells of burned houses sitting amid blackened fields. Some were obviously old and abandoned. But one house, that of Edith Curry Tanner's nearest neighbor, was still emitting thin wisps of smoke from its charred, silent surface.

Curry sat in his saddle and stared for a long minute before swinging easily from his horse and walking around the skeletal structure. His boots crunched the charred earth like dried leaves.

"Couldn't have been more'n a day—two days," he said in a cold voice when he returned to the spot where Hugh waited with the horses.

"How near is your sister's place?"

"About three, four miles."

He looked moodily in the direction of the woods, his face an emotionless mask.

"I expect we'd better be pushin' on."

Hugh followed along, staring at Curry's impassive back and wondering what they were going to find at the Tanner place. It was possible that the family heard the commotion or saw the smoke and fled to safety. Or, if Robert Tanner was not there, the marauders might have left Mrs. Tanner and her children unharmed. Though he knew that all his misgivings were just as much a concern of his companion, still Curry said not a word all the long way.

The acrid heaviness of the air told them before they emerged into the clearing that the Tanner house had not been spared the fate of its neighbor. Curry kicked his horse up the small rise to where the house stood only partially damaged. Behind it the barn and two outhouses were a smoldering shell. Making a soft clucking sound with his tongue, Curry swung off his horse and walked toward the open door of the cabin.

"House don't look too bad," he muttered, more to himself than to Hugh. "Maybe she got away with the young'uns."

Slipping off his mount, Hugh tied the reins to the broken spar of a fence rail. Then he followed Curry into the yard and up to the house. The door hung half off its hinges. Inside, in the first darkness, he could barely make out the disheveled clutter of broken furniture scattered about the tiny room like kindling. The air was cool and abnormally still—as though the movement of the world was temporarily suspended. It might have been the emptiness of a home when its owners are away except for the overpowering stench that was so strong it was like walking into a wall. He recognized that odor. It had saturated his nostrils during the long morning following the assault by the French and American soldiers on the Spring Hill redoubt. He stood, reluctant to follow, while Curry, moving hurriedly, stomped the room, scattering the shattered furniture.

They found Edith Tanner's body sprawled before the fireplace, caked with blood from innumerable hackings by knives and tomahawks. It was Hugh's first sight of a scalping and he had to turn away to fight the nausea that choked his throat. Morrel Curry stood in the half dark looking down at his sister for what seemed half a lifetime, then slowly, softly, violently he began to curse. Every blasphemous malediction Hugh had ever heard and a few he had not Curry called down in those few moments of emotion. Having gone through them once, he started again, adding a few more. Then, as though he had said all there was to say, he began to rummage about the room until he found a tattered quilt which he spread over his sister's body. Only then did he begin his slow exploration of the property. Thankfully, Hugh followed him out into the open air, loping behind as they circled the house.

They found a baby's body lying at the foot of a live oak tree. Its head had been bashed against the trunk which still bore the gruesome evidence on its bark. Near the banks of the river they came across a twelve-year-old boy, scalped, with his throat slashed. The body of another, about eight years old lay half charred among the still smoldering timbers of the barn.

"She had two little girls," Curry muttered, bending beside the boy's body. "They must have carried them off with them."

Hugh could take no more. He left Curry and stumbled back to his horse, pulling out his canteen to swish some whiskey around his mouth. Turning his face from the wreckage, he wished he could blot out the images he had seen as easily. But he knew they would be with him forever. He had seen men die in duels and in battle. He had seen their bodies maimed by cannons and grapeshot. But this was a woman and her children. He wanted to cry and pray and curse as Curry had done, all at the same time. The pit of his stomach felt as though it had taken a cannonball.

When Morrel joined them his face was as bleak and devoid of emotion as a frozen pond in winter.

"I'd be obliged if'n you would help me bury them."

"Of course."

It was the longest hour's work Hugh could ever remember.

Although it was nearly dark by the time they finished, Hugh and Morrel, by mutual consent, set off down the trail at once, eager to put as much distance between themselves and the house as possible. They slept in the woods, taking turns on watch in case either Tory marauders or Whig partisans should happen by. At this point Morrel distrusted both and Hugh was inclined to agree with him.

By the middle of the next morning they arrived at a ramshackle tavern on the banks of the river where two ancient Indian trails converged. There were small groups of people huddling there, families from outlying districts who had fled their homes when word of the raid reached them. From them they learned that it was Daniel McGirth and his men together with a party of Cherokee braves who had cut a swath through the countryside, attacking every known rebel homestead. Although it was obviously the Indians who had hit the Tanner farm, McGirth must have known it would happen and bore the brunt of the blame. A group of McGirth's men had wreaked similar atrocities on another notorious rebel family, murdering the eldest son and an old woman and wrecking the entire farm.

It seemed to Hugh that each family had a worse tale to tell. When Curry finally pulled him aside and asked him if he wanted to stay the night or start back to Ebeneezer, he couldn't answer fast enough. All he wanted now was to leave the backwoods with their death and hatred and get back to civilization.

"I'd be obliged if you'll wait until tomorrow and travel with the McCleary family. They have people in Savannah they're tryin' to reach."

"What about you?"

Curry's eyes moved restlessly toward the oiled paper curtain on the nearest window. "I figure to go after Edith's little girls. If they get carried away to the tribes over the mountains, they may never see a white face again. It's the least I can do for my sister."

He paused. "You're welcome to come along, if'n you've a mind."

"No," Hugh said quickly. "I'd only be in your way and, to be frank, I haven't the stomach for it."

"Best you go back to town then," Curry said without rancor. He laid a hand on Hugh's shoulder. "Thanks for helping me bury my kin. Good luck to you."

"And to you," Hugh answered, thinking to himself that Morrel Curry, for all his woodsmen's skill, was going to need it.

Chapter 12

THROUGH THE LONG trip back to Savannah Hugh carried the image of Louisa's gracious parlor in his mind like a balm to his sore soul and once back in town he hurried there as fast as his legs would carry him.

"It was horrible!" he told her as they sat together, for once without any other guests to disturb their privacy. "A white woman hacked to pieces and scalped, little children murdered, a baby dashed against a tree—I've never in my life seen such horror. And all of it carried out in the King's name. Even though it was done by Indians, it was Tories who were behind it, people like you and me who want to keep these colonies English."

Never had he been so thankful that Louisa was not a fluttering, fainting kind of girl. His common sense told him that it was not proper to describe such terrible scenes to a lady of quality and breeding, yet he was driven to it by his need to share all he felt with her. Far from being horrified or even surprised, Louis listened to his emotional outburst with a calm patience.

"Daniel McGirth is a Tory because the rebels whipped and imprisoned him."

"Does that justify the things he did? Does he have the right to murder women and children, steal, burn, destroy, all because he was once badly treated?"

"Of course not," she said in her quietly level voice. "But you should understand that so much of the hatred and violence prevalent now in the backcountry is spawned by a desire for revenge. Mark Dawson rides with McGirth and was probably along on this raid. Dawson's entire family was murdered by a gang of rebel partisans out to avenge a similar incident on one of their own. Even Colonel Brown, who has fought valiantly for the King's cause, carries hatred in his heart for rebels because of the way they abused him in Augusta in '75."

"I don't believe that gives him *carte blanche* to murder!"

"Hugh, my friend, have you ever seen a man tarred and feathered? It's ghastly. First he's stripped, then covered all over with hot, sticky tar, even to his eyelids and lips. Then, over that, he's plastered with feathers and often carried around town straddling a sharp fence rail."

"Louisa! That you should be familiar with such things—"

"Oh, bosh. Of course I'm familiar with them. I saw them happen often enough right here in this town before we went to England. A mob is a terrible thing—mindless, blind and with such power."

"All the more reason for common sense and order to be restored. What will happen to this country if such men gain control?"

"Why, Hugh. I didn't think you cared what happened to this country."

Hugh looked away from her half-amused gaze and drew a hand across his face in embarrassment. "I don't really. It's just that the more I see of war the more stupid and senseless it all becomes. Why can't people solve their differences without having to resort to hacking away at each other."

"Then we would have no use for armies or generals

or—" She looked teasingly up at him from under her long lashes. "Duels."

His look was full of chagrin. "Rob must have been talking. Or was it Elizabeth? But I won't be put off. It is wrong that innocent people have to suffer because of the hatred and ignorance of vengeful men."

"Not all the men among the rebels are ignorant or vengeful. There are some very fine gentlemen who truly believe this country ought to be independent of England, who are convinced it will only find its true destiny alone. I knew many of them when I was a young girl growing up here in Savannah. They were not the vulgar men who make up the mobs. Besides, England is not blameless in all that has happened. There was a time when this issue might have been settled amicably through understanding and compromise. Parliament and the King threw that opportunity away. There were also times when the Continental Army could have been easily destroyed—in Boston, on Long Island and Kip's Bay, for example—and the English Generals threw those opportunities away. Now independence has a momentum of its own and every year it becomes more difficult to stem the tide."

Hugh listened to her long impassioned speech with eyes that grew ever wider. "Why, Louisa. You talk like a rebel. These fine gentlemen, as you call them, have been the cause of more distress than any one mob. Name one good man who would stoop to treason to justify his political convictions."

"James Jackson. The younger Habersham, William and Benjamin Few. Oliver."

That rang a bell. "Oliver? Oliver who?"

"Just Oliver. No one knows his other name. Even that one is probably false."

"I overheard the men in Sallette's camp talking about an Oliver. They were waiting for word from him before they decided what to do with us. I thought he must be someone like Sallette or Clarke, with a partisan group of his own."

"No. He's supposed to be a sort of spy who moves about behind British lines and sends information to the rebels.

Perhaps Sallette was not certain who you were and wanted some kind of confirmation."

"You mean Oliver might be living right here in Savannah?"

"Or Augusta. Or Sunbury, Midway or even St. Augustine."

"Then he's nothing more than a common spy."

Absently Louisa fussed with the wide lace ruffle on her sleeve. "If Sallette had to wait to hear from him before he knew what to do with you, then I would say he's far from being a common spy."

"But a spy nonetheless. And spying is a dirty business."

"Sometimes honorable men are compromised by events. Or maybe they come to believe that a worthwhile result is more important than the means used to achieve it. I'm told that often happens in a war."

In a sudden motion she sat forward in her chair. "Come now, enough of this dismal conversation. Let's talk about something pleasant. My father has volunteered me to help plan an assembly in early March and I insist that you help me with it. It shall be the most delightful, gay, carefree ball of the season, I am determined."

Her eyes sparkled with vivacity. There was a time when her high spirits would have swept him along, eager to put aside grim reminders of the war that was raging outside the city. But now Hugh found it difficult to dismiss those images of the Tanner farm as just something that happened to other people. The frivolity that had always been so important in his life now seemed empty and foolish compared with the suffering he had witnessed. He was also confused by Louisa's defense of rebels as "fine gentlemen." He found these Americans nothing but a heap of contradictions: Farmer-militia who would throw down their guns and run at the first fire while beside them a ragged Continental line was fighting bravely against overwhelming odds. He had seen both in the ditch before Spring Hill. The vulgar sweepings of the street who would tar and feather any good citizen who disagreed with them locked in a bind with educated men of honor who gave reason and high purpose to the cause of rebellion and treason. Uneducated country yokels like Morrel Curry with a deep sense of pride and independence who quietly assumed they were as good as the next man, even when his father was an Earl.

Louisa tipped her pretty head at him as his thoughts tumbled on.

"So serious! Won't you help me plan my ball?"

Her smile was so teasing and so charming that he instantly gave in.

"Of course. Tell me all about it."

In early January Savannah loyalists were thrilled to receive confirmation that General Sir Henry Clinton had sailed from New York with a huge flotilla of men and horses destined for the conquest of Charleston. It was the best news in many months, for it meant that at last the British high command intended to move the war into the southern provinces. Since the fall of Savannah, the Oath of Allegiance to the King had been accepted by most of the rebels living between the coast and the interior. Whether they meant it or not, and there was much skepticism about the question, it meant that most of the active Whigs were confined to Wilkes County beyond Augusta or had left the province entirely. To all intents, Georgia was now back in the fold, an English colony. Now, if only some kind of similar victory could be achieved in the other southern states, the rebellion must receive a blow from which it could never recover.

After a fearful journey through stormy waters that was even harder on the horses than on the men, Clinton's flotilla crept into Edisto Inlet below Charleston where they disembarked on John's Island.

The siege of Charleston had its effect on Savannah when a number of British soldiers were ordered north to assist Clinton's army. While Governor Wright and his Council wrung their hands, young men like Hugh and Rob looked toward South Carolina and debated whether or not to follow those long lines of red-coated regulars. The excitement of camp life and the old lure of battle made the blood rise even as sensible men tried to tell themselves it was all a foolish and vain attraction.

Though Arabia was aware of the siege—how could she

be daily in the taproom and not know of it—yet her interest
in it went only so far as her fear that Hugh might go running
off to join the Army. Even she, however, could not fail to
see the difference General Clinton's arrival in South Carolina had made on the streets of Savannah. It was the one
thing about the world around her she noticed as, early one
afternoon, she made her way back to Tondee's from another
fruitless visit to Mrs. Strickland's boarding house. She lingered deliberately along the streets, partly out of a reluctance
to go back to work and partly to calm her distraught emotions. The breeze off the river had a cool nip in it yet the
air was warm for February. Because there had been no rain
for several days the streets were sandy and walking difficult.
She cut down to Bay Street and ambled along the edge of
the bluff, studying the boats moored at their wharves, their
top masts barely reaching to the top of the bluff. There were
many pedestrians crowding the walks but the crowd had
changed since General Clinton landed in Charleston. There
were not as many soldiers as there used to be and many
more refugees in tattered clothing with gaunt, sallow faces.
Since the fighting up-country had taken such a grim turn,
more and more dispossessed people seemed to end up in
Savannah seeking help from the British authorities. They
seldom got it and in the end only added to the overcrowding
and short supplies that regular residents had to deal with.

Yet what did she care about nameless people uprooted
by the war. What did she care about politics and fighting
except as they involved Hugh. All this talk about liberty—
when had she ever been free? Toby was not free and for
certain he would be no freer if the rebels won. Margery
would always be a cook, Toby a slave and she a tavern
wench and there was no liberty from that for any of them.
She pulled the ends of her shawl tight across her bodice,
gripping them in frustration. She would gladly give up this
whole country and all the freedom in the world just to have
money and position like Louisa Culpepper had. Surely then
Hugh would love her and want to marry her and keep her
with him always.

It had been useless to go to his rooms today—she had
known that it would be before she went yet something drove

Sandenny   **189**

her to seek him out anyway. He had been in a hurry to leave and though he would not say where he was off to, she knew the answer well enough. Didn't he spend all his time these days with Louisa Culpepper planning a big, fancy ball? Planning a ball! It was not difficult to figure out what they were really doing. And then today, when he told her he was thinking of going to Charleston to involve himself in more fighting, her frustration had led her to tears and recriminations. Of course that was a mistake for it had only pushed him further away.

"It's that Louisa Culpepper!" she muttered bitterly to herself. Hugh would never go off and leave the golden Louisa if he thought there was a chance she would love him. Yet she, Arabia, who loved him so much, could be easily thrown aside like an old piece of clothing. It wasn't fair!

The tears were hot behind her eyes. Determined not to give in to them, Arabia turned from the bluff, putting it and these hopeless thoughts behind her. At least work at Tondee's kept her too busy to think and there was some consolation in that.

Walking into the kitchen of the tavern was like stepping into a Dutch oven. A huge fire raged in the hearth, spitting with the juices of a whole pig turning on the spit above it. To one side a bored Toby sat listlessly plying the gearshift. Framing the fire were two iron pots sitting on slender legs over a circle of searing embers. Margery, the sweat streaming down her broad face and her skirts pinned up around her ample petticoats, greeted her with a wave of a tin ladle.

"Misses is askin' for you," she said. "I'd hustle up there if I was you."

Groaning, Arabia tied an apron around her waist and adjusted a starched white mobcap that was hanging on a peg near the door. Then she climbed the narrow creaking stairs to the first floor of the tavern where Mrs. Tondee was sitting at a desk in the central hall working at some bills.

"You're late, girl," the woman said without looking up.

"Sorry, Ma'am," Arabia replied. "I walked back by way of the bluff and got quite caught up watching the ships at the wharf."

Mrs. Tondee's level eyes fastened on Arabia. She suspected that her servant had been off to see that handsome Englishman and the puffiness around her eyes suggested it had not been a pleasant meeting. When would the girl ever learn to accept her place and give up this hopeless obsession?

"I don't pay you to stand gawking at the ships, now do I? If all of us did that where would the custom be? We'd all be out in the streets destitute as one of them up-country loyalists. I haven't managed to keep this place going since my Peter died through Rebel and Tory governments alike, by standing around admiring ships in the harbor, now have I?"

Arabia studied the carpet, trying to appear chastened. The truth was she and Mrs. Tondee understood each other very well. She was a good worker when she wanted to be and pretty enough to draw men to the taprooms and gamerooms. Mrs. Tondee, though she liked to sound severe, had a good nature and was even somewhat fond of Arabia. She gave her a place to live and a modest salary and enough free rein to make her want to stay. Plenty of girls working in this town had it worse.

"There's a gentleman wants to see you in the private room upstairs," Mrs. Tondee said and went back to peering at her lists.

Arabia hesitated. "Who is he?"

"Go on up, girl. You'll know soon enough. You've nothing to worry about—he's not interested in fondling you. He just wants to talk to you."

"Is he sober?" she asked, remembering the first time she met Hugh.

"Yes, yes. I made certain everything was above board. Run along, now, and make sure you're pleasant to him. We want no trouble with the authorities."

Arabia moved upstairs lingering over each one. What could any of the authorities in the city have to do with her? She knocked lightly at the closed door and heard a muffled voice answer. Pushing it open, she stepped inside with trepidation in her heart.

The elegant gentleman facing her across the room was

vaguely familiar. She had noticed his lean, pinched face among the Governor's entourage who infrequently visited Tondee's. The expensive cut of his satin coat, the elaborate wig decorated with tight curls and ribbons, the long ebony cane he held in one hand, all bespoke a person of wealth and position. The long fingers of his other hand rested on the table before him around the stem of a crystal wineglass. He looked up at her through eyes cold as frozen cod.

"Well, come in, girl, and close the door," Ralph Stoakes said sharply.

Arabia did as she was told, then moved to stand in front of the table trying not to look intimidated. All sorts of unknown crimes, unwittingly committed, went racing through her brain.

"You are Arabia Tillman?" Ralph's chin went up, giving him the appearance of staring down on her even though he was seated and she was not.

"I am."

"I am, Sir."

A corner of Arabia's mouth lifted in a sardonic smile. "I am, SIR."

"I am Ralph Stoakes, one of His Honor, Governor Wright's, Commissioners of Claims. I have some authority in this town and am a close friend of both Sir James and Brigadier General Prevost. I mention this to impress upon you that I intend to have my questions honestly answered. Anything less and you could very well come to grief. Do you understand what I am saying?"

Did he think her feeble-minded? "Yes, SIR."

A thin eyebrow shot upward at the inflection in her voice. "And I'll brook no insolence from a common serving wench such as you."

Arabia hung her head so he could not clearly see her face.

"Yes, sir."

"Now. You are acquainted, I believe, with a certain Hugh Sandenny. Is that correct?"

Her head came up and her eyes widened in surprise. It was the last thing she had expected to hear.

"I know him."

Stoakes tapped the end of his cane on the floor impatiently.

"Tut, tut. You do a good more than simply 'know' him, unless you speak in the Biblical sense. You are his *immoralité*—his mistress, is that not correct?"

Arabia turned her face away from his penetrating eyes. How she wished that were true! But she was not going to enlighten this unpleasant, snobbish fellow. Let him think what he wanted.

"Well, sir," she said hesitantly, as though embarrassed. "I do not think . . ."

"Don't attempt to be modest with me. I know everything about that young man, including who he sees and how often. It is not unusual for young men to make mistresses of serving girls or actresses so let us not waste time with false denials. It can only serve to irritate me and to more serious consequences for you."

Arabia shifted on her feet, defiantly crossing her arms over her waist. "Well then, so what if I am," she lied.

"So what indeed. Who you choose to sleep with does not interest me in the least but Hugh Sandenny does. I want you to get some information out of him for me."

Arabia looked at him blankly. "Information?"

"Yes. I have reason to believe that 'Sandenny' is not this gentleman's actual name. Nor is 'Hugh.' I want you to find out who he really is and why he is in Savannah. If you bring me this information you shall receive a handsome reward. How does ten guineas sound to you?"

Her mouth fell open. "You want me to spy on Hugh? My dearest and best friend? What kind of a person do you think I am?"

"No better nor no worse than others of your class."

"I love Hugh. I would die before I would do anything to hurt him or to help you either."

Stoakes gave a short, bitter laugh. "My dear girl, you delude yourself. Mr. Sandenny's charms have obviously blinded you to the reality of your situation. The truth is he has his eye on far higher game than you, in spite of your obvious charms. He would give you over in a minute if he thought he could win that other woman."

Arabia's eyes went dark, her face sullen, and Stoakes knew at once that he had hit a sensitive nerve. It was the chink in her armor he had been hoping to find. Lackadaisically he drew a single round eyeglass from the fob pocket of his waistcoat and peered at Arabia through it, satisfied by the anguish on her face that she knew of Hugh's interest in Louisa and resented it deeply.

"You look like a sensible girl," he said sympathetically. "I should hate to see you make the mistake of taking a rakish young man's dalliance too seriously."

"Dalliance?"

He laid his cane on the table and leaned toward her over it. "He is just amusing himself with you."

"Hugh is not a rake."

"Very well, then. A 'spirited' young man. But that does not alter the fact that he is using you while behind your back he pays court to one of the town's loveliest and wealthiest young women. Perhaps you and I can be of mutual help to one another. You find out what I want to know and, by learning the truth about Mr. Sandenny, you may be able to hold him by promising silence."

"And all the time I'll be telling you."

"Ah, yes. But I shall not use the information to harm the young man. I simply want to know who it is we have among us. It is not unusual, for example, for rebels to pretend to be Tories and move freely about the city. Then they carry what they learn back to the Continental Army. Those of us in positions of authority must always be vigilant if we are to protect our cause and keep the King's peace. And ten guineas, you must admit, is ample recompense for such a trifling duty."

"Then why don't you get the information yourself? Why not just go up to him and ask him his real name?"

Abruptly Ralph sat back in his chair, his face a frozen mask. "Because the gentleman and I do not get along. I fear I would be the last person he would entrust with the truth."

"So you want me to weedle it out of him. Well I won't do it. Not for twenty guineas. I don't like your proposition, Mr. Commissioner of Claims, and, what's more, I don't much like you either. So, if that is all you want with me, I'll be pleased to be excused."

She turned on her heel and stalked to the door.

"If Mr. Sandenny should find himself confined to jail for refusing to tell us his rightful identity, it would do very little for your *vie amour*."

"Horse feathers!"

"On the other hand, Miss Culpepper might be willing to help us discover who he really is. Her heart is loyal to the Crown above all else."

Arabia's hand stilled on the door handle.

"Then why don't you offer her ten guineas?"

"Think it over, Mistress. You don't have to make a decision this morning. I'll give you until tomorrow, the same time."

"I don't need any time. I won't do it."

She stalked out the door, slamming it behind her. Stoakes watched her go then sat twirling the ribbon on his glass, smiling to himself. He had learned a few things from his conversation with Arabia, more than the girl herself suspected. All of them were pieces of a mosaic which, when completed, were certain to give him the information he needed to avenge his nephew and put this annoying Sandenny out of his way forever. He could not be more pleased.

C h a p t e r 13

BY THE TIME Louisa walked out onto the porch of the Council House it was already a few minutes past noon. The meeting had gone well. All the long hours spent planning the ball seemed at last to be worth it and as the ladies toured the Council House long room and supper room, they each felt pleased with the results. The decorations—spring greens, flowers and festoons of ribbons in pastel colors—were appropriately beautiful; the food was planned down to the last sweetmeat and bowl of Flip; and the small orchestra rehearsing in the alcove off the ballroom, gave promise of lively jigs and contredanses. There was little left to do now except to walk home, stopping by the booksellers to pick up a copy of the first volume of Dr. Johnson's *Lives of the Poets* which had only just arrived for her on a ship from London. She would have just enough time to accomplish that errand and still get home in time for the midday meal with her father.

"Good morning, Miss Culpepper," said a familiar voice.

"How fortunate that I should come across you just at this moment."

Louisa looked up from under her sunshade and saw Ralph Stoakes making her an elaborate bow in the doorway of the Council House. His velvet tricorn hat was perched on the curls of his white wig and he held his ever present walking stick in one hand. Was he leaving or arriving, she wondered, very much afraid it was the former.

"Sir Ralph. Good morning to you."

In a quick bound he was down the stairs and by her side. "I am just on my way from a meeting with the Governor's Council. Have you been here long?"

"Yes. The Ladies' Planning Committee was making last minute preparations for the ball tomorrow. We are so anxious that everything go well."

"With such talented hands as yours assisting, I feel certain it can go no other way. Do you have your carriage waiting or may I offer you the use of my own? I am on my way home and would be honored to take you to your door."

Louisa hesitated. "That would be kind of you, Sir Ralph, but I have made plans to stop by the booksellers before I go home. He has a volume for me that I have been waiting for quite a long time."

"Oh, that's no problem. I will be happy to wait for you there until you complete your purchase."

"But I should not like to put you out of your way."

"It would be my pleasure."

He reached for her hand to lead her across the road to where his carriage stood waiting, taking no heed of her reluctance. Louisa went, wishing she had been more quick-witted but resigned to the ride. At least it was a handsome carriage, open to the air, with a gilded coat of arms painted on the doors, and pulled by a striking pair of bays. Stoakes' liveried driver helped her up and she settled as far from her host as possible on the tuffed seat, resting the handle of her sunshade on her shoulder as the carriage rolled smoothly down Bull Street.

Stoakes sat back looking as though he owned the world and oblivious to the dust stirred into life by the horses' hooves and carriage wheels.

"How the town has changed since General Clinton landed in South Carolina," he remarked to Louisa. "Have you noticed the difference it has made?"

"Only that there are far fewer soldiers and many more refugees."

"Governor Wright was quite beside himself when His Excellency ordered so many of the troops to the Carolinas to support his siege of Charleston. He was forced to call a whole regiment of Georgia loyalists from the area around Augusta. Colonel Brown is on his way here with them now."

"I suppose he was afraid we would be so undermanned that the rebels would be encouraged to strike at Savannah again."

"Oh, that is very unlikely. To all intents and purposes the entire province, with the exception of that wild, untamed western country, is now loyal to the King. And a good thing too."

"But there is a Continental Army just across the border. Is it not possible that they would use the excuse of an unprotected city to march back into Georgia?"

"My dear girl, where do you hear these things? They are idle rumors and not at all the sort of gossip that usually concerns young ladies. Besides, the American forces are too busy right now trying to hold Charleston. If that city falls, the whole South will soon follow."

Louisa twirled the handle of her sunshade impatiently.

"I think you are too optimistic, Sir Ralph. Governor Wright knows that many of those who took the Oath of Allegiance only did so for expediency's sake. I feel sure he would not trust most Georgians to support the British if it seemed for a moment that the rebels could win. He knows them too well. Even now, right here in Savannah, it is impossible to tell who is truly loyal and who is not."

"You are referring, no doubt, to that detestable 'Oliver' who passes information to the rebels right under our noses. He is nothing but a common spy. One among many, if the truth be known. But we will catch him sooner or later as we have all the others."

He leaned forward, reaching for her free hand. "But come. This is not a proper conversation between a beautiful lady and her admirer. We should not be talking of politics at all. Not on such a beautiful spring day. Your lovely head should be full of nothing but the ball and its pleasures. You will promise me the first dance, will you not?"

Louisa pulled at her hand but he held it fast. "Why, I have already promised it."

"The second then, and the third—"

He edged along the carriage seat until he was against her, pinning her in. His long, narrow face was close enough that she could feel his breath on her cheek. There was a look in his eyes she did not like at all, too interested and too hungry.

"My dear Louisa, if I could only tell you what is in my heart . . ."

With a shove Louisa pushed him back across the seat. "Please, Sir Ralph. May I remind you that we are in an open carriage. This is not at all proper!"

At once he slid back to his corner, as conscious of convention as she and mentally chiding himself for getting carried away so easily. It was her intoxicating nearness and the fact that he almost never had an opportunity to be so close to her or to speak to her alone. The broad back of his Negro driver reminded him that, in fact, they were not alone. He looked around at the pedestrians whose eyes followed his fancy carriage. It almost made him wish he had an enclosed, nondescript leather hack.

They pulled to a stop in front of the bookstore where Louisa stepped down and quickly retreated inside to purchase her volume, grateful to be away from Stoakes' devouring eyes even for a few minutes. She dawdled inside as long as possible but eventually was forced to go back to the waiting carriage. At her appearance the driver jumped down to hand her up, smiling broadly. She had just set her foot on the carriage step when her eye was caught by a familiar figure standing under the sign outside a hatter's shop across the street. It was Arabia Tillman, wrapped in a long fringed shawl with a straw bonnet on her dark head. Waiting for someone. She saw Arabia look up and for a moment they stared at each other. Louisa waited for a sign of recognition but Arabia only looked away, scowling.

She had barely settled in her place once again as far from Ralph Stoakes as possible and the carriage was rolling gently down the street when she caught sight of Hugh striding across the road in their direction. He glanced up just as they rolled past, doffing his hat as Louisa smiled at him. Overcome with curiosity, Louisa swiveled around on the seat, desperate to know if it was Arabia Hugh was on his way to meet. She watched until the carriage rolled around the corner, just catching a glimpse of Hugh as he stopped underneath the hatter's sign. Then she turned back, staring straight ahead.

Beside her, Stoakes took in the whole scene, scowling and affronted. He had been asking Louisa about her new book but it was obvious she had not heard a word, so absorbed was she in following Hugh Sandenny's progress. All at once it was very clear that her objection to his own impassioned words had nothing to do with propriety or the open carriage. It was her obsession with this handsome, foolish coxcomb that kept her from appreciating his suit. He cut short his comment in mid-sentence, glaring at his driver's back while the dislike and annoyance he had felt toward Hugh for so long slowly bubbled into full-fledged hatred.

"I'm sorry, Sir Ralph," Louisa said politely. "You were saying?"

"It was nothing," he snapped. Prodding his stick into the driver's back, he sharply commanded:

"Hurry on there, you lazy fellow. We don't have all day. Miss Culpepper has to get home to her dinner."

Louisa, quite aware that she had offended him, rode the rest of the way in silence, offering only an occasional friendly comment by way of a peace offering. But Stoakes was not to be mollified. A deep, simmering fury had replaced his former buoyancy which she took to be directed at herself. She was sorry to have things left like that for her common sense told her that the way things stood right now it was to her advantage to be on good terms with Sir Ralph. When the carriage rolled to a stop at her front door she made one more effort.

"Won't you come in and join us for dinner," she asked

in her most sincere voice.

In spite of himself Stoakes softened. "Thank you," he said a little less icily, "but I really must get home. I have a number of dispatches to get off for the Governor."

"Oh, yes. Colonel Brown's brigade. You mentioned it."

"No, that is already taken care of. The Governor expects them to arrive by the Ebeneezer road late tonight. But there are others. Always others. I would not have him think I shirk my duties, even for so tempting a diversion as yourself."

"Of course not. But do come some other time. Perhaps for tea early next week. Monday?"

Stoakes unbent enough to take her hand. "Thank you. I should be most pleased."

"Excellent. It's all arranged then." With a flourish of skirts and petticoats, she was handed out of the carriage. Smiling back at the Commissioner, she thanked him again for the ride and watched as his carriage rolled away in a swirl of sand. Then, her smile changing to a grimace, she turned and walked up the steps and into her house.

The front hall was empty except for Olana's young son, Jerral. He had been lounging in a straight-backed chair listlessly waving away the flies with a palmetto fan. When he saw Louisa coming through the door he hurriedly jumped up to take her sunshade and hat.

"Is my father home, Jerral," Louisa asked as she pulled off her knitted mitts.

"Yes, ma'am. He upstairs. He say to call him when the dinner's on the table."

"Good. What have you been doing to keep yourself amused this warm morning?"

"Why, nothin' a'tall, Miz Louisa, except maybe helpin' cook with that load of cabbage palms and alligator steaks we got this mornin'."

Louisa fussed with a tiny pearl button. "Oh, did old William send us a new order?"

"Yes, ma'am. Wagon came in a'fore first light."

"Good. It's been too long since the last. Where is the driver? Has he gone back yet?"

"No, ma'am. I believe he in the kitchen now eatin' his dinner."

"Very well. Take this book upstairs to my room, please, Jerral, then come back down to the hall." She started toward the entrance leading off to the kitchen but soon stopped and turned back. Jerral was halfway up the stairs when she caught him.

"Jerral, if Mr. Sandenny should stop by this afternoon, I want you to tell him that I have the headache and can see no one. Can you remember that?"

A frown creased the boy's dark face. He liked Hugh who always teased him a little before seeking out Louisa's company.

"Do you hear me, Jerral," Louisa said more emphatically. "I am not at home to Mr. Sandenny."

"Yes, ma'am. I remember."

"Good. See that you do."

To Louisa's consternation, her small revenge went for nothing. Hugh did not stop by that afternoon and she had all evening to think back on an image of him walking off with Arabia's hand on his arm, a picture which, try as she might, she could not blot out. Was Arabia his mistress? Probably. It would not be the first time a lusty young man took a beautiful serving girl into his bed yet she was both appalled and annoyed that it should matter so much to her. It was not as though Arabia was real competition. For all her beauty and sensuousness she was only a serving girl. There was not the slightest chance that Hugh would marry her while, on the other hand, she had every expectation that he would eventually seek her hand. Yet the thought of that girl in his arms...

Angrily she threw aside the embroidery she was trying to work and stalked to the window. Why was she doing this to herself? Why should she care at all? Who was this Hugh Sandenny that he should upset her ordered life this way? She knew next to nothing about him. He never mentioned his family in England. Perhaps he was not even a gentleman but a commoner masquerading as one. He was free. She had no claim on him. He could live with whomever he wanted. Why should she even care?

But she did care. She forced back the hot tears that

blurred her view of the street through the window. Of all
the women in Savannah Hugh could have chosen for a
mistress why did it have to be Arabia Tillman? That enigmatic child who had once been her friend and had then
turned against her. The woman who met every overture of
good will with hostility and anger.

Don't be foolish, Louisa, she chided herself. It would
make no difference if it were any other girl, be it stranger
or friend. It would hurt terribly, no matter who it was,
because you want it to be yourself. You want him to love
you and you alone. But you, Louisa Culpepper, the proper,
marriageable, well-bred daughter, must not let him know
how you feel. You are the prisoner of convention and responsibilities. You are not free to live openly with Hugh,
cannot share his bed or his life in any abandoned, wild way.
Any relationship he has with you must be weighed down
with commitment, propriety, legality.

How she envied Arabia her freedom. Perhaps that was
what was tearing at her so badly—jealousy. Jealousy of
Arabia Tillman. And envy. Certainly envy. And anger. At
Hugh for looking at another woman and at herself for caring.

Feeling completely the victim of her emotions, she finally
gave up and went to bed. The next morning she found that
much of the turmoil was gone and her old, balanced equi-
librium had returned. When Jerral knocked at her door and
walked in carrying a bouquet of spring flowers with a note
from Hugh that he looked forward to escorting her to the
ball that evening, she was able to smile in anticipation and
pleasure. She knew those tempestuous emotions of the night
before were bound to return again, but for the present, they
were tucked back in the recesses of her mind where they
belonged. She swung her feet over the bed, digging her toes
into the carpet and stretching her arms high over her head.

It was a beautiful day and there was a wonderful party
ahead. And she was going to enjoy it!

The word raged through the city, passed along by word
of mouth from one street to another. It was the topic in
every taproom and coffeehouse. Small groups of men stand-

ing on street corners shook their heads solemnly and pulled at their chins.

Colonel Brown's Rangers had been set upon on the road from Augusta outside Ebeneezer by a band of Sallette's Georgia Partisans. A fierce fight had left four dead and twice that many wounded, most of them from Brown's corps. Striking swiftly and using the advantage of surprise, Sallette had cut down the Rangers almost before they knew what was happening. By the time they regrouped and set out in pursuit the Whigs were gone, swallowed up by the night and the marshes. Though he had not been wounded, Colonel Brown was in a towering rage, furious at the way his every movement was known and at the ease with which the rebels could attack him with impunity.

Ralph Stoakes heard of the attack that morning when a dispatch came from Governor Wright calling his Council together in an emergency session. This setback only reinforced the Governor's conviction that Savannah must not be left with only loyalist defenders and his first order of business was to dispatch a letter to General Clinton outside Charleston demanding that a brigade of Regulars be returned to the province before the Whigs were able to snatch it back from the Crown.

Stoakes sat at the polished mahogany table listening as the Governor and his aides drafted the letter, running a feathered quill along the mirrored surface of the wood. A most curious thought had just clutched at the corners of his mind and he was examining it with more interest than anything in recent days. A broadside had been left behind after this raid with the infamous "Oliver's" name prominently displayed.

Suppose, just suppose this thorn-in-the-flesh Oliver was actually Hugh Sandenny. The thought was not so farfetched as it first seemed. After all, no one had ever heard of Oliver before Sandenny arrived in Georgia. And though Hugh Sandenny tried to give the appearance of a foolish young rake, that could easily be a masquerade. His name was actually Hugo St. Dennis, wasn't it, and even the change of name might be part of an elaborate disguise to be of service to

the rebellion. It was true he had fought for the King during
the siege last fall, but there was so much confusion during
that affair that he might well have been helping the other
side and no one would have been the wiser.

Stoakes' cold eyes narrowed and his lips fell into a slitted
smile. It was really not so impossible as it seemed. In fact,
this might be just the coup he needed to dispose of Sandenny
once and for all and to solidify his own position in the Royal
government. It only needed a little evidence to confirm,
then a quick decisive stroke and—*voilà!* And with Hugh
gone, Louisa might be his for the asking.

Glancing around he realized that he was the only man
around that table who was smiling. Hurriedly he pulled some
papers toward him and bent over them, giving them all his
earnest attention.

Louisa heard of the raid as she entered the Council House
that evening.

"God's truth, I never saw so many glum faces at a party
before," Hugh muttered as he took her arm to lead her into
the grand ballroom. Beside him, Rob Earing offered his
sister, Elizabeth, an elbow and smoothed back the elaborately powdered wig he had donned for the occasion.

"It's that Sallette raid. Look at the Governor. For all his
splendid green satin coat his face is as withered as last
week's dinner."

Louisa looked around the room, her eyes shining. "I
won't have any talk of politics tonight, gentlemen," she said
deliberately. "It's bad enough that we hear it every ordinary
day and night. This is a time to forget war and armies and
hatreds. We are going to dance and flirt and eat sweetmeats
and drink punch and have a gala time of it. I insist on it."

"Oh, if only we could," Elizabeth sighed. "Forget the
war, I mean. If it would only just go way."

Hugh smiled down at Louisa who was looking particularly lovely in a pale blue damask dress with an overskirt
elaborately embroidered with tiny white roses. Her carefully
waved silver wig was emblazoned with white camellias and
a pink feather. A dark beauty patch near her lip set off her
perfect features.

"It's going to be deuced difficult to forget the war with all these uniforms about," he said dryly, noting the splashes of scarlet coats everywhere in the room, the Highland plaids and Hessian blues weaving among them. "But I'll do my best to obey your command on one condition."

Louisa playfully tapped his arm with the tip of her fan. "And what is that?"

"That you confine your flirting to me and me alone."

"Now that's not fair. Not with all these handsome officers about."

A small orchestra at the other end of the room launched into the sprightly lilt of "Sir Roger Coverley."

"Well, you cannot say I didn't try," Hugh answered, frowning as he saw Sir Ralph Stoakes detach himself from a group of people near the center of the room and head straight for Louisa. Stoakes had decked himself splendidly in white satin and pale green with silver buckles on his satin shoes and yards of Mechlin lace at his throat and wrists. Making Louisa a bow, he somehow managed to convey the impression that Hugh was not standing there at all.

"My dear Miss Culpepper, how perfectly dazzling you look tonight."

"Thank you, Sir Ralph," Louisa answered graciously. "You know Mr. Earing and Miss Earing, of course. And Mr. Sandenny..."

The wave of her hand took them all in, emphasizing Hugh.

Ralph made a slight bend in Hugh's direction. "Of course. Your servant."

"May I say how perfectly dazzling you look tonight, Sir Ralph," Hugh said pointedly, his eyes alight with mischief. Louisa gave his arm a pinch.

"You won't forget that you promised me the first dance after your father," Stoakes said, ignoring Hugh's remark.

"Oh, but I'm afraid I've already promised that one to Hugh, and the next as well. But after that..."

Stoakes turned to glare at Hugh. "But surely, Miss Culpepper, a prior commitment must take precedence. Don't you recall our conversation in the carriage yesterday morning?"

"You heard what the lady said," Hugh answered, stepping between them. "A gentleman never questions a lady's judgment."

Stoakes' eyes flared. "I do not think I need you to remind me of the duties of a gentleman. Especially not you."

Hugh's irritation was beginning to get the better of him. He knew he should move off and let well enough alone but there was something about this hateful man that drove him to throw caution to the wind. Stoakes' open contempt and overbearing arrogance made the temptation to goad him into speechless fury simply too strong.

"And why not especially by me?"

"Gentlemen, please," Louisa interrupted. "I won't have this lovely evening spoiled by petty quarrels. Come now. Be friends."

Stoakes continued to glare at Hugh. "A gentleman customarily sees fit to be known by his real name."

"Not necessarily," Hugh said, a thin smile lingering about the corners of his lips. "Any man can use his proper name and wear fashionable trappings. But underneath the names and fancy clothes there is often no gentleman to be found at all. Honor is of the heart and spirit. It is not a surface thing, no matter what name it goes by."

The flesh around Stoakes' narrow lips went stark white. "Sir, are you calling . . . ?"

"Here now," Rob said loudly, grabbing Hugh's arm and propelling him forward into the room. "There's the first minuet. Come along, ladies. We don't want to be the last group on the floor, do we?"

Hugh followed along, looking back at Stoakes standing in frustrated rage behind him. Then he added insult to injury by laughing out loud.

"Another minute and I'd have called him out."

"I know. Only too well I know," Rob hissed back at him.

It was all Louisa could do to be civil to him as she stepped into the line beside Hugh, muttering that he had better put on his good graces or this would be the only dance he'd share with her that entire evening. That she meant every word was all too evident.

"I was only goading him a little," Hugh said, lifting her

hand and pointing one toe in the first steps of the dance figure.

"He is not a man to make an enemy of," Louisa whispered back.

Hugh flashed her his handsome smile. "Nor am I."

To Arabia's relief the entire town seemed to be concentrating on the ball at the Council House that evening. She had been afraid that Mrs. Tondee might schedule a similar event in the long room of the tavern, as often happened, and she would be tied up all night serving punch and toddies. Not only was she spared that but so many patrons of Tondee's were engaged at the Council House that the landlady closed the barroom early so that she and her more prominent guests might go along to enjoy the first brilliant social soiree of the season. Arabia slipped upstairs, combed her hair, put on her best dress—a calico stripe that Mrs. Tondee had outgrown and cut down for her—fastened her cloak about her shoulders and went quietly outside to make her way through the darkened streets to the brilliantly lit garden of the Council House. She had been tempted to wear the lace shawl and Spanish comb which Hugh had given her in St. Augustine but on second thought had decided not to. She had no intention of competing with the elegant ladies in their rich dresses who would be there tonight. All she wanted was to find a quiet corner behind the shrubbery where she could watch the couples come and go as they took a breath of air after the rigors of the dancing. With any luck she would see Hugh and watch him as he moved easily among the wealthy and grand folk where he was so much at home and she was not. Never had the difference in their respective stations lain so heavily on her heart as this night. She knew that was the real reason why she had no wish to compete but was content to settle for a dark corner where she could stare and envy. As she made her way through the quiet streets she began to pass the waiting carriages of the guests long before she reached the house itself. Light streamed through the long windows from hundreds of candles and lanterns bobbed in a gentle breeze in the garden behind the house. There was a brick wall surrounding that garden but

Arabia knew how to get through it and slip inside. She even knew the best places to hide—behind a row of heavily scented boxwood near the southeast corner close by the path that led to the Ogeechee Gate.

It was a warm evening for March, and the mosquitoes were already beginning to be pesky. Yet she did not mind, so glorious a sight was it that she glimpsed through the branches of the hedge. Though her corner was dark compared to the lantern-lit paths in the center of the garden, still there was enough light to make out the flamboyant colors and rich fabrics in which both men and women paraded before her. Jewels twinkled like stars in the dancing light. Some of the men wore heels several inches tall and the women wigs three feet high, festooned with all manner of plumes, ribbons and artificial flowers. The ladies wore hoops that made their skirts stand out from their sides so far they could only turn by scattering their friends, and several of the men wore coats so stiff with jewels and silver lace they were unable to bend. They came striding down the low steps from the open doors of a room behind them which spilled light as bright as though it was the portals of heaven itself. Music, far richer than the one or two fiddles she was accustomed to hearing, floated merrily from the house to fill the garden, punctuated by laughter, the hum of conversation and the comforting clink of glasses and china.

It would be paradise to move among that crowd, Arabia thought. To wear a rich gown and jewels in her hair, striding around that room with her hand on Hugh's arm, basking in the admiration that glowed in his eyes. A dream. Her dream. And as hopeless as her life itself.

Pulling her cloak around her, she shrank back against the cold brick of the wall as a couple approached her, closer than any before. As they passed by, talking some nonsense about the merits of the musicians, she forgot her caution and leaned nearer to peer at and admire the glistening folds of the woman's embroidered skirts.

It was well into the evening when Hugh left Louisa to try his hand at the gaming tables. The card room was a

popular place and all evening traffic had been streaming in
and out of its French doors. The room was filled with tables
set for whist and faro, each of them surrounded by a crowd
of onlookers watching the players as they concentrated on
their cards. In one corner a group of officers was loudly
waging a bet on who could stack the highest pillar of dom-
inoes. Waiters in satin smallclothes weaved among the crowd
with their trays positioned over their heads, the glasses
sliding precariously.

As Hugh entered the crowded room he was briefly di-
verted by a remark from Rob Earing behind him. He moved
ahead without looking and stumbled into a group just leaving, nearly knocking one of them over. Quickly he reached
out to grab the gentleman and saw it was Ralph Stoakes,
glaring at him.

He thinks I did it on purpose, Hugh thought, and was at
once consumed by that old devilish delight in tormenting
the man.

"Your pardon, sir," he said, fully aware that the grin on
his face conveyed anything but repentance.

Stoakes yanked his arm away and stalked off without
answering, the fury in his eyes fully conveying what he
thought of Hugh's apology.

"Dear me," Hugh muttered and moved on to one of the
tables. Though he tried to get interested in the game and
even sat down briefly for two hands of faro, he found that
his eyes kept straying to the ballroom, searching for Louisa's
silver wig. When he finally spied her, twirling in the figures
of the dance and laughing at something her partner said, he
found that the gaming room had lost its attraction. Returning
to the ballroom, he stood leaning against the wall, his arms
folded across his chest, and waited until the long, complicated dance was done. Then he made his way to her side
once more.

"I believe the next one is mine," he muttered to Colonel
Munroe, her partner, taking Louisa's arm to lead her away.

It was on the tip of Louisa's tongue to protest when she
realized she was winded enough to be glad of a break.
Folding her arm in Hugh's she walked with him toward the
open doors that led to the terrace.

"I think a walk in the garden would be more pleasant than another dance," she said, snapping her fan open and fluttering it at her face. "It's becoming rather too warm in here."

"I would prefer that too," Hugh answered, laying one hand on top of her fingers.

"Why? You have not danced the last three sets."

"No, but I've had to watch other men squiring you, and that is every bit as fatiguing."

She smiled up at him provocatively. "Why, Mr. Sandenny, I do believe you have made me a compliment."

As they moved off through the open doors and out into the garden, Ralph Stoakes stood across the room watching them leave with narrowed eyes. Twice this very evening he had been insulted by that insolent cub, once in front of the woman he most wanted to impress. Now, to see him lead her off into the soft, romantic darkness of the garden was too much. He had had enough of this Hugh Sandenny. He might not have the actual proof that he was Hugo St. Dennis but, he decided abruptly, his suspicions were all the proof he needed. After all, they were living in a small outpost far from the revered halls of London's Inner Court. By the time his justice was carried out it would be too late to determine whether or not a mistake had been made.

With an almost imperceptible movement of his hand he summoned one of the brigadiers who was standing guard near the terrace door.

Arm in arm Hugh and Louisa strolled down the low steps on the terrace to the graveled walk dappled by the lanterns swinging gently overhead. In the bronzed shadows of the moonglow and lantern light, Louisa looked more beautiful than Hugh had ever seen her. On an impulse he threw caution to the winds.

"I wasn't just making you a compliment," he said softly. "I'm trying to tell you that I love you. That it drives me to distraction to see other men with their arms around you, teasing and flirting with you. I want your smiles, your laughter, your hands, your whole self to be mine alone."

Louisa caught her breath, a little overwhelmed by this sudden, impassioned speech. Though she had half expected to hear some such declaration from Hugh some day, here, now, she was not prepared for it. They moved farther along, deep into the shadowed recesses where the high boxwood hedges blocked the light from the lanterns.

"You must have guessed," Hugh went on, too carried away to back off now. "You must know by now how I love you, how distracted I am by your beauty, your charm . . ."

"Hugh!" Louisa cried, glancing around to see if there was anyone close enough to hear. "Please . . ."

Hugh drew her into the end of the garden where they were hidden by the hedges. In the dark the planes of her face were almost indistinct. Encouraged by the darkness and the solitude, he pulled her into his arms.

"Don't ask me not to speak," he whispered. "I love you, Louisa. I love you to distraction. Tell me you love me too or my heart will break."

Gently he stroked the line of her cheek with his hand, cupping her chin and lightly brushing her lips with his. Louisa's protest died under the sensual warmth of his lips and the tingling smoothness of his fingers. Her tense body went slack in his arms as she let herself enjoy the arousing touch of his body while he searched her face with his lips until at last he crushed her to him, kissing her long and fiercely. His hand moved insistently on her back, his body was hard against hers.

"Oh, Hugh," she sighed when he released her. Her arms went about his neck. "Oh, yes. I do love you. I have loved you for so long—"

"Arrest that man!"

A lantern held aloft threw jagged shadows around them. Men seemed suddenly everywhere, intruders pulling them apart. Louisa gasped as Hugh was jerked away, chagrined and embarrassed that her private moment had been glimpsed by others.

Hugh's arms were pulled behind him and he was swung roughly about. Two soldiers, one on either side, gripped him in a vise as Ralph Stoakes walked into the circle of light, a smirk of satisfaction on his narrow face.

"What does this mean," Hugh cried. "Take your bloody hands off me," he said, trying to yank free.

Stoakes nodded and the soldiers released him.

"Hugo St. Dennis," Stoakes intoned, "you are under arrest for the willful murder of Pelham Stoakes, my late, lamented nephew."

"My name is Hugh Sandenny," Hugh said defiantly, straightening his coat.

"Your name is Hugo St. Dennis, the second son of the Earl of Lindsay. I have a mittimus for your arrest stating who you are, and that you fled England after murdering my nephew in an illegal and unlawful duel."

"Prove it."

"I don't need to. I am the law here. The King's justice reaches to the King's colonies or did you think to escape it by leaving England?"

Louisa looked from one to the other. "I don't understand."

Stoakes moved closer to her. "This gentleman has defrauded you, my dear Louisa, by attempting to make something of himself which he is not. To whit, an honorable man."

"How would you know an honorable man? It takes one to recognize one."

"You go too far," Stoakes cried, goaded into an easy fury by the memory of that kiss he had just witnessed. Drawing his sword, it occurred to him that he could save the government the trouble of a trial by dispatching this insufferable rogue on the spot.

Hugh glanced wildly around. They were at the end of the garden with only the brick wall beyond the hedges. Though Stoakes had spoken clearly enough to them, he had not created enough noise to bring an audience running. It was obvious to Hugh that once Louisa was gone Stoakes could easily run him through and explain later that he had tried to escape. He stood between the two soldiers, both of them looking at Stoakes, searching helplessly for a way out. Even Rob, who would surely come to his aid, was too far away to hear him call. And if he tried to run for it, that would be all the excuse Stoakes needed to kill him.

"Go into the house, Louisa," Sir Ralph commanded.

"No. I won't. You cannot just arrest Hugh like this. It isn't right."

"This is a necessary and unpleasant business and I beg you to remove yourself from it."

"Don't go, Louisa," Hugh said, knowing that as long as she was there he might still have a chance.

Reaching quickly out, Stoakes grabbed Louisa's arm and pushed her back toward the house. "Please leave. You are not needed here."

It was all the momentary diversion Hugh needed. Lunging, he knocked against one of the soldiers, sending his musket flying, then turned to grasp the other, grappling with him. Stoakes, when he saw what was happening, moved to strike at Hugh with his sword but was suddenly careened backwards by a dark figure that threw itself against him, knocking him over and sending the sword clattering on the walk. At the same moment Hugh got a grip of the second soldier and knocked him to the ground.

"Hugh. Take this!"

Arabia's voice. Hugh glimpsed her standing over Stoakes just as the first soldier came crashing back against him. Quickly ducking, he was able to knock the man off balance, then smash his fist against the soldier's face. He reached out for Stoake's sword which Arabia had grabbed up.

"Follow me," she cried and disappeared into the shadows of the hedge. Throwing Louisa one quick look, Hugh went blindly after her, lost in the darkness until he felt her hand grasp his, leading him through the hedges to a break in the wall and from there, into the street beyond.

Behind him Louisa stood in utter confusion as Stoakes, cursing, picked himself up from the ground.

"Go after him, you idiots," he cried, shoving the soldiers in the direction Hugh had fled. "Don't let him get away!"

The two men were swallowed by the darkness. Stoakes stood brushing his coat while Louisa watched, too stricken to move.

Who was this man who only a few moments before had been swearing his love and moving her to declare hers? Hugh? Or Hugo? Why must he take an assumed name, if indeed he actually had. And Arabia. Why was she here? Where had they gone and how could Hugh return now that he was under the threat of arrest?

Stoakes lightly touched her arm.

"Please accept my humble apologies, my dear, for subjecting you to so painful a scene. This was not at all the way I wished to handle this. Allow me to take you back to your father. You do not look yourself at all."

Moving like one asleep, she let him lead her back toward the house.

Chapter 14

IT WAS SEVERAL weeks after their arrival in Charleston before Hugh and Rob were attached to the military unit they wanted—Tarleton's Loyal Legion. For Hugh this assignment offered not only relief from the monotonous siege business of digging and shelling but it also held the promise of some real action since the British Legion was famous for its sorties against the entrenched Americans. It also provided him with an excuse to purchase a horse he had long admired—a dark brown gelding with a black mane and tail and an intelligent, spirited eye.

The British camp was a busy place even in the middle of the afternoon. Women bent over campfires, their skirts hitched up to guard against the cinders. Beside the open door flaps, small groups of soldiers huddled over a card game or a backgammon board. Some sat polishing their muskets while others worked over small fires pouring melted lead into molds for musket balls. The siege of the southern town had settled down now into an almost mundane routine except for those frequent cavalry skirmishes around the edges of the city. There were rumors every day that a sizable American army was on its way to relieve the Continental forces pinned down within the town but so far they had proved to be only rumors.

As he neared the area of the officers' marquees Hugh's attention was drawn to a group of four men arguing loudly over some sort of wager, not unlike the kind that he used to involve himself in without a second thought. He smiled to himself but never broke his long stride. Time was when he would have hurried to join them, not out of concern for the wager itself but simply for the fun of the game. He was amazed at how his priorities had changed since coming to America. He looked back on his obsession with foolish pride that had so often led to challenges and duels—those silly confrontations where he had so cavalierly laid his life on the line—and wondered how he could have been so shallow. Life seemed an easy thing to throw away in those days and a point of honor more important than anything. But that was before he knew he had it within himself to be a better man. And that was before Louisa.

At the end of the row, not quite a part of either the officers' tents or those of the regulars, was the one he shared with Rob and two other young men who had come up from Georgia to join the siege. Mentally he calculated how long it would take him to retrieve his hoard of silver from its hiding place, then get back across the cantonment to the stables where his horse was waiting. Lifting the tent flap he concluded there was just enough of the afternoon left to purchase all the supplies he needed and rejoin the Legionaires by supper.

The interior of the tent was muggy and dim and at first Hugh did not recognize the figure who rose from the camp bed to stand in the center. Then he stopped, not believing his eyes.

"Arabia!"

She stood there with a small clutch of belongings bundled in a cloth under her arm. Her straw hat was tied over her mobcap and under her chin and her eyes were looking everywhere but at him. It was obvious that she did not know what kind of welcome to expect.

"Hello, Hugh."

"Arabia. What on earth are you doing here?"

"Here in Charleston or here in your tent?"

"Well, both . . . I'm surprised, very surprised to see you. How did you get here?"

Arabia edged closer to Hugh where he stood still near the tent flap. "I asked a woman with a baby which was your tent and she showed me. You don't mind, do you, Hugh? I had to see you. I had to know if you got away all right."

He moved toward her and she threw the bundle of clothes on the cot and reached for his hands.

"I was so worried. Tell me you're glad to see me."

"My dear girl, of course I'm glad to see you, but . . ."

"I've been in such a fit of the blue devils and I thought a visit to see how the siege was going would be just what I needed." She hurried on without taking a breath. "Savannah is so dull right now with everybody gone. No excitement at all."

"Arabia, you shouldn't have come. There is a war going on here and all our efforts and concerns are involved with it."

"Oh, but I won't distract you. There are lots of other women in the camp—I saw them as I walked around. I just want to be with you, Hugh, to take care of you, watch over you. There must be times when you want a woman—a friend—nearby."

Gently Hugh disengaged her hands. "It's not that simple, Arabia."

His lack of enthusiasm was beginning to have an effect. Arabia sank onto the cot, staring at her hands in her lap, her head drooping noticeably.

"You want me to leave, don't you."

"Of course not," Hugh said, sitting beside her and laying what he hoped was a brotherly arm around her shoulders. "It's always nice to have a pretty girl around," he added lamely. "We'll have to find you some place to stay. Perhaps Sergeant Simpson would let you move into the tent his daughters share. You'd be safe there. I wouldn't want you to be around those trollops who are known camp followers."

"I thought I could stay with you," Arabia said in a small voice.

Hugh shook his head, "It's not possible. I've only just today been given a place with Tarleton's Legionnaires. That's why I'm here. I have to purchase the best horse I can find this very afternoon and then get to the Legion's quarters by supper."

"But won't you be back?"

"I don't even know that. Tarleton is a commander who moves fast and frequently and he waits for no one." At the crestfallen expression on her face something within him took pity. "However," he added cheerfully, taking her hand, "when I am here we can take supper together. And I will let it be known immediately that you are under my protection. That is, unless you'd rather look for someone else. This place is thick with handsome officers who would take on a beautiful girl like you in a minute."

His compliment softened her disappointment for the moment and she threw her arms around his neck, burying her face in his shoulder.

"Oh, Hugh, I don't want anybody in the whole world but you. You know that."

Hugh held her for a moment, enjoying the good feel of her soft, pliant body against his. For one instant he almost regretted that his love for Louisa prevented him from caring for Arabia in the way she wanted so desperately. But the moment was swiftly gone. The heart has its own reasons and that is the way it is. He was only sorry that by giving in once to her intoxicating presence he had led her to expect more of him than he was willing to give.

"Now," he said, turning his thoughts to more pressing matters. "Let me dig out my last hoard of coins then we'll go and find Sergeant Simpson. I promise I'll try to get back later to see that you're properly settled. Agreed?"

She looked up at him with soulful eyes under her thick fringe of lashes. Though she did not relish the idea of living with silly girls, still it might be worth it in the end just to be near Hugh again. Only time would tell if she would be able to make more of being near him than seemed likely right now. She had not yet given up hope.

"Agreed."

* * *

While Hugh was escorting Arabia around the British camp outside Charleston, Louisa stood at her parlor window staring out at the riotous glory of the garden in the rear of the house. Spring was in full dress and everywhere tender green was splashed with the bright colors of flowering shrubs and vines. Ordinarily she loved this time of year when the natural beauty of the earth awoke in her a warm response, a sense that this world must mirror the loveliness of heaven.

But not this year. Through these last two glorious weeks she had borne such a weight of heavy anguish that the whole world seemed painted gray. As though the trees and shrubs and flowers were singing to the glory of God while she stood apart, looking on from behind a dark curtain.

There was a soft clink behind her as Ralph Stoakes laid his teacup on the table. His silence was loud with his anger. And yet it was not her fault. He should have known.

His voice was clipped. "I do think you might have given me more indication of how you truly felt."

Louisa sighed and turned to face him squarely. He was very white about the lips and his narrow eyes looked almost black.

"Can you deny that beyond polite cordiality I ever gave you reason to hope that our friendship could be anything more?"

"But the times we spent together. The walks, the teas, the balls—"

"Please recall, Sir Ralph, they were most of them because you sought me out."

"But that was only proper."

"Perhaps, yet never did I attempt to suggest that I had any feeling for you beyond regard for your station and rank."

The mention of both these assets seemed to restore his equanimity. He flicked at his satin sleeve with a long fore-finger. "My station and rank are yours to share. I beg you not to turn them aside lightly. I feel certain that I have a future here, even to possibly replacing Sir James when he retires. You would be the wife of the Royal Governor. Surely that must tempt you a little."

Louisa stared down at him through narrowed eyes of her own. "I would think you knew me well enough by now to know that my heart is not to be bought by titles and worldly goods."

"Ah yes, your heart. That is really the problem, isn't it." Abruptly he rose from the settee and walked over to stand before her. The black patch on his cheek stood out starkly against the chalkiness of his skin. "Your heart has been beguiled and deceived by that base Hugo St. Dennis. That is really the problem, isn't it, dear lady. That worthless scoundrel, that rake who threw away his patrimony on gambling, whores and duels, who broke his good father's heart—he has blinded you to the true worth of a gentleman's offer. But it is a foolish dream, Louisa. I must tell you that there is not the slightest chance of a life with that man. Justice will seek him out eventually. *I* will seek him out, since it is my family honor that is most at stake."

"I do not know any Hugo St. Dennis," she answered stonily turning back to the window.

"You know well who I mean. There is not the slightest doubt that that fellow calling himself Hugh Sandenny is actually the worthless second son of the Earl of Lindsay. He has been a rake from his cradle and he will earn a rake's reward. I beg you not to waste your tender feelings on such a man, especially when far more worthy men would lay their hearts at your feet."

"You, for instance."

"Yes," he answered, drawing himself up. "I do not readily offer my regard to any woman and I am acutely conscious of the fact that I have revealed more of my feelings to you than to any woman alive. And, I might add, with little enough return for it."

"Please, Sir Ralph," Louisa said, her voice softening. "I did not seek this proposal from you nor did I at any time attempt to encourage you in it. Unlike some women, I do not enjoy collecting bruised hearts. I am truly sorry if this has caused you any pain."

He turned away, flicking his lace handkerchief and reaching for his enameled snuffbox in the wide pocket of his coat.

"Egad, dear Louisa, don't imagine that I shall die of a broken heart, not for you nor for any other lady. However,

I do feel that my honorable offer is not being given the consideration due it. And, after all, I did speak to your father and he gave me leave to hope—"

"I do not think he did. My father would never speak for me in these matters. I feel certain that he told you only to put your offer to me directly."

Stoakes raised a pinch of snuff to his nostrils, then flipped the lid of the box closed with a snap. "A wiser father might act for his daughter in matters which are to her advantage."

"Perhaps," Louisa said coldly. All his fussing with the expensive snuffbox and the waving of lace handkerchiefs did not fool her. He was furious with her, the more so because he could find no way to get her to change her mind. He was not a man to take humiliation lightly even when it was tempered with polite respect. How her head ached. If only he would go away so that she might go upstairs and draw the blinds and lie down. To her dismay he took his place again on the brocade settee.

"May I bother you for a second cup of tea," Stoakes said, raising his cup.

"Oh, of course. Forgive me. I am forgetting my manners."

Hurriedly she walked to her chair on the other side of the table and poured the tea. He accepted it, then sat back stirring a fragile silver spoon around the cup.

"That fellow will never get away, you know. He managed to escape Savannah but he cannot escape the law forever. I'll find him eventually."

"Perhaps he went west to the frontier," Louisa answered, concentrating on a small dot of tarnish on the tea tray. "It is not unusual for men to lose themselves there, the country is so wild and untamed."

"That is true, but somehow I cannot see a fop like young Sandenny felling trees and roasting game over a campfire. More likely he is with the army laying siege to Charleston. That town should fall very soon, they say, and then justice will catch up with young Hugo."

"But I understood General Lincoln to be very well entrenched."

"Oh, he is. And the planters and townsfolk with him are

desperate to have him defend the town. But his position is untenable. He has let himself get boxed in between the rivers and Charleston neck and there is no place for his army to go. He will have to surrender eventually and when he does, what a glorious victory it will be for the King. The entire south should soon follow."

"How wonderful," Louisa murmured.

"At any rate, I should soon get some word about Sandenny. I have my spies up there, you know." Leaning forward, he set down the cup, no longer interested in tea. "Dare I hope that once he is out of the way—"

"Sir Ralph, would you mind terribly if I—that is, if we, you see, I have such a bad headache—"

He sat back as though she had struck him. "Oh. Well then, I would not trouble you for the world."

His voice dripped sarcasm and it was all Louisa could do not to stalk from the room. Instead she offered him her hand, her face stony and cold. He would not look her in the eyes as he raised her hand two inches below his narrow lips.

"I do hope we can continue to be friends," she began. But he interrupted her.

"I shall endeavor to remember that this conversation was carried out when you were not yourself. We shall talk again."

Before she could answer he turned on his heels and left the room. Louisa stared as the door closed behind him wondering how she had managed not to throw something at it. The arrogant, cold-blooded fool. She would as soon marry a snake. Wife of the royal governor indeed!

Hurrying up to her room, she drew the blinds, stepped out of her dress, slipped a silk banyan over her chemise and stretched out on her feather mattress, yet still she could not sleep. Her churning mind would not or could not cease its constant treadmill. Where was Hugh? For that matter, *who* was Hugh? Had everything he told her been a lie and, if so, then what kind of man was he? Was he actually the second son of the Earl of Lindsay, a wild, immoral rake with a black reputation in England? Was his light, irresponsible relationship with Arabia just part of an old, dissolute pattern of debauchery?

And yet she remembered how bravely he had fought during the siege last fall. How much she had come to depend on him for witty conversation and thoughtful analysis of the terrible rebellion that raged around them. And, most of all, she remembered that kiss in the garden just before he was forced out of her arms and away from the city. His words sounded in her mind like a constant echo— "I love you to distraction. Tell me you love me too or my heart will break—"

Over and over it went until at last she heard her father's voice in the hall downstairs. Rising, she rang for Olana to help her dress then went downstairs to find him in his study, his feet propped on a needleworked footstool, half dozing over a book.

He was soon wide awake and conscious of how deeply he had offended his beloved daughter.

"How could you, Papa! How could you encourage that man to offer for me."

"But Louisa, I never speak for you in these matters. I only wish you to follow your own heart. I thought we were agreed—"

"Yes, yes, I do appreciate your sensibilities in that regard. But Papa, surely you must have known that Ralph Stoakes is the last man I could ever marry! Indeed, if he were the only choice, I should not marry at all!"

"But he has breeding and wealth," Thomas Culpepper said lamely. "And his station is, well, not exalted but certainly respectable."

"Bah! And when have I ever cared for station, wealth or rank. Breeding, yes, but a hundred men qualify for that. You should have told him there was not the slightest possibility I would agree."

"Well now, I did rather hint at that. But he was unwilling to believe me. He is a rather firm-minded gentleman, as you know."

"Oh yes. I know." She stopped pacing the room, now that her anger was dissipated a little, and sat down opposite her father. When her worried Papa noticed the shadows under her eyes and the unusual lines around her lovely mouth, his heart hardened a little toward Stoakes that he should have caused her so much distress.

"Papa, what is the situation like in Charleston?"

A little taken aback by her abrupt change of subject Thomas had to collect his thoughts. "I believe the city is rumored to fall very soon. General Lincoln's army is surrounded and he will be forced to capitulate. In fact, I heard some conversation to that effect in the coffeehouse just this morning."

"Well, when it comes and the King's forces are established in the city, I want us to go there."

"Leave Savannah? What ever for?"

"Charleston was ever a lively city and with the bulk of the army there, it is bound to be again. Cousin Cecily would put us up, I'm sure of it."

Thomas' round little eyes crinkled in a knowing smile. "I see. You want to be near those handsome young officers. Just like a young girl."

"Can we go? Please?"

He reached over and patted her hand. "Of course, my dear, just as soon as it is safe. Whatever you wish."

She jumped up and kissed him lightly on the top of his carefully dressed grey wig.

"Thank you, Papa. You are very good to me, in spite of the way you encouraged Ralph Stoakes."

She resumed her seat, immeasurably comforted by the thought of leaving both Savannah and Sir Ralph Stoakes behind. If Hugh was in Charleston she would find him, and with any luck she would be able to warn him about Stoakes and his spies. Perhaps she would even be able at last to find some answer to the riddle of who Hugh Sandenny actually was. Perhaps she might even have a chance to be in his arms once again.

Thomas Culpepper picked up his book again and settled his feet back on the footstool, relieved to see the shadows lift from his daughter's face and the suggestion of a smile flutter about her lips. Why Charleston should do this for her he had no idea. But women were ever beyond comprehension.

* * *

On the eleventh of May General Lincoln surrendered the town of Charleston to the British. On the twelfth, as the American drummers beat a sad "Turk's March" the American forces limped out of the city—looking to many British soldiers like the most ragged rabble they had ever beheld. Over two thousand Continental soldiers and seven generals laid down their arms that morning. The militia, who were allowed to return to their homes to put in their crops, refused to parade with the beaten army but scurried from the city in small groups the next day.

Hugh walked away from the spectacle of the defeated Americans long before the end of their ranks came in sight. He had expected to feel triumph, vindication or, at the least, joy that that victory had been won. Instead he was filled with an unsettling uneasiness, as confusing as it was disturbing. The sight of men, tears streaming down their faces or eyes black with defeated pride had not brought the expected pleasure. Never had he seen a more unmilitary group of men. Their uniforms were an assorted collection of civilian clothes and tunics of every conceivable regiment and color, including a few British cast-offs. One whole, complete uniform was hardly to be found even among the several generals of rank. Most of them, from their clothes to their arms, were tattered and disheveled and yet they had pride! They were a proud collection of gentlemen and farmers who in their recklessness and daring, he suspected, were not too different from himself. It was their country, when he came to think of it, and he was hard put all of a sudden, to know why he was here trying to force a parliamentary system down their throats—a system he himself had scoffed at for many a year.

He had seen enough of the British army now to realize that, polished as it was, it represented all the best and the worst of the military system—courage, bravery, wit, and honor on the one hand; on the other, arrogance, obsession with rank, snobbery and that slavish militancy and harsh discipline that had so distressed him in his own father. For the first time in months he recalled the spectacle of those French troopers at the siege of Savannah, blindly walking into a barrage of fire because their officers ordered it. Brave, yes, courageous and honorable, and oh, so foolish. And such a waste!

Oh yes, he had enjoyed the few forays he had made along with small groups of Tarleton's dragoons around the city trying to prevent Lincoln from escaping. He loved his horse who had proved to have spirit and stamina and who was swift as the wind. Up until now he had seen little of his mercurial commander and was still unsure if the rumors about him actually fit the man. But though riding with the dragoons had made his life among the army seem worthwhile, now, all at once, he was not so certain that he really wanted a commission at all.

Through the long line of tents he could see Arabia sitting before the door of the one she shared with Sergeant Simpson's daughters, her red skirt billowing around her, her face turned up to the sunshine. Would she understand this strange reaction, he wondered. Probably not. She had been anxious for the city to fall so that she might find proper lodgings in a house once again and get away from these hordes of soldiers and camp followers. Well, at least, she would get her wish soon enough. She was a child of this country and yet she did not seem to care whether it remained a colony of England or became independent. Why on earth should he?

He shuddered as if to shake off the seriousness that troubled him. There was going to be a lot of celebrating in Charleston tonight and he wanted a share in it. He would tell Arabia to put on her best dress and wear the lace mantilla he bought her in St. Augustine and they would go into the town and have supper at the best restaurant they could find. Time enough later for such solemn deliberations.

Nearly a week later, on a brilliant Sunday morning, a special service of Thanksgiving for the deliverance of Charleston was held at old St. Philip's on Church Street. Hugh and Arabia were late arriving and as they neared the gates they could hear the voices inside intoning prayers from the prayer book. It was obvious from the small crowd of people who stood outside the door that the church was already full.

"Oh, dear," Arabia sighed. "And I did so want to see General Clinton and General Cornwallis in their military wigs and gold lace. Then too, they say the ladies of Charleston dress the most fashionable of any place in the South, saving perhaps Virginia."

Hugh doffed his hat at a portly lady passing by on the arm of a gentleman in a green frock coat. The patch on her lip proclaimed her a Tory and the warm smile she was beaming at every English uniform in sight confirmed it. He was filled with good will and a strange sense of contentment. At last he had a place with the military, he had found decent rooms for Arabia in the town and there was no Ralph Stoakes with which to contend. The brightness of the day mirrored his own satisfaction.

"So that was why you wanted to come to church. It was not to see the generals at all."

"No, no, I want to see them too. Sometimes they have been known to outshine the ladies."

"It's too early for dinner. Why don't we wander the streets for a while or pass the time in the churchyard until the service is over. Then we can join the gawkers as the gentry emerge."

"Oh, Hugh. You're gentry too."

"So I am."

And that is what they did, ambling the narrow paths to the end of the street where the blue harbor sparkled in the morning air, then wandering back to browse through the graveyard, reading the weathered stones, some of which were over a hundred years old, young by English standards. When the bell began clanging the end of the service they moved back to the entrance to join the small crowd near the door.

It did not take Arabia long to realize her hopes for a fashionable display were going to be disappointed, for the ladies of Charleston were still suffering the effects of the rebel embargo on imported goods and their brocades, satins and damasks bore the telltale signs of long and frequent use. Their husbands fared no better. Only the British officers were up to her expectations resplendent in their scarlet coats, highland plaids, yards of gold and silver lace, gleaming silver buckles and gorgets, reams of exquisite Flemish lace at their throats and wrists, sashes and tassels, fancy engraved swords and spotless military brigadier wigs. When a tall, heavyset officer came striding down the low steps sur- rounded by a retinue of lesser officers, Arabia recognized the thick features of Lord Cornwallis and was appropriately overwhelmed. So overwhelmed that it was a moment before she realized Hugh, standing beside her, had frozen. Tearing her eyes from the smiling, effusive laughing general, she saw just emerging from the church behind him a familiar figure. She was dressed in sky blue brocade that set off the gold of her hair and her hand rested lightly on the arm of a portly gentleman in black silk walking sedatively beside her.

Louisa Culpepper! Quickly Arabia turned to Hugh who was staring at Louisa as though he could not get enough of her face.

"I've seen enough," she said hurriedly, pulling at his arm. "Let's go now."

"No—" he tore his eyes from Louisa's face and looked back at the stricken girl beside him. "General Clinton has not come out yet."

"I don't care. I've seen enough. Please, Hugh, let's go now."

"Arabia, behave yourself," he muttered. "It would not be seemly—I really must wish them a good morning."

"Why? It will only mean trouble. Remember how you left Savannah!"

But he had torn his arm from her grasp and was moving toward the crowd at the foot of the steps. Miserably Arabia watched as he stepped in front of the Culpeppers, father and daughter, and touched his helmet, bowing politely.

She could not see Louisa's face under the wide brim of her bonnet but her voice was clear enough, as was the shock and delight in it.

"I was not aware you were in Charleston." Hugh mut- tered, his lips lingering over Louisa's fingers.

"We only just arrived. I . . . I wondered if you were in the city. I heard . . . that is, it seemed likely you might be."

"Yes, I'm with the army. Tarleton's dragoons, to be exact."

Thomas Culpepper looked around him. "My boy, is this wise? After all you did leave Savannah a little under a cloud."

"I have nothing to hide," Hugh said briskly. "Ralph Stoakes has a personal vendetta against me. What he accuses me of happened long ago in England and there is no way he can prove it."

"Nevertheless—"

"Where are you staying?" Hugh said turning back to Louisa. "May I come and see you?"

"Why—"

She was interrupted as Arabia stepped up beside Hugh making her presence obvious yet not daring to speak or take his arm. Some of the color drained from Louisa's face.

"Good morning, Arabia," she muttered.

Arabia nodded, glaring at the girl from under her dark lashes.

"We'd better be going, Papa. So good to see you again, Mr. Sandenny."

"But—"

Hugh stepped aside as they pushed by him, taking some of the satisfaction he had felt with them. And he hadn't learned where they were staying either.

Arabia slipped her arm through his. "We'd better be going if we too want dinner."

Hugh looked down at her as though just remembering she was there. What a nuisance that she should be with him now when all he wanted was to follow Louisa. Yet he could not leave the girl standing alone here. That would be too cruel and unmannerly. "Yes, I suppose we had," he muttered, thinking that it would not be too difficult to discover where the Culpeppers were staying. And once he had a chance to talk with Louisa again he could clear up some of these misunderstandings.

Beside him Arabia walked with her eyes on the cobbles and her lips clammed together, fighting back her anger and tears. Of all the churning emotions she felt none was more poignant or painful than the consciousness that Hugh had made no move to introduce or acknowledge her to the Culpeppers. In fact, it was only too obvious that her presence had embarrassed him. Everything had been so lovely until *she* showed up. Why did she always have to spoil everything!

It took Hugh three days to discover that Louisa and her father were staying at the home of the cousin he vaguely remembered from the voyage of the *Windward* a year ago—Cecily Davenport. It took him one more to finagle an invitation to one of Cecily's afternoon salons. It seemed that Cecily, when she wasn't seasick, was one of Charleston's more popular hostesses and her afternoon soirees were already attracting many of the young officers who swarmed about the town in search of entertainment. He entered the gilt and gold upper drawing room of the Davenport town house that afternoon his eyes searching the crowd of scarlet coats and short green jackets for the bright sunshine of Louisa's hair. Almost at once he spotted her across the room talking with two military gentlemen he faintly recognized but before he could reach her he was waylaid by Cecily herself, half-prone on a brocade settee, instantly alert to a new face entering her salon.

"Mr. Sandenny, I do belive," she said, extending one languid arm. "I remember you from our lamentable voyage together. That dashing young Tarleton told me you would be stopping by today. So pleased you could come."

"Your servant, ma'am," Hugh said, bowing over her hand. The woman who eyed him so thoroughly could hardly have been more removed from the bland, seasick invalid he remembered. Though Cecily affected a bored, indifferent air he knew enough about such postures to realize that behind them usually lay a shrewd personality very aware of the currents coming and going through the room. He had seen such people often enough in London parlors. Cecily's sharp little eyes confirmed his hunch. She asked him a few careless questions which he answered without giving his full attention, always conscious of the way her eyes darted between his and the end of the room where her cousin sat quietly.

Louisa heard Hugh's voice before she saw him striding across the room and with his first words she froze. Suddenly all the voices around her went silent as she grew conscious only of the tingling of her skin and the confusion within her breast.

Yet wasn't this what she wanted—to see him again? Hadn't she dragged her father up here to the city in the hope of finding him and warning him? Why such a strong reaction now? Why such a powerful wish to run from the room?

Thomas Fortesque, a captain in the 76th Highlanders bent over her, close to her face.

"'Pon my soul, Miss Culpepper, I don't think you've heard a word I said."

"What? Oh, I'm sorry Captain Fortesque. Forgive me— I was thinking of something far away. What was it you asked me?"

"Only if you would enjoy visiting the parade some afternoon. It's a bonny sight and with the pipes and all I think it would give you pleasure."

"Why thank you, I'd love that."

By this time Hugh had paid his respects to his enthroned hostess and was making his way to where Louisa sat nervously fluttering her fan.

"Miss Louisa," he said, bowing politely.

"Why, Mr. Sandenny, how nice to see you." Her eyes looked everywhere but directly at him. "Do you know Captain Fortesque?"

"We have met," Hugh said indifferently.

"And Lieutenant Goodsel."

A thin, gangly youth with hair powder dusting the shoulders of his scarlet coat gave Hugh a smart military bow.

"Lieutenant." His fingers closed over Louisa's and he bent close to her face as he raised them toward his lips.

"I have to talk with you," he whispered. "Alone."

"These gentlemen have been telling me about the siege of Charleston." Louisa went on airily. "It sounds as though it was very different from that of Savannah."

"Having lived through both I can assure you there is no comparison. You can see by the comparative wholeness of this town how little it was affected by our guns while Savannah was badly damaged. And the fighting was nothing to speak of here—"

"Well, sir," Lieutenant Goodsel interrupted, "we may have had an easier time of the siege but I'll wager you've never had a voyage like the one we undertook coming here from New York. It was as bad as any battle I've ever seen."

Hugh looked the youth up and down. "Have you seen a battle yet Lieutenant Goodsel?"

"Well no, but there could never be one any worse than that vile sail. Storms, waves, so many horses hurt that we had to throw them overboard—"

"Oh dear," Louisa said.

"See here, Goodsel," Fortesque interjected. "You're distressing the lady. No more about the voyage."

"Oh. So sorry," Goodsel muttered. "It was only the truth."

"Nevertheless—"

While the two men went on arguing the subject Louisa finally raised her eyes to Hugh and found him staring at her with an intensity that made her blush. A few moments later when Goodsel, having been roundly chastized by his superior, wandered off, she made a pretext of sending the Captain to fetch her a glass of punch. Once he was gone she rose, took Hugh's arm and walked with him toward the doors which opened onto a long piazza. There was no one there and though they were in full sight of the room, they could speak without being heard. Hugh stood as close to her as he dared while Louisa pointed out some of the more exotic plants and trees in the enclosed garden below.

"You see that poor half-burned stump over there in the west corner? That was a lovely lime tree my cousin had expressly brought from the Keys below Florida. How carefully she had always cultivated that little tree for the fruit was very special. But one of the shells that landed in the city hit this garden, very close to that tree and ruined it."

Her fingers rested on the balustrade as she spoke. Hugh laid his hand over them, stepping in front so as to block the view from inquisitive eyes within the salon.

"Louisa! You cannot know how I've longed to be standing here with you again. It's been my constant thought and dearest desire."

Pulling her hand away Louisa turned to face him. "Why

were you with Arabia Tillman yesterday? Do you live with her?"

Such a question was the last thing Hugh had been prepared to hear and for a moment he did not know how to answer her. "No, I don't. She followed me here against my wishes."

Louisa studied him in a way that suggested to Hugh that she did not believe what he said. "Why would she follow you without some encouragement? Arabia is a beautiful girl. She could have any man she wanted."

"That's true enough. But she has an affection for me that seems to blind her to other men's charms for the time being. Believe me, I have not tried to encourage her. She helped me out of a bad spot back in Savannah and I'm grateful to her, but it's you I love."

Louisa frowned as though she was struggling to believe him. "There must have been something . . ." She caught the quick flash of guilt in his eyes.

"Well, perhaps there was once. But that was before I knew how much you had captivated my heart and mind. How can I convince you there's no room now for anyone but you, Louisa."

Turning away from him Louisa stared out over the garden. "I know Arabia Tillman. I've known her since we were girls. Her mother worked in our home years ago. We were even friends once but after her mother died she seemed to develop a resentment towards me which no amount of kindness on my part has ever been able to lessen. Yet I am still fond of her in a way." She paused, turning back to Hugh. "I wonder if you know her at all."

"Really, this is impossible! You know I love you. I told you what was honestly in my heart that night in Savannah. And I believe you love me too. If we hadn't been interrupted by that ridiculous business—"

"Was it so ridiculous? I don't know who you really are."

Her eyes darkened with distrust. He turned away, staring out at the blackened lime tree in the garden. "Does it matter? Hugh or Hugo, my feelings for you would be the same."

Cecily Davenport's lighthearted voice came ringing out

to the balcony. "Louisa, my dear, don't let that nice Mr. Sandenny monopolize all your time. Your other admirers are positively fuming in here."

Louisa gave her cousin a wan smile and turned to go back into the room.

"I must see you again," Hugh said, desperation in his voice. This had not turned out at all like he had planned.

"I don't even know your true name . . ."

Ignoring the curious eyes from the salon Hugh laid a hand on her arm. "Trust me, Louisa. Perhaps I haven't been completely frank about my life back in England but there is a reason for that. Once it is cleared, I promise you you shall have the whole story. In the meantime, I have been truthful about Arabia. I love you and I don't want her to come between us."

"I want to believe you, Hugh, but . . . I don't know. Everything is so complicated."

"What other complications can there be?"

"Please, we can't discuss this here. Everyone is watching."

"Then I must see you alone some time."

"Not now. Perhaps . . . Come to call some afternoon."

She moved away and Hugh followed wondering how an afternoon call could be any more private than this, considering the number of friends Louisa had among the military.

Inside the doorway Louisa paused to smile at a tall young man who was passing wearing the blue tunic of the Continental Army. Hugh took a closer look and recognized the orderly who had taken them to General Lincoln's tent the night before the siege.

"What on earth is he doing here?"

"He's on parole. The American officers signed them just yesterday. His family has known my cousin's family for years so it is not unexpected that he would show up at her salon."

"I should think it would be deuced awkward."

Louisa snapped her fan open and fluttered it at her throat.

"You'd better get used to such things," she muttered and left Hugh standing at the door.

C h a p t e r 15

ARABIA HAD SURMISED from that first dismal Sunday at St. Philip's Church that Louisa and her father were staying with her cousin, Cecily Davenport, since she remembered meeting that lady years ago at the Culpepper house in Savannah. Yet she was slower than Hugh to make her way across town to Cecily's attractive house. She readily guessed that Hugh was attending those popular afternoon soirees at drawing rooms around the city where officers gathered to ogle the well-born beauties of Charleston, and the thought that he might be meeting Louisa among them was almost more than she could bear. She was drawn to the Davenport home like a moth to a flame and though she fought the urge successfully for a few days, in the end she had to know whether or not Hugh was there.

When at last she stood across the street watching the door that opened onto the street on one side and led to the long piazza on to the other she realized she must have chosen an afternoon when the party was being held elsewhere. After

a short while Cecily herself emerged in a swarm of feathers
and lace to climb into a carriage and roll away and Arabia
resigned herself to coming again tomorrow. At least there
was no Louisa rolling off for the latest round of social
engagements. Either Arabia had guessed wrong and she was
not staying with her cousin or she had chosen not to go out
this afternoon. Which was it?

Determined to look further, Arabia made her way around
the walled garden toward the corner from which the carriage
had come. There was a kind of narrow alley with each side
enclosed by a high wall, the nearest one obviously belonging
to the rear of the Davenport house. As she slipped around
the corner she stopped suddenly as she spotted a man in a
blue military coat standing far down the alley. He did not
look up and Arabia melted into the thick shadows of a large
magnolia tree standing near the stone wall, watching him
as he pushed open a small wooden door and disappeared
inside.

She gave him a moment and then quickly followed, more
curious than ever. The ancient, worm-eaten door stood
slightly ajar and quietly she pushed it open far enough to
slip inside.

She was in a garden, deep in shadow from the thick trees
and lush vegetation growing everywhere. The scent of wild
jasmine and roses was heavy in the air. An ancient live oak
whose thick limbs made a canopy for the door in the wall
trailed its Spanish moss like sleeves of silver lace nearly to
the ground. Avoiding the graveled walk which would be too
noisy, she slipped along the thick grass between overgrown
shrubs. Ahead she saw a small white summerhouse, sheathed
with tiny pink roses growing wild over its latticed sides.
Carefully she drew close enough to hear voices whispering
inside.

"But I must see her," a man's deep baritone.

"Misses can't come. She got the headache."

Arabia recognized that voice immediately. Jerral, Olana's
young son and Louisa's page.

"Look here, young man. This is very important. I have
a very important message for Oliver."

"Oliver? We don't know no Oliver."

The man's whisper grew more intense. "You don't have to play these games with me. I know that you're the same Jerral who goes to the Turtle River for those cabbage palm hearts and alligator steaks that Miss Louisa loves so well."

"Please, mista'."

"You don't have to worry about me. I'm all right. I just want you to tell Miss Louisa to come out here."

"I don't know nothin'."

"Jerral!"

Arabia shrank deeper into the protective shadows as she heard Louisa's voice calling from the terrace of the house. There was a shuffling of feet along the graveled walks and whispers too faint to be understood. Then, after a short silence, she heard Louisa's voice from inside the summerhouse.

"Why are you here? Don't you realize how dangerous it is?"

"I had to come. I overheard some information which ought to be passed along to Oliver. Look, here is a list of the regiments and the number of men His Excellency General Clinton plans to draw off Savannah to support Lord Cornwallis in his push through South Carolina."

"He's drawing off more troops?"

"Yes. Surprising, isn't it. I suppose he feels Georgia is safely in the King's net so there's nothing to worry about. Don't you see, it's our best chance since Savannah fell."

"Yes. I do see."

"Can you get this information to Oliver? Then if he'll pass it along to Sallette or Elijah Clarke perhaps we can manage to coordinate some kind of united push.

"Clarke is leaving for Tennessee but he can probably reach William or Ben Few. Thank you for bringing it but please, please don't come here like this again. It's far too dangerous. Anyone might see you."

"Don't worry. We'll be leaving the city soon anyway. That's the reason I was so anxious for you to have this."

Arabia watched, hardly daring to breathe as the two of them exchanged a few more hurriedly whispered words. Then the soldier slipped out of the summerhouse and back to the door in the wall. Although he was very careful to look outside before he stepped through the door, he obviously felt the garden was safe and did not even glance around as he passed where Arabia was crouched.

Arabia expected that Louisa would quickly leave but instead she heard her call Jerral and tell him to bring her writing desk. There was a soft scratching of the quill on paper, then Louisa spoke to Jerral again.

"You want me to go to Savannah, missy?" she heard the boy say.

"No. Not this time. I think this calls for someone older. I want you to go to the wharf and find Captain Jameson. He should be there near the sloop, *Restless*. Bring him here to me. Can you do that?"

"Missy, you knows I can do that. I can even go to Savannah you want me to."

There was a patient kindness in Louisa's voice. "No, I think not. Just bring Jameson here this afternoon and that will be service enough. Tell him I have some seedlings to send back to our house in Savannah and it is most urgent that they sail on the next tide."

"Yes, missy. I'm goin'."

He was off in an instant, his shoes clattering on the gravel. Arabia held her breath as Louisa sat in the quiet of the summerhouse several moments then closed the lid of her box with a snap and slipped off down the walk, her skirts rustling softly. Arabia waited longer just to be certain that the garden was deserted then finally eased her way back to the narrow wooden door. Slipping through it, she leaned against the stone wall for a moment taking long breaths of air, then hurried down the alleyway and around the corner to lose herself in the busy traffic of carriages and sedan chairs.

It was not until she neared the street where Hugh had taken lodgings that the enormity of all she had overheard really came to her.

Louisa Culpepper—a rebel! And with some kind of connection to the infamous Oliver, the scourge of the British in Savannah. Some kind of significant connection too or why seek her out in order to send him information. What would Hugh think of his lovely Tory beauty if he only knew?

What did it mean and how could she use it? She could see no way now but she felt certain that she would in the end. For the first time she began to hope that she had a hold over her rival at last, and one which might well turn Hugh away from her in disgust.

Intent on her thoughts, Arabia came hurrying around the corner and ran straight into a tinker, just as intent on hurrying toward a house where he had heard there was a pot that needed mending. Both were knocked back on their heels and Arabia had to clutch at the wall of the nearest house to keep from falling. The tinker, not so fortunate, went down on his knees amid the clatter of his bellows, hammer and box all flying in different directions.

"Why don't you watch where you're going," he cried, vastly irritated.

"I'm sorry..." she began, reaching for her hat which had been knocked off in the dust. Just as she straightened up she caught sight of a familiar figure near the other end of the block and her words froze.

Hugh! With Rob Earing close behind, just turning into the doorway under the colorful sign of the Cocoa Tree, a popular coffeehouse. She listened absently to the tirade of wrathful scorn being vented by the tinker, a spindly little man with ragged clothes and a stubble of beard on his pointed chin.

"I'm sorry," she muttered again, brushing the dust from her hat. But you were not looking around the corner either. So, just stop your scolding. You're as much to blame as I am."

Setting her hat briskly on her head she pulled at the strings and moved quickly down the street.

"The least you could do is help pick up all this—" the tinker called after her. But Arabia paid him no more mind. She was delighted to have spotted Hugh, for now she could tell him about Louisa's big secret. She could hardly wait to see his face when he heard of his idol's defection. Dodging the strolling pedestrians, she weaved her way quickly to the doorway and pushed it open to step inside. After the sunlight the room was like a closet but in the dimness Arabia could make out clusters of tables with men bent over them and potboys wandering between carrying trays over their heads. It took her a moment to spot Hugh's dark head against the deep brown paneling of the taproom sitting with Rob and another gentleman in a military coat and brigadier wig. The table was across the room in one of the corners near the windows and Arabia had to push her way through the crowd to reach it. She plopped down in a chair across from Hugh breathless and expectant but her excitement died as she saw his eyes widen and his lips fall in a frown. Arabia went cold. He was not even attempting to disguise his dismay at seeing her suddenly appear at their table.

"Why, Arabia," Rob said in his friendly way. "I didn't realize you were to join us."

"I didn't expect you," Hugh said lamely.

"Something in his tone irritated her. "I was out taking the air and I saw you coming in so I thought I would have a cup of chocolate. How are you Mr. Earing?"

Rob, who had risen as she sat down, gave her a little bow. Across from him the gentleman in the military coat also rose to his feet eyeing Arabia with an intensity she well recognized.

"I don't believe I've had the pleasure," he said, ogling the low cut of her bodice.

"Miss Arabia Tillman," Hugh said, "Major Stryker."

"Your servant, ma'am," the Major replied, reaching for her hand and leaning over the table to raise it to his lips. "The devil, my dear, but I don't recall seeing you at any of these afternoon soirees the Charleston belles delight us with. And I'm very certain had I seen you I'd not have forgotten so sweet a countenance."

Arabia smiled thinly at the compliment which she accepted with a barely concealed contempt. She was growing far too perturbed at Hugh's attitude to take the Major seriously.

"You are too kind," she muttered.

"Miss Tillman is a special friend of Hugh's," Rob said in a vain attempt to clear the waters. It seemed to have little effect on the Major.

"Well then, where have you been keeping this lovely

child, Sandenny? Buried in some stuffy cantonment? Selfish of you, man, I do declare."

"Miss Tillman does not often go out into society," Hugh muttered.

"Nonsense. Why, my dear Miss Tillman, I'll wager you'd enjoy Charleston society and I know they would enjoy you. See here, Hugh, why don't you bring her along to the dinner party Colonel Miles is giving tonight? I expect you would enjoy it, Miss Tillman, though it's only a small supper party with a middling orchestra of just three pieces. But you'd shine like the moon among all us stuffy military men. What do you say?"

"Oh, Major Stryker, I'd love—"

Arabia turned to Hugh and her words died in her throat at the warning look on his face. The excited sparkle in her eyes grew dulled and her smile faded into a grimace.

"Look, Major," Rob broke in, pointing toward a crowd of men who had just sauntered through the entranceway. "Isn't that Tarleton who just came in? I've not seen him in here before."

The Major's head shot around.

"Didn't you say he owed you some money? Here's your chance. It isn't often that the Commander of the Loyal Legion deigns to come into a place like this. Why don't we join them? . . . It looks as though they're ready to start a game."

Stryker watched the slim figure near the door as he sauntered to a table followed by several laughing young men who jerked chairs around. A deck of cards was thrown on the table and dice rolled on the wooden planks as they settled themselves, some of them straddling the chairs. "Hmmn," Stryker said, pursing his lips. He looked back hopefully at Arabia but it was obvious that his trend of thought had been interrupted. "Well, ma'am, my invitation stands if you can get this rascal here to bring you along."

"Thank you, Major," Arabia said, glaring at Hugh who was suddenly absorbed with fussing with the cuff of his sleeve. "Perhaps it can be arranged."

Rob was already on his feet, going around the table.

"Come along, Major, or we'll be too late to get in the game and there will go your best chance to get even."

Stryker, though longing to get away, took a moment more to speak directly to Hugh. "What do you say, Sandenny? Bring the lady along?"

"It may not be possible tonight. Perhaps another time."

"We'll discuss this further, Ma'am, after I've had the opportunity to relieve the Legion commander of some of his ill-gotten gains. Good day to you."

Arabia nodded silently as they moved from the table. She was so furious with Hugh that she could not speak. There was a heavy silence between them.

"I suppose you'd like to be off there as well gaming with the Major and your friend Rob," she muttered.

"Not particularly," he answered.

"If it weren't for me sitting here you would be off directly, wouldn't you."

"Now Arabia, that is a ridiculous comment. There would be nothing to hold me if you were not sitting there."

"There's nothing to hold you here anyway," she said through clenched teeth. "Not here, not when you're off at those afternoon parties dancing attendance on all the other women . . ."

"That's not fair."

"Isn't it? Where were you today? Not on the parade grounds, I'll wager. Whose drawing room? And tonight, whose rout? Why do you never take me with you? Why don't you introduce me to your friends?"

"I do."

"No. Only when you have to, like today."

"I didn't ask you to come here today. I certainly do not object to introducing you to Stryker though why you should want to know him is beyond me. His interest in you is not that of a gentleman," he added lamely.

"And yours is of course. You don't want me but you don't want any other man to have me either."

"Certainly not a rake like Stryker. Please, Arabia, this is not the time or the place to discuss these matters."

"Then when? And where? It's never the time or the place!"

She jumped to her feet, grabbing up her recticule. "I'm going."

"You're acting like a goose. Come now—"

"No." Whirling on her heel, she turned and hurried toward the door. Hugh watched her leave, feeling such a mixture of emotions that he could barely sort them out.

Reluctantly he reached for his hat and followed her. She was not a girl to take rejection lightly and he was unsure of what she might do. And certainly he did not need anything further to embarrass him at this point.

He could just manage to see her wide leghorn hat bouncing among the crowd of people on the street ahead of him. He followed her back to the small house where she had a room, relieved that she was going there and not someplace less private. When he finally knocked on the door to the tiny room and cautiously opened it, she was sitting in a chair near the window, twisting her hands in silent despair and fury.

"Arabia," he began but she turned on him, her face an angry grimace.

"You were ashamed," she hissed. "Ashamed of me. I could tell. It was obvious to everyone. It embarrassed you to say you knew me, to have me sitting with you . . ."

"That's not true. It was just that I didn't expect you there in a coffeehouse filled with men. You took me by surprise."

"Don't make excuses. Ever since I came here you've shunted me off to some dark corner as though you didn't want to be seen with me."

"Be fair, Arabia. Haven't I given you my protection since you arrived in Charleston? Haven't I squired you and chaperoned you? Didn't I find a place for you to stay?"

"A place where you never come. And then when Louisa Culpepper arrives, you don't want to be seen with me at all. You don't care anything about me!"

"That's not true. I have an affection for you and I'm deeply conscious of all that you've done to help me."

"Help you! I've been paid in full for all I've done, haven't I." Stalking to the chest of drawers, she yanked one open, rummaged through it and drew out the lace mantilla he bought her in St. Augustine, throwing it at him.

"Here! Here's my payment, returned to you in full. I want nothing from a man who is ashamed of me."

It was on the tip of Hugh's tongue to remind her that he had not asked her to come to Charleston in the first place but the anguish in her dark eyes held him back. He wished he could spare her any further hurt and yet at the same time he was irritated and annoyed that she forced him into these painful scenes.

"I must go," he muttered. "There's no point in talking about these things now. Perhaps when you're calmer."

She watched him turn away and open the door and deep within her a fierce despair crystallized into a resolve to remove herself from this desperate situation. As long as she stayed near Hugh she was destined to know only heartache and hurt. Especially when Louisa was there too.

Without a word of good-bye she let him walk away, closing the door behind him. Reaching out, she drew up the crumpled mantilla and buried her face in its silken folds. She wanted to cry but her tears were bottled up within her by her fury and anguish. Underneath all she felt lay the one inescapable, terrible fact that out of all the words they had exchanged, he had never attempted to deny her charge that he was ashamed of her.

He was gone now. He might come back but he would not find her waiting for him. Arabia Tillman was not the woman to sit around waiting for any man to throw her a few crumbs of his affection. She had done well enough without Hugh Sandenny before and she would again. To the devil with him!

From where she stood in the narrow street fronting the busy wharf Arabia could hear the bells in St. Michael's tower tolling six o'clock. It had taken her longer than she expected to gather up her courage to leave this town where she had shared many pleasant moments with Hugh. She carried her few personal belongings in a bag made of heavy woven straw—the few things Hugh had given her she deliberately left behind. Then after making her way here she had found it difficult to locate the *Restless* among the scores of British ships lining the docks. Now she stood staring at it from across the street where it was moored in the Cooper River, gathering up her nerve for the last effort required which would once and for all separate her from Hugh Sandenny.

It was a depressing boat, so small and unkempt that she wondered how it would manage to survive the journey to Savannah. Gathering up her courage, she crossed the street, dodging the small boys and the sailors seeking the nearest taverns, and stood at the foot of the narrow gangplank.

"Are you Captain Jameson?" she called to a man standing at the top of the plank, inspecting the sheets.

"Aye," he answered, looking down over the stub of his pipe to examine her with brittle black eyes. "What do ye want of me?"

"I wish to book passage on your boat for Savannah. I can pay you whatever you ask—within reason."

"Can ye now. Suppose I'm not bound for Savannah."

"But I was told you were. And I must get back to the city immediately."

The captain lowered his hands from the ropes and walked to the end of the plank to stare down at Arabia. She drew her shawl closer around her shoulders at his inquisitive stare, and glared boldly back at him.

"Have you any objection to taking a poor widow home to her brother? You'd be doing an act of Christian charity. I'd be much obliged."

"Widow is it. How?"

"In the last shelling before the city fell. A mortar hit my little home and my poor John, he was killed along with our babe. There's no one but me now and I long to return to my brother in Savannah who will take care of me."

Lowering her head she wiped an imaginary tear from her eye. Jameson studied her as though he was not really sure whether or not to believe her story. At length he shrugged.

"Very well. But it'll cost you five shillings."

"Five!" Her head shot up, then she quickly lowered it again. "Oh, I cannot thank you enough, Captain. You have a warm heart."

"My heart's a deal warmer than my head, I think. But

come on aboard. You don't have a maid with you, do ye?"

"No," Arabia said climbing quickly up the gangway. "But I'll keep to the cabin and stay out of the way. You won't even know I'm here."

"See that ye do," Jameson said, dismissing her for more pressing matters. His most dependable mate, who had a tendency to get drunk the closer they came to sailing time, was still ashore. If he caused them to miss the tide—

Ordering a young cabin boy to show her the way, the Captain sent Arabia below to stow her gear in one of two tiny cabins. It was close and narrow and dark but somehow the gloom of it suited her mood and she did not mind. The boy left her there and hurried back to the deck where his exacting master would be waiting for him. There was a tiny connecting door between Arabia's little box and a slightly larger one which was obviously the Captain's quarters. It had a latch which she started to fasten but then thought better of. Pushing the door she found it ajar and stepped into the Captain's cabin. It was the usual cramped room, with dark wood, a bunk built into the wall, a lantern fastened to the low ceiling, a sextant and several books on the table in the corner. What caught her eye, however, was a dark recess behind the head of the bed. On it stood a chest with a rounded lid studded with brass knobs and striped with leather bands.

The boat creaked gently as it rocked back and forth on the water. Above her head she could hear the dim voices of the crew and the soft shuffling of their feet on the deck. Yet for all the activity above it, the interior of the cabin was dark and still and quiet.

Cautiously Arabia stretched out a white hand to the chest and tried the lid. It was unlocked. Carefully she opened it.

After leaving Arabia Hugh decided that he had had enough of women-problems and in an effort to clear his mind, he saddled his horse and rode out into the environs of Charleston. He spent the afternoon alternating hard rides with sedate canters around the area where he had lived when he came north to join the British camp. It was good to be in the open after the closeness of the town and his horse seemed as satisfied as he himself to be riding free. By the time he returned to his lodgings he had made up his mind to be frank with Arabia and suggest that perhaps it would be best if she returned to Savannah. At least then he could pursue his chances with Louisa, maybe even convince her to marry him. It would certainly make life easier and simpler with Arabia gone.

He was bending over the washbowl in his room, getting ready to dress for Colonel Miles' supper party when he heard the noisy clatter of boots on the stairs. A moment later the door was thrown open and Rob Earing came running in breathlessly.

"Thank God you're here. I was afraid I'd have to search half the drawing rooms of this town to find you."

Hugh turned, his face dripping and reached for a towel.

"Another twenty minutes and I would have been on my way to Colonel Miles. Why aren't you dressed?"

"No time for social pleasures tonight, dear boy. Get your coat. You're riding with the Legion." As he spoke his eyes searched the room until they found Hugh's green jacket which he grabbed up and threw at him. "We've just got word that an American brigade on its way here to relieve Charleston has turned back for Virginia. Tarleton's been ordered out to catch and scatter them. If you hurry we can go along."

The towel was quickly thrown aside as Hugh grabbed for his coat.

"Do you know where they are? How many?"

"Near the North Carolina border, about three hundred strong. It should be a cracking fight. I wouldn't miss it for anything. But we've got to hurry. This is one commander who doesn't allow the grass to grow under his feet when he smells a battle."

Boots, belt and sword were hastily thrown on. Hugh was ready and almost out the door behind Rob when he remembered Louisa.

"Wait up a moment," he called. "There's something I must do before I leave."

"Come along, man. We don't have time."

"You go on, Rob. I'll be right behind you."

Rob needed no urging. He was back down the stairs before Hugh was able to drag his writing desk out from under the bed. Hastily he scrawled on the foolscap paper:

> "My dearest Louisa. I cannot be with you to-
> night as I am off with the Legion. When I return
> I will ask A. to go back to Savannah. I pledge
> my love to you as always and hope and believe
> I carry yr's with me.
>
> H."

Hurriedly he sanded, folded and sealed the paper. Grabbing up his hat he ran downstairs and gave a coin to a young lad to deliver it to the Davenport house by seven o'clock. Then, with a rising excitement he could barely contain, he went running off to the barracks.

Chapter 16

LOUISA READ HUGH'S note while Cousin Cecily called from downstairs that the carriage was at the door and would she please hurry or they were sure to be late for Colonel Miles' supper party. She laid the paper he had so recently held in his hand against her cheek, trying to recall his touch. She was both relieved and disappointed. She wished more than anything to see him, and yet, as she reminded herself yet again, the last thing she needed right now was to let herself fall head over heels in love with an Englishman.

As Cousin Cecily's voice began to rise on a shrill note of impatience, she slipped the letter in a drawer of her escritoire and ran downstairs to join her. During the ride across town to the Colonel's rented house she sat silent and reflective, half listening to her cousin's chatter and conscious of her father's thoughtful eyes upon her from the opposite seat. When they pulled up before the brightly lit doorway, Cecily alighted in a flurry of satin and watered silk. When Louisa moved to follow, her father laid his hand gently on her arm.

"Are you quite well tonight, my dear?"

Louisa hesitated. "Yes, Papa. Why do you ask?"

"You do not seem yourself. Are you certain you would not prefer to go back home? I am quite willing to take you."

"Thank you, Papa, but I will be fine. It's just a little touch of the vapors."

She gave her hand to the footman and stepped down from the carriage thinking how she must make more effort to appear her usual self. Determined she followed Cecily into the house to join the rather large group of guests at the Colonel's table.

It was a pleasant group for all its size. Most of them were familiar to Louisa either from her days in Savannah or her afternoons at the frequent soirees in Charleston drawing rooms. But it turned out to be an interminable meal of twenty-five covers and long before the last sweetmeat was served she found her good intentions flagging. Her companion on the left was a dour little major in the 76th Highlanders. He was a lowlander Scot who had little use for the colonies and once he learned that she was born and bred in Georgia his comtempt was only slightly tempered by his attempts to be polite.

The gentleman on her right was much more helpful since he was inclined to carry the conversation and listened very seldom to anything she said. His florid face gave an indication of his fondness for port and good fellowship and his loud, guffawing laugh sometimes attracted more attention to their end of the table than she might wish. But he was pleasant and entertaining. He introduced himself as Major Stryker.

Stryker was a great talker and without the least concern over her ties to the Colonies he dwelt at length and lovingly on what a miserable country this was and how easily the King's forces would soon have everything back under control now that Charleston and Savannah were theirs.

"But I have heard that the people in the interior are sympathetic to Congress for the most part," Louisa said tentatively. "And South Carolinians especially tend to be extremely stiff-necked in their prejudices."

"Nonsense, my dear. Why the countryside is thick with

loyal citizens who long to be rid of this devilish rebel crowd and return to the peaceful, useful life they once knew. Good Englishmen to the core, most of them. If it were not for this small rabble of fanatics who stir things up we'd have no problem at all."

Louisa pushed her Charlotte Russe around with her spoon and said softly: "I think perhaps you underestimate the extent of the problem."

"Not a bit of it," Stryker replied, holding up his glass for one of the many servants to refill. "Take my word, Miss Culpepper, Lord Cornwallis will have the King's peace restored from Charleston to Baltimore within a few months at the most."

"Lord Cornwallis? What about General Clinton? Does he not wish to get credit for putting down the rebellion? I've heard the two are very much in competition with each other."

Stryker leaned close to her and lowered his voice. "That's true. But his Excellency, General Clinton, feels that Mr. Washington and his rabble are too great a threat to the Hudson and New York City for him to linger long in the Carolinas. He's done the bulk of the work down here. Now he must go back and deal with that army, leaving Cornwallis to clean up the South. After all, with Lincoln's forces taken prisoner and the militia disbanded, there is no rebel army of any size in these southern provinces to fear.

"Well, I'm sure you must know better than I."

Stryker beamed and lifted his glass. "Indeed I do. I won't say I have the General's ear but I'm pretty quick to detect which way the wind is blowing. You have to do that when you make the army your career or you'll never get ahead at all."

Louisa looked up at him from under her lashes, getting up her courage to ask a question she had been longing to all evening.

"Since you are so familiar with what is happening in the army, Major, I wonder if you know anything about the raid that Colonel Tarleton went upon this afternoon. I ask, you see, because I have a friend who went along—Hugh Sandenny."

"Oh, yes, Sandenny. Saw him earlier today sitting with the most stunning dark-eyed beauty I've ever laid eyes upon. Are you certain he's with Tarleton? Perhaps he simply decided to stay home with and keep her company. Couldn't blame him if he did."

He laughed heartily at his little joke while Louisa miserably studied her plate. Catching her frozen stare, Stryker grew more serious.

"I only heard that the Legion went flying off to catch a force of rebels who had been marching to the relief of Charleston and turned tail for the border when they learned it was fallen. They'll no doubt fade into the mist before he ever catches them—especially if they hear he is coming. There's probably no danger involved at all."

"Oh, I'm not worried about Mr. Sandenny. He knows how to take care of himself."

"No man rides with Tarleton who does not. As for that little filly he was with, why I don't think she meant anything to him. I tried to convince him to bring her along tonight and he was very reluctant. By the time they left she was as angry as a wet hornet. I'd not give that little lady a second thought."

Louisa smiled faintly as she recognized Stryker's poor attempts to relieve her anxiety. "Thank you, Major, but I assure you that whatever Mr. Sandenny does and whoever he does it with is strictly his own business. It matters very little to me."

One eyebrow on Stryker's florid face climbed upward. He had heard such protestations before. All at once he began to wonder what there was about Hugh Sandenny to attract two such lovely women. He must look into the matter when the Legion returned.

Somehow Louisa got through the rest of the meal. Directly after the men had left the table and joined the ladies in the parlor, she cornered her father and got him to drive her home without waiting for the cards, or musical entertainment. Pretending a headache grown suddenly severe she sat quietly in a corner of the carriage trying not to think back on Stryker's conversation.

"Louisa," her father said as they were nearing the Davenport house, "I've been thinking that perhaps we should go back to Savannah. I find all this socializing somewhat wearying and I begin to think you do as well. I was only staying on your behalf anyway. What do you say? Shall we return to Abercorn Street?"

Louisa sat straight up. "Oh, I don't think so, Papa. Perhaps not just yet anyway. Actually I long to go home again as much as you but perhaps not for a few more days. Do you mind waiting that long?"

"Of course not, my dear. Whenever you are ready, I will be ready. It certainly is not my wish to deprive you of this entertaining existence but I wonder if it is not taking too much of a toll on your health. I don't want that to happen."

"Perhaps I shall cut down on some of the social activities, and try to get a little more rest. It's just that there is so much to do and so many attractive invitations."

"And so many attractive men, I dare say. You young girls must have your parties and fancy balls. I know that. Very well. Just let me know as soon as you've had enough and are ready for the quiet and peace of Savannah."

"I shall, Papa. I promise."

The fog hung like a shroud over Savannah harbor. Pinpricks of light from lanterns swaying from the yardarms and pier were visible only from a few feet away. The *Restless* moved down the river at a snail's pace, one of her mates hanging from the bow swinging a lantern before him to guide her into a berth at the far end just above Yamacraw. There were not too many ships moored here since it was a seedier section of the wharf, one which even sailors tended to avoid. On a good night there would be a few pedestrians roaming its cobbled walk frequenting the dingy taverns. On a night like this there was no one.

The sloop responded to Captain Jameson's deft handling of the tiller. With a grinding of wooden sides against the pilings, she maneuvered into a slip, just managing to avoid a collision with a British scow undergoing repairs. The watch on the scow called out a curse as the crew clambered onto the wharf and began throwing the mooring ropes over the posts and rings.

"All secured, sir," one of them called to the Captain.

"Good. Now get back aboard and make sure the sails are bedded."

"Aye."

The two men scrambled back on the boat while Jameson, anxious to get ashore and on his way, checked the last of the chores required to leave his boat moored. He was about to step down the hatch to his cabin when all at once he heard the sharp stamp of boots on the wharf. The pier was filled with running men, their lanterns swinging like a horde of fireflies in the fog.

"What the devil's going on?" he said, peering into the darkness. Suddenly the deck of the boat was swarming with men who poured off the gangway. Before the Captain realized what was happening he was grabbed roughly and shoved against the cabin, his arms pinned behind him and the muzzle of a brass handled pistol shoved in his face.

"What do you think you're doing? Get off my—"

A fist crushed against his jaw.

"Shut your mouth, rebel, or I'll blow your brains to kingdom come!"

"There'll be none of that," said a cultured voice, thick with authority. Jameson turned to stare at a tall figure, indistinct in the fog though he was only standing six feet away.

"Are you Captain Jameson?"

"Aye. What of it."

"You're under arrest by order of the Royal Governor, Sir James Wright. This ship, the *Restless* is impounded."

"By what right! I've done nothing!"

"That remains to be seen. You are accused of transporting seditious correspondence and material aid to men who are in rebellion against their King. Need I remind you that is a treasonable offense."

"I've done nothin' of the kind."

"Search the ship," the voice said dispassionately. "And put this fellow in irons."

"You can't do this! You've got no right—"

He was pulled off toward the pier, protesting. Behind

him one of the men climbed up from the hatch and called to the officer in charge:

"You'd better come below, sir."

In her cabin Arabia heard the pounding of feet on the deck floor and the muffled cries of the Captain and the men swarming over the ship. She sat on her narrow bunk, her bundle of belongings clutched in her arms and wondered what trouble she had blundered into now. The trip to Savannah had been so rough and unpleasant that many times she had regretted her hastiness in leaving Charleston. Yet when they finally entered the river and drew near the dock her relief in going ashore and being home again made it all seem worthwhile. And now this. Whatever was happening she knew it meant trouble.

When her door was thrown open and a grungy seaman in a tattered scarf and a stubble of beard on his face stared in at her, her heart sank. For one moment she thought she was fallen into the hands of pirates. Then he disappeared only to be replaced a moment later by a tall figure resplendent in cranberry brocade carrying an ebony cane in one hand. Arabia gave a sigh of relief.

"Sir Ralph! Thank heaven it is you."

"Why, I do believe it is Miss Tillman. I must say I never expected to find you here. What are you doing on this boat?"

"Trying to get home to Savannah."

Stoakes studied her through his glass, obviously trying to decide if she were lying or telling the truth. Arabia stared boldly back at him but she did not try to leave the room, or even rise from her cot.

"This boat has been impounded," Stoakes said, resting his cane on one corner of the table. "Jameson is arrested and carried to jail."

"Oh. For what?"

"He is a rebel who for some time now has been using this sloop to transport letters and information from spies behind the British lines to the partisan leaders in the interior. We've been biding our time, waiting for the right moment to catch him and we think this is it."

"Why are you looking at me like that?"

Stoakes shrugged. "I am trying to decide whether or not I should arrest you as well. It is extremely suspicious, you being on this sloop at this time."

Arabia rose from the cot, clutching her bundle to her chest. As she was about to answer, Stoakes was called from the room by one of the men searching the cabin. When he was gone she jumped on the cot and stared out the tiny porthole wondering if she might crawl through it to try her luck in the waters of the river. Then he reappeared and she stepped down.

"Did you find what you were looking for?"

"Not yet, unfortunately. But we will."

"Suppose I help you. Would that make me appear less suspicious?"

He looked sharply down at her.

"And could you?"

"I might. Look here, Mr. Stoakes, I am no rebel. I don't care one way or the other about this war. I only wanted to get to Savannah and—well, just to get back to Savannah. But I happen to know that Captain Jameson has a letter in his possession and it might just be the one you're looking for."

"What kind of a letter?"

Arabia laid her bundle down on the cot and walked to the door, closing it.

"Before I left Charleston I overheard Louisa Culpepper talking with an American officer from Lincoln's army. He told her that some of the men here in Savannah were going to be pulled out to reinforce Clinton in Charleston. She seemed to think that was very interesting information. Then, after he left, she wrote everything in a letter which she had her boy, Jerral, take to Captain Jameson. That's how I knew the *Restless* was leaving for Savannah last night. I wanted to get home so I paid him to bring me along."

Stoakes stepped closer staring down into her eyes. "You must be mistaken. Louisa Culpepper would never—"

"Oh, wouldn't she: Well, I heard her say so with my own ears. And I saw her write that letter and say she meant it for Oliver. You know about Oliver, don't you? Well, that is who the letter is for."

For a moment she thought he was going to grab her arm but that quickly passed. With a face hard as flint he stepped back.

"I should have allowed Jameson to deliver the letter and had him followed. Well, too late for that now. Where is this missive you saw Louise write? We've not been able to find it."

"It is in the Captain's chest at the head of his bed. I saw it there myself."

Stoakes' thin lips fell into something representing a sneer. "Your jealousy of Louisa Culpepper is getting the best of you. We searched that chest and there was no letter there."

"It has to be. It must be."

"Come along." Pushing her by the shoulder he shoved her ahead of him out into the narrow dark walkway and into the Captain's cabin. Everything in the room had been thrown around, littering the floor. A layer of feathers from the ripped mattress lay like a thin dusting of snow. Stoakes searched through the debris until he found the chest, its lid half torn off.

While his deft fingers searched its carved surface he threw questions at the man standing near the door.

"You searched Captain Jameson?"

"Aye, we did. And found nothing. He could not of had no letter on him save he ate it and that we'll only know by servin' him a purgative."

"See that you do."

Stoakes almost grinned as he caught sight of Arabia's white face. "It's very common, my dear. A letter in a tiny empty vial, swallowed. Many a message has been recovered that way."

"Ugh!"

"Ah, what have we found here now," he said with satisfaction as he heard a tiny click. Nimbly he maneuvered the lid of the chest to slide back a thin sliver of the inlaid carving and reveal a narrow cavity built into the lid. With the sharp edge of a knife he pried out a piece of paper from the recess.

"See. I told you," Arabia crowed.

With a barely suppressed smile, Stoakes broke the seal

on the letter and spread it on the table under the lantern. Bending over it, he ran a long finger down the page. Arabia moved to stand as close as she dared, staring down at the paper.

Years ago she had spent many hours sitting beside Louisa in the cramped schoolroom on the top floor of the house on Abercorn Street picking up the rudiments of reading and writing. The shared lessons ended when her mother died but she carried away enough of them to be more literate than most girls of her station and she still retained enough ability to make out most of the words in Louisa's letter. Her eyes skimmed over the brief cluster of words and the columns of numbers and names. But it was the signature at the end of the letter that caught her attention. She fully expected to see Louisa's neatly formed name, or, at the least, the letter "L." Instead she looked, and looked closer, almost leaning on Stoakes' shoulder, as mesmerized as he by that signature. Slowly Arabia spelled out the letters—O L I V E R.

"Oliver?" she said, looking into Stoakes' cold eyes, nearly on a level with her own, their depths like winter ice.

"So it would seem," he answered, in a voice as frigid as his look.

Two days later on a warm, lazy southern evening, Louisa sat restlessly reclining on the satin chaise in her bedroom trying to lose her thoughts in a novel that her Cousin Cecily had loaned her. The hour was late but she had long ago given up any hope of sleep as an impossibility. Nor did the book help much. Her own concerns were clamoring at the corners of her mind far too strongly to lose herself in the farfetched high-jinks of Mr. Fielding's Master Jonathan Wild.

She had about decided to blow out the candle and stretch out on her bed in an attempt to at least rest if not sleep when she heard the soft clatter of gravel against her window. It was so gentle and delicate a sound that it took her a moment to separate it from the familiar evening murmurs. When it came again she laid down the book and moved to the shadows of the long window looking down over the garden below.

In the coppery moonlight she could just make out a figure standing near the summerhouse—a tall man swathed in the folds of a long cloak with a tricorn hat pulled down over his face.

"Louisa!"

The whispery call sent a brief thrill through her body. Leaning out the window she answered:

"Hugh?"

"Yes. Can you come down. I must talk with you."

"But—"

"Sh-h-," he cautioned. "Keep your voice down. I don't want anyone to know I'm here. Please, come down, Louisa."

It was on the tip of her tongue to ask him why he could not come inside but the urgency in his voice answered her question.

"I'll be there in a moment," she whispered and hurried back to her room for a robe to slip over her nightdress. The hall outside her door was empty and quiet. Thank heaven Cecily's room was at the other end of the house or her inquisitive cousin would have sniffed an intrigue before Louisa even knew Hugh was there. Making her way softly down to the parlor, she quietly opened the long French doors that gave out onto the piazza, slipped down the stairs and went silently across the grass to the summerhouse. He was there, waiting to take her in his arms almost before she was up the low steps.

"Louisa, Louisa," he muttered, burying his face in the softness of her streaming hair. She gave herself fully to his warm embrace, savoring the firmness and warmth of his body and the good feel of his arms holding her close before pulling back a little.

"Hugh, what's wrong? Why couldn't you come inside? Why are you here at night like this so secretly?"

He took both her hands in his and sat with her on one of the benches lining the open trellis of the summerhouse walls. The heady fragrance of the climbing roses hung like a perfume in the air and the moonlight fell in lacy patterns through the lattice and along the floor. It was so beautiful and so good to be here in this lovely place with him and yet there was something in his manner that cautioned her against giving her emotions full rein.

"Louisa, I'm in trouble. The Legion is looking for me and if they find me I'm sure to be thrown in jail, maybe even shot."

"Hugh! But why?"

"It's that damned devil, Tarleton! He is the one who ought to be shot, not me. I wish I'd never gone on that accursed raid."

She had forgotten the raid. Impulsively she threw her arms around his neck and hugged him fiercely.

"Oh, but you did go and you came back safely. I was so worried you wouldn't."

He kissed the soft curve of her cheek then pulled himself away, laying an arm around her shoulder.

"It would have been better if I had been killed. As it is, I feel so confused I don't know who I am anymore."

"Hugh, what on earth happened to put you in this state? Nothing could be so bad—"

"It was bad. It was terrible." Releasing her he leaned forward, resting his arms on his knees and twisting his hands together. "We rode like madmen trying to catch up with Bufort's Virginians, ruining our horses, fighting through swamps, abusing the natives who, as it turned out, were not happy to see us in the least. When we finally caught up with the rebels we had to commandeer horses from the locals to make the attack. The rebels put up a strong first defense but when they saw they were outnumbered they raised a flag. It turned out that just as the flag went up Tarleton's horse was shot out from under him. That was all the excuse he needed to give full vent to his barbarous nature. Against every honorable rule of war, he ordered 'no quarter.' What happened then was a sight I'll never forget as long as I live!"

Louisa laid her arm about his shoulder. "You don't have to talk about it if you don't want to."

"No. I do want to. I have to tell somebody. Make somebody understand. The Ensign who advanced with the flag was shot down immediately. Then the dragoons—those dashing soldiers of whom we are so proud—went through the lines cutting down every man that moved, thrusting their bayonets sometimes through two or three at once to get at the man underneath. To cry 'quarter' was only a signal to be run through with a sword or a bayonet. I've never seen such carnage, such indiscriminate slaughter, not even last year during the siege."

"Oh, Hugh," she whispered. "How horrible—"

He sat back and reached for her hand. "It made me sick to the soul. I've killed men in duels, Louisa, and I certainly caused my share of casualties on the parapets of the Spring Hill redoubt last autumn. But to stab a man when he's looking up at you, crying 'quarter'—you have to be a barbarian to do that."

"Perhaps you just have to be more committed to a cause than you are to Tarleton's."

"There was an American officer, a captain, I think. I saw him surrender and be cut down with a shot to the face. I tried to reach him but before I could get there two more dragoons stabbed him with their bayonets. His face was just a bloody pulp when I reached him but he was still alive. Something snapped in my mind and I began pulling the others away and trying to protect him. Tarleton saw me and came roaring up, ordering me to get back to the business of his private slaughter. I—I told him he was a bloody butcher and I'd have no more of it, and—I struck at him with my sword."

"Oh, Hugh!"

"I didn't hurt him. He deflected the blade easily then was off to some other bloody business. But he didn't forget. When the sport was done, he ordered his butchers to find me and shoot me on the spot for insubordination. Rob warned me of it quickly enough that I was able to slip away. But the Legion is returning to Charleston on my heels and if they catch me before I can leave the city I'm done for. He'll never forgive or forget. At least I was able to save that American's life. He may never be able to speak clearly again but he survived, thanks to me. I stayed long enough to make certain of that."

"But Hugh, you're not commissioned in the regular army. The Legion Commander has no authority over you."

"What does that mean to a man like Tarleton. I was

serving under him and I am guilty of gross insubordination. That's all he needs for revenge. I tell you, Louisa, I don't understand what this war is all about anymore. It started out for me as just a lark. Now, I've seen these rebels more closely and I wonder at the stupidity of the King and Parliament that they ever attempted to handle such a problem in this way. This is a rich, fine country and our British intransigence is losing it for us as clearly as if we wanted it lost."

Laying her hand on his cheek Louisa smiled into his eyes. "Hugh you cannot know how happy I am to hear you say these words. I feel the same way. This is a stupid, vain, useless war. The colonies deserve to be independent and they surely will be. If it isn't achieved by conquest of arms then it will come with time. We are too far from England to suffer her arrogance forever."

Hugh's eye's widened. "Why, Louisa. Are you a rebel?"

"Yes I am. I'm fond of England—she's our 'mother' Country and always will be. But I love America more than England or King George."

Hugh took both her hands and raised them to his lips, opening them to kiss her palms. "Then hear me, my dearest love. Come with me, Louisa, away from here. Away from the army and the war and rebels and loyalists and Whigs and Tories. Come with me where we can be safe to start a life together without the interference of British officialdom or old hatreds."

"You're going away?"

"I must. And I want you by my side."

"But where? There is no place to escape this war right now."

"Yes, there is. Out beyond Augusta. I'm told the lands there are rich and beautiful and no British authority reaches that far."

"Hugh, Augusta was just recently taken by a British battalion. It is true that Wilkes county to the west is almost entirely rebel in sympathy but beyond that lies Indian country, wild and savage. You would only be escaping one kind of barbarism for another."

"But I would be free. *We* would be free, and safe. Say you'll come with me."

Gently Louisa drew her hands away from his urgent clasp. "I cannot come with you, Hugh. I wish I could more than anything in the world. But I have—responsibilities here and I cannot turn my back on them."

"What responsibilities? More parties and routs? New dresses? Flirtations? Is that the life you cannot leave?"

"You know that is not the reason. We all have things we have to do and they will not disappear simply because we walk away from them."

Abruptly he rose and walked to the other side of the small enclosure, leaning a hand on the lattice work. "You know how I feel about you. I love you more than anyone in the world. Indeed, you are almost the only person in this world that I do love."

"What about Arabia? Did you send her away?"

"No. She left of her own accord before I could talk to her. But she left knowing that my heart belongs to you. Louisa, why won't you come with me? What could possibly hold you here? I can only think that you do not care for me as much as you say you do."

"That's not true. I do love you, Hugh, but there are people here who depend on me."

"What people? Your father? Your servants? Those foolish beaus who fawn over you and flatter you? Does their society mean so much more to you than mine?"

Even in the moonlight he could make out the agony on her face. Whatever her reason, it was obviously deeply felt and was causing her a great deal of pain. But he wanted her with him so badly he would not allow her anguish to soften his heart. Life without her stretched ahead so bleak and empty.

Louisa spoke softly, all the more intense for her quiet way. "You asked me to trust you once, Hugh. Now I ask the same of you. Please try to accept the fact that I must stay here for now even though it almost breaks my heart to see you go away without me."

There was a soft clatter near the gate followed by hurried

footsteps on the gravel. Louisa recognized Rob Earing's anxious whisper:

"Dragoons on the road, Hugh. If they spot the horses I don't know how long I can hold them off. Hurry it up, please."

"Coming Rob. Just a moment more."

With a few strides he was across the enclosure, fiercely gripping her shoulders with his hands. "I love you, Louisa, and I would marry you in a moment if you would only come with me."

She slipped her arms around his neck, staring up into his face. "Oh, Hugh, I can't. I can't. Please try to understand."

There were tears in her eyes. They glistened in the dim moonlight like deep, dark pools of brooding water. He pulled her to him, pressing her body against his, as though to let go of her would be to lose the only order and sanity left in life.

"I don't know if I will ever see you again!"

"You will. You must. This will all be over some day and then, if you don't come back to me my heart will break for certain."

"But so much can happen. I know it isn't fair to ask you to go off into a wild unknown life but I'm so afraid I may never be able to ask you again. If you truly loved me..."

"I do. I do so much. You must never doubt that for a moment. Always believe that I'm waiting, thinking of you, loving you wherever you may be."

His arms tightened about her and his mouth sought out her face, her neck, her lips. "I don't understand you. Why?"

"I can't! I can't!"

Digging his fingers in her shoulders he pulled away to look down into her distraught face. "Then this is farewell. I hope, I pray I can come back."

Louisa laid her hands on either side of his lean face and lightly kissed his lips. "Oh, my love, I pray so. God keep you."

Clasping his arms around her he kissed her roughly, almost angrily. Then with his dark cape swirling about him, he was gone, leaving her to clutch at the trellis, staring after him into the darkness.

"God keep you, Hugh," she whispered into the silence.

Chapter 17

FROM ACROSS THE river Hugh could just make out the low, jagged stones of the parapet of Fort Cornwallis with its Union Jack fluttering languidly above it in the mild after-noon breeze. A sentry's sharp bark carried softly across the water accompanied by the muted fluttering of a military drum. The river was wide here, swift, with the color of churned mud. With Rob's help Hugh had planned to put together a small raft of timbers similar to the ones he had used on that long ago trip to St. Augustine but it seemed wiser to build it downriver where the current could not carry them under the guns of the Fort and a foe who had long ago learned that in this wilderness you shoot first and ask questions later.

Hugh was not anxious to cross the river at all. His disgust for British regulars had not lessened on the long trip from Charleston, and the town of Augusta was under the control of Thomas Brown, a man he was not anxious to meet again. However, the countryside surrounding it was heavily Whig and it was on this interior region that he had set his sights. The hamlet of Augusta would serve well enough for rest and re-equipping. If he could manage to keep his burgeoning Whig sympathies from surfacing, it might even turn out to be pleasant. After so many days sleeping under the trees of the forest, he looked forward to a bed in an inn no matter how uncomfortable.

Crouched in the thickets that grew so luxuriously along the banks, he slapped at the gnats that swarmed around his face and waited for Rob to return from scouting below. The sweat ran in rivulets under his linen shirt, much the worse for wear by now. Even in the shade he could not escape the oppressive heat or the flying insects which seemed drawn to him like a walking side of beef. When he finally caught the light tread of Rob's boots pushing through the overgrown thickets, he rose, filled with relief.

"I had about given you up."

Rob crouched beside him, breathing heavily. "Good news for a change. I found a road and a farmer with a wagon headed for Augusta. He says there is a ferry a few miles away. From what I could gather it is a primitive thing— little more than a flatboat and ropes, but it should serve."

"Do you suppose it is safe? What if we meet some of the men from the Fort?"

"It's a chance we'll have to take. He says it would be insane to try to swim our horses across. By the time we reach the ferry it should be nearly evening and most of the traffic will be gone."

"That's true. But we'd better have some sort of story ready for the military as long as we're walking right into the lion's mouth."

"What do you suggest?"

"Not the truth, that's for certain. We can say we're new arrivals from England who have come to see what the Indian country is like."

"That should do. Unless they become suspicious or we meet someone who knew us back in town."

"We won't stay around long enough for that to happen."

Hugh took one last look at the stubby ramparts of the Fort topping a hill lush with greenery rising high above the river. It was probably unwise to go anywhere near that outpost of British officialdom. Only his longing for a decent bed and a civilized meal led him to take such a risk.

"All right. We may as well get started."

"Look, Papa," Louisa said, leaning out the window of the Culpepper carriage as it rounded the square in front of Christ Church. "They've still not repaired the damage from the siege."

"We were not gone that long, my dear. You cannot expect to see too many changes in the short time we were in Charleston." Beaming, he settled back against the cushions. "My, but it is good to be home. And what a pleasure not to see soldiers everywhere. There were times in Charleston, I confess, when I felt as though I was living in an occupied city."

"But we were."

"Perhaps, but it was a friendly occupation, you must admit that."

Louisa did not answer. Instead she stared over the top of the half-opened leather curtain at the familiar streets and comfortable houses of this city that she loved above all others on earth. Not even London with its vibrancy and glitter, its extremes of poverty and wealth, its excitement, entertainments and shops could replace the affection she felt for these brick and plaster buildings, these sandy streets, these lush trees and shrubs with their heavy tropical flowers. Savannah was home and no matter where she might go, her heart remained fixed on this place.

Even her father was anxious to return to his old haunts. "I am just going to see you inside, my dear, and then I think I shall run around to the Merchant's Exchange and see how trade has been doing in my absence."

Louisa smiled over at him. "And perhaps stop in at the coffeehouse as well?"

"You know me too well. I confess I have missed the pleasant camaraderie of the place even though half the members were in Charleston along with us. You don't mind, do you?"

"Of course not, Papa. I have some people to catch up

with as well. I'll see you for supper."

While Nathan handed down her boxes to the waiting house servants, Louisa walked up the steps to her front door and entered the hall. The servants had done a good job of opening and airing the house, removing the furniture covers and setting up vases all around heaped with flowers from her gardens. She might have just returned from an afternoon's social engagement. It was so good to be home again, she thought as she handed her bonnet to Olana.

"You like to wash you' face and change you' dress, Miz Louisa," the woman said, taking Louisa's shawl from around her shoulders.

"Perhaps I shall, Olana. Can you take my striped dimity out of the press and air it a little. It's warmer here than it was in Charleston."

"I sure will, Miz Louisa. An' you maybe lie down and rest for a while first. You been exertin' you'self too much lately."

"Now don't start acting like a mother hen, Olana. I'm not the least tired. Just a little hot and damp." She started up the stairs with her servant at her heels. "Just to take off some of these petticoats will be sheer bliss. I don't need . . ."

Voices behind her in the hall stayed her steps on the stairs. Louisa looked down and was startled to see two soldiers just entering her front door followed by Ralph Stoakes, wielding his ebony came like a baton. He spotted her standing on the stairs, and swept off his hat.

"Miss Culpepper. I heard you had arrived. Might I have a word with you, ma'am."

Suppressing her annoyance, Louisa answered civilly: "This is a most inopportune time, Sir Ralph. I only just returned from South Carolina and would really prefer to get out of these dusty clothes. Could we make it this evening? For supper, perhaps?"

Ralph Stoakes laid a gloved hand on the newel post and stared up at her. There was something in his face she had not seen before. A severity he usually reserved for others but had never shown her.

"This is not a social call, Miss Culpepper. I am afraid I must insist you see me now. And if your father could join us as well, it would be for the best."

"My father has already left for the Merchant's Exchange. But very well. Since you feel it is so important, I will see you."

She started regally down the stairs. "Olana, please ask Jerral to bring some refreshment to the parlor. What would you like, Sir Ralph? Lemonade, or cherry punch? Or would you prefer tea?"

"Nothing, thank you."

"Well, I must say I am quite dry from the street dust. Bring me some lemonade, Olana, as cool as you can make it. Won't you step this way, Sir Ralph, please."

With an aplomb that masked what she was actually feeling inside, she led the way into the parlor. The long French windows were open and the wild jasmine in the garden beyond filled the room with its heady scent. Louisa beckoned Stoakes to a brocade chair standing before the open window and then took the one opposite, sitting very primly.

Stoakes refused the chair and remained standing as though he was admiring the view, his hands clasped behind his back.

"I must say, Miss Culpepper, that it grieves me to be the person who comes to you on such an errand. You know my feelings for you—I have made them plain in the past. To have to be the one now who—no matter. Duty must come before the heart."

Louisa stared at him, thinking how his tone of voice was in direct contrast to his words. There was something in it which suggested he was almost enjoying having her at a disadvantage. Her contempt for him grew even deeper than before.

He turned away from the window to face her squarely.

"It is my painful duty to inform you, Miss Louisa, that you are under arraignment from this moment."

"What!" She attempted an incredulous laugh but Stoakes had so little humor or lightness about him that she knew well enough that he would not make such a statement unless he meant it. As if he read her mind he went on:

"Please do not attempt to deny your guilt. We impounded the *Restless* the moment she dropped anchor and we now have Captain Jameson in jail. The incriminating letter was discovered hidden in a chest in his cabin."

"What letter? I have no idea what you are talking about."

"It will serve no purpose to make these useless denials. This letter is proof without a doubt that you are secretly in sympathy with the American rebels. Furthermore, you have been passing information to the rebel partisans who then used it to harass our forces. In short, Miss Culpepper, you are a spy."

"This is preposterous. You cannot possibly be speaking seriously. I know Captain Jameson, of course, but I am quite willing to swear on the Bible itself that I sent him no letter bearing my name. Especially one carrying information about the King's forces."

"Ah, but you did send him one bearing the name of 'Oliver' and I am quite certain you recognize the significance of that *nom de plume*. You wrote that letter, Miss Culpepper, for we have an eyewitness who saw you do so. And I am quite certain that when we search your rooms we will find the seal that letter bore. In fact, my soldiers are doing so at this very moment."

Louisa turned away from him, her mind racing. Who? It could not be Jerral. The American officer? But surely he would not be a turncoat. No, for he had left the garden before she ever wrote the letter.

"This is ridiculous," she said in as outraged a voice as she could muster. "I knew that you were insulted when I refused your suit but I never thought you would go to such lengths to gain such a small revenge. Really, it ill becomes you as a gentleman."

He gave her a thin smile. "Clever, my dear, but unfortunately my arresting you has nothing at all to do with my feelings for you. Naturally, I would prefer not to have to do this but duty must take precedence. Being rid of 'Oliver' is worth more than all my tender feelings for you."

He stopped, cocking his head to one side as he observed her with an expression both calculating and cold. "So many things make sense to me now," he went on. "How many times did I inadvertently mention the movement of troops or decisions of policy that were passed along to the enemy?

The attack on Colonel Brown on the Ebeneezer road, for example. It never occurred to me that an innocent conversation with a society miss could have been the source of all our trouble."

Louisa sat primly looking down her nose at him, no longer trying to hide her contempt. "I don't know what you are talking about," she said, more as a refusal to admit guilt than as a protestation of innocence.

Stoakes smiled thinly, indulging her in her little game. "How did you pass along the information you weedled out of all these poor gullible Tories? Sallette would not dare show his face in Savannah and I don't recall you making any forays into the swamps. What was your line of communication? Hugh Sandenny?"

Louisa was betrayed into a moment's surprise but quickly went back to studying her fingernails, not even bothering to answer. She felt certain Stoakes could not know whether or not Hugh was involved and was only baiting her, hoping to find out. A short rap on the door brought her head up and her heart plunged when she saw one of the grenadiers standing there holding her writing box. Stoakes motioned him to set it on the table.

"Found this among the lady's things," the man said as he put it down. With dexterous fingers Stoakes ran over the surface of the box, then lifted the lid and examined the interior. It took him only two minutes to locate the spring that opened a small pocket in the lid where the brass seal bearing an ornately engraved 'O' was hidden.

"Good work," he said, dismissing the man. "Now, Miss Culpepper, if you will just come along with me."

Louisa jumped to her feet, dropping her protestations of innocence. "Really, Sir Ralph, what would it serve? And I to be confined to jail? Do you plan to have me shot at sunrise tomorrow?"

"Spies are customarily hanged."

"Yes, but am I a spy or simply a patriot who longs for her country to be free? Could I not give you my word and stay here in my house on parole as the captured American officers do?"

"That luxury is not usually afforded spies. And, since

these colonies are still under the rule of His Most Sovereign Majesty, George the Third, and you are actively working against him, you most certainly shall be considered a spy. It will save us both a lot of trouble if you come along quietly."

She saw she would get nowhere with him. And yet she could not believe that she had lost the power to move him.

"But, Sir Ralph, what have you to gain by making a public spectacle of me? If you prevent me from acting as Oliver, I assure you someone else will be ready to take my place. You will never be rid of him, you know. And think how ridiculous it will make you look when everyone knows a mere woman led you such a dance for so long."

"That is my concern. You may take a few clothes with you and your woman may come as well. That much I will grant you out of the affection I still feel for you."

"You are too kind."

All at once Louisa's knees began to tremble so that she had to lower herself uneasily back onto the chair. "Must my father know," she asked, speaking very quietly.

"He is to accompany you. At this moment two of my men are seeking him at the Merchant's Exchange. You will find him waiting for you when we finally arrive at our destination."

"Oh, no. That is too cruel. He knows nothing of this."

"Perhaps not. But his is guilt by association. I remember saying once before that he should have exercised a father's stern hand on his willful daughter. Such laxness only leads to trouble."

Louisa glared at him. For whatever reason—and it could be as mundane a one as wanting the use of her house— Stoakes was determined to put both her and her father in jail. She could still not believe he would actually execute her but even that might not be past him. For herself she did not mind disgrace, imprisonment, even death. But for her father, who had never borne anyone any ill will . . .

"I trust you are now beginning to regret your impulsive shenanigans," Ralph said in his prim voice.

"Never!" she cried, her eyes finally betraying the disgust and anger she felt for him. "We will win, in spite of people

like of you. These colonies will be free and independent
and if anything I have done helps to make them so, then
my life will have been worthwhile, even though I may lose
it."

"Very noble. This is the kind of mischief that occurs
when young ladies are encouraged to think for themselves.
Come along, Louisa. I have wasted enough time here."

With a sinking heart Louisa followed him into the hall
where Olana, her eyes enormous in her dark face, waited.
Louisa directed her to go upstairs and quickly put a few
things in a valise while she stood beside Stoakes who refused
to allow her out of his sight. When they left the house there
were already a few people clustered around the doorway,
mouths gaping as she was led to the carriage, murmuring
to themselves as she passed. She barely noticed them. On
the long trek to the jail, her thoughts churned around only
one question:

Who could have watched her write that letter?

"I won't do it!" Arabia cried, staring down at the quill
and paper lying on the table before her. "You can't make
me do it. It's a cracked idea anyway. He'd never believe
it."

She could feel the firm pressure of Stoakes' hand on her
shoulder, pushing her down into the chair. Everything in
her wanted to get up and run out of the door, down the
stairs, back to the harbor. Anyplace but here. Yet she knew
she could not move. He would never allow her to.

"You'll do as I say, Arabia. Come now, you've done your
work very well so far and this last step is all that's needed
to complete our bargain. Pick up the pen and write what I
tell you. We're going to need three copies and I don't have
all day."

"You never said I would have to do anything like this.
"I've already helped you enough. Besides, Hugh would
never believe anything I wrote. He'd probably not even read
the letter once he knew it was from me."

"Ah, but it won't be from you. It will be from Louisa.
You know how to copy her signature, you told me so yourself. That's all you have to do now."

"But I don't write well. I never had the schooling she did. He'll never believe it."

"We are wasting time," Stoakes said grimly, digging his fingers into the soft flesh of her shoulder. "You are as involved in this now as Louisa herself. If you do not wish to be shot along with her you will pick up that quill at once."

Arabia lunged out of his grip, darting to the other side of the room and glaring angrily at him from across the table. "You can't shoot me. You have no cause. And even if you did, I wouldn't care. Maybe then I'd get a little peace."

He realized his mistake at once. "Now, Arabia," he said soothingly, walking around the table to take her hand and lead her back to her seat. "Remember the hatred you bear Louisa Culpepper. Remember how she took the man you adore away from you and how he willingly followed her. They have both done you a terrible injury. This little task I am asking you to perform is the best, perhaps the only, revenge you shall ever have upon the two of them."

He could see his words hit home. Like someone in a trance Arabia moved back to her chair and picked up the quill.

"But he'll know it's not her handwriting," she said. It was almost more of a question than a statement. Stoakes laid both hands on her shoulders, squeezing them gently and leaning over her to whisper soothingly:

"Does he recognize her handwriting? How many times can he have seen it? Not many, I should think. Then too, she will be writing him from jail with the threat of execution hanging over her. Under such circumstances one's handwriting is not likely to be as precise as usual. Don't you agree?"

For a long moment Arabia's dark eyes bored up into his cold, pale ones. Then, turning back to the paper, she dipped the point of the quill in the inkwell.

It was nearly dusk when Hugh and Rob finally walked their weary horses into the main thoroughfare that ran through the village of Augusta. Dim pinpricks of light wavered behind the thick windowpanes of the low log buildings. A faded sign squawking on rusted hinges above a group of men and horses announced the main hostelry of the town and it was there that Hugh and Rob headed. The crowd was interesting to Hugh because of the number of Indians on its outskirts, their feathers and turbans bright splashes of color in the gathering dusk.

Tying their horses to the post, they pushed their way inside. At the far end of the room a flabby man in a dirty smock worked behind a caged bar. Hugh, assuming this was the owner, started across to him but within only a few steps was brought up short by a tiny woman in a starched mobcap who stepped into his path.

"'Evenin', gentl'men. Pray what would you be wantin'?"

Hugh stopped, looking down into a pair of the keenest green eyes he had ever seen.

"Good evening, ma'am. Have I the honor of addressing the proprietor of this worthy establishment?"

"If you mean by all that am I the owner, well, that's my husband Jake, over there behind the bar. He's busy drawin' ale for you fellers so he leaves me to handle the details. What will it be?"

"A bed," Rob breathed.

"And a meal," Hugh quickly added.

"This way then," she said moving back to a tiny wooden table near the door and pulling out a worn logbook from a drawer underneath. Running a pudgy finger down the scribbled inkblots, she made a clucking noise with her tongue.

"We be pretty full up but you can share a bed with two other fellers, if you've a mind. Be a little close, but that's neither here nor there. As to supper, we've a pigeon pie and a syllabub still left to serve. Nothin' more though so if'n its fancier fare you'll be wantin', you'll have to seek elsewhere."

"And where is elsewhere?" Rob said over Hugh's shoulder.

"Unless you're invited by Colonel Brown up to the White House there an't no elsewhere."

"This sounds fine," Hugh said quickly. "What do we owe you for it?"

"One and fourteen, for lodging and supper. Two, if breakfast. To be paid in full now.

"That's a high price for poor fare," Hugh muttered, nevertheless reaching for his purse.

"You can go elsewhere," Mrs. Jake said, peering at him from under the ruffle of her cap. "It's neither here nor there to me."

"We'll stay." Hugh counted out the coins. "Anything is better than spending another night in the woods."

They followed her upstairs to a long narrow room with three full-sized beds along one wall. For a primitive public room, obviously occupied by several people, it was remarkably neat and clean, giving Hugh hope that the sheets would not be too damp or the bed too flea-infested.

After brushing the dust from their clothes and washing some of the grime from their faces, the two men hurried back to the dining room to see if Mistress Jake's pigeon pie was as satisfying as her housekeeping.

They took their place at the one long table, nearly empty by this hour, and greedily dug into the whole pie that was put before them. Hugh had barely broken the pastry with his knife when a familiar voice arrested his hand in midair.

"I thought I recollected you. Saw you from the barroom next door."

The speaker was a man standing in the doorway, a bottle in his hand. The moment Hugh looked up and saw his lean face and lanky form he recognized him. It took a moment more to recall his name.

"Morrel Curry!" he exclaimed, rising to extend his hand. Curry gave him a firm clasp with one hand and with the other set the squat green bottle on the table. Swinging one leg across the seat of a chair, he sat opposite Hugh.

"Go on with your supper. Mrs. Jake's pie is none so bad when it's hot but somethin' gets lost as it cools down. You'll join me in a dram?"

"We'd welcome it. What have you got there? Rum?"

"Blackjack brandy, smuggled off'n a schooner from Jamaica. Good to see you again, Sandenny."

"It's good to see you as well," Hugh answered between mouthfuls of the pie. "This is Rob Earing, an old friend from England."

At Rob's quizzical look he went on. "Morrel is a scout

for Colonel Brown. We went on a mission together once when I was still in Savannah."

"What on earth you doing this far west?" Morrel asked. "Not still working for that fellow who always looks like he smells something rotten, are you? What was his name? Stoakes?"

"Stoakes, yes. And no, I'm not working for him. Just doing a little wandering on my own. I thought I'd see what the frontier is really like. What brings you here?"

"Oh, the same. Scouting for Colonel Brown out of Fort Cornwallis. You picked a rare time to go travelin'. The country west of Augusta is rabid with rebels and beyond that, it's all Cherokee. To the south is pure Creek. Go out there explorin' and you're like to leave your scalp behind."

"Is it that bad? I thought the savages were on our side."

"An Indian don't know no side but his own. Can't trust one no further than you can throw an axe."

The hardness on Curry's face brought vividly back to Hugh that terrible scene in his sister's house so long ago.

"Did you find your nieces?" he asked softly.

"No."

His eyes said it all. Hugh quickly motioned to a Negro potboy to bring them three pewter cups and changed the subject to a less painful one. For nearly an hour they lingered at the table. With a little encouragement and between long draughts of the blackjack, Morrel regaled them with descriptions of Colonel Brown's latest forays into Whig territory as Hugh and Rob continued to stuff themselves on the pie and syllabub. As the evening wore on they began to get not a little drunk over endless discussions of the safest way to explore the mountain country to the west. By the time the bottle was finished Curry was ready to take them over to the Fort where they would be certain to find good company, another bottle and probably a game of cards or dice. On the excuse that they were too exhausted for anything but sleep, Hugh and Rob managed to beg off and head upstairs.

"That was a little too close," Rob whispered as they entered the long room with its row of beds, its quiet punctuated by the snores of several men already asleep.

"He's safe enough," Hugh whispered back. "But I was not anxious to go into Fort Cornwallis with him. There's certain to be someone there who knows of me, even in a godforsaken outpost like this."

Rob sat gingerly down on the edge of the bed, shoving a hump in the middle over to one side.

"God's blood, I wish we had this to ourselves. I feel like a piece of pickled beef in a keg." He pulled off one boot. "Do you think we can avoid the Fort tomorrow?"

"We'll just have to say that we decided to move on without waiting here."

"Just as I was beginning to enjoy civilization again."

"It can't be helped. If we linger around Augusta there's no way we can avoid being drawn to the Fort."

Hugh had just begun pulling at one of his boots when there was a sharp rap on the door frame. Looking up he saw Curry leaning wobbily against the wall for support.

"Almost forgot," he muttered, then quickly lowered his voice at the irritated shushing that came from one of the beds.

"Almost forgot," he whispered loudly. "Got a letter for you, Sandenny. 'Twas given me by a sergeant at the Council House afore I left Savannah."

Hugh stared at him. "A letter?" Who on earth could possibly be writing him here from Savannah? Who would even know he was in Augusta?"

"Yeah. Said 'twas given him by Thomas Culpepper, askin' if he knew of anyone comin' west to pass it along. Never thought I'd get a chance to deliver it."

He handed Hugh a greasy, much mangled piece of paper in which the wax seal was the only thing left intact.

"I'm grateful to you," Hugh said, trying to remember if he had told Louisa where he was headed. If so . . .

His heart missed a beat. What if this was from Louisa herself? He moved to the window at the far end of the room where a candle burned desolately in a tin holder. Leaning close to the flame, he broke the seal and strained to decipher the marks on the paper. Curry, restraining his curiosity, murmured, "I guess I'll be goin' along then."

The paper was so creased and the ink so faded that Hugh

could barely make out the words. But the signature was enough to cause him to forget everyone else in the room—the low snoring, the coughs, and Rob sitting with one boot poised in his hand, watching him intently.

At Hugh's breathless exclamation, Rob moved to peer over his shoulder.

"What's in it?"

"I can't believe it! By God..."

"Has something happened?"

"It's from Louisa. She's been arrested."

Rob laughed quietly. "That's absurd. You must be mistaken."

"She says so, right here. That villain Stoakes has arrested her and her father, accusing them of being spies for the rebels. She says he intends to have her executed."

"Oh, come now, Hugh. Not even Stoakes would do that. I'll wager this paper is false. It's probably not from Louisa at all. Stoakes is using it to try to lure you back to Savannah. Or it may be Tarleton. One of them, though."

Hugh bent closer to the page. The handwriting looked familiar but was it Louisa's? He could not be certain. There was only one way to find out.

"I'll have to go to her."

"That's insane!" Rob cried, hissing under his breath. "Think, Hugh. This could be a trap. You'd be doing exactly what they want you to."

"No. Louisa would never write me like this if she were not really in trouble. If she says she's been arrested, then it must be true."

"But you can't be sure she even wrote this letter. Anyone could have."

"It looks like her handwriting and it's certainly her seal. Besides, how will I ever know unless I go back. And the thought that I might not be there when she really needs me is too terrible to bear. I can't take that chance, Rob."

"Let me see that letter."

"No. It's mine and it's private. Will you go with me? You don't have to if you've a mind to stay here. I'll understand. You could push on west without me or wait in Augusta until I return."

Rob made a soft clucking sound with his tongue. "Do you think I'd let you go back into what is most likely some kind of trap without me? No. We'll go together or not at all."

There was a rumble on the nearest bed as its occupant heaved himself over on his side.

"Goddammit! If'n you two fellers want to have an argument then go downstairs," he yelled. "It's hard enough to sleep in this here cattlebarn!"

Hugh glared at the man then folded the paper to put away.

"I trust we can at least wait until morning," Rob whispered seeing his vision of a civilized bed fading away.

"All right," Hugh whispered back. "Though I doubt I'll get much sleep now."

Chapter 18

THE SHARP BARK of the sentries from the Council House
across the street brought Louisa to her feet. Jumping up on
the cot she strained to peer through the jail house window.
Though the sun was beginning to come out, the stones of
the prison still held the coolness of the night before and she
shivered through the thin fabric of her dress.

"Here, Miz Louisa," Olana said, seeing her mistress rubbing her arms for warmth. "Yo' wrap this blanket around
yo'self. Won't do nobody no good for yo' to take the ague
and all, here in this awful place."

Without arguing, Louisa drew the thin flannel around
her shoulders and went back to staring across the street.
There was a lot of movement over there but it might be
only the daily routine of the guard being replaced. The early
morning crowd in the street seemed larger than usual and
for one terrible moment she feared an execution was about
to take place. This would be the right time for it.

Behind her Olana fussed with the sparse furnishings of

the cell, arranging the bedding on the other cot and muttering under her breath:

"Disgrace, that what it is! Disgrace that a white lady like yo'self be put in such a place. I say it from the first and I say it still. It a disgrace!"

"Hush, Olana," Louisa cried. "I want to hear what they're saying."

"Can't be sayin' nothin' no lady should ought to hear. Dat no-count Mr. Stoakes, he ought to be fried in oil to put a lady in a place like this for thieves and no-goods."

"Olana, please! Oh, what's the use. They're only re-placing the guard."

Desolately she stepped down and huddled on the cot with the blanket around her. "What are we going to do, Olana? It's bad enough to be under house arrest but this—this is just too awful. And my poor Papa. I'm so worried about him."

"You ought to worry 'bout yo'self. How we goin' to get you out of here?"

"No. I'm strong and I knew what I was doing when I took the risk. But Papa is innocent. He knew nothing about my helping the rebels and would not have condoned it if he had. Why does Sir Ralph want to make him suffer for my wrong-doing? It's too hard a punishment."

Olana sat down beside her mistress and smoothed back her hair as she had done many times when Louisa was a young girl.

"He only tryin' to hurt you with yo' Pa. Don't you see? He know how it make it so much more bad for you to be worryin' 'bout your Papa. That no-count white man!"

"Well, he's certainly succeeded," Louisa said, rubbing dejectedly at her forehead. "And there's nothing I can do to stop him. Nothing."

"Yes, there is. You get yo'self up now and wash that pretty face and let Olana comb yo' hair nice. When that no-count Stoakes come, yo' stand with yo' head high and act like he dirt under yo' pretty feet. Which he be, for sure."

Louisa smiled up at her. "I can do that well enough but I don't see how it will help Papa."

"Least he won't know how he gots to yo' and that's somethin'!"

An hour later she sat on the cot waiting for Stoakes' usual morning visit ruminating as she had every day over whether or not it was folly or true patriotism that had brought her here. Her role as a spy called "Oliver" had been so easy for so long that she had probably grown too sure of herself and maybe even a little careless. Learning the movements of the British was not difficult at all and once Robert Sallette had worked out a way to send messages inside the cabbage palm hearts the system had gone perfectly. Writing the broadsides was easy—it was Robert who saw that they were printed and distributed. And it was one of Robert's men who drove the load of palm hearts and alligator steaks that served as a means of exchanging notes regularly into Savannah to her house.

But where had she slipped up? Who had seen her write that note in the garden of Cecily's house in Charleston and how had Ralph Stoakes learned it was aboard the *Restless?* Had she failed her country and her friends through carelessness? Had her love for an Englishman blinded her to a traitor's presence somewhere in the crowd of pleasant admirers who surrounded her? She would give a deal to know.

And her father, loyal King's man that he was, would he ever forgive her for siding with the rebels? But of course, they were not really "rebels." They were Americans who sought only self-rule for their own country. And they were the people she had known and respected all her life. Never would she willingly have betrayed them.

The sudden turning of a key in the door interrupted her thoughts. As she heard the voices of the guard outside she was grateful she had followed Olana's advice and made herself as presentable as possible. When Ralph Stoakes walked in she met him with the regal dignity of a queen.

"Where is my father?" she demanded before Stoakes could get out his intended polite greeting. He gave her a short bow and answered primly:

"I have told you before he is lying in a cell such as this just down the hall."

"I don't believe you. What have you done with him? Why can't I see him?"

"Up until now that has been quite impossible. However, I have some good news for you. You will both be allowed out into the yard for exercise later this morning and you are free to talk with him as you wish."

Louisa slumped visibly. She had longed to see her father for so long that the thought of finally being with him again made her knees feel weak and she had to reach out a hand to the wall to steady herself.

"That's something, at least," she said, struggling to regain the strength she had lost. "But you've no right to bring him to this place. He's committed no crime. You are only trying to punish him for my mistakes."

Stoakes motioned her to sit while he stood with his arms folded across his chest, watching her closely. She remained defiantly standing while he went on.

"I don't see why you should blame me for something which you yourself brought about. Could you have been so naive as to think your father would escape any repercussions for your spying? I would have thought better of your reasoning, my dear."

"I thought I was dealing with gentlemen."

"Sallette—a gentleman? Bosh! I've no doubt that if you were in his hands as a spy for the Crown both you and your father would be dead by now."

"That's not true. It only shows how little you know about him and about all rebels."

Stoakes dusted a lace handkerchief across the thin bedding on the other cot and sat down, crossing his silk hosed legs.

"I did not come here to discuss the characteristics of rebels. Have you reconsidered my offer? It still stands."

"Never," Louisa snapped, glaring at him. "I will never betray my friends. Nor do I have any idea where Hugh Sandenny is. I told you that from the first and I meant it."

"My dear Louisa, I don't think you quite realize what a dangerous position you are in. I admit it is not customary for a woman to face execution but in wartime it is not unheard of. It might well happen to you."

"Let it. I would never betray my friends to save my own life. Others have died for their country. I can do so too, if I must."

"And your father?"

Louisa flinched under his cold, blue eyes. "You wouldn't! You wouldn't dare."

"Oh, but I would. All I have to do is convince the Council that he is as guilty as you yourself and the sentence is certain to be carried out against both of you."

"But he is innocent."

"So you say. I rather tend to think that a woman alone could not have put such a plan into operation, much less carry it out unaided. You would have to have help. Not only from your father but from others as well. Hugh Sandenny, for one."

"That's really what this is all about, isn't it," Louisa said bitterly. "You want to destroy Hugh through me and my father."

"I am also anxious to be done with 'Oliver,' who has become a trifle too much of an irritant. Come now, isn't it worth helping me if it means forgiveness for you and your dear Papa?"

She sank down on the cot. "What would happen to us if I did help you?"

"Exile. You would have to leave Georgia, probably for the West Indies. Possibly England. But certainly somewhere outside the Colonies."

For a long moment she was silent. "I'll consider it," she said softly. "I'll give you my answer tomorrow."

"Please do not wait too long, my dear, or you might well run out of time. If I do not have your answer by tomorrow I shall be forced to go before the Council with these charges. After that I cannot guarantee what will happen."

"In the morning."

Rising, he reached for her hand and raised it to his lips, ignoring the way she shrank from his touch.

"Until tomorrow, then."

He was halfway out the door when Louisa jumped up. "Did you really mean it when you said I would see my father today?"

Looking back he gave her a thin smile and walked out the door, slamming it behind him.

She waited, filled with anxiety, all morning until the sun was almost at its noon height. Then a guard appeared to open her door and lead her outside into the walled courtyard of the prison. Across the yard she saw the pudgy figure of a man whom at first she did not recognize. Then with a cry she flew into his arms. Thomas Culpepper, looking strangely unkempt and confused, held his daughter tightly, clinging to her for the strength that was in her. Then he pulled out a gray handkerchief and wiped at the tears that ran down her cheeks.

"Papa, I'm so sorry," Louisa sobbed.

"It's all right, my child."

"How have they treated you? Has it been too bad?"

"Not so bad. Not what I am used to, of course, but it could be worse. Now that I see you and hold you again, everything seems so much better. Come and walk with me. It is so pleasant to be out in the sunshine again. Dry your eyes now and hold up your head bravely."

They stayed together nearly an hour before the guard appeared to lead them back inside. Louisa returned to her tiny cell more distressed than ever, for though her father seemed in decent health and had not been physically abused, something in his mind and spirit had suffered. He had lost the ebullient good nature he had always possessed and seemed confused and shaken to the core by the abrupt change in his fortunes.

She sank onto the cot with her head in her hands, thinking again of Stoakes' offer, of Hugh's face and strong arms, of her own stubbornness in helping Sallette without ever considering what would become of Thomas Culpepper if she were caught.

"It's my own fault," she moaned. "I'll have to give in. I'll have to agree to his conditions. There is no other way."

It seemed to Arabia that the noise in the low-ceilinged taproom of Tondee's Tavern was more strident than ever. A courier had ridden into Savannah that afternoon with the news from Charleston of another skirmish in which Tarleton's Legionnaires had scattered the rebels like chaff before the wind. It was all that was needed as an excuse to celebrate and all the taverns had been packed earlier than usual with boisterous revelers. Smoke filled the rooms like a fog off the river, making it difficult for her to breathe as she carried innumerable trays back and forth from the kitchen to the public rooms. The clatter of wooden and earthenware dishes, the clanking of pewter tankards on the hard oak tables, the frequent outbursts of raucous laughter, the closeness of the fetid air, the loud choruses of "The Volunteers of Augusta," all the hilarity was so in contrast to the heaviness of her own heart that it left her with a pounding headache.

She had just entered the kitchen bearing a large tray heaped with dirty trenchers and cups when Mrs. Tondee appeared at her heels, long rivulets of perspiration streaming from under her mobcap.

"Where have you been, girl," she scolded. "Three times those officers in the upstairs supper room have sent for their meal and I know it's been ready this half hour. Why haven't you carried it up as I told you?"

Arabia set the heavy tray on the table and leaned against the edge for support.

"Let one of the potboys carry it up to them."

"I can't spare a potboy," Mrs. Tondee answered, her voice rising in irritation. "Besides, it's your job. Get to it."

Arabia turned to face her employer, her eyes blazing.

"I won't!"

The pink blotches on Mrs. Tondee's face stood out under the white paste she habitually wore. "What do you mean, you won't?" she spluttered.

"I won't go up there again. It's bad enough being pawed half to death in the public rooms. Going upstairs alone with those officers is asking for trouble. They've only one thing on their minds and it isn't their supper. They were already half-drunk the first time I served them and it was only by God's good grace that I was able to get out of there without my skirts thrown over my head."

"Now look here, girl—"

"No! You look here, Mrs. Tondee. I have been serving you for a long time and I've always been loyal and done what you asked. But I won't be put at the mercy of a lot of drunken louts no matter how much they call themselves 'gentleman.' Let Toby serve them."

"Just who do you think you're talking to?"

Angrily Arabia untied the strings of her apron and balled it up in her hands.

"I don't care if you was the archangel Gabriel hisself tellin' me to go up there. I won't go!"

Throwing the apron on the cluttered table, she stalked to the door that gave off onto a narrow alley and garden behind the tavern, disappearing into the dark.

"Go after her," Mrs. Tondee demanded of the cook, Margery, who had been standing by the hearth listening to the whole scene.

"Mayhap she's right not to go up there alone, Mistress," Margery said gently as she stirred a wooden ladle around an iron cookpot. "Give her a few minutes and she'll be back as ready as ever."

Mrs. Tondee laid her hands on her ample hips and sighed.

"Well, perhaps you're right," she said, pursing her lips and staring at the empty darkness of the doorway. "But if she sulks longer than five minutes, you go after her. That's an order!"

Margery nodded and bent over her pot while Mrs. Tondee moved back into the smoky taproom. From outside Arabia saw her leave then walked down the dark alley away from the lighted kitchen where she leaned against the tall boards of a high fence, wiping at her sticky skin with the edge of her overskirt. It was cooler out here and quieter. After her angry outburst she felt empty and drained, weary beyond measure. Although she would never admit it to Mrs. Tondee, she knew well enough the real reason she refused to serve those drunken officers. It was too reminiscent of the first time she met Hugh and reminded her too poignantly that she no longer had anyone to protect her from such situations. The thought brought stinging tears to her eyes and she leaned against the rough boards, her crying choked in her throat, as she struggled not to give way to it. It hurt her so much to think how she missed him.

"Arabia!"

She was so absorbed in her feelings that at first she failed to hear the thin whisper at the end of the alley.

"Arabia," it came again.

Her head shot up as she turned toward the black void at the end of the fence.

"Arabia, come down here."

"Who is it?"

She strained to make out a shape in the darkness.

"It's me, Hugh. Don't cry out! Come down this way."

Arabia caught back a gasp. Hugh! It couldn't be. Sidling along the wooden fence, she eased her way to the end. As she drew nearer she could make out the figure of a man swathed in a long cape, a battered round hat on his head. With every nerve tingling she recognized the height, the set of his shoulders. She moved slowly nearer, stopping before she was close enough to reach out her hand and touch him, straining to see into his face.

"It's me, right enough," Hugh whispered. "I've been waiting here since nightfall, hoping to see you."

"What are you doing here? You're crazy to be in Savannah."

"That's not a very warm welcome."

"It's as warm as you're going to get." Deliberately she held herself back though she longed to throw herself into his arms. Since she refused to come any closer, he took a few steps toward her, standing just inside the fence and bending over her.

"Arabia, I need your help."

"Go away. It's not safe for you here. Don't you know that Tondee's is full of Englishmen right at this moment. And the Royal Governor has a mittimus out against you. I saw it myself."

"I know. But I had to come." He tried to lay his hand on her arm but she shrank from him. "You are the only person in this town I can turn to. Don't send me away, Arabia. For the sake of our friendship."

"I never meant anything to you," she said bitterly. The shadows of his lean face grew more distinct in the amber light as a weak moon came from behind a cloud. Underneath his cloak she glimpsed a woodsman's fringed buckskin shirt.

That and the battered old hat were so unlike the natty man she had known before that even now she was almost afraid someone was trying to trick her.

"That's not true. You meant a great deal to me."

"Lies. Always lies. Go away. I don't want to help you ever again."

In spite of her harsh words she made no effort to turn back to the safety of the house. Encouraged by that, Hugh drew closer to her though he did not attempt to touch her.

"I know you are still hurt and angry with me, Arabia, but believe me, I never meant to hurt you. I gave you as much of myself as I could. If the situation were not so desperate now I would not ask anything of you again. But it *is* desperate and there is no one else."

She struggled not to look into his eyes but could not resist being drawn to them. She tilted her face upward, her voluptuous lips slightly parted, her large eyes liquid in the moonlight, her anger wavering.

"Oh, Hugh," she cried, and fell soundlessly into his arms. He held her close to him, smoothing back her hair, lightly kissing her forehead.

"Arabia, you've helped me before. Help me now. Help me save Louisa."

She stiffened suddenly and pulled away, though he gripped her arms tightly.

"I should have known."

"Don't go, please," he cried, holding on to her arms. She struggled against him, inching her way toward the kitchen.

"Listen, Arabia. Louisa is going to be executed unless I can somehow get her out of the town. You can't just stand by and let that happen. She has always been kind to you and she doesn't deserve this."

"She does. She's a spy and spies deserve to be shot. I don't care what happens to her."

"But I do. Do this for me if not for her."

"That's even more reason why I should not help you. I hate her for taking you away from me. It was always like that. She gets everything and I get nothing. Let her die. I'm glad of it."

"Arabia," Hugh said more gently, "people cannot force their hearts to act the way they want. It's true I love Louisa but I care for you too."

"It's not the same."

"No, it's not. But I never tried to pretend that it was. I was honest with you, wasn't I? Please, out of friendship's sake now, if not out of love, help me to save her."

He had never asked anything of her before, certainly not with such sincerity. Arabia hesitated, calculating, standing quietly for a moment. If she gave him away now, he was certain to be shot along with Louisa.

"Even if I wanted to help you, I don't know how. There is nothing I can do."

Hugh's fingers dug into the soft flesh of her arm. "Yes, there is. Tell me where she is being held, then help me find a way to get her out. I know she's not under house arrest because I've watched her home long enough to be certain she's not there."

"She was there, at first. Then Sir Ralph had her moved along with her father."

"Where?"

"To the old prison opposite the Council House," she lied.

He bent closer to peer into her face. "Are you certain? I watched there too and could tell nothing."

"That's because there are so many others there as well. Sir Ralph thought the new jail would be the most obvious so he put her in the old one."

"That dank, fetid place. Poor Louisa. And poor Mr. Culpepper. I hope they haven't already come down with jail fever."

"I haven't heard it."

"Arabia, how can I get her out? Is it really possible that Stoakes means to execute her? Do you have any idea when?"

"It is not beyond him, by any means," Arabia answered, rubbing at her bruised flesh. "I don't know what he plans but I could probably find out and let you know."

"Is there any way we can save her?"

She shrugged. "Where there are men there is always a chance for bribery. But it would take a lot."

"I'll get the money somehow. If you can make the arrangements, I'll find the means."

Once again he leaned closer to her, his breath soft on her cheek. "I make no promises," Arabia said sullenly, as her flesh began to come alive at the nearness of his body.

Gently Hugh tipped her chin up and kissed her warm, full lips. "I'll be grateful to you forever, my dear."

"What do I get from this? To stand by and watch while you set off with Miss Louisa for a life in some peaceful haven? You ask a lot of me, Hugh Sandenny."

Hugh dropped his hands and stepped away, still speaking in a soft whisper.

"I have nothing to offer a lady like Louisa now. I'm an outlaw and an outcast, at least until this rebellion is resolved. I don't know where she will go but I shall strike out for the western frontier. If you still want to go with me, then..."

"You'd take me?"

He did not answer at first. Then he gave her a thin smile. "Yes. If you want to go."

The bright light from the kitchen was suddenly obscured as Margery's ample bulk filled the doorway. "Arabia," she called. "Ye'd better be gettin' back or Mrs. Tondee's goin' to be comin' after ye."

Shrinking back into the darkness, Hugh hid his face under the brim of his hat. Quickly stepping in front of him, Arabia called:

"I'm coming. Tell her I'll be right there. I was just in the necessary house."

Margery waved and waddled back inside the kitchen.

"Go now," Arabia whispered. "Don't come here again. I'll meet you tomorrow night. Where are you staying?"

"I don't want you to know that. It could be dangerous for you. I'll meet you near the old dueling ground around midnight. Will you be able to get there?"

"Don't worry about me. I know my way around this town, even at midnight."

With a quick, impulsive gesture, he bent and kissed her hand. "Thank you, Arabia. Thank you with all my heart."

"Take care..."

He melted into the darkness. Arabia strained to see the dark outline of his body as long as she dared, then turned and walked back toward the kitchen, her heart only slightly less heavy than it had been when she came out earlier.

Twenty-four hours later, Arabia stood under the eaves of General McIntosh's stables, looking diagonally across to where a sentry stood leaning on his long rifle in bored lethargy by the old burying ground gate. Down the street she could just hear the voice of the watchman crying the hour of midnight. The General's house was dark and quietly tucked up for sleep—a disappointment since she had hoped perhaps a late night party there would make it easier for her to slip by the sentry. Getting here had been no problem. Swathed in the folds of a long, dark blue cloak, the hood pulled down to obscure her face, she had slipped along the quiet, dark streets, sliding from one darkened doorway to another in order to avoid any late night wanderers. Knowing the city as she did, it had been a simple matter to get this far undetected. Getting past this sentry might prove more difficult.

There was nothing to do but wait, even though it increased the possibility that Hugh might think she wasn't coming and leave without seeing her. She fought down her anxiety as the moments slipped by and the sentry leaned against the wall, whistling quietly to himself. Then, just as she was desperately trying to think of a way to distract him, fortune came to her aid in the form of a drunken old tanner, his clothes reeking of his occupation, who came wobbling down the street singing at the top of his voice and waving about a bottle of black-strap. He stopped on the other side of the gate nearly ten yards away and fell with a thud on an empty keg.

"Here, now," the sentry called. "You can't stay there. Get along with you."

The tanner waved his bottle in the guard's direction. "Jus' havin' a rest," he cried. "S'death, can't a man have a rest when he needs it. Come and share this wi' me. Mayhap it'll make it worth it to you to let me have a little rest."

Though the soldier looked longingly at the bottle, he stayed at his post.

"Odd's blood, if I was to get any closer to you, the fumes

would kill me. Throw that bottle over this way."

"Oh, no, my good sir," the tanner said, wobbling about on the keg. "You want it, you come and get it."

With a sudden clatter he fell off the keg, the bottle clanging on the cobbles while tanner and barrel went over in a heap.

Muttering curses to himself, the sentry moved to where the man lay sprawled on the street, still blaring out the verses of his song. Stepping around him, he searched for the black-strap bottle. Behind him, Arabia slipped unnoticed through the open gate and outside the town. She looked back long enough to see the sentry bend to pick up the bottle, and nudge the tanner with his boot. Then she was gone, swallowed by the darkness of the woods.

It was only a short distance to the old burying ground and beyond that to the dueling field but the overhanging trees, the tilted headstones and the thick marsh grass gave a gloomy desolate aspect to the dark path. By the time she reached the open plot of the dueling ground, coppered by the thin moonlight, she was almost eager to see another human form. Searching the darkness, she strained for some sign of Hugh waiting there for her.

She heard his low whisper before she saw him step from behind the thick trunk of a moss-hung oak. Standing for a moment, she clasped her cloak tightly around her face before she moved over to where he stood.

"I'm late," she whispered. "Had a difficult time getting past the sentry. I'd be there yet if it hadn't been for some drunken rustic who happened along."

"I know," Hugh answered softly beside her. "That was Rob. We thought you might get held up so he was waiting to cause a diversion. It must have worked."

Arabia's eyes widened in surprise. "That was Rob? I'd never have known it. Yes, it worked very well."

"Do you have some information for me?"

She hesitated. "Yes. Not much, but enough to help you get what you want. It's here," she said, reaching inside her cloak for a folded piece of paper. Carefully she opened it up. "It's too dark here to see. Come a little out into the moonlight."

Eagerly Hugh reached for the paper and stepped out of the shadow of the tree's overhanging branches. Kneeling on the ground, he held the paper up to allow the moonlight to fall upon it, turning it every way in an attempt to make out the writing.

"What does it say?" he asked Arabia who had stepped up behind him. "It's too dark to read."

"Have you any kind of light? A lantern, perhaps?"

"No. You'll have to tell me what's in it."

"It's too complicated. The young private who gave it to me was very specific about what had to be done. Here, I've brought the stub of a candle with me and a flint. You light it and I'll hold my cloak up thus, to hide the light."

"I don't know," Hugh said, looking around. "This is a little too out in the open—"

"And who is watching, pray? No one knows you're in Savannah. We'll only light it long enough for you to read the letter and send back instructions."

Moving back to the oak tree, Hugh reluctantly took the flint and struggled with it until he got a thin flame. He put the light to the candle, then knelt to hold it up to the letter while Arabia made a wide arch with her cloak. He was so intent on reading the carelessly scrawled words that he did not hear the soft scrambling noises around him. When he looked up he saw that Arabia had stepped away and her cloak was hanging limply over her shoulders. The sound of running feet was almost upon them.

"What—?" Hugh said, scrambling to his feet and reaching for his sword. It was half out of the scabbard when his arms were gripped and he was pulled nearly off his feet. Suddenly soldiers were everywhere, pinioning his arms behind him, gripping him ever tighter as he struggled wildly against them. Lanterns appeared, casting a ghostly glow to the dangling Spanish moss trailing the oak's limbs. Then, materializing out of the darkness, Ralph Stoakes stood facing him, a sardonic smile on his lips.

"So, Mr. Sandenny. At last justice will be served."

Hugh looked from his smug grin to Arabia standing behind him, her face gaunt in the moonlight.

"You did very well, Miss Tillman," Stoakes said, as if

to answer the question in Hugh's eyes. "Very well, indeed. Your service to the King will not be forgotten."

With a small groan, Arabia turned away, unable to look at Hugh.

"Why?" he asked though he knew the answer well enough. Her anger at him, her hatred and resentment toward Louisa— he should have known they would be stronger than any lingering sentiment she might still have for him.

"You are under arrest, Hugo St. Dennis," Stoakes said officially. "For the murder of Pelham Stoakes in an illegal duel and for insubordination and desertion in the service of your King. You will be punished accordingly. Take him to jail."

The order was brisk and was carried out with brutal efficiency. Half dragged back into the city, Hugh felt as though he had entered some kind of waking nightmare. It had all happened so quickly and with such surprise that there was an air of unreality about the quiet streets and the dark massiveness of the prison. Even when he was stripped of his coat and thrown onto the damp stones of the cell floor, he could still not believe Arabia had betrayed him. Even now, he was more hurt than angry at her. She had more than taken her revenge, for worse than anything that could happen to him was the knowledge that now he could do absolutely nothing to save Louisa.

At first light the next morning Louisa came awake in an instant, when her cell door was opened with the familiar clanging of keys. Sitting up on her cot, she smoothed back her disheveled hair and watched in amazement as Ralph Stoakes walked briskly in.

"Please get yourself up and dressed, Miss Culpepper," he said without any prior greeting. "And get your things together. You are going to be transported back to your house in just a few moments so you have no time to spare."

"I—I don't understand," she answered, pulling her robe around her shoulders. "Why?"

"Because your being here has served the purpose for which it was intended."

"But—my execution?"

"Pshaw! Did you really think, Miss Louisa, that your petty little exploits were enough to cause the justice of the King to send a woman to the gallows? Irritating, yes. Annoying, certainly. But hardly deserving of such uncivilized treatment. No, I brought you here for one reason only—to apprehend Hugh Sandenny. And that I have done."

"Hugh!" Louisa cried. "Here?"

"In a room only just down the hall. You may look in on him as you leave, if you wish. It shall most assuredly be for the last time."

"Oh," she groaned. "He came back to help me. I know it."

"I believe there was some such cavalier idea in his head. In.fact, I counted on it."

"You are unspeakable! Why do you hate him so? What has he ever done to you to deserve this?"

"Aside from murdering my nephew—no great loss to the world, I admit—he is an unprincipled, arrogant rake who has always got what he wanted no matter who stood in his way. Well, in getting in my way he has gone too far. But I have no more time for idle conversation, Miss Culpepper. Get ready to leave at once."

He was nearly out the door before Louisa remembered. "My father?" she called.

Stoakes turned and eyed her with a benign contempt. "I am not a vindictive man, Miss Culpepper. Your father will be put under house arrest with you. He is waiting outside now in the carriage."

"Thank you for that, at least," she said softly. "What will happen to us?"

"Exile, I suspect. I shall inform you of the details as soon as they are worked out. Good day, Miss Culpepper."

With an officious bow he left her there, scrambling to put on her clothes and throw together her few belongings. With Olana's help, muttering under her breath how it was about time that man came to his senses, she was fully though not very neatly dressed by the time two guards appeared at her door. Walking between them down the hall, Louisa strained at every locked door to peer through the opening. Most of the cells were empty but at the one nearest the entrance there was the shadow of a man's face looking through the bars.

"Hugh," she called, recognizing him. "Oh, Hugh." Darting away from the soldiers, she ran to the door, reaching her fingers through the bars to touch his face.

He gripped her hand as much as was possible through the small opening.

"Louisa. Where are they taking you?"

"Here, now, Miss," one of the guards said darting after her. "Come along now."

"Oh, just one minute, please," she begged. "Then I'll go quietly, I promise."

"It's not allowed—"

"Please," Louisa pleaded, her eyes filling with tears.

They worked their magic. "Well, one minute more I suppose won't hurt," the man said, looking sheepishly at his companion.

"I'm going home to be under house arrest," Louisa said, clinging to Hugh's fingers.

"Thank God for that. I was afraid—"

"No. Ralph Stoakes never meant to kill me. He only said that to get you here. Oh, Hugh. I'm so afraid for you."

"Don't worry about me. As long as you are safe and well, I don't care what happens to me."

"But you came here to help me and now . . ."

"Come along now, Miss," the guard said, untangling her hands from the bars. "We really must get along."

Straining against her guards, she was dragged up the steps.

"I'll do something, Hugh," she called back. "Don't worry. I'll do something to help you, I promise."

"Good-bye, Louisa."

His last words echoed in her mind all the long way through the sandy streets to her house. Her father, sitting on the seat beside her, had recovered something of his old elan now that he was back out in the world again and going home. He could not understand how Louisa could be so unhappy.

Chapter 19

MRS. TONDEE CAREFULLY laid two elongated bottles on a bed of thick straw in a basket on the kitchen table. Covering them with a clean, starched linen cloth, she tucked the edges around them and covered the top of the basket.

"There. That should do it. But you must walk carefully, my girl. This here is my finest Spanish sherry and I wouldn't have it come to grief for the world. Besides, Captain Emory has paid handsomely for those bottles to arrive safe."

Arabia tied the strings of her straw hat under her chin. "I don't see why I have to be the one to carry them around. Let somebody else do it."

"Stop your grumbling. You know well enough that there is no one else right now. The Captain will see that you're well recompensed for your trouble, have no fear. Ain't that right, Jerral?"

Louisa's young page shifted his weight nervously under the Madam's firm gaze. "He be generous, tha's for sure," he answered hoping they wouldn't press him for more information. His mother had been firm about ordering him to make certain Arabia brought the sherry back and nobody else and so far it looked as though he would succeed. If Arabia should talk the Madam out of going now he did not know what he was going to do.

"I don't want to go to that house," Arabia said, making one more attempt. "You know that."

"Tut, tut. There's no reason for you to feel that way. All you have to do is deliver this sherry to the Captain and come right back. There is no reason you should even see Louisa Culpepper if you don't want, though why you should avoid people who treated you and your ma so well is quite beyond me. Now get along, the two of you. And make sure you are careful with that wine."

Muttering to herself, Arabia took up the basket and followed Jerral out through the kitchen door to the street gate. Once there she insisted he walk behind her as she briskly made her way to Abercorn Street. Her only consolation for this unwelcome journey was the fact that Captain Emory was known to give handsome tips and he had a special fondness for her. If she could get in and out of the house quickly she would have extra money in her pocket and still not have to face anyone there.

Her first disappointment came when she walked into the Culpepper's spacious kitchen and came face to face with Olana.

"Take me to Captain Emory at once," Arabia said imperiously.

Olana glanced at her son in the doorway and motioned for him to run along. "You follow me," she said, ignoring Arabia's haughty attitude though it irritated her beyond measure.

"What room is he in? I can find the way myself."

Olana was already on the first step of a narrow stairwell built into the wall of the kitchen.

"I take you," she said and disappeared around a sharp turn.

"I can find it—Oh, bother!" There was nothing to do but follow the woman up the stairs. Once inside the narrow wall, they climbed up two floors, Arabia protesting all the way that the Captain would never have allowed himself to be situated on the top floor of the house. But when Olana pushed at the door that opened onto the old nursery and schoolroom, she grudgingly stepped inside, thinking that housing in Savannah must be truly desperate for a military man like the Captain to be satisfied with such quarters.

To her surprise the old rooms still bore the trappings of the schoolroom, dust-ridden and decayed from lack of use. Situated under the roof, it was stifling in the summer heat. The shutters on the windows threw mottled stripes of light across the wide plank floors. Arabia caught her breath as she saw a woman standing in the middle of the room and recognized Louisa.

With a cry she turned and started back through the low door but it was quickly slammed in her face by Olana on the other side.

"Open this door, you black witch!" she cried, rattling the handle. "Let me out of here!"

"It's no use, Arabia," Louisa said quietly. "You've got to stay and talk to me, for a few moments at least."

Arabia turned and leaned against the door. "Where is Captain Emory? I have a basket to deliver to him. That's all I came here for."

"The Captain is not at home. I ordered that sherry because I had to see you, had to talk to you. I knew you would never come if I sent round a note asking you to, so I had to plan some way of getting you here."

"This was all a trick! I should have known."

"Not such a bad trick," Louisa said, moving nearer the girl. "You can keep the sherry. It's paid for. All I want is a little of your time."

Warily Arabia moved away from the door to the window where she laid the basket on a small desk thick with dust. There was a stool near it but she did not sit down.

"I have nothing to say to you," she said without looking at Louisa directly. "You've simply wasted your time and your money."

Louisa stepped to the other side of the desk, looking across it at her old antagonist. "Arabia, I know how you feel about me, but please, for a little while, put your prejudices aside. It's Hugh who needs our help now. He's in desperate trouble and if we don't do something he will certainly die."

Arabia's lips pursed into a tight line. She still could not look Louisa directly in the eye. "I don't care about Hugh," she muttered.

"I don't believe that. He's been arrested and is in jail. Ralph Stoakes intends to have him shot—he told me so himself. There is nothing I can do because I am so tightly guarded here, but you could. You're still free to move about the town."

Finally Arabia looked up into Louisa's pleading eyes. "You don't understand. It was me who had Hugh arrested. I told Sir Ralph where he would be. I gave the signal. He's only in this situation because of me."

To her surprise Louisa showed no sign of shock or amazement.

"I know that. Ralph Stoakes told me that as well."

Arabia's eyes widened. "He told you? You knew it was because of me that Hugh is going to die and still you ask me to help? You must have lost your senses."

"No. I haven't lost my senses. I've known you since we were children, Arabia, and I don't believe you are the kind of woman who would betray the man she loves out of sheer meanness. I think Hugh hurt you so badly that you wanted revenge. But I also think you still love him and you don't want to see him die."

Under Louisa's gentle words the hardness Arabia clung to so stubbornly began to waver. Her eyes filled with tears. Easing herself down on the stool, she leaned across the desk.

"He came to me asking me to help save you. Always it was you he cared about—never me. After I left Charleston I was dying to see him again, to tell him how sorry I was for getting so angry and upset. Then when he did come to me, all he wanted was help for you. I was so hurt and so angry . . ."

Louisa studied Arabia's bowed head, wishing she could touch her, comfort her, but knowing it would be the wrong move to make.

"I understand," she said quietly. "Truly I do. In your place I might have done the same thing. But that is not what matters now. We must do something to help him get out of that jail and out of Savannah before it is too late. Please, won't you help?"

Arabia shook her head. "He won't ever forgive me, no matter if I did help. He hates me now, for certain."

"No. That's not true. Can't you see? If you save him now it does away with the hurt you've caused him and he's caused you. It will give you both a chance to start over. My father and I are going to be sent away, probably to the West Indies. I'll be gone, Arabia, and Hugh will need you in the way you've always wanted him to. If he dies both of us will be left with only grief."

Timidly she reached out and touched Arabia's arm lying on the dusty desktop. "Please, Arabia. I won't ask anything of you ever again if you will only help me save him."

Arabia looked down at Louisa's hand. Here in this place where they had once shared happy times and warm bonds of friendship, her resentment and anger seemed suddenly without strength, as though in the space of an instant it had grown old and empty. She slipped her hand in Louisa's, allowing herself to remember for a moment the love and concern that had once been so strong between them.

"Oh, Louisa. My life has been so useless."

Louisa gripped her hand. "What's done is done. If it helps us to be friends again then it was all worthwhile. And if we two can give Hugh back his life, what more could we ask. Will you help me, Arabia?"

"Do you really think he will forgive me?"

"I believe he will."

"But how do you know you can trust me?" Arabia said with something of the old glint of anger in her eyes. "I might go straight to Sir Ralph again and tell him every word of this conversation."

"I do not believe you will, Arabia. Don't you remember how close we once were? You were my sister and my friend. I simply do not believe you are the kind of person who would do such a thing."

Arabia's body tensed and she jerked her hand away.

"I'm not your friend," she said with the old bitterness in her voice. "But I will help Hugh. I betrayed him once. I shall never do it again. All right. Tell me what you want me to do."

The message bearing the wax seal of the Magistrate's office came late in the afternoon. Louisa read with a sinking heart how she and her father must be ready to leave Savannah in a few hours. They were allowed to take one portmanteau each and nothing else. Olana could accompany her mistress and Thomas Culpepper's valet might wait upon him. Otherwise all the servants, including Jerral and Nathan, must stay with the house.

She laid the paper in her lap, wondering for the hundredth time if Arabia had kept her word or gone straight from the upstairs schoolroom to Ralph Stoakes' office at the Council House. It had been nearly a week and she had not heard one word from the sullen girl she had once called her sister. Though she clung stubbornly to the belief that Arabia would not betray her, as each day passed with no indication of what was happening, her faith seemed more and more unfounded. And now, in just a few hours, there would be no more time. What was she to do?

For the third time that week she dispatched Jerral to Tondee's Tavern with a note for Arabia. When he returned an hour later saying he had not been able to find the girl anywhere, Louisa began to despair. Listlessly she threw some clothes, some of her best jewelry and a miniature of her mother in the portmanteau then sat down to wait for the summons.

It did not come until early that morning, just before dawn. Olana shook her awake in the chair where she had fallen wearily asleep a few hours before, saying that two soldiers were downstairs demanding that she leave.

Instantly awake, Louisa pulled her cloak around her and went down to greet her father, only half-awake, standing in the hall. With a last look at the house where she had lived most of her life, she embraced Jerral, gave him a silver spoon for his own, shook Nathan's hand, spoke a quick good-bye to the other servants, then went quickly out into the dark where a carriage waited to take them to the wharf.

As she bent to enter the cab she was surprised to see Ralph Stoakes sitting inside the carriage, his long fingers resting on the ebony handle of his cane.

"I hardly expected to find you here," Louisa said bitterly, taking her seat opposite him. With despondency in every line of his body, her father settled himself next to her, Stoakes leaned out of the window and spoke to the driver and the carriage rolled off down the street.

"I could not let you leave without saying farewell," Stoakes said. "In spite of what you may think of me, I am very much concerned for your welfare."

"How touching. I am more disposed to think that you're concerned to make sure we really sail."

"Perhaps. That is my responsibility too. However, I beg you to remember that I could have sent a formidable guard to accomplish the same end."

Louisa refused to be mollified. "Where are you sending us? What kind of ship? Are we to be put in irons?"

"My dear lady, surely you must realize by now that you are under my protection. I would never allow you to suffer any more discomfort than is necessary. Indeed, it is my hope that once this accursed rebellion is over and peace restored, I might be able to return you to your home and even to something of your former estates."

Thomas Culpepper gave a sigh. "Oh, dear. Do you suppose that is really possible?"

"I shall certainly do my best to make it so."

"Please don't bother," Louisa snapped. "I for one do not wish to live in a country where liberty is so dearly bought."

Stoakes gave a thin laugh. "You may change your mind after a few months in the West Indies."

Only the darkness prevented the dismay on her face from showing. "So that is where we are headed."

"Yes. There is a ship, the *Aurora*, waiting to leave on the early tide. Though she is largely a cargo ship she has room for a few passengers. The Captain, George Malloy, will see that you get the best care possible under the circumstances."

"You are too kind."

They rode the rest of the way in silence. It was still too dark to see out of the window or Louisa would have dwelt lovingly on every old building of the city that she loved. As it was, she knew the way well enough to be aware when the carriage started the long descent down the bluff adjacent to the public stairs. Her grief lay like a lump of dough in her throat. The thought of Hugh lying in some dank cell— if indeed he was still alive—led her to speak once more to Ralph Stoakes.

"Mr. Sandenny. What will happen to him?"

Stoakes looked through her as though she was not there.

"Is he still alive?" she asked quietly, thinking that if Stoakes told her he had already been shot she would go to her exile in complete despair. And yet, she clutched at some desperate thread of hope that he might still have a chance. After all, Arabia could have done something to help Hugh without telling her of it.

"Mr. St. Dennis is being taken care of," Stoakes said curtly. The carriage rolled to a stop, the door was pulled open, and Sir Ralph stepped out. He turned to offer Louisa his hand which she took some satisfaction in refusing. It was so dark she felt as if she was stepping into a cave. A seaman with a long stiff pigtail and loose trousers appeared, holding aloft a tin pierced lantern. It was enough to light their steps down the wharf to a gangplank that bobbed with the movement of the ship in the water. The sailor went ahead, offering her a hand across the narrow plank. Gingerly she stepped over it and onto the deck then turned to help her father. Behind him came Stoakes. There were several other sailors standing across the deck, shadows in the darkness, and a first mate in a short jacket and seaman's cap standing beside the hatchway steps. As soon as Stoakes' buckled shoes touched the deck this man moved forward, touching his cap. As the thin light from the lantern fell on the caverns of his lean face, Louisa stifled a gasp.

"Where is Captain Malloy?" Stoakes barked. "He was told to await me here."

"He's below in his cabin, sir. First Mate Windsor here, sir. He asked me to see that the lady was come aboard proper."

"That was not the arrangement. Take me to him at once. And see that this lady and her father are locked in their cabin."

"Aye, sir. We will."

The First Mate motioned to the men waiting on the other side of the deck. With a few silent steps they were upon the group, shoving Louisa and her father aside while three of them pounced on Stoakes, grabbing his arms and stifling his exclamation of surprise with an enormous handkerchief. Moving swiftly, they bound his arms behind him and firmly thrust the kerchief in his mouth as a gag while the First Mate stepped closer to peer into his face, chuckling softly.

"Done proper, are you? Sorry to disappoint you, Master Stoakes, *sir,* but it is the Captain who is locked securely in his cabin. And you, Sir Ralph, are my prisoner. Are you all right, Louisa?" he said, turning to the speechless girl. "He didn't harm either of you, did he?"

"No, no," she said, recovering her voice. "But Robert— how did you—"

He laid a finger on her lips to caution her. Though they had moved quickly, it had all been accomplished with so little sound that the soldiers waiting beyond the carriage had not looked up.

The First Mate made Stoakes a short bow. "Robert Sallette, your servant, sir," he whispered with mock civility. Snatching up Stoakes' cane, he bared the rapier in the head. Then he reached under Sir Ralph's brocade coat and removed his short sword from its scabbard and handed it to one of the sailors.

At the mention of Sallette's name Stoakes began to squirm, mouthing sounds. Robert made a motion and one of his men tightened the gag, turning his face purple in the dim light.

"You'd do better to be quiet, Mr. Stoakes, if you wish to get out of this alive. I've no wish to kill you if you behave yourself. Let me have that pistol, Ned."

One of his men handed Sallette a long handled pistol which he poised between Stoakes' eyes.

"This thing makes a terrible roar when it goes off and quite a mess of anything in its way. It is all primed and ready and if you don't want me to dispatch it against your head, you'd better do as I say. Exactly as I say."

Immediately Stoakes grew quiet though the fury in his eyes shouted murder. Sallette waved the barrel of the pistol toward the dock. "Louisa, you and your father go back to the carriage. We'll be right behind you. Go quickly and don't call attention to yourselves. The driver and the two guards are my men but those soldiers at the other end of the wharf are not and we don't want to arouse their suspicions.

Without answering Louisa made her way back across the gangplank, taking her bewildered father's hand then linking arms with him and walking with lowered heads back to the carriage. Holding her breath for fear her father might begin to ask questions, she hopped up the steps and into the dark recesses of the cab, sinking back against the leather seat. A moment later Sallette threw Stoakes, still securely bound, into the carriage then crawled in after him as they rolled away.

"Olana?" Louisa whispered to Robert.

"My men will see that she and your father's valet get safely back to the house. You'll both have to learn to do without them for a while, I fear."

She nodded. As long as they were safe, what did it matter.

As the horses pulled up the steep incline of the same bluff she had gone down with such despair only a short time before, Louisa listened as Sallette explained in his quiet voice that they were headed for the seldom used old colonial jail where Hugh was being kept. Louisa's heart gave a bound as she realized that not only was Hugh still alive but that Robert did not intend to leave Savannah without him. The outraged man sitting tensely bound and gagged on the carriage seat opposite her was their one hope of accomplishing that goal.

As the road grew level and the carriage straightened, Sallette leaned toward Stoakes, pointing the cold brass circle of the pistol barrel at his temples.

"When this carriage stops I want you to order the guard to bring Hugh Sandenny out. Make some excuse that you are taking him to the jail at the Council House—I don't care what you say but make certain you get him inside this carriage. If you by so much as a raised eyebrow betray who we are, I shall blast your head away before anyone can get to us. Is that clear, Mr. Stoakes?"

Ralph glared at him above the gag.

"My men are dressed in grenadier uniforms for a reason. Have your guards turn Sandenny over to them. Now, I am going to remove this handkerchief from your mouth."

"Oh, Robert," Louisa whispered. "Do you think you should?"

Sallette's eyes never left Stoakes' face. "I think Mr. Stoakes here is a reasonable man who values his life. If he does as I say he will be released unharmed outside the town. If he does not—" he dug the end of the pistol into Stoakes' temple. It seemed to have the desired effect. Sir Ralph settled back into the seat, his eyes murderous but his lips closed.

As the carriage rolled to a stop Sallette's men sitting beside the driver bounded off the cab and stood at attention by the door. A sleepy looking guard, his bayonet at the ready, made his way toward them. When he spotted the coat of arms painted on the door of the coach, he lowered his musket and came to attention. After a pause that seemed endless to Louisa, Ralph Stoakes leaned forward so that his face was framed by the window.

"You, sentry," he barked.

"Sir."

"I have come to transport a prisoner, Hugo St. Dennis, to the Council House for questioning. Take these guards with you and bring him out."

"But Sir, do you have written orders?"

"I don't need orders, you dolt! I write the orders. Be quick now and do what you're told before I reprimand you for sleeping on the job."

Since the clatter of the horses had indeed wakened the sentry from an early morning doze, he quickly decided it was wiser to forget about the requirement for written orders. Motioning to Sallette's men, he disappeared down the ancient lane behind the jail.

As the sound of their boots on the cobbles grew fainter,

Louisa sat twisting her hands in her lap, hardly daring to breathe. So much could go wrong. Stoakes' conversation seemed innocent enough but had he found some way to warn the sentry that everything was not what it seemed? Was the man intelligent enough to realize how unofficial Stoakes' demand actually was? The quiet minutes dragged on and she waited, afraid to hope that Robert's plan would really work. She was intensely conscious of Stoakes' eyes boring into her face.

At last she heard the sound of the soldiers returning accompanied by the light clink of a chain, similar to that prisoners sometimes wore on their wrists. Stoakes leaned forward again, but she peered around him and saw a bewildered Hugh standing between the two bogus guards. Behind them two genuine members of the 63rd Grenadiers had accompanied the prisoner. The sentry stepped up and saluted smartly.

"Prisoner delivered, sir. Anything more?"

"No. Put him above."

Sallette dug the pistol into the back of Ralph's neck and he spoke up quickly.

"On the other hand, it might be safer to have him inside. I want to talk to him."

Using his free hand, Sallette slipped up the door handle as his two men jerked it open just far enough to shove Hugh inside.

"Drive on," Stoakes said in response to another lunge of the pistol against his neck and the carriage rolled away even before Hugh could sit down. He fell against Louisa and her father and before he knew what was happening he was in her arms.

"Hugh, you're safe! I can't believe it," she cried, hugging him fiercely.

Still trying to get his bearings, Hugh leaned against her wishing his hands were not fettered. Even in the darkness of the cab he recognized Stoakes at once. Sallette took a little longer.

"What's going on?" he asked, then spotted the pistol Robert was still holding against Stoakes' head. "How did you get here? How did I get here?"

Louisa untangled her arms from around his neck. "It was Robert. He rescued Papa and me and now he's saved you as well. Dear Robert. How can we ever thank you?"

"We're not rescued yet," Robert warned. "Nor can I take all the credit if we do make it. We must still get past the sentry at the town gate and that will not be easy. The guard at the prison might believe our friend Stoakes here was transporting Hugh to the Council House in the early morning hours but I wonder what the sentry at the gate will think of his taking so notorious a prisoner outside the town."

"Perhaps Sir Ralph can come up with a plausible excuse. That ought not to be too difficult for a rogue like him."

"Such ingratitude," Stoakes said scathingly. "Never fear, Sandenny. You may get off this time but you'll get what you deserve yet."

"Stop it, both of you," Sallette hissed. "You will not be released unharmed, Mr. Stoakes, until you've got us well away from Savannah so you'd better start thinking of some kind of a believable story."

For a moment Stoakes' rage threatened to get the better of him. "And if I don't?" he said vehemently.

"Then prepare to meet your Maker. Ahead of us!"

"I could be more convincing if my hands were free."

"No, I won't risk that. You'll simply have to do your best without them."

"It's impossible. You ask too much."

The carriage slowed as it neared the old garden gate on the south side of the town. "Who comes," a sentry called and stepped up in its path. The driver pulled the horses to a stop while the guard walked around the team and up to the coach window.

"Oh, Sir Ralph. I didn't recognize your coat of arms. You're up early, sir."

Leaning forward, Stoakes recognized the young man as one of the sentries who was usually on duty at the Council House, with whom he had often exchanged pleasantries. A stab of hope went through him. He leaned farther out the window, staring at the man without speaking.

"I hadn't heard you were to leave the city this morning," the sentry said, wondering at Stoakes' silence.

"St. Augustine," Sir Ralph muttered. "Yes. The garrison at St. Augustine. Just a little business . . ."

He sounded so unlike his usual imperious self that instantly the guard's suspicions were aroused. Stepping closer to the coach he peered into the Commissioner's face.

"Is anything wrong, sir."

"Wrong? Why—Why, no—"

The sentry attempted to look around him and peer into the darkness of the cab.

"Are you certain?"

"Why—"

All at once a girl's lighthearted laugh broke in.

"Oh, there you are at last, Sir Ralph. I do declare, I was about to think I had been left waiting at the gate like some old cast-off bride. La, such a time I've had of it—"

With a flourish of skirts, Arabia Tillman came bounding up to the cab, thrusting herself between Stoakes and the sentry. "And here I was so looking forward to seeing St. Augustine again. Why, I've heard it's simply the liveliest city, especially for a girl like me."

Quickly the surprised sentry jumped back while Arabia wrenched open the door and went flouncing in, slamming it behind her and leaning back out the window, completely obliterating Stoakes.

"Drive on, driver! Let's be off—"

"I understand, sir," the guard muttered, suppressing a wink at his superior. Fancy him, that arrogant aristocrat, stealing out of the city before dawn with a piece of flimsy from a tavern taproom!

"Drive on," he said, thinking he was doing Stoakes a favor by not prolonging his embarrassment.

With a cry from the driver, the team lunged forward and started at a brisk pace down the packed dirt road south toward Thunder Bluffs. The six people inside the coach, crammed together in its small space, sat without speaking until the gate of the town was far enough behind them that they knew they had not been followed. Then Sallette said softly,

"Well done, Miss Tillman." It was echoed by Louisa's heartfelt, "Thank you, Arabia."

Arabia, who had crammed herself down next to Stoakes, looked across at Hugh, all her hopes for his forgiveness in her eyes.

"Yes," Hugh said, "well done, Arabia."

With a clink of the chains on his wrists, he reached out and took her hand, squeezing it in his own.

"Oh, Hugh. Can you forgive me," she said quietly, oblivious to the presence of the others.

"I should like to know how much longer I have to endure this," Stoakes snapped. "We are out of the town now. I've done my part. I demand my release."

Sallette jammed the end of the pistol in the Commissioner's neck. "I think we will just travel together far enough so that we shall be well gone by the time you make it back to town," he said. "You shouldn't mind. After all, you're in such excellent company."

Stoakes clucked his tongue in disgust. "This is intolerable," he muttered. When no one bothered to answer they rode on in silence, the thud of the horses' hooves on the sandy road and the rattle of the wheels their only accompaniment to the loud roaring of the insects. When Sallette finally leaned out the window and called to the driver to halt, it was as though he knew where they were by the length of time they had traveled rather than any recognizable spot on the road. The coach pulled up and Sallette directed them all to disembark. Hugh went first, then attempted to hand out the ladies though hampered by the chains on his wrists.

Through the faint dawn light Louisa caught glimpses of sequined silver beyond the trees and knew they were near the coast, though where she could not be sure. Sallette ordered his men to unharness the horses then turned to Stoakes.

"You will have to walk back to Savannah, Mr. Stoakes. So sorry about the inconvenience but I'm sure you can understand the reason for it. Actually, you are not far from Beaulieu plantation. Far enough, however, to allow us to be well gone by the time you reach it."

While Robert was speaking to Stoakes one of his men worked skillfully at knocking the fetters from Hugh's wrists.

"You are too kind to him, Sallette," Hugh said as he held out his arms. "Stoakes should thank his stars that he is allowed to walk back to Beaulieu. Had our positions been reversed, we should all be lying dead by the side of the road by now."

"I've no doubt that were it up to you that is where I should be," Stoakes answered, the hatred thick in his voice.

"I should certainly give the matter serious consideration."

"Stop it, Sandenny," Sallette snapped. "We've no time now for private quarrels. You are to go with Powell here through the woods. I shall take the ladies and Mr. Culpepper by water. Powell will lead you to our rendezvous."

The chains were thrown aside and Hugh rubbed his chafed wrists as he met Stoakes' bitter gaze with a hatred of his own.

"Go back to Savannah, Sir Ralph," he said. "For my part I never intend to enter the place again, so you can forget me. Your nephew was a silly fellow, hardly worth all this burning revenge."

"I shall never forget! You may think you've won now but I shall hound you till your dying day. I'll catch you somewhere and I'll make you pay for your arrogance."

"You are hardly the man to talk of arrogance."

"Both of you stop!" Sallette said with a deadly quiet. "Get along, Hugh. The ladies are coming with me." Taking Arabia's arm he gently pushed her toward the edge of the bluff while the two horses were led back to where Hugh stood, still facing Ralph Stoakes.

"I don't want to go with you," Arabia cried, pulling back. "I want to go with Hugh."

Louisa laid a hand on her arm. "You can't walk through a swamp, Arabia. Do as Robert says."

"But you told me—"

"You'll see Hugh again at the camp. He can take you with him then."

It took her a moment to recognize the wisdom in Louisa's words. Giving Hugh a last look, she started with Robert toward the path that led down the bluff.

"Wait," Stoakes called. "You cannot leave me like this. At least free my hands."

Sallette hesitated, looking back at the man standing near the abandoned coach. Then he waved the barrel of his pistol, directing one of his men to untie the bonds on Stoakes' wrists. It was done in a moment and the two women and four men turned back to the bluff while Hugh and his guide started toward the horses, leaving Stoakes alone in the road.

It was more than Ralph Stoakes could bear to watch the man he hated and the woman he loved slip out of his life with no retribution of any kind. With an almost inhuman cry he rushed at Hugh, throwing himself on his back and clawing at his throat. Caught off-guard, Hugh was knocked to the ground. Then, his fury every bit as strong as his adversary's, he rolled over, forcing Stoakes under him and pounding at his hated face. Of the two men, Hugh was the younger and stronger but the enforced idleness of prison had sapped some of his strength, making them closely matched. Both were fueled by the same hatred and in the darkness of the road, each had as little visibility. Grappling, they twisted in the dust, rolling over again as their fingers clawed to reach the other's throat. Hugh's grip tangled in the lace cravat Stoakes wore, tearing it but unable through it to gain a grip on his windpipe. Shoving with the heel of his hand, Hugh pushed the man's chin upward, hoping to hear his neck crack. Stoakes, in a frantic effort to break his hold, dug his fingers into Hugh's eyes until he was forced to turn his head away and loosen his grip. Gasping, they rolled over again, bumping against the wheel of the coach, this time with Hugh on top. Sitting astride the man, he grabbed a fistful of Stoakes' collar and, using it as a lever, began pounding up and down, battering Stoakes' head. When he felt his body slacken he doubled up his fists and hit him again and again in the face, hoping to knock him cold.

Sensing that at last the fight had gone out of his enemy, and finally heeding Sallette's cry to stop, he sat back, the breath heaving in his chest.

"I ought to kill you, Stoakes," he gasped. "Instead, I warn you never again to come at me or I promise you I will kill you with the first weapon at hand. Leave me alone, do you hear! I never want to see you again or, so help me God, I will kill you first and ask questions later."

With every muscle in his body protesting, he dragged himself off the prostrate man in the road and to his feet. Then he turned his back and walked toward his horse.

He had nearly reached it when he heard Arabia's sharp cry.

"Hugh! Look out!"

Somehow Stoakes had got to his feet again. Moving quickly, before anyone was aware of what he was doing, he had spied the ebony stick on the floor of the coach, had pulled away the sheath from its rapier and sent it flying like a javelin at Hugh's back.

Hugh stood frozen. There was a blur of motion as a body flew across the road, an explosion, a burst of fire, then the sulphurous odor of saltpeter hanging on the air. In the dim light of the new morning, Hugh stared at two bodies sprawled before him: Stoakes lying in a crumpled heap near the open door of the coach and, nearer him, nearly at his feet, Arabia sinking to her knees, the long shaft of the ebony cane protruding almost obscenely from her chest.

With a terrible cry Louisa flew across the grass to Arabia's side. Before she could reach her Hugh was kneeling, cradling the girl's body in his arms, not even aware of his voice crying.

"My God! Arabia, what have you done? Dear, sweet God . . ."

"Oh, oh, oh," Louisa cried trying to help him hold her. "Help her, someone. What can we do? Robert. Papa . . ."

Robert knelt beside her. With a swift, deft movement he grabbed the shaft of the cane and jerked it out of Arabia's chest much as he had pulled Indian arrows from wounded men. Arabia gave a cry, her back arched then went slack and she slumped in Hugh's arms.

"Arabia, my poor girl. Please, speak to me," Hugh cried, pressing the girl's limp body to his chest, stroking her hair and cheek, kissing her brow. Almost as though he had called her back through his force of will, she opened her eyes and looked up at him.

She watched with wonder the tears brimming in his eyes.

"Oh, Arabia," he said, "why did you do such a foolish thing? Why?"

Robert handed Louisa a wad of cloth quickly torn from his sleeve. "Take this and staunch the wound. It's bleeding fast."

The bodice of Arabia's dress was already sticky and wet. Louisa, ignoring the anguish that choked in her throat, worked to bandage the deep wound, pressing down against it to stop the terrible flow of blood.

Arabia tried to raise her hand to wipe the tears on Hugh's cheek but her limbs felt so lethargic and heavy they refused to obey. The dizziness in her head almost obliterated the searing pain in her chest but both dimmed beside the knowledge that she was back in Hugh's arms and he was bending over her and his lips were on her cheek. She was conscious of nothing so much as the certainty that this was where she had wanted to be for so long. This was where she belonged.

She tried to speak but her lips could barely form the words she wanted so much to say: that what she had done was not foolish at all.

Louisa understood her but Hugh, sick and distressed, was only aware of how beautiful she looked with the pale light on her face, her full lips trying to smile up at him, her eyes filled with that old all consuming love he had seen so many times. Then, even as he watched, the light seemed to dim, shadows moved across her face like a veil quietly laid. Her eyelids closed and her head slumped against his shoulder.

He held her tightly, rocking back and forth, the words he wanted to cry out—of forgiveness, of how sorry he was—caught fast in his throat. He was only barely aware of Louisa sobbing beside him.

Chapter 20

IT WAS NEARLY daylight by the time they left the clearing. Because of the two deaths Robert made a quick change of plans. Both Stoakes and Arabia were quickly buried in the woods where, with any luck, their graves would not be discovered for a long time. Though time was precious Louisa insisted on a brief committal service with several prayers partially remembered from the burial service. Then Sallette sent two of his men with the horses while he and the others cast off in a longboat hidden in the underbrush and followed the long, treacherous inland water route into the interior.

Louisa and her father clung to each other sitting in the stern while Hugh sat alone near the bow, now and then helping to navigate but mostly lost in his own preoccupations.

By midday they reached the camp where they found Rob waiting for them. One look at Hugh's face and he knew something had gone terribly wrong. When Louisa told him what had happened he started after his friend in an attempt to help him but Louisa held him back.

"I think it's better to leave him to himself for a while," she said. "He's hardly spoken since the accident."

For a moment Rob seemed about to disagree. Then, realizing she was probably right, he nodded and walked the other way.

Louisa was all at once aware that she had had almost no sleep during the long night. She asked where Robert wanted her to stay then threw herself down on a pile of furs in the tent and stretched out, so tired that she slipped almost at once into a fitful sleep. When she woke several hours later the camp was unusually quiet. Someone had placed her portmanteau in her tent so she hurriedly changed her dress and combed her hair then went looking for Hugh only to find that he had been out all day riding the woods with Sallette and some of his men. It was nearly sundown when they finally rode in, Hugh near the back looking disheveled, his face drawn and tired. Louisa exchanged a brief conversation with Sallette while Hugh removed his saddle and bedded down his horse. Then she made room for him near the fire where the contents of an iron pot bubbled over the flames, giving off pleasant aromas.

"Is that really pine bark stew I smell," he asked. "I'm famished."

"It is indeed. Let me get you some."

She filled a wooden bowl and watched as he greedily downed the thick stew. "You look exhausted," she said. "Did you get any rest at all?"

"No. It seemed wiser to keep moving. That way you can't think."

Louisa studied his face, stark and lean in the firelight with none of the mischievous glints she was accustomed to seeing. She laid her hand gently on his arm.

"Hugh, it wasn't your fault. You mustn't blame yourself."

"Oh, I don't suppose it was all my doing. Yet it was because of me that all of you were there in the first place. It was me Stoakes wanted to kill."

"But we wanted to be there. We chose to be there. And Arabia wanted to save you more than anything."

"I don't believe she wanted to die. I cannot even understand why she took such a risk."

"Because . . . because she loved you. I only wish I had been quick enough to be there in her place."

Hugh laid his arm around her shoulder and pulled her to him in a quick embrace, his lips lightly brushing her forehead.

"I never wanted Arabia to make such a sacrifice for me but I'm glad it wasn't you. That would have been truly unbearable."

Abruptly he let her go, running his fingers through his hair in a nervous, impulsive gesture. Louisa, a little disappointed asked casually:

"Where were you riding this afternoon? After Tories or Indians?"

"No. Sallette was anxious to see if there were any unusual murmurings from Savannah over Stoakes' disappearance."

"Surely they wouldn't be missing him yet."

"I doubt it. If the guard believed he was bound for St. Augustine on a tryst with Arabia then it should be a week at least before they begin wondering why he hasn't returned."

Hugh frowned, trying to shut out the painful image of Arabia's bleeding body, then threw his bowl aside. "Tell me about your plans. What does Sallette propose to do with you and your father?"

"He thinks we should leave in the morning for Philadelphia. He feels we should stay there until the war is resolved one way or another. We have friends who will offer us a home and it is far enough out of the sphere of English influence that repercussions from Sir Ralph's death—assuming there are any—will not touch us."

"So soon?" It was almost a whisper.

"There is a sloop we can board waiting now at the coast. Robert says that if we miss it it will be at least two weeks before he can put us on another and that would be taking too large a risk."

Hugh rubbed his chin, rough from lack of shaving. "It sounds like a wise idea. I'd like to think that you were safe and well cared for."

"And what will you do?"

"Rob and I shall head for Augusta again. After that, who knows? Perhaps the west country, perhaps the Continental Army. I haven't made up my mind."

"You'd fight with the rebels?"

"Yes. Does that surprise you? It surprises me also. But I think I've seen enough of jolly old England to last me a lifetime. I like this country with its wild, free ways and I think I should like to make my home here. What better way to become a patriot than by lifting my sword for America."

Louisa fought down a growing sense of distress. "What about your father and your estates?"

"The estates are my elder brother's and my father has no wish to set eyes on me again. He told me so many times."

Absently Louisa picked up a narrow twig and dragged it across a bare patch of dirt beside her feet.

"When will you go?"

Though he had not thought about it all at once he knew. "Tomorrow. Early. Before you and your father cast off."

They sat staring into the fire while Louisa struggled with her emotions. Back and forth the twig went making an intricate, meaningless pattern in the sand. At length she said very quietly:

"Philadelphia is a pleasant city but I would rather go with you. Take me with you, Hugh. Please."

He looked up in surprise. "I only wish I could, Louisa, but it would not be fair. I'm going into untamed, savage wilderness. There are no niceties for a lady like you."

"But women do go there. Many have. I have even known a few."

"And have you seen them after they've lived there a year or two? They work alongside their men clearing the wilderness and scratching out a living. Most of them are old before their time with the work, the sickness and the danger. I wouldn't have that happen to you for three lifetimes."

"You would have taken Arabia."

"That was different. Arabia was not a gentlewoman. She knew hard work and expected it. She did not expect coddling."

With a sudden snap the twig was broken in two. Angrily

Louisa threw the pieces at the fire.

"And I do?"

"I'm sorry. I did not mean you any disrespect. You are gentle, beautiful and soft—a lady in every sense of the word. I would not change that for anything."

"But Hugh. I love you. I want only to be with you."

"And I love you, Louisa. When things are straightened out I promise I will come for you. Can't you wait for me until then?"

"But anything could happen to you. I might not even know . . ."

"All the more reason you should not share such dangers."

"You asked me to come with you once," Louisa went on, stubbornly. "In Charleston, remember? Why not now?"

"Because now I know more about what I am going into. It will be a comfort to me to think that you are safe and in pleasant surroundings in Philadelphia until I can make a home somewhere for us. Can't you accept that?"

She stared at the fire, fighting back bitter tears. "I suppose I can if I must."

Louisa sat by herself long after Hugh had disappeared watching the flames die down and struggling to calm her unsettled emotions. The racket of the night creatures in the woods around her was incessant, broken only now and then by the soft hooting of an owl or the far-off chilling howl of a wildcat. As the fire died the air began to grow cool and she wrapped her thin shawl tightly around her shoulders and rose to make her way across the camp to the tent where her father was already asleep.

She had nearly reached the door when she heard Robert Sallette and his men come riding into the camp. Spotting her, Robert dismounted, handed the reins to one of his men and came striding across to her.

"I have arranged passage for you and your father," he said, in his low, matter-of-fact tone. "The sloop, *Splendid*, will take you on at the coast and carry you to Philadelphia. Can you be ready to leave at first light tomorrow?"

"It really has to be so soon?"

Something in her voice touched him. "It's better this way,

Louisa. I don't want to chance having you here if Stoakes' body should be discovered. Besides, it's disconcerting to my fellows to have such a lovely woman about." He smiled mischievously. "Even one they are accustomed to calling 'Oliver.'"

Louisa dug the toe of her shoe into the soft sand at the door of the hut. "It's just that I—well, I don't really want to go to Philadelphia, Robert."

Lightly he laid a hand on her shoulder. "It's better that you do, my dear. Trust me in this."

She had no reason not to. For several years now he had managed to be a thorn in the flesh to the British without ever endangering those who followed him. She would only be in his way if she insisted on dallying here.

"Very well, then. We'll be ready."

"Good girl."

Louisa knew it was important that she get a good night's rest but it seemed to her during the long hours that followed that the harder she tried, the more sleep eluded her. Tossing on her bed of fur skins, worried over the separation that faced her with a tenacity she could not shake. How could Hugh allow her to walk out of his life without making any effort to win her back? How could he be satisfied with loneliness and hardship when he knew all she wanted was to be by his side, helping him to build a new life. It might be years before they found each other again—perhaps they never would. The western country was a wild, dangerous place and there were at least ten different ways he might be killed out there and she would never even know it. How would she be able to live the rest of her life wondering if he were alive or dead?

Near dawn she finally fell into a fitful sleep from which she was awakened by the first stirrings of the camp. With heavy eyes and an even heavier heart she woke her father and tried to make him understand that they had to face another journey. Then she pulled together their belongings, dressed, combed her hair and stepped outside.

Hugh had changed to a blue checkered shirt and leather vest and was sitting with a group of men around the fire eating a meager breakfast. He gave her a wan smile, toyed

with the food on his plate, cast it aside then rose and walked
to the other side of the camp where two horses stood saddled
and packed for the journey. With a pang Louisa realized
that in a few moments they would be saying good-bye, with
no idea of when they would see each other again.

While she picked at her breakfast she could hear Rob
and Hugh as they worked over the horses and packs exchanging low comments about their trip and the direction
they would be traveling. Robert, who never seemed to need
sleep, appeared bright-eyed and eager to be away. He barked
orders in all directions, particularly to Louisa, hurrying her
and her father to the inlet where a longboat waited to carry
them to the coast. Slipping her cloak around her shoulders
Louisa stepped over to where Hugh was fastening a saddle
girth.

"We're about to leave," she said. "Won't you walk down
to the water with me to say good-bye."

"Of course." When he turned to look at her the misery
in his face belied his casual manner. Keeping a little apart
from the others he walked with her toward the water's edge.

"I don't suppose you would write to me after you get—
wherever it is you are going?" she asked. The light touch
of his hand upon her arm seemed to burn into her flesh.

"As soon as I can. It may be difficult at first, especially
if I end up with the Continental Army, but I promise I'll
try."

"I'd like to know where you are."

"I promise. And you'll write to me? I'll let you know
where to send it."

The smile she gave him was more like a grimace, "Every
day. Even when I don't know where you are."

He traced the line of her cheek with his finger. "You'll
watch after yourself," he said lightly. "And after your father."

"Oh yes. He depends on me."

"We all do."

"And you'll take care? There is so much danger—so
many things can happen—" A slow flush spread over her
cheeks. "I suppose I worry too much."

Hugh tried to smile. "Soon you will probably be so busy

enjoying all the social attractions of Philadelphia that you'll forget all about me."

Her eyes locked on his. Neither was able to pull away.

"I'll never forget you, Hugh. It breaks my heart to leave you. I shall only live for the time when you come back to me."

With a choked cry he caught her in his arms, burying his face in her hair.

"I will come back for you, I promise. Wait for me, my love."

"Louisa!" Robert called from the boat. "Hurry along now. We have to catch the tide."

She could no longer hold back her tears. His lips sought her cheek, her throat and finally her lips and he kissed her long and hard, trying to burn the memory of her soft flesh in his mind.

"God keep you, Louisa," he muttered.

"Louisa!" Robert called again. "We must go."

Abruptly Hugh dropped his hands and turned away, walking off toward his horse. With eyes too blurred to see, Louisa moved toward the boat, groped for Robert's hand and crept into the wobbling craft to sit next to her father. The last of the oarsmen climbed aboard and the longboat glided into the dark water.

Looking back toward the shore Louisa's vision cleared long enough for her to clearly see Hugh standing beside his horse, leaning against the saddle, his head on his arm.

"Don't row into that alligator," Robert said from the bow, pointing to what looked like a log slowly sliding by ahead of them. "We've only an hour to reach the coast and we don't want to lose time."

Gently the bow began to turn in the brown water, cutting a slow arch through its placid surface. Out on the river a fish came leaping up, showering droplets and slapping the surface before disappearing into its depths. A horse whinnied from the far side of the camp while a cormorant dipped suddenly downward flapping its wings before it swooped up, bearing its breakfast triumphantly in its beak.

"Captain Wilder doesn't like to be kept waiting," Robert went on in his matter-of-fact way as he took his place beside one of his men and the shore began to slip away.

"No!"

Her sudden cry brought all heads in the boat around.

"No! I won't go. I won't let him send me away like this. Take me back, Robert. I'm not going."

"My dear," her father said beside her, frowning in confusion. "What can be the matter..."

Robert stared at her. "We don't have time for this, Louisa."

"I don't care. Papa can go with you if he wants but I'm staying. I'm going with Hugh."

Robert clicked his tongue in exasperation. "Louisa, you don't know what you are saying. I can't let you..."

Louisa rose to her feet setting the boat wobbling uncertainly in the water.

"If you won't take me back then I'll go by myself."

With a quick motion she jumped overboard into the shallow water that rose only up to her knees. She clutched at the hem of her skirt which drifted to the surface of the stream while the men in the boat dived frantically for the sides.

"What the devil! What's come over you, Louisa?"

Without answering she went striding for the shore while the alligator, responding to all this unusual agitation went gliding smoothly off toward the middle of the river. Clutching her skirts aloft, Louisa climbed back on the shore leaving the flabbergasted men sitting in the boat. She had moved so quickly in spite of her wet skirt that she was standing before Hugh before he realized what had happened.

"Hugh Sandenny, I won't let you do this," she exclaimed, pounding him on the shoulder with her fist.

He caught her arm in his hand, the surprise on his face almost comical.

"What the devil..." he started, but she gave him no chance to go on.

With eyes flashing, Louisa jerked her arm away. "I won't allow you to send me away like this. I won't go. You don't give me enough credit, Hugh. I will simply *not* accept your decision to ruin both our lives because of some conception you have of me as a 'lady.'"

Over her shoulder Hugh caught the circle of eyes staring

at them. The few men still seated around the fire held their plates suspended in their hands, their eyes glued to Louisa's angry back. In the water the boat sat idle, its occupants watching them, still uncertain what to do. Even Sallette's face was more curious than perturbed.

"Really, Louisa, everyone is watching," Hugh said, taking her arm and guiding her around the horse's rump where they were at least blocked from the view of the camp.

"I don't care." She lowered her voice slightly. "I don't care if they hear me. That's not important. *We* are and I won't have that ruined. This is one time you are wrong, Hugh. You were wrong about Arabia and you are wrong about me."

His face hardened. "You don't have to tell me I was wrong about Arabia. I should never have allowed her to leave Savannah."

"That's not what I mean. Oh, Hugh, don't you understand anything? She gave her life to save yours because she loved you so much. Even when she betrayed you it was because she was so hurt that you could not see how much she loved you. You find that difficult to believe, don't you? You think that because she was a serving girl and worked in a tavern she had no character. Well, she did. She had courage and devotion and, in her own way, integrity. And she loved you with all that she was. At least give her credit for that now that she's gone. Accept her sacrifice and her love."

Hugh looked away, distressed by her words. She went on relentlessly.

"You've done the same thing with me. Because I am a gentlewoman and have education and manners you think I have no strength. Well, you're wrong, Hugh."

In her effort to reach him, she gripped his arms, peering up into his face.

"Look at me, Hugh. Am I a simpering, silly piece of fluff, cooing 'la-de-da' and fainting at the sight of blood? No! I have as much courage as Arabia. I can stand hardships and hard work. I'm healthy and I love a challenge and—dear God—I'm just as lusty and full of passion as Arabia ever was, if only you'd give me the chance to show it. And I love you," she went on. "I would have gladly taken that rapier in Arabia's place if God had wanted me to. But He didn't. I'm alive and I'm here and, by heaven, you are *NOT* going to pack me off to Philadelphia!"

A smile began to tremble at the corners of his lips. "Louisa. My dear Louisa."

Some of the determination went out of her firm, lithe body as she saw her words were getting through to him. She stepped back.

"Louisa," he laughed. "I never really wanted to send you away. I simply wanted what I thought was best for you."

"Say that you'll take me with you."

"But, your father? And the trip is so difficult and so dangerous. And suppose I join the army. I would have to leave you alone in Augusta."

"Papa can stay in Philadelphia until it is safe for him to go back to Savannah. Robert can fetch Nathan to look after him. And if you leave me to join the Continental Army, I'll wait for you. I'll open a tavern or something to keep busy until you get back."

"By God, I believe you would."

"As for the journey, if you don't take me with you I'll follow you anyway. When I can walk no farther, I'll crawl! All the way into Augusta if I have to. You won't ever be rid of me so you might as well accept it!"

He stood, his hands at his waist, watching the play of hope and determination on her features, this bedraggled lady, hair blowing, the hem of her dress dripping around her ankles. All his good intentions cracked like glass and slid shattering to his feet. Throwing back his head, he laughed aloud.

"Louisa, my dear Louisa. Every word you have spoken is true."

"I'm glad you can admit it," she said, half-sheepishly.

He looked her up and down. "I suppose since you are going to follow me through pine barrens then you'd better have a horse. You won't last a mile in those shoes."

Her body seemed to slump as the force of her resolution went out of it.

"Oh, Hugh," she said, smiling up at him. "I love you so."

"My dearest girl. I expect you to spend the rest of your life telling me so."

He opened his arms and she fell against him, both of them so lost in their embrace that they barely heard the good natured huzzas and applause of the men around them.